THE

BLOODSTONE'S

CURSE

The *Son of Avaria* Trilogy
The Thief's Relic
The Bloodstone's Curse

THE BLOODSTONE'S CURSE

ANGELA KNOTTS MORSE

AN ENCOURAGING THOUGHT PUBLISHERS

To my husband,
From the character motivations to the plot points to the very title,
this story is yours as much as it is mine

Praise for *The Bloodstone's Curse*

"Even better than the first! The line between light and dark grows thinner by the page in Angela Morse's captivating tale of corrupting power and enduring love that will leave readers eager to uncover secrets and join the rebellion."

-Kayla Ann, author of *Well of Dreams*

"Welcome back to Sarieth! The sequel to *The Thief's Relic* doesn't disappoint. Morse layers politics, magic, darkness, and light as our heroes navigate new relationships and heavy responsibilities. Questions are answered—and more questions arise, ending in a show-down that's worth the wait."

-Amanda Auler, author of *Daughter of the Sun* and *Children of the Earth*

PRONUNCIATION GUIDE

PEOPLE

Eamonn	AY-mun
Leyna	LAY-nuh
Dorylss	DOR-ulss
Hadli	HAD-lee
Kinrid	KIN-rid
Gilleth	GILL-eth
Taran	TAIR-an
Teiyn	TAYN
Imrilieth	im-RILL-ee-eth
Tandriel	TAN-dree-ell
Rafella	ruh-FELL-uh
Galicia	guh-LEE-sha
Taularen	tuh-LAH-ren
Javorak	juh-VOR-ack
Vinnerod	VINN-uh-rod
Ree	REE
Rothgard	ROTH-gard

PLACES

Sarieth	SAH-ree-eth
Avaria	uh-VAH-ree-uh
Idyrria	ih-DEER-ee-uh
Teravale	TAIR-uh-VAIL
Miren	MEER-in
Farneth	FAR-neth
Wolstead	WOHL-sted
Holoreath	hu-LOR-ee-ath
Nidet	NIY-dett
Rifillion	ri-FILL-ee-un
Braedel	bray-DELL
Caen	CAYN
Erai	AIR-eye
Amrieth	AM-ree-eth
Iyer	EYE-ur

OTHER

Kaethiri	kuh-THEER-ee
Réalta	RAYL-tuh
Arithnyx	uh-RITH-nix
Rovis	ROH-viss
Bardan	BAR-dun

ONE

THE WOUNDS WOULD HEAL, but the scars would remain. Each long, ragged gash on his back would forever remind him of a time he only wanted to forget.

A mere two weeks had passed since Eamonn was rescued from the crumbling fortress of Holoreath, where he had endured endless torture at Rothgard's hands. Two weeks separated his past life from his present one. Because that was what it was, now. A past life.

The entire world felt different to Eamonn. Heavier, but also somehow lighter. The torture he'd endured changed his perspective, but at the same time, the threat of Rothgard had been eliminated from their country of Sarieth. Eamonn had left the island of Nidet a changed man, hoping he'd be able to find a place for himself in the world before him.

"We'd best get going, lad, if we're to arrive in Rifillion by nightfall."

The voice of Eamonn's mentor, Dorylss, broke through his reverie in the stables after Eamonn's hands had stilled in his work to saddle Rovis, who had returned to Braedel after running off in an ambush. Eamonn craned his neck over his shoulder to see Dorylss's eyes turn up at the corners, a fan of lines spreading out beside them. Even though an unruly auburn beard largely hid his mouth, Eamonn knew Dorylss smiled. Layered under the man's features was another, more subtle emotion: relief. To see Eamonn strong. To see him well. To have his honorary son returned to him, whole.

Of course, Eamonn didn't feel entirely whole.

Eamonn pulled the straps tight against his new leather bag, its rich scent filling his nose. Dorylss and Leyna had shopped for him during their stay with Taran and Teiyn in Braedel, purchasing new clothes as well as the bag. The old clothes he'd been wearing upon his rescue—bloodied, sweat-stained, and ragged—had been burned.

The thought of Leyna, who lingered in the inn eating her breakfast, gripped Eamonn's heart. Something about her had changed as well. She'd risked her own life to save Eamonn by invading Rothgard's hideaway with Dorylss and the twin magic-casters, Taran and Teiyn, so Eamonn wasn't surprised she'd been affected, but he hated himself for it and took the entirety of the blame for the weight she now carried.

Every now and then, she'd had a conversation with Dorylss or one of the twins, but then she would go back to quietly tending Eamonn's wounds or reading one of the books in the house. She hadn't been entirely closed off, though; sometimes Eamonn would notice her eyes on him—kind, compassionate, and caring—but when she met his gaze, she would look away.

Was it because he had betrayed her? Leyna had traveled across provinces and through clear danger for the sole purpose of rescuing him, only for Eamonn to give her up to the enemy, but neither brought that up.

A horse snorted, and Eamonn worked faster. He was getting too lost in his thoughts.

"There's no way Leyna can ride this mare the rest of the way. She can barely support her own weight, much less Leyna's." Dorylss shook his head as he stroked the horse's nose. "That fall was too much for this old girl."

They'd purchased the senior cream-colored mare in Braedel for Leyna to ride, only able to afford her because of her age. Right after they entered the village of Dorca, the horse had twisted her ankle in a muddy divot in the road concealed by recent rain.

"What will we do?" Eamonn dropped his hands from Rovis's saddle as Dorylss turned to his own horse to work on his tack.

With a hopeless shrug, Dorylss said, "Leave her here. Sell her for what we can. Someone in the village might be willing to nurse her back to health for the right price."

"We can't afford another horse."

"No, we can't."

Leyna was again without a horse. A rippling warmth nestled in Eamonn's stomach as he considered how Leyna might travel.

Leyna. There she was again in his mind. His heart ached with the thought that she might be angry at him. Maybe Dorylss knew something he didn't. He hadn't had the opportunity before to ask if Dorylss knew of something bothering her, and the lack of her presence in the stable had Eamonn itching to bring her up.

"Uh... Dorylss," he started, his voice low, "how's Leyna doing?"

Dorylss caught Eamonn's gaze briefly, his narrowed eyes curious. "I believe she's all right, given the circumstances."

The word "circumstances" hit Eamonn's gut like a rock. So something *was* wrong.

"What do you mean?"

"She was determined to save you but had no idea what she was walking into on that island. Capture may have meant imprisonment or torture or... death." A softness washed over Dorylss's features. "She carried your pendant, and with it, the weight of what would happen should it fall into the wrong hands."

Which it did. The rock in Eamonn's gut dropped, heavy and horrible. It was because of him. Eamonn had condemned her before she'd set foot on the island.

"Does she... does she resent me for it?" The words barely managed to scrape out. He kept his eyes on Rovis's saddle, ensuring the straps were secure.

Eamonn thought back to the last time he'd carried on a conversation with Leyna shortly after they'd arrived in Braedel. He'd told Leyna he saw his father in the tower and that Florin had sent Hadli to help Eamonn, explaining the significance without going into detail.

He'd also briefly described what he'd undergone at Rothgard's hand. Though he kept the specifics of his torture to himself, he did confess to breaking under duress and giving her up to Rothgard as the one who carried his pendant.

Eamonn had betrayed her. He'd broken her trust to save his own skin and make the torture stop. Granted, he had hoped it would also save Leyna's life, but he should have guessed Rothgard was not a man of his word. It only made sense that Leyna should resent him.

"Lad." Dorylss's voice was authoritative, pulling Eamonn's gaze upward. "Why don't you talk to her? It would do much more good than asking me."

Eamonn looked to the saddle again, still fiddling with the straps even though he didn't need to tighten them any more. "I guess I think coming from you, it'll hurt less."

"Give her the benefit of the doubt. She might not know what to say either. Maybe she's waiting for you to say something first."

Dorylss was probably right. He usually was, about most things.

"And I don't think someone who resented you would put as much time and effort as she did into helping you heal." Dorylss gave the mare another gentle pat. "I'm going to speak to the stable master and see if he'd be interested in buying the old girl here and finding a new owner."

Dorylss exited the stall, his last words about Leyna on repeat in Eamonn's mind. Although more reserved, Leyna had been by his side ceaselessly the last two weeks, which had to be a good sign. He hoped he hadn't done something to create a rift between them or ruin their friendship. Maybe it was selfish of him after all she'd been through for his sake, but he couldn't deny his growing affection for her. It was true he'd already been attracted to her, but her determination to save him from Rothgard and then her kindness and attentive care after his rescue had rooted those feelings.

Once Dorylss returned with a small sum from the sale of the mare, they led their horses out into the open air to find Leyna leaning against the stable wall, her arms wrapped around herself as her breath appeared in short-lived puffs. A lightning bolt shot upward through Eamonn's core. He expected her to wait for them inside the warm inn.

"Ah, there you are," Dorylss said, stopping in front of Leyna. "I'm afraid your mare isn't fit to ride after her fall. The stable master knows someone who will buy her, so we at least have some money back for her." He offered the reins to his own horse out to her. "You can ride on Bardan."

"No, don't." Eamonn heard the sudden urgency in his tone and cleared his throat. Trying again, he spoke more evenly. "There's no reason we can't all ride. You can sit in front of me on Rovis."

Leyna's lips parted and her eyes flicked between Eamonn and Dorylss. Eamonn's heart sped up and his stomach twisted. Did she not want to be close to him that badly?

"I can just ride on Bardan, if Dorylss is offering."

"Dorylss is being overly generous. He can't walk all the way to Teravale."

"Give me some credit!" Dorylss interrupted with a chuckle. "I'm not as old and brittle as you seem to think I am."

Leyna pressed her lips together and asked Dorylss a wordless question with her eyes.

"It's up to you," Dorylss replied with a shrug. "I don't mind walking, but Eamonn is right. We could all ride."

Leyna's chest rose with a slow inhale. "Dorylss, you can take Bardan. I'll ride with Eamonn."

The way she'd said it only made Eamonn's stomach knot tighter. Riding with her would be a good time to talk to her, as Dorylss had suggested. But even then, Eamonn knew the words wouldn't be easy to find.

Eamonn held out his hand to take Leyna's bag, attaching it to Rovis's saddle opposite his. She mounted first, settling herself at the front of the saddle. Eamonn grasped the pommel in front of her, his thumb unintentionally brushing her knee and sending his pulse into a frenzy.

In a swift movement, he swung his leg over the horse and tucked into the saddle behind her. His chest pressed into her back for a fleeting moment before he pulled away, allowing a hand's breadth of space between them.

The warmth of Leyna's body banished the cold in front of Eamonn. She reached to her bound strawberry-blonde hair and pulled it over her shoulder, revealing the pale flesh of her neck. Leyna took the reins and Eamonn rested his hands on his legs, conscious of her personal space and respecting it how he could. He was conscious of everything about her.

The morning sun peeked over the bustling city, spreading across the tall buildings enclosing narrow, muddy streets. Thin clouds drifted through the sky, a cold breeze pushing them along with the scents of cookfires that warmed the crisp air. Idyrrians, bundled to their necks in clothes of bright colors, filtered into the streets as they began their day.

As the group set off on the road south, Leyna sat ahead of Eamonn as stiff as a board, holding the reins and guiding Rovis down the road. Her natural flowery scent drifted to Eamonn's nose, and he lost himself in the comfort and familiarity of her presence. She was safety. She was home.

In the midst of Leyna's soothing closeness, something decidedly unnerving touched the back of Eamonn's mind. It was foreign and unwelcome and dark. Where it had come from, he couldn't fathom, so he pushed it away until only the peace from Leyna remained.

The trip back home to Teravale would take several days, especially if they kept a slow pace to keep Eamonn's nearly-healed injuries from regressing. Eamonn was eager to return, but he didn't mind the prolonged travel time as much if Leyna would be riding with him the rest of the way.

Dorylss had suggested that Eamonn stay home in Caen as he went off with the caravan market for their next months-long journey, allowing his body to fully heal and letting him spend some time with Leyna, but Eamonn had resisted. As much as Eamonn liked the idea of several months of rest with Leyna, he knew how restless he would get if Dorylss and the other merchants they worked with left him behind. He needed to be out there, traveling through the country, getting his life back to normal.

Not to mention, Eamonn hoped to stop by Avaria as the caravan traveled through Idyrria. On the boat ride back to Braedel, Leyna had recounted her interaction with the Queen of the Kaethiri—the magical beings who dwelled in the forest realm, one of whom had been Eamonn's mother. In his previous life, Eamonn would have had trouble believing her, but after everything he'd seen, none of it came as a surprise. He wished he'd had the chance to meet with Imrilieth himself. He had so many questions to ask about his mother, about his magic, and he wanted to use the caravan journey as an excuse to visit Avaria himself.

Leyna's back curved against Eamonn's chest as she relaxed in the saddle. He sucked in a breath that caught in his throat, and his heart jumped to meet it. He prayed she couldn't feel the rapid hammering against his ribcage.

Movement to his right pulled Eamonn's gaze, and he saw Dorylss watching them, the glimmer of a smile playing on his lips. It confirmed to Eamonn that his offer for Leyna to ride Bardan had been intentional in order to spur Eamonn into sharing his horse.

That man knew exactly what he was doing.

"Doing all right over there?"

Leyna's head turned to the sound and her spine straightened slightly in response, separating her from Eamonn.

"Yes."

Eamonn could glean nothing from Leyna's single-word response. At least she didn't say no.

"So far, so good," he replied, catching the twinkle in Dorylss's eye. Eamonn's eyelids fell low over his eyes as he spoke through them to Dorylss. He knew the man would pick up on his meaning. *I'm on to you.*

Dorylss no longer suppressed a grin, but, with any luck, Leyna wouldn't grasp its true meaning. "Good, good. We have quite a way to go before we arrive at the kingdom."

Rifillion, Idyrria's kingdom, was their only lengthy stop between Braedel and Caen. They would take the time to rest well, refresh their supplies, and help spread the news about Rothgard's defeat. After two weeks, Dorylss hoped word had started to make its way through Idyrria and beyond. Kinrid and Gilleth—the Farnish ex-soldiers who had led a small force against Rothgard's followers on Nidet—should have long since left the island and sent their fighters home to their corners of the country with the news. The people needed to know Rothgard would no longer be a threat to their provinces, monarchies, or families, and hopefully, life across the cities he'd influenced would return to how it had been.

Eamonn had expected Kinrid and Gilleth to be right behind them leaving Nidet. They had said they had questions to ask Eamonn and would meet up with them in Braedel, but they never showed. Weeks ago, it would have made Eamonn uneasy, but with their common enemy vanquished, nothing should pose a threat to them. Perhaps they had other business to attend to after taking care of Rothgard's supporters that delayed them.

The sun crept up the sky, like it was in no rush to carry on with the day. Eamonn needed it to go faster. At least Leyna's proximity helped keep his mind off thoughts that always seemed to drift in when Eamonn was otherwise unoccupied: thoughts of his father and Hadli and the events on Nidet that still haunted him. He closed his eyes and breathed in deeply the sharp air tinged with Leyna's sweetness, willing those images away. They plagued his nights enough as it was, his nightmares forcing him to relive his torture; he didn't need them encroaching on his days.

Unbidden, the same unease from before crept back into his mind, heavy and foreboding. Eamonn wanted to believe it was the memory of his trauma, but no. This was new. Dread washed over him as the unease spread from his mind to his core and settled there, sending a low rush of warmth through his veins.

Fear curled in his gut, but Eamonn didn't know why. Nothing was amiss. Leyna sat in front of him. Dorylss rode beside him. Rothgard was defeated. There was no obvious reason for the apprehension that caused sweat to bead on the back of his neck.

His whole body shook—which he could pass off as the cold—and his fingers curled into fists on his thighs as he attempted to bury the fear deep within him. But instead of him controlling the dread, it took root inside him, dragging him down into the darkness of his trauma.

TWO

LEYNA HAD FORGOTTEN HOW stiff and sore a full day of riding could make her.

The cold didn't help anything, either. The bitter chill of the wind tore through Leyna's layers and bit her skin. She wished they could have taken a longer break before setting out again, but Dorylss said they had no time to lose.

Her one consolation was that she now rode with Eamonn.

She chided herself at the thought gliding over her mind as she sat on the horse in front of him, resisting the desire to lean back into his warmth, to melt into the blanket of his embrace. The longing was new and exciting and confusing all at the same time, and she wasn't entirely sure what to do about it.

Leyna knew when she latched onto the idea of rescuing Eamonn, leaving her family behind with no warning, that her motivation was more than the pursuit of saving a friend. Something else was responsible for the irrational decisions that landed her in the heart of a battle where she didn't belong. Until their return to Braedel, enough had distracted her from slowing down and considering what had driven her into unnecessary danger.

Even from their first meeting, Eamonn was thoughtful and always polite, and she admired his grand dreams for the future. Not to mention, he was compassionate to a fault. Medicine for her mother had shown up on her doorstep only two days after Leyna had told Eamonn about her illness. She knew it came from him.

"You're not about to fall asleep and slide off that horse, are you, lad?"

Leyna turned her head as far as she could to catch a glimpse of Eamonn. She hadn't noticed him slacken behind her or give any indication that he was drowsy.

"No, it's...nothing. Never mind." Eamonn shook his head as he squeezed his eyelids shut.

Leyna returned her attention ahead, noticing with a passing glance Eamonn's white-knuckled fists against his thighs. Something was bothering him, but she didn't imagine it was fatigue. Was he ill? Had he eaten something that didn't agree with him?

Or had he gotten lost in reliving his recent horrors?

In the midst of Leyna's new, undeniable feelings for Eamonn, another certainty refused to be ignored: the way her heart hurt to look at him compared to the man she had met. The bruises had started to fade and the lashes on his back transformed to puffy pink scars, but he still bore his trauma. She could see it in his eyes: the faraway look of someone haunted. Much of his old personality had returned, but the effects of his suffering lingered.

She wanted to ask him more about it. She wanted to know what had happened to understand and empathize with him—as much as he was willing to share. Leyna had only experienced a fraction of his tribulations, and the terror that had gripped her heart while she was in Rothgard's clutches was never far from her mind. Eamonn let on that he'd put it all behind him, so Leyna didn't know how—or whether—to ask. Combined with the feelings that always arose now when in his presence, her hesitation in bringing up Nidet caused her to keep her distance.

After what Eamonn had described of his torture, of the surprising actions of Hadli and his father, he never brought it up again, but a new affection for him arose from the ashes of his pain.

The muscles of Eamonn's chest went rigid behind her, and Leyna turned her ear to her right shoulder in an attempt to check on him. From the corner of her eye, she saw the tightness of his jaw and minuscule beads of sweat along his hairline.

"Is everything all right?" Her voice was a murmur, low enough to remain between her and Eamonn.

"Fine, just... a headache." Eamonn's clipped words provided little reassurance to Leyna, but she accepted his explanation. As Eamonn shifted and adjusted the position of his arms on his legs, Leyna's eyes were drawn to Eamonn's hands, trembling against the fabric of his trousers.

She dropped her right hand from the reins and placed it tenderly on Eamonn's, and the trembling stilled as she stroked the back of it with her thumb. Her heart beat like a hammer in her chest at the choice to reach out and touch him. The contact was so intentional, so forthright, that Leyna second-guessed herself and returned her hand to the reins, finding a new nervous trembling in her own fingers.

The day didn't lend itself to conversation, with icy gusts that prompted Leyna to pull her thick Idyrrian scarf over her mouth and nose, and she was grateful. She feared too much engagement in conversation would open the floodgates of questions she had in her mind, that they would all come spilling out and make things between her and Eamonn even more strained.

By the time the sun hung low on the horizon, Leyna had gone numb. Dorylss assured them that Rifillion lay close up ahead, but she would only rejoice when she saw the tall white walls surrounding the kingdom and the golden-domed palace sitting proudly at the top of the hill, its needle-like spires piercing the sky.

The ground turned icy in spots where rain from the recent storm froze over as the temperature dropped. Frozen grass sparkled in the twilight, catching the sun's last rays.

Most of the puddles in the road crunched under Rovis's hooves, but one thin enough to turn into a sheet of ice sent the horse sliding. He tumbled forward, jostling his riders. Leyna gripped the reins, hoping to steady him, and she pressed her legs into his sides to keep herself in the saddle. Eamonn's arms wrapped firmly around her waist and he held her close, pulling her body into his.

All of Leyna's breath escaped her lungs. The strength in Eamonn's arms shocked her, especially considering he'd been starved and beaten for days on end only two weeks before. The quick flutter of his heart thumped against Leyna's ribcage, and his puffs of nervous breath blew loose strands of her hair. Even after Rovis found his footing and righted himself, Eamonn didn't release Leyna. She pulled a long breath of sharp air through her nose and closed her eyes. Though her grip didn't slacken, her muscles loosened, and she let her body relax into Eamonn.

Dorylss had dismounted Bardan and rushed up to them in an instant, speaking calming words to Rovis and stroking his neck before turning his attention to the riders. "Are you all right?" he asked, trying to keep his tone soothing. "Are you hurt?"

"I'm fine," Eamonn answered, and he unwound his arms as though suddenly aware of the tightness of his grasp around her. "Leyna?"

She wanted to tell him she was too shaken, that he needed to put his arms back around her. Instead, she eased her hold on the reins and sat up straighter, pulling her body from Eamonn as if she'd ripped a piece of fabric into two.

"I'm okay," she answered in a murmur, opening her eyes. She flexed her fingers and dropped the reins.

"Here," Eamonn said, almost in her ear, his voice a whisper. "Let me take them for a while."

He reached around her and picked up the reins, his arms encircling her. Leyna took a side of her cloak in each hand and pulled it together, tempted to lean into Eamonn's chest and feel his heartbeat again. She trembled, but not from the cold. She didn't notice it anymore. Phantom arms pressed into her waist and held her close. Her heart jumped again.

Even without a moon, the distant golden domes of Rifillion's palace glittered in the darkness. The light of the city cast it in a dazzling spectacle. Leyna smiled and the tension in her shoulders eased. Respite awaited them.

The guard presence outside the kingdom's walls was greater than Leyna remembered from their trip north. Dorylss rode ahead to speak with them and gain entry, their dialogue brief. Leyna didn't hear what was said, but she didn't care. All she wanted was warm food and a warm bed.

As soon as the gates opened and they rode through, Leyna noticed the difference in Rifillion. She pushed her shoulders back and perked her head up as she examined the city. What she saw—or rather, didn't see—made her stomach uneasy.

The normally vibrant city, typically swarming with people from all over the country even late into the night, greeted them with silence. A few people here and there hurried through the city, keeping their eyes straight ahead with no regard for the travelers. Individual sets of footsteps thumping on the road could be heard approaching and departing rather than the steady hum of hundreds of people crowding the busy streets.

"Dorylss," Leyna began tentatively, flashing her eyes to him before returning to survey the empty city, "what's going on?"

When he didn't answer, Leyna turned her head toward him, finding his eyebrows knitted together and his mouth in a frown.

"The guards didn't say anything. They bid us safe and swift travels..."

Leyna locked her eyes on him. "And?"

"And they seemed on edge."

Eamonn tensed behind her. "Something's not right."

Leyna's throat went dry at the warning in Eamonn's voice.

Dorylss shook his head. "We should be pushing our way through the city right now, much like we did in Braedel. Rifillion's never asleep, not like this."

The shift in Dorylss's tone sent ice down Leyna's spine. "Is it... is it not safe here?"

"We'll find out at the inn," Dorylss replied, picking up Bardan's pace and taking the lead. "We don't have much of a choice but to stay here for the night."

Dorylss guided them up the gentle slope of the desolate city, keeping Bardan at a trot. Leyna glanced around them as they rode but found no signs of life, even in the residences. Windows were dark or shuttered tight. Debris blew through the empty streets with the wind. Every now and then, she caught the weak glimmer of a flame through a window, even though it was about time for the evening meal and residents were presumably inside eating.

It seemed all of Rifillion had gone into hiding.

They entered the plaza where Leyna and Dorylss had first met Kinrid. He'd stood on a platform in the center of the circular plaza, giving an impassioned speech in hopes of gathering followers to help take down Rothgard. Now, the platform stood empty. No crowd gathered. Even vendor stalls had disappeared. At least here, lights illuminated some of the windows.

The clack of their horses' hooves on stone rang out in the silence and bounced off the walls of the buildings surrounding the plaza. Leyna shivered violently with the breeze that tore through the empty space unhindered. She leaned closer to Eamonn, allowing his body to shield her from the wind, and her stomach flipped as his arms tightened around her in response.

After coming to a stop just outside the stables in the plaza, Eamonn released the reins and hopped off of Rovis, staying close beside the horse. Leyna swung her leg over and lowered herself from the saddle, her back to Eamonn. Hands rested delicately on her waist as she descended, as though ready to steady her should she stumble, and a flurry of butterflies took flight in Leyna's stomach. Her heart threatened to fly out of her chest.

As suddenly as his gentle hands had found her waist, they fell, and Leyna faced him. Eamonn met her gaze without a word.

"Get that horse settled," Dorylss called from within the stables, breaking their stare. "I'd rather not linger."

Eamonn followed Dorylss into the stables, where they quickly untacked the horses and rejoined Leyna.

"Let's make haste to the inn," Dorylss said, stepping out into the plaza. "I'm curious to see its current state."

Leyna kept by Dorylss's side, with Eamonn bringing up the rear, hoping some deliberate separation from Eamonn might help clear her head. The bottom of her gray cloak flapped around her ankles and cold wind found its way underneath. *Only a few more steps*, she thought, imagining the fire that awaited them in the inn. A fire, warm food, a soft bed... Her mind latched onto the hope and promise of all that the inn could provide.

A wooden sign with the brightly painted emblem of a shield hung over a fine, polished wooden door, signaling The Golden Shield Inn. Dorylss turned the iron handle and pushed the door open. Warmth burst through the doorway, its source a cheerful, crackling fire in the fireplace on the far wall. The fire, it would seem, was the liveliest part of the inn.

Leyna stopped short just inside the room, enough for Eamonn to fit inside and shut the door behind them. Except for two patrons minding their own business in a shadowy corner of the hall, the main room of the inn was unoccupied. Leyna had thought surely she would find people in the inn, tucked away behind walls and doors and enjoying the company of others. But no—the inn was nearly deserted.

The innkeeper approached them, his eyes darting all over and around them, his hands clasped tightly in front of him.

"Ah, Dorylss, wonderful to see you again. I take it this is your return journey back to Teravale?"

"Yes, but—"

"We have several rooms available. In fact, you can take your pick!"

"Thank you for the offer. Do you—?"

"And plenty of warm food to fill your stomachs and make you comfortable."

"Hallivand," Dorylss interrupted, his tone commanding. Hallivand stopped talking and wrung his hands together. With the man silenced, Dorylss softened his voice and murmured, "What's going on?"

Hallivand swallowed, his throat bobbing. His eyes darted to the corner where the two other patrons sat in shadow. "I believe you'd better talk to them. They've been waiting for you."

Leyna peered into the darkness but could make out nothing distinguishing about the figures. They sat opposite each other, in profile to Leyna, with hoods over their heads. The hairs on the back of Leyna's neck stood on end as a cold wave of fear rushed through her body.

Leyna stayed a few paces behind Dorylss as he strode to the corner, Eamonn in step with her. Though she kept her eyes ahead on the shadowed figures, she saw Eamonn glance at her from her peripheral vision. Was her fear written all over her face?

Before Dorylss had reached the patrons' table, the two stood, turning to them and dropping their hoods to reveal their faces, the whites of their eyes bright against their dark skin.

The sigh that escaped Leyna's lips was unintentionally audible, making her relief apparent to the entire room. Any apprehension vanished from her being and the corner of her mouth tipped up into a smile.

"We have much to discuss," Kinrid said, his grim tone reflected in his expression. Gilleth, too, appeared distressed and weary.

Dorylss's features had brightened at the appearance of their Farnish friends, but Kinrid's words wiped the cheer from his face. "What's happened?"

Kinrid leaned in toward Dorylss, though no one else was present to overhear. When he spoke again, his voice had lowered into a harsh whisper.

"Rothgard has taken Idyrria."

THREE

"THAT'S NOT POSSIBLE." EAMONN crossed his arms. "I sent him over that cliff to his death. There's no way he survived that fall."

"Come, sit with us," Kinrid offered, stepping aside and gesturing to the bench beside the table. "We'll tell you what we know."

Dorylss and Eamonn filled the bench beside Kinrid, and Leyna sat next to Gilleth. Kinrid lifted his hand in the air, catching the attention of Hallivand behind the bar, and requested three ales. He took a long swig of his own before setting it back down and staring intently at the rough wooden table.

"That was not the end of Rothgard," he said, keeping his voice quiet. "He assumed Idyrria's throne just two days ago."

Eamonn shook his head in disbelief, blinking rapidly. His gut churned with a strange mix of anger, and hate, and fear. *It's not possible.* He repeated it to himself in hopes of making it true.

Blood ran hot through his veins, his heart pounding loud and heavy in his ears.

"We're not entirely sure what happened." Gilleth's voice pulled him back into the present. He had stopped listening, but now, he needed nothing more than to know whatever they could tell him. "The best we can determine is that when you sent him over the cliff, his own human survival instincts kicked in. He must have used magic to save himself. Even without your amulet, he can still wield great power."

Eamonn squeezed his eyes shut and dropped his head to his hands, pressing his fingers into his forehead. *Stupid, stupid, stupid.* He should have known better. How else could Rothgard have kept himself alive in that burning tower until the connection between his and Eamonn's minds broke? Eamonn had commanded him to stay in the tower, and he had, but apparently it wasn't enough to keep Rothgard from trying to survive the fire.

"It's my fault," he whispered, opening his eyes. He looked up to meet Leyna's gaze across the table, intent and unwavering. Eamonn searched her face, attempting to see into her thoughts, but—as usual—her expression gave nothing away. He couldn't tell if the blue-eyed stare that bore into his soul accused him or pitied him.

Eamonn tore his eyes away, finding Gilleth, Dorylss—anyone who wasn't her.

"It's all my fault," he repeated when no one contradicted him. "I don't know how to use this magic. I allowed Rothgard to save himself."

"You did the best you could." Though a subtle trepidation widened his eyes, Dorylss rested a compassionate hand on Eamonn's shoulder. "You saved all of our lives, which was no small feat."

Eamonn sighed. Dorylss always had a way of seeing the positives. "But what happened on Nidet after we left? You were supposed to meet us in Braedel." Eamonn glanced between Kinrid and Gilleth. "You'd declared victory, hadn't you?"

Kinrid took another drink from his tankard, but Gilleth nodded. "Yes, we had, after he fell. Most of the fighting ceased when the tower crumbled and Rothgard started attacking you with magic. People on both sides were watching you."

Hallivand appeared with the drinks and distributed them around the table. Leyna took a hearty gulp of hers, and when she put the mug down, her gaze didn't return to Eamonn. A pit formed in his stomach. Somehow, this was worse than the unreadable stare. He imagined she must be remembering the battle, the fear of almost certain death.

"Rothgard's people laid down their weapons when they saw you push him over the cliff," Gilleth continued. "Without him—without his power and influence—they were lost. Many of them fled on their own ships, but some we captured and held within the fortress for a few days. We determined them not to be a threat without Rothgard, so we released them. Our purpose was to take down Rothgard and liberate those under his influence, not wipe them out.

"It was only when some of our people were helping them board their last remaining ship that they heard Rothgard's right hand mention a rendezvous location in Nos Illni. A backup plan, it seemed. By the time word got to us in the castle from the docks, they were long gone."

Hadli. Eamonn's grip on his tankard tightened, turning his knuckles white. Of course Hadli wouldn't accept defeat. He'd made it plain to Eamonn where his loyalty lay, and he wouldn't give in even though his leader had fallen.

"Is that when you left? When none of Rothgard's force remained in Holoreath?" Dorylss asked.

Kinrid still did not speak.

"We pillaged, of course, and gave the mercenaries their payment from Rothgard's stores. And we searched the fortress for anything of value to Rothgard—books, plans, letters, anything. Anything that might provide further clarity to all he knew and what he'd hoped to accomplish. Whatever might have been in his tower was lost, but we did find a text and a few scrolls in a meeting room that may yet prove useful."

"Can I see them?" Dorylss asked.

Gilleth shook her head, the tight braids bound together at the back of her head swaying. "We didn't bring them here. They are under guard, just to be safe, but you may see them later if you wish. Right now, they are our only insight into Rothgard's goals."

"We *know* his goals," Leyna said miserably.

Eamonn's head shot up in surprise at her interjection. He leaned closer to the table, not wanting to miss a single word.

"He wants to take over Sarieth. His exact word was *overlord*, I believe." Her eyes flashed to Eamonn for a moment, no doubt recalling the instance in the tower when Rothgard declared his intentions. She stared at her mug and sighed. "If he is still alive, that's what he's trying to do."

"Those are his long-term goals, yes." Gilleth's dark eyes rested kindly on Leyna. "What we don't understand is how he's doing it without Avarian magic. We're hoping these documents might shed some light on his plans or methods if he never obtained Eamonn's amulet. The practical magic he taught himself isn't enough to overthrow any province, which is why he never has before now."

A silence settled over the table. Only the crackling wood in the fireplace could be heard. Eamonn watched as Leyna absently swirled the contents of her mug. She put the drink down without taking a sip and rested her forehead in one palm, never looking up.

The weight of the silence manifested into a rock that nestled itself in the bottom of Eamonn's gut. Guilt filled him until it was overflowing, but then Dorylss's words replayed in his mind. He saved their lives. He got them all out of there, even if it was only a setback for Rothgard rather than a defeat. The way things had been going, making it off that godforsaken island hadn't seemed like a real option. At least he could rest in that and counter some of the responsibility he felt for Rothgard coming back.

"What do you know of Rothgard's rise to power?" Dorylss asked, keeping his voice low in the quiet room. Kinrid finally lifted his head and spoke.

"Not much," he replied, his deep voice heavy and rich. "All of his ships departed with the exodus of his followers after the battle, so it's possible he made his way to one. When the last of his people departed Holoreath, we did a sweep of the fortress and left.

"We took our time leaving Nidet, and when we arrived in Braedel, we assumed you had already moved on. We stopped at every village from Braedel to Rifillion, only arriving here a few days ago. Amid our declarations in the plaza here that Rothgard was no longer a threat, the devil himself strode through the crowd with a few followers in his wake." Kinrid paused and ran a hand over his bald head. "He caught my eye, the smug bastard. And then he smiled, like he knew I thought I was seeing a ghost."

He stopped and swallowed, the movement in his throat obvious. Gilleth watched Kinrid with compassion as he spoke, reaching across the table and placing a gentle hand on his forearm. Kinrid laid a hand of his own on top of Gilleth's and squeezed it softly before returning it to his tankard.

"I followed Kinrid's line of sight, and so did the rest of the crowd," Gilleth continued as Kinrid drank. "Some had not seen Rothgard before, but enough recognized him and began to spew curses at us. Called us liars and tricksters. Some accused us of the worst—that we'd pledged our allegiance to him."

Kinrid rubbed his thumb along the mug's handle, his gaze lost to its contents. "Rothgard must have believed we weren't a threat, because neither he nor his followers attacked us. They strode through the plaza toward the palace in broad daylight. They wanted us to see him."

"Why didn't you attack him?" The words came out of Eamonn's mouth louder and sharper than he intended. He softened his voice as he added, "He was right there, out in the open. You could have stopped him!"

"We were looking at a dead man walking." Kinrid's head shot up and a deep crease formed between his eyebrows. "The shock froze us. Even so, innocent civilians separated us from Rothgard, and we would not risk their lives in a melee." With a sigh, Kinrid relaxed some of the mounting tension in his shoulders. "There was nothing we could do."

His voice broke, and Gilleth picked the story back up. "We set up camp outside the city and sent scouts to the walls near the northern road, tasked with keeping an eye out for you in case there was any chance you hadn't yet passed through.

"The next news we heard was that King Trinfast had stepped down, and Rothgard sent out a proclamation to all of Rifillion that he was now king." She shifted her gaze to Dorylss before continuing. "We came here, expecting you to stay at this inn as before."

Eamonn drew his brows together in thought. "The king *stepped down*?" His eyes flicked between Kinrid and Gilleth. "Are you sure he's still alive?"

Gilleth nodded, but Kinrid replied. "We've seen him. He rode through the kingdom, shouting, 'All hail King Rothgard!' The news that he'd stepped down came from his own mouth."

Leyna shared a look with Dorylss, her lips parted and eyes wide. "He was in league with them," she whispered as she leaned into the table. "Well, maybe not 'in league,' but he made a deal with them. He provided supplies and they didn't take over Idyrria. I heard it myself in the palace when we came through before."

Dorylss frowned, his thick eyebrows shadowing his eyes. "The arrangement must have gone south, for some reason. Perhaps Rothgard thought your attack was orchestrated by Idyrria, so he considered the deal broken."

"Surely the king would have denied it," Eamonn added with a shake of his head. He couldn't fathom the King of Idyrria giving in to Rothgard so easily. "The army wasn't his. They didn't bear Idyrria's crest."

"Half of our army were mercenaries," Gilleth pointed out. "Crest or no crest, Rothgard might have accused the king of hiring mercenaries for the invasion. They couldn't necessarily be traced back to him that way, which would be a tactic the king could have employed considering this arrangement with Rothgard."

Eamonn tried to accept Gilleth's explanation, but something still didn't sit right in his mind. Rothgard could have tried to take

Idyrria's kingdom before, when he had a stronger force behind him. Now, his followers were scattered. He might have used his learned magic against the king, but Trinfast could have deployed the whole of Idyrria's army to resist him. They could have killed him and been done with him. No, they were missing a critical detail.

"I want to see what you found in the fortress," Eamonn said suddenly, a thin layer of sweat rising on his hairline. "Rothgard knows something we don't. And I have a bad feeling about it."

Kinrid nodded thoughtfully. "As do I. We have two of our contingent spying on the palace's night patrol to see what they discover. There's more to these happenings than we yet comprehend." Kinrid stood, and Gilleth followed suit. "You must stay in our camp tonight. Gilleth and I will wait outside and keep watch while you have your meal, and then we will accompany you to the camp."

With that, Kinrid and Gilleth made for the exit, pulling their hoods over their heads once more.

Eamonn tipped up his mug till the bottom faced the ceiling, draining the ale. He motioned for Hallivand, requesting another and some food for the table. Dorylss emptied his tankard and ordered another as well, but Leyna sat silent, picking at a rough spot on the tabletop, her drink still half-full.

Eamonn wanted to ask what she was thinking. Maybe he should tell her that he was unsettled, too. Torn apart inside, as though everything that had brought them to that point had been in vain. But his throat was a desert, regardless of the drink he'd downed, and he couldn't seem to unseal his lips.

"I'll go see about our food." Dorylss stood from the table as if he'd sensed Eamonn's internal struggle and had given him more time to reconsider his decision. Eamonn flashed his eyes up at

Dorylss as he walked away, hoping the intense wrinkles between his eyebrows conveyed just how much he didn't want the man to leave them alone. But Dorylss merely shrugged as he passed, tilting his head toward Eamonn as if to say, *You know what you have to do.*

Eamonn watched until Dorylss had reached Hallivand at the bar, then turned his head back to Leyna. He caught her gaze resting on him for a moment before she cast it back down to the table. Maybe he needed to say something, after all. Maybe she was waiting for him to speak first.

He cleared his throat, took a sip, and cleared it again. *It should be easier than this*, he thought. *It's not like you've never talked to her before.*

Eamonn settled his eyes on Leyna from under his brow. After sucking in a slow breath through his nose, he huffed it out and asked, "What do you think?"

Like a bolt of lightning, Leyna whipped up her head and met Eamonn's gaze. She turned her face a fraction to the side as though confused, but her eyes didn't leave his.

"What do I think?"

"Yes," Eamonn replied, sounding a little too eager. "About Rothgard. How he's pulled this off."

"You really think he survived?"

A breath left Eamonn's lungs in defeat. "I believe Kinrid and Gilleth. I don't know how he survived, but he did." Questioning how it happened didn't matter; figuring out what to do next was all Eamonn could focus on.

Leyna's shoulders raised in a shrug. "If he's truly alive, he must have come to Idyrria to threaten the king with retaliation if he didn't give up the throne."

Eamonn chewed on his bottom lip. "That just doesn't really answer all the questions though." He lowered his voice and dipped his head toward her. "He wouldn't even have his entire former force behind him. Magic would only get him so far."

Leyna studied him, the cornflower blue of her eyes bright and shining. Thoughtful. Eamonn could see her mind working behind her eyes, and he found himself holding his breath for her response.

She rolled her lips together and wet them before speaking again. "What was he doing in the time before he came to Rifillion?" she whispered. Pressing her stomach into the edge of the table and bringing her face closer to Eamonn's, she said, "That's what we need to find out. Kinrid and Gilleth mentioned a rendezvous point at Nos Illni. Maybe he went there."

Eamonn nodded, a slight movement but enough to express his agreement. "We've got to see the documents Kinrid and Gilleth recovered from Holoreath. Right now, that's our only lead."

"But what will we do then? Go on home? What's to say Rothgard doesn't still want you as his captive?"

He hadn't thought of that. Eamonn stared at his clasped hands on the table. He might dare to hope that Rothgard no longer needed him, having secured a kingdom on his own. But Eamonn's heart sank as a new reality flooded his mind: Rothgard had become a much more real threat to the other provinces. The chance of organized resistance from one or two of the provinces was high, which meant Rothgard needed an edge.

The same edge he'd needed before.

Eamonn.

"He can't find out you're close," Leyna murmured, a new fear in her voice. "We can't linger here. He may be tracing your magic as we speak."

Eamonn squeezed his eyelids shut and lowered his head to his hand, pinching the bridge of his nose. He thought he'd finally escaped this nightmare, thought his life might return to normal. Yet here he was, not even home again and already back to where he'd been a few weeks ago.

"Eamonn."

He peeled his eyelids apart to look at her, surprised to see her eyes glistening. She tried to hold his gaze, but she faltered, blinking repeatedly. Her interlocked fingers tightened around each other and her lips parted, but no sound came out.

"Eamonn, I—"

"Here we are," Dorylss announced, returning to the table with bowls of steaming stew. His expression shifted the moment he saw Leyna. With a question in his eyes, he turned to Eamonn.

"Lad?"

Eamonn took another glance at Leyna before meeting Dorylss's gaze. He let out a breath: weary, resigned, and a little fearful. "I'm not safe anymore."

FOUR

THE COLD PINK LIGHT of dawn greeted the camp as a new day emerged. A dusting of snow rested on tree branches and fallen leaves, the slightest smattering that would dissolve as the sun climbed above the horizon. Eamonn breathed the crisp morning air that bit his nose and cheeks as he sat outside the tent he'd shared with an Idyrrian soldier. The scent of clean, cold earth mixed with the aroma of fresh wood burning with the morning's first fires. Some of the Farnish and Idyrrian fighters remaining with Kinrid and Gilleth were already up and about, like Eamonn, warming themselves by the crackling fires and setting up kettles for tea.

Under the cover of night, Eamonn, Leyna, and Dorylss had made it safely out of Rifillion, led west of the city by Kinrid and Gilleth, where the remnants of their forces had set up a temporary residence. A dozen or more white canvas tents dotted the gray-brown winter landscape, clustered together in a glade surrounded by dense forest.

Although in the company of their allies, Eamonn had lain awake most of the night. Dreams transformed into nightmares that froze his limbs and shot panic through his veins. Even in his sleep, he felt the whip on his back, the strain on his joints, the stabbing in his hip. The torture he had escaped lived on within him, a place where he would never be free.

He'd bolted upright in a cold sweat more times than he could count. Thankfully, the Idyrrian on the other side of the tent never seemed disturbed, snoring with fervor throughout Eamonn's wakings. Every time Eamonn awoke, the same nauseating fear from their ride into Rifillion clenched his stomach and drove his heart to a mad thundering. The anxiety lingered well after he returned to reality, taking up residence in the back of his mind—a part of Eamonn, but also not. With the nightmares overshadowing everything else, the foreign unease was harder to shake than before, and eventually, Eamonn decided it was easier not to sleep at all.

After arriving in the camp, Dorylss, Eamonn, and Leyna had decided to get some rest before meeting with Kinrid and Gilleth in the morning to review the documents in their plunder from Holoreath. Eamonn mindlessly traced a stick through the dirty snow at his feet, waiting for the meeting to begin.

The slap of canvas met his ears as a tent flap fell closed near him, and Eamonn looked up toward the sound. Leyna exited the tent she had shared with Gilleth, still dressed in the same clothes as the day before. As if drawn by an unseen force, Leyna's head turned toward Eamonn and she met his gaze. She paused and changed direction, approaching Eamonn instead of the fire closest to her tent.

Eamonn tossed his stick into the fire and watched the flames swallow it. The involuntary acceleration of his heart with her appearance surprised him, and he inhaled slowly through his nose to counter it. She didn't make him nervous in the same way as the inexplicable fear. No, Leyna's presence always ushered a sense of calm into Eamonn's being after the initial heart lurch.

"You're up," she said before she reached him.

Eamonn swallowed past a dry throat. "Yeah." He didn't want to get into a discussion of the night before, not then.

"Are you ready to go to Kinrid's tent?"

"Yes, I was just waiting for—"

Dorylss's bulky form burst through the tent to Eamonn's left, taking up his vision.

"Wonderful! You're both about." Dorylss beamed at them, eyes crinkling at the edges like an unfathomable threat didn't loom just beyond the city's walls to the east. "Let's go on, shall we?"

Eamonn stood, wiping dirt off the back of his trousers, and the three crossed the clearing to Kinrid's tent. Gilleth arrived as they did, opening the flap for them and allowing them entry ahead of her.

The tent didn't seem larger than the others in the camp, but the inside was unexpectedly spacious, given the table to one side that the entire group could fit around and a bedroll pushed to the other side, clearly the less important item from the inhabitant's perspective.

Kinrid greeted them, then knelt beside a bolted wooden chest with metal fittings underneath the table, unlocking it with a key hidden within his clothes. Out of it, he gathered papers, scrolls, and books, laying them on the table as Gilleth lit a lamp and set it in the center.

Eamonn scanned the documents, looking for anything that might grab his attention. The only thing that stuck out to him was the worn book, its leather cover scratched and distressed and its pages browned with age. Any lettering that might have been imprinted on the spine had long since worn away. Nothing about it looked particularly special, but it reminded him of the ancient texts Leyna's father had procured, the ones Leyna had used to help convince Eamonn that magic was real. He turned the book toward him, his fingers gentle on the delicate pages, and began to peruse its contents as Kinrid and Gilleth pointed out their findings.

"These look like notes taken during a meeting, or a personal reflection of a meeting after the fact," Gilleth mentioned, her finger pressed onto a small stack of papers. "They don't seem to have been compiled by Rothgard personally, but he is mentioned and was present for the proceedings."

"What does it say?" Dorylss asked, a heavy crease forming between his eyebrows.

"Mostly, it discusses supplies, inventory, recruits, and such." Gilleth looked at each person in turn around the table. The lamp light in the dim tent cast eerie shadows across her face. "It does get into a bit of strategy at the end. Rothgard mentioned his plan to use Eamonn's 'life matter,' as he calls it, as the only way to wield the amulet. So this meeting occurred after Eamonn was captured, but before the rest of us arrived at the island."

"But that seems to be his only course of action. He needed Eamonn and the amulet to further his plans, according to that set of documents. This," Kinrid added, unrolling a scroll and setting stones on the edges to hold it down, "would appear to be something Rothgard referenced when making his plans."

The old scroll was brittle and yellowed, patterned with wrinkles and inscribed with a fading, sloping script. Perhaps it was something Rothgard had recovered from the vault in Erai's library when Eamonn had seen him there with Hadli a few months before.

"'The magic... of Avaria... can master a... person's very will,'" Dorylss read, tilting his head and leaning closer to the scroll to make out the words. "'This magic can... only... be accessed by... the Kaethiri themselves.'" He lifted his head and found Eamonn. "We knew this already. But I suppose this is where he got the idea in the first place."

"It goes on to describe the amulet each Kaethiri has—their Réalta—and how it channels their magic through it," Gilleth continued. She rifled through some papers, stopping on one and pulling it to the top for everyone to see. It contained a sketch of an amulet similar to Eamonn's Réalta, surrounded by barely legible notes scrawled in incoherent groupings. "We found this, too. It's hard to decipher what was written, but we think Rothgard was describing what he'd learned about the amulets. What's clear, at least, is that he knew he needed one."

Eamonn set the old book aside for a moment and picked up the paper with the sketches. It didn't share the same ancient qualities as the book or scroll. Nothing about this paper told of age, except for a few creases and curled edges. Eamonn held the paper closer to the lamplight, curving his neck to see the scribbled words more clearly. One of the groupings was a list of gemstones: *Topaz. Tanzanite. Amethyst. Jade. Jacinth. Arithnyx.* Some of them had been crossed out, but the last one, Arithnyx, had been circled.

The other gems Eamonn knew, but Arithnyx was unfamiliar to him. Was that the stone in his mother's Réalta? Eamonn reached up to touch the pendant around his neck, then took the necklace off, laying it on the table beside the paper with Rothgard's drawing.

Side by side, the differences between the two were magnified. Where Eamonn's had curves and swirls, Rothgard's sketch had points and harsh edges. In the sketch, the pendant enclosed a stone pointed at both ends, contrasting Eamonn's oval one.

"Maybe Rothgard didn't know as much as we thought," Eamonn said, pulling everyone's attention to the pendants. "What he was going off of isn't the same as mine."

"Hmm." Dorylss glanced back and forth at the image and Eamonn's pendant. "Perhaps not."

"Wait."

The intensity behind the word drew everyone's gaze upward to Leyna, whose eyes were locked on Dorylss. "When the brigands attacked us on the way back to Braedel from Avaria, Taran found a paper on them with a sketch of the Réalta. It's how they knew what to look for."

"And, if I remember rightly, that pendant *did* look like Eamonn's," Dorylss added.

Leyna nodded vigorously, her forehead wrinkled and her lips pressed together.

"So, then, what is this?" Dorylss asked to no one in particular, gesturing to the paper.

Eamonn bent over it again, studying the scrawled words and trying to make sense of them. He could make out a heading that said *Properties of the Stone* and some of the phrases that followed, such as *bend light* and *four planes*. At the bottom of the list, underlined, was written: *conductive*. Most of the other notes around the sketch referred back to the amulet's gemstone, with low emphasis on its metal casing.

"He seemed to have more interest in the stone," Eamonn said as he straightened again and replaced his pendant around his neck, not answering Dorylss's question, "which makes sense.

The stone glows as it channels magic, so I'm assuming it's what really matters."

Leyna picked up the book Eamonn had examined and carefully turned its pages. She frowned, her eyebrows knitted together as she pored over the text. Eamonn watched her for a moment, wondering what she was thinking. Something in the concentration behind her eyes made him think she was following a hunch.

Dorylss turned to Gilleth. "What else is there?"

"Not much of significance," Gilleth replied with a shrug. "More inventories, rosters, things of that sort. I don't believe most of this was personally Rothgard's. It's more likely anything of his would have been in the tower."

"This was the only other indication of his plans that we found." Kinrid produced a small stack of papers. "The writing matches the hand on most of the other documents, so it's unlikely Rothgard penned it himself. I think the sketch of the pendant is the only document we recovered personally written by Rothgard."

"You sound as though there isn't much insight into his schemes," Dorylss said as he crossed his arms.

Kinrid shook his head. "No, there isn't. The author lists the most recent provisions sent from King Trinfast as well as what they most desperately lacked and planned to request. All it mentions by way of strategy is the intent to take Idyrria first after departing the island, and even then, it would take place only after Rothgard were to obtain Avarian magic. He was dependent on it."

"Hold on," Eamonn interrupted, his body weight pressed into his hands on the table. "They mentioned the supplies from Idyrria, so the arrangement had been made with the king, but they still planned to take Idyrria first." He scoffed and pushed himself back. "Rothgard never intended to honor their agreement once he had Avarian magic."

"You're right." Gilleth tapped the stack of papers. "He was using them for the supplies and the security on his island. Once he had the magic, all bets were off."

"That explains why he came for Idyrria but not how he took it for his own." Dorylss rubbed his bearded chin. "We're still no closer to determining a strategy that doesn't include magic."

Eamonn sighed. Maybe it wasn't necessary for them to be fully aware of how Rothgard came to take Idyrria's throne because, no matter what, at least two truths remained: Idyrria wasn't Rothgard's end goal, and Eamonn posed a threat to him. Rothgard would be on the move soon enough. They might better formulate a plan for their next steps if they had more insight into his strategies, but it looked like they had reached a dead end.

"Well, I guess we'll start on our way again," Dorylss said, stepping away from the table. "We can't go into the city for supplies, but perhaps we can make it to—"

"This doesn't make sense."

The words came out in a breath from Leyna's mouth. Across the table, she frowned at the ancient book he'd been glancing through moments before.

Leyna set the book down in the center of the table for everyone to see, open to the page she'd been studying. In the midst of a neat, fading script covering the page was a rendering of the Réalta—Eamonn's Réalta—the details almost identical to the pendant around his neck. He stooped over the book, trying to read some of the words around the image. He hadn't made it that far in his perusal of the book before.

"You believe this was in Rothgard's possession, yes?" he asked, meeting the dark, curious eyes of Kinrid and then Gilleth.

"We have no reason to believe it wasn't," Kinrid replied. "It's an ancient magical text that we presume he used to help teach himself the magic he knows."

Eamonn found Leyna again. "If this was his... if this was how he learned about the Réalta in the first place..."

He couldn't form the words. His gaze never left Leyna, and she seemed to read his thoughts in his eyes.

"Then he *did* know what it looked like," she finished for him, her forehead creasing as her eyebrows lifted. "The sketch here might be his own depiction."

Eamonn grabbed the paper with the sketch and brought it alongside the open book. His eyes flicked between the two images, catching their similarities as well as their distinct differences. A sliver of worry crept up his spine, lodging itself in the back of his neck and making the hairs there stand on end. "Does anyone know what Arithnyx is?"

Around the table, the others shook their heads. Eamonn's heart rose to his throat as he compared the two images and studied the writings around each. Rothgard's sketch included mostly hastily scribbled notes, some of which paraphrased the descriptions in the book. He'd been studying the Réalta, no doubt. Eamonn caught the words "life matter" at the bottom, just as Gilleth had mentioned, with a curved line connecting the phrase to the image. If he could make out the rest of Rothgard's compressed, slanted scrawl, he might be able to learn more, but the writing on his sketch was even more difficult to read than the lines of text in the ancient book.

"That's all we have, though," Gilleth said, breaking the silence. "It's simple enough to assume that Rothgard will attempt to rebuild his forces. It's understood he was the cause of the fall of Wolstead's monarchy, and rumors say that he was involved in the death of Farneth's king, but taking over a province for himself is new. Other provinces might mount an attack. Rothgard could even move on to another province soon—Teravale, perhaps. He seems to know something we don't, so we need to be ready."

Leyna stepped back from the table and folded her arms over her chest. Eamonn knew she had to be imagining Rothgard coming to her home province, removing the king, declaring himself ruler. What it might mean for her family. He felt Dorylss's eyes on him, so he set his jaw and faced his mentor.

"We need to make haste for Teravale," Eamonn said. "I doubt Rothgard is ready to move yet, so we have the chance to make it there before he does. We can warn the people and rally their army."

Gilleth inclined her head toward Eamonn. "I'm sure they've heard. Or they will before you arrive. Word travels fast in this country, especially word of this kind."

With another sidelong glance at Leyna, Eamonn said, "Well, we at least need to warn *our* people. Make sure they're safe."

Leyna's eyes flitted up to him. He could see the worry behind them, the fear of what may happen to her family should Rothgard claim Teravale. Eamonn dipped his head a little, an acknowledgment of how she must be feeling. Her mouth pulled in a mix between a grimace and a smile in reply.

Dorylss nodded in agreement to Eamonn's proposal. "We'll quicken our pace to Teravale."

Kinrid gathered the documents on the table, collecting them into a neat pile and returning them to the chest underneath. "We've sent emissaries to Farneth to inform the new king of the developments here and make a case for bolstering the military. It's the least that needs to be done. Till now, the new King Vinnerod has been opposed to taking up arms against Rothgard, regardless of his potential implication in his father's death—but usurping Idyrria's throne changes things. If he agrees, we've proposed creating alliances with whichever provinces are willing for a united attack."

"We'll remain here for a few days awaiting their response." Gilleth led the others out of the tent. "If the king agrees to strengthen the military, we will return to Farneth and join the cause."

"And if he doesn't?" Dorylss asked.

"Then he's a fool."

Metal clattered and murmurings pervaded the camp as the fighters suddenly came to attention, drawing weapons and facing the woods to the east. The rising dull thud of quick footsteps on the frozen ground added to the clamor of the camp, and in an instant, a man and a woman—both Idyrrian—came into view. The soldiers in the camp relaxed, lowering their weapons.

"It's Parthelle and Nylir," Gilleth said as Kinrid stepped forward to meet them. "Our spies."

"Captain," the man said, coming to an abrupt stop in front of Kinrid and dropping forward with his hands on his knees to catch his breath. "We have news."

"What is it?" Kinrid asked as the man gulped air, but when he started to cough, Kinrid turned his attention to the woman. "Parthelle?"

Parthelle, who was having remarkably less difficulty regaining enough breath to speak, said, "We think we know how Rothgard took the throne."

A fearful curiosity stabbed Eamonn's heart, and he took two steps closer to them, desperate to find out what they had learned.

"A couple members of the night guard at the point farthest from the palace began to speak of it," Parthelle answered. "They were cautious and spoke quietly, so we only picked up a few words. But from what we understand, they claim Rothgard made it King Trinfast's own idea to relinquish the throne."

"How?"

Kinrid asked the question, but Eamonn already knew the answer. His stomach bottomed out with the realization as everything clicked into place. How had he missed it in the tent? The answer had been scratched on a piece of paper in front of his very eyes.

"He has an amulet, Captain." Nylir choked out the words as he straightened. "A glowing red amulet."

"They say the amulet is controlling the king... or, the former king."

"The amulet isn't what's controlling him," Eamonn said, his voice grim as he came alongside Kinrid. The words from the sketch floated in his memory. "But it is channeling his magic. *My* magic."

A sharp intake of breath from behind him made Eamonn swivel his head to where Leyna stood. Her round eyes told him her thoughts were in the same place.

Rothgard had his own Réalta.

FIVE

LIFE MATTER.

Rothgard had written those two words underneath the drawing of the strange Réalta and his insight into its properties. He might have been attempting to create his own amulet longer than they realized.

"The papers, the notes you have," Eamonn murmured as he locked eyes with Kinrid. "It was right there in front of our noses. Rothgard made a Réalta."

"How is that possible?" Kinrid asked under his breath.

Gilleth's lips parted in surprise, her usual soldier decorum falling with the revelation. "He'd been researching it. Studying it. It was all through those notes, just not overtly."

Kinrid thanked the spies and dismissed them, then directed their group back into his tent. Once the flap had closed behind them, he faced the group with folded arms.

"How can Rothgard be using your magic, Eamonn? How could he create one of these amulets?"

Kinrid didn't move to unlock the chest and retrieve the papers again, so Eamonn reconstructed the sketch in his mind's eye.

"Rothgard could have been planning this for a while. He'd seemingly learned everything he needed to know to create a Réalta, but he was still missing something. I was that missing piece. He must have needed my 'life matter' in the amulet to connect it with my magic."

He tensed as he spoke the words from Rothgard's hand, almost spitting them out with the revulsion of the memory attached to them: Rothgard sneering as he strapped Eamonn down to the hard table, the thick needle that pierced Eamonn's flesh and bone, the victory in Rothgard's eyes as the tool pulled the marrow from Eamonn's hip. Emotion built in his throat and he coughed to clear it, forcing the feeling away. He wouldn't let the horror overtake him, not now.

Eamonn felt Leyna's gaze on him, but he didn't face her, afraid of what she might see if she met his eyes. He only breathed again when Dorylss spoke and drew Leyna's focus.

"It's hard to believe, but the documents do seem to corroborate." Dorylss's eyes flicked between Kinrid and Gilleth. "And given that the King of Idyrria supposedly stepped down of his own accord, it does, unfortunately, line up."

Dorylss rested a large hand on Eamonn's left shoulder, but Eamonn couldn't determine if it was an attempt at reassurance or consolation.

"So," Leyna began, "if Rothgard has a Réalta..."

The rest of the sentence died in her throat.

Eamonn finished it for her. "If Rothgard has a Réalta, I'm the only one who can stop him."

She whipped her head to him, the firmness of her stare this time arresting him where he stood.

"You're the only one standing in his way," she argued, her tone grave and pointed.

Leyna wasn't wrong, but neither was Eamonn. A surge of hatred rose in his body with the thought that Rothgard was still alive, Rothgard had a Réalta, Rothgard was succeeding. Eamonn didn't just have to stop Rothgard—he wanted to. His deep-seated loathing for Rothgard returned at full force, bringing with it a need for drawn-out, painful revenge.

But Leyna didn't know what went through his mind once the Réalta had returned to him in the castle tower, how badly he'd wanted to rip Rothgard limb from limb. Eamonn had suppressed that overwhelming desire solely for her sake.

"We'll make haste to Farneth. This requires an immediate audience with the king." Gilleth pushed open the tent flap and made to leave, as though she was about to pack up camp right then. "We can send word to you in Teravale if we learn anything."

"We can't go to Teravale any longer."

All eyes turned to Leyna. Her words stopped Gilleth in her tracks and she let the canvas fall. "Then where will you go? Surely you aren't staying here."

"Will you be accompanying us to Farneth?" Kinrid asked.

Leyna shook her head. "We have to go to Avaria."

"What?" Eamonn's eyebrows rose up his forehead. Was she serious? Of course, Eamonn wanted to visit Avaria, but not like this. Leyna had been longing to see to her family, to go home. He wouldn't let himself stand in the way of her returning to them now.

Leyna leveled her gaze at him. "It's the only place you'll be safe. You have no greater protection from Rothgard in Teravale than you do there. Maybe you could even learn more about your magic."

"But your family—"

"We can send them a message. Maybe Kinrid and Gilleth know of someone going to Teravale." She faced the Farnish soldiers with a question in her eyes.

Kinrid and Gilleth shared a glance. "We'll have to send a team to Teravale to speak to King Javorak about these developments," Kinrid confirmed.

"Can they carry a message to my family in Caen? Tell them we had to change our plans, that I'll be later coming home, and make sure they're aware of the danger."

Kinrid dipped his head in answer.

Leyna shook her hair back from her face, her chin tipped up. "There, it's settled."

"Nothing's settled!" Eamonn wanted to fling out his arms in frustration, but their cramped quarters in the tent prevented him. "There's no need for you to go to Avaria with me. Dorylss can accompany you to Caen. You could even go with the contingent sent to speak with King Javorak." Eamonn looked to his mentor for support or a word of agreement. Instead, Dorylss met him with a heavy sigh.

"We can't let you travel to Avaria alone, lad," the older man said. "The last time you fled to a forest, you ended up Rothgard's captive."

"And the two of you are going to prevent that from happening again?"

"There's strength in numbers." Dorylss shrugged. "I know we're not much, but we make three instead of one."

"I can travel with some of these soldiers. Surely there are a couple Kinrid and Gilleth could spare."

Gilleth opened her mouth to speak, but Dorylss's reply came first. "No one else needs to know where you're going or what you're doing. We don't need rumors spreading around the camp and beyond."

"But Leyna doesn't have to come. She can still return home."

Dorylss angled his head and crossed his arms. "You want to keep her safe?"

In his peripheral vision, Eamonn saw Leyna drop her gaze to the ground, and a resigned breath passed from her lips. "Yes."

"She will be safest in Avaria."

Leyna's head shot back up, and she smiled softly at Dorylss.

With a huff, Eamonn closed his eyes and rubbed his hand across his face. "Fine. We'll do things your way."

Leyna directed her smile to Eamonn before she turned away from him, the expression enough to send a flutter through his middle, rippling gently like wind carrying a snow flurry. Maybe she didn't blame or resent him after all.

Gilleth pushed open the flap again and exited the tent, the others close behind. Kinrid stopped just outside and surveyed the soldiers. Low rumbles of quiet speech hummed in the air as the soldiers no doubt discussed the spies' news amongst themselves.

"We'll break camp and head straight to Farneth's kingdom," Kinrid said, his focus across the crowd as he waved his hand in the air. "Titus, Jacynn, Halfast; to me! And bring our friends' horses."

Gilleth tightened the leather straps of her baldric and checked each of her weapons, as though she were suddenly afraid to lose them. "We can send a messenger to Braedel and request for Taran and Teiyn to rejoin us. We're still close enough to them that they ought to be able to catch up quickly."

A woman and two men appeared before them, answering Kinrid's call. The two men led Rovis and Bardan from their tie-off with the rest of the forces' steeds and handed the reins over to Eamonn and Dorylss.

"Gilleth and I will lead the others to Swyncrest to meet with the Farnish king," he instructed, his fierce eyes settling on each one in turn. "I'm making it your duty to meet with King Javorak of Teravale and request his presence in Miren. We'll gather the monarchs in Amrieth to ensure they are aware of the truth behind Rothgard conquering Idyrria and insist they form an alliance against him."

Eamonn inserted himself into their conversation. "Why meet in Amrieth if you're going to Swyncrest? Why not just have King Taularen join you and King Vinnerod in Farneth?"

Gilleth crossed her arms and set her jaw, the disgust in her face giving Eamonn a partial answer despite her holding back words. Kinrid flashed a look at her and the same sentiment briefly passed over his face. He waved off the three he'd called, each heading to nearby tents, then straightened and almost imperceptibly tipped his chin up.

"For one, Swyncrest is far less stable than Amrieth right now. The damage left in Rothgard's wake is still proving problematic for Farneth as a whole, but especially the kingdom. He has supporters there, so it's more dangerous. And," Kinrid added, propping a hand on the hilt of his sword and gripping it, "the King of Miren is not likely to attend. If we meet him on his own ground, he has a harder time escaping it."

Eamonn's brow furrowed, and he tugged on the reins to steady Rovis, who grew impatient. "He doesn't see Rothgard as a threat?"

"Hardly." Gilleth nearly spat the word out. "The Mirish army ran Rothgard out of the province with little effort, which, unfortunately, means that King Taularen has one more accomplishment to build up his ego."

"What Gilleth *means*," Kinrid interrupted, holding Gilleth's gaze long enough for her to relax her crossed arms, "is that King Taularen feels invincible. Foolishly, of course. Just because his army was able to dispel Rothgard once doesn't mean they can again."

"But it makes him feel stronger than the kings of the other provinces who fell. It gives him a sense of power that he has no claim to."

Another warning look from Kinrid shut Gilleth's mouth, and she turned away from the group, stalking to her tent and flinging the opening flap wide.

"Is the Mirish king really all that high and mighty?" Leyna asked, her eyes on the tent where Gilleth had disappeared.

Kinrid said nothing, so Dorylss filled the silence. "He's not the humblest of people, you might say. Just what I know from my limited experience with him."

"Makes sense." Eamonn shrugged. "He's not just Mirish, he's their *king*. All the Mirish think they're better than everyone else. It comes with the territory."

"Not all," Kinrid countered. "There are many who don't fit the stereotype, just as there are plenty of Idyrrians who don't care for higher education. Princess Karina, the King of Miren's daughter and heir to the throne, has a much more agreeable disposition."

"Well, it's a shame it's not her we'd be working with." Dorylss let out a sigh and mounted Bardan. "I have a feeling Taularen is going to be our roadblock. I'll go on ahead to Miren after accompanying these two to Avaria and seek an audience with the king on Teravale's behalf while we wait for King Javorak to arrive."

"You can do that?" Eamonn asked as Leyna hoisted herself onto Rovis. "You don't have the authority."

"Erm—" Dorylss's massive shoulders raised in a shrug. "I do, in fact. Many years ago, I fought with Idyrria in the War with Cardune. To make a long story short, I used diplomacy with the Cardunians, talks that brought about the war's end. A skill from negotiation as a merchant. King Javorak learned what I had done and granted me a position in his palace as an ambassador, but I refused. I preferred my life as a merchant." Dorylss's eyes twinkled and one cheek lifted in a smile. "The king said the position was mine no matter what. So, technically, I can request an audience with Taularen on authority of the King of Teravale."

Eamonn huffed incredulously and titled his head at Dorylss before pulling himself into his horse's saddle. "I can't believe you never told me that."

"It wasn't important," Dorylss said with a small shake of his head. "I never planned to do anything with it."

Kinrid dropped the grip on his sword's hilt. "Well, I'm grateful for it. Perhaps you can meet with the Mirish king while we are in Farneth speaking with King Vinnerod." He offered Dorylss a curt nod. "We'll meet again in a fortnight."

Eamonn shot a glance to Dorylss as the older man turned his horse's head and dug his heels into the stirrups. "So you won't go to Avaria with us?"

"As I said, I'll accompany you," Dorylss answered, the lines around his eyes fanning out as he smiled warmly at Eamonn. "But lad, I never intended to go inside the forest with you. I won't want to once we get there. The magic keeps out anyone who doesn't belong there." His gaze shifted from Eamonn to

Leyna. "I've actually wondered if Leyna will be able to enter again."

Eamonn knitted his eyebrows together, and he tried to lean around toward Leyna to catch sight of her face. "What? You might not be able to go back into Avaria?"

Leyna turned her head and met Eamonn's questioning stare from the corner of her eye. "Just what Dorylss said. The magic of the realm prevents anyone who doesn't also possess the magic from going inside. I was able to enter last time because I wore your Réalta. Dorylss, Taran, and Teiyn all wanted to turn back once we arrived at the forest's edge."

With a scoff, Eamonn leaned back on the saddle and returned his attention to Dorylss. "You failed to mention that."

"I didn't think it relevant," Dorylss replied, eyebrows raised in innocence. "It won't be a problem for you. Leyna may be able to enter again since she has before, and if not, you can have her wear the pendant again."

Eamonn trotted Rovis up to Bardan's side, closing the distance between Dorylss and himself. "So, you never intended to go to Avaria? Just to take us there?"

"I'd serve no purpose in the forest with you, lad. My talents are much better utilized in convincing the King of Miren to hold a council and ally with the other provinces."

Eamonn sighed and slumped a little. "I don't like the idea of you traveling alone. You didn't want me to do it. It's a long way from Avaria to Amrieth."

"Do you forget that I know this country like the back of my hand?" Dorylss chuckled, and Eamonn couldn't resist the smile that rose on his face. "I'll travel by main roads and stay where I trust the innkeeper." His eyes twinkled at Eamonn. "Don't you dare worry about me, my boy. It's the last thing you need to do."

Leyna looked at Dorylss as he spoke, a grin creeping up her cheeks as well. Eamonn pulled a deep breath in through his nose, catching the scent of her that was now so familiar to him. He allowed himself to relax a bit for the first time that day, taking hope in their plans and dreaming of answers in Avaria.

A sensation washed over him without warning—a pressure rising within his chest into a dull ache behind his breastbone—and a momentary panic passed through Eamonn. His first thought was that the fear he couldn't explain was returning, but it took only seconds to realize this was different.

This sensation was comforting and familiar. A foreign presence filled his mind and spirit but didn't invoke fear. He recognized it—he'd felt it before while they were on Nidet. Eamonn had heard a voice coming from somewhere deep within himself, and he knew it was the voice of a Kaethiri. It was clear he had uncovered some connection to them, and it was that connection now that tugged at his being and filled in the answers as he thought the questions.

Did they know he was coming?

Yes.

Were they eager to see him?

Yes.

Would they teach him how to control this magic?

Yes.

SIX

THE DAYS BECAME BITTER as frigid air blew in, unseasonably cold for autumn. After leaving Kinrid and Gilleth's camp behind, Eamonn, Leyna, and Dorylss didn't return to Rifillion or rejoin the main road. Instead, Dorylss led them to a lesser-used trail that cut through the wilderness, keeping them more concealed within trees and through hills. Their path passed Nos Illni on the eastern side before approaching the forest realm of Avaria.

"It's not the best time to be traveling this far north," Dorylss told them on their first day of travel as Leyna shivered beside a fire, closing her eyes to the minimal warmth it offered. "Especially not for sleeping out of doors."

The trail Dorylss followed brought them to a village here or there, where they would stop to have a hot meal and warm their numb extremities. They'd managed to avoid snow so far, which was a blessing, but the air was dry, and an ever-present icy breeze stung their skin. Leyna trembled atop the horse in front of Eamonn as they rode, her shaking worsening the longer they were away from a fire. Eamonn offered her his riding cloak more than once to layer over her own, but she refused every time.

"I'm already wearing everything I have with me," she said, hugging her arms tightly around her middle. "One more cloak won't make a difference, and you need to keep warm yourself."

"Well, in that case..." Eamonn shifted on the saddle so that he sat flush against her, pressing his body gently against hers to share his warmth. He adjusted his hold on the reins to pull his arms closer around her, enveloping her with his body heat. His stomach flipped when she leaned back into him and rested her head on his shoulder.

"Any better?" he asked, unable to raise his voice above a murmur for fear that Leyna would hear his nerves behind it.

"Yes."

The single word sent a blade of fire through Eamonn's core that warmed him more than any true flame could. She didn't push him away or tense at his touch. How much of the distance between them had come from his own mind, his own perception of how she regarded him?

They rode like that for hours, and at one point, Eamonn wondered if Leyna had drifted off to sleep. Her breathing grew rhythmic, and her head bobbed against his chest with every step Rovis made. He locked his arms around her, giving himself the excuse that he didn't want her to slip off the horse as she dozed. When she awoke a little while later, she didn't move or shift away from him.

As the sun dipped closer to the horizon, taking the last of its light and heat with it, Leyna sat up and a blast of cold filled the space where she had been. Eamonn sucked in a breath and fought the urge to ease her back against him.

"Please tell me there's another village before we turn in for the night." She fixed her eyes on Dorylss riding beside them, a mixture of expectation and dread swirling in their cornflower-blue depths.

"I'm afraid not," he replied, apology flooding his features. "We'll have to camp tonight."

She huffed and fell back into Eamonn, the position familiar now. Easy. It still shot Eamonn's heart rate up, and he willed it to slow so Leyna wouldn't feel how rapidly his pulse thrummed.

Once they found a small clearing, they stopped the horses and prepared their camp. Eamonn and Dorylss moved through the tasks effortlessly: cutting any low brush from the area, starting a fire, spreading out their bed rolls, hanging the tarp above where they would sleep. Dorylss stalked off into the woods to find some small game for them to eat, leaving Leyna and Eamonn alone by the blazing fire.

Even after three days of travel, Eamonn and Leyna's conversation had remained at a minimum. Mostly, they rehashed what they knew of Rothgard, the new Réalta, and how he might be stopped. If the discussion fell away from their current mission or their travel to Avaria, Leyna drifted out of it.

But after their ride earlier that day, after the comfort with which Leyna relaxed into Eamonn, he couldn't keep his thoughts to himself anymore. They'd only begun to get to know each other before he'd been captured by Hadli and taken to Rothgard, but the events in the tower at Holoreath—and even before, simply knowing that she had been dragged into his mess and was in danger—eliminated the need for formalities and a proper courtship.

Courtship? A thin layer of sweat rose on his palms at the thought. He glanced in Leyna's direction as she stared into the orange flames, but the moment her eyes met his, he flicked his gaze back down.

Yes, in other circumstances, he would have courted her. He'd already felt the desire back in Teravale. He could have seen himself spending his off months from the caravan taking her for walks in the meadows beyond her house, bringing her flowers from Nani's shop in Caen, even treating her younger brother and sister to sweets when he came by. Eamonn lost himself in a vision of a trip to Lake Elaris, where he reclined in the grass on a blanket laden with a picnic, Rovis tied to a tree nearby, and Leyna's head in his lap as they laughed about something frivolous, maybe some conundrum Dorylss had gotten himself into.

A pop from the wood as the fire bit into it drew Eamonn back to the present. The vision evaporated, and along with it the likelihood of that scenario ever happening. Even if something changed between them, would life ever be that carefree again? Would Eamonn? He could never go back to a life that hadn't known Rothgard, hadn't known the torture or trauma by his hand.

Eamonn drew away from the thoughts, not wanting to squander this moment, not while he had the resolve, not while they were alone. He clasped his hands together, elbows on his knees, and wrung them furiously.

"Leyna." His voice barely made it past his tightening throat, gritty and low.

Leyna looked at him again and pulled her eyebrows together at the odd way he spoke her name. His eyes fell to the fire.

"I know things have been...difficult...the past few weeks. I know I'm the reason you got caught in this mess in the first place, and I—" He swallowed back the guilt and sorrow he carried.

"I'm so sorry. It's fair if you resent me for it. Really, I would probably resent me too. I mean, I broke. I told Rothgard you had my pendant. You have every right to hate me forever. We can find a way to get you back to Teravale safely instead of you staying in Avaria with me."

"Resent you?"

Leyna's words pulled Eamonn's gaze to hers, and the look on her face sent a wave of shame through his core. He couldn't stand to see the pity in her eyes. The hurt. As though it pained her that he would say such a thing. In that instant, any thought that she could be angry or upset at him vanished, and he felt foolish for ever imagining she might be. And now, the last thing he wanted from her was her pity.

Eamonn didn't want to be pitied, not anymore. He'd never move on.

"I don't know, I just thought that—"

"I could *never* resent you." Sincerity hung in her words, and she waited a beat with their eyes locked before she spoke again. "Of course, I wish neither of us had gone through any of it, but it's not something I hold over you or blame you for." Leyna straightened and tossed her hair over her shoulder. "I made my own decisions, and I'd make the same ones again. And..." She paused, her throat bobbing. Her voice was less even when she spoke again. "I see what he did to you, even if I don't know all the details. I can't believe you endured any of it just for me. I can't fault you for breaking."

A weight lifted inside Eamonn, a burden that had been heavy on him since they'd arrived in Braedel and Leyna closed herself off. He'd been so certain she saw him as the cause of her own troubles. Now that she'd admitted it wasn't the case, a new thought came to him, and he frowned.

"I just don't understand," he murmured, his foot tapping out the rhythm of his heart. "If that wasn't it, then what?" He swallowed past the cotton in his throat.

Leyna broke their gaze and her eyes found the fire. Something like turmoil filled her expression, as though it was her turn now to pick and choose her words. Her hesitation caused a pit to form in Eamonn's stomach, his insides pulling into a knot that grew tighter with each passing second. What could be so bad that she'd wanted to withhold it from him?

"I didn't know what to say," she finally said, her words a whisper over the crackle of the fire. "I couldn't empathize with what you'd been through, so I didn't want to bring it up. I haven't known how to talk about it, or even if you would be okay talking about it. And I was terrified of saying the wrong thing, something that would bring the pain back for you." The firelight glinted in the tears welling in Leyna's eyes, and she swallowed. "It changed you. All of it. After you told me some of it, you didn't bring it up again or act like it was bothering you, but I could see the change. I could see how it affected you."

Her voice came out tight, as if the words fought to stay inside, remain unspoken. A tear freed itself and ran like an arrow with charted precision down Leyna's cheek as she lifted her eyes to Eamonn. After a shuddering breath, she began again. "I've wanted so badly to let you know that I'm here for you, that I want you to feel safe and open with me if you need to talk about any of it, or if you don't, that I will sit in silence with you. I wish I'd said something sooner, but I've had such a hard time knowing what to say, especially since—"

She cut herself off, finding the fire again and pressing her lips into a hard line. A pink flush that had nothing to do with the heat of the flames crept over Leyna's cheeks.

Eamonn leaned toward her, eager, the knot in his stomach gripping him even more. He needed to know the end of that sentence. "Especially since what?"

Leyna tilted her head back, her face to the sky. She wrapped her arms around her knees and released a heavy breath. A white puff appeared in front of her mouth. "After you were captured, I was so scared. When I saw you in the tower, it absolutely broke me. Eamonn..." Her voice cracked as she said his name. "I only ever want to take your pain away and be there with you through it all. And in realizing this, I've had to admit that my feelings for you are more than..."

Sparks flew off the fire beside them, and Eamonn's insides mimicked the crackling flames. Sharp tingles shot from deep within to his fingertips, his toes, every nerve alive and vibrant. The feeling flooded him with a new wave of resolve, and he scooted closer to Leyna, undaunted by the reservations holding either of them back. She looked up at him but didn't move away, her face still flushed and her eyes glistening.

Eamonn swallowed hard, but his throat might as well have been sand. "Leyna," he said in a rough whisper, surprise emotion choking him. "I thought you hated me. My life has been agony thinking I had ruined yours. That you wanted nothing more than to get away from me. You didn't have to go through any of what you did—*any* of it—but you did it for me. And I can never repay you for that."

Leyna couldn't hold his gaze. She rolled her lips and stared at the ground. Eamonn ducked his head closer to her, lifting her chin with gentle fingers and bringing her eyes back to him. He hadn't finished what he wanted to say, and he needed her to hear him. He needed her to *see* him.

"I've been dealing with the same things you have. The same feelings. I couldn't stand to see you hurt. And thinking about what Rothgard might do to you sent me into a new level of rage that I didn't know was possible."

Eamonn trembled with the memory of Rothgard shoving Leyna through the tower door and then holding her feet in place with magic. Rothgard hadn't released her after obtaining the Réalta, as he had promised, but Eamonn wasn't really surprised. The fear of not knowing what Rothgard might actually do to her had coursed through his weak frame and sent him to his feet to protect her, but Rothgard had struck him back down.

Pushing the memories from his mind, Eamonn found himself back in the moment and struggled to catch his breath, his chest heaving.

"The truth is, ever since I met you, it's like you were this invisible force drawing me towards you. I couldn't resist the pull. I don't know how else to describe it." His words came out in a hurry now, unbidden, spilling from his mouth before he could think to stop them. "Thoughts of you have consumed me ever since we met. Once I knew you were coming to Nidet because of me, I only ever worried about you. Leyna—" he said again, this time stopping to swallow and slow down his speech, lowering his words to a murmur. "You sparked a fire in my soul that I can never quench. I've been tortured these past weeks thinking I had lost you forever."

He shifted his hand to cup her jaw. He noticed the flick of her eyes to his lips, expectant, and she didn't withdraw. Eamonn's heart pounded like a mallet against his ribcage, picking up speed as he lost all his inhibitions and opened himself up to her.

"I started to feel this way in Caen shortly after we met, but ever since the island, it's consumed me. You are always on my mind, and I always want you near."

Eamonn studied Leyna's face, hoping to get some indication of her reaction to his confession. Her eyes shone in the firelight, dragging Eamonn far into their vivid blue depths. She sniffed once, her lips parting, but she made no move to speak. Eamonn released her cheek, but before his hand could fall, Leyna lifted hers and caught his, pressing his fingers against her skin once again. His heart jumped at the movement and he took it as an invitation, bringing his other hand to her free cheek.

A small smile curled Leyna's lips and made her dimples appear, and she ran her hand down from his hand at her cheek to rest past his wrist. All of Eamonn's insides were ready to burst. His heart threatened to explode from his chest, its rapid beat sending warm blood coursing through his veins and causing his limbs to shake with anticipation.

Leyna dropped her eyes to Eamonn's lips again, and this time, she let them linger. Willing his pulse to steady so he could do this properly, Eamonn leaned in toward Leyna, taking his time to ease in close to her. Her loose curls brushed his fingertips as he held her face in his hands, and he ran a thumb over her cheek, marveling at her impossibly soft skin. The minimal space that had remained between them was now all but eliminated. Eamonn breathed deeply, letting Leyna's scent fill his lungs as he closed his eyes and brought his face to hers.

Heavy footsteps came crashing through the woods behind them, crunching dry leaves and cracking brittle twigs. Eamonn and Leyna jumped apart. Their eyes locked for one moment more before Leyna turned away, sucking the wind from Eamonn's lungs as she did. She stuck her hands out to the fire and shivered. Eamonn couldn't tear his eyes from her. He searched for something in her expression, hopefully disappointment or perhaps even desire, and nothing like regret, embarrassment, or—dare he think it—humor. But her countenance was steel as she faced the fire and let the orange glow warm her skin.

The rhythmic stomp of one man's footsteps continued and grew louder as they approached the camp, and Eamonn turned in their direction to see Dorylss faintly illuminated by the fire-light. He carried two hares by the legs in one hand and an unsheathed knife in the other.

Dorylss must have noticed the tension in the air and the smaller space between Eamonn and Leyna than there had been when he left. His eyes brightened, and he caught Eamonn's gaze, a mischievous grin on his lips.

"You don't seem pleased to see me!" he called, coming into their clearing and dropping the hares on the ground. "I've brought us all food, but you're looking at me like I just stepped on your dinner!"

"Just give one here," Eamonn demanded as he reached for one of the limp animals. His tone was as sharp as the knife he pulled out of his belt to clean the hare.

"No 'thank you?'" Dorylss chastised, but his eyes still glittered. "We might not be eating at all if not for me going off to find this brace of hares while you two were—"

"*Thank you*, Dorylss." Eamonn cut him off, narrowing his eyes knowingly at his mentor.

Leyna busied herself with readying the spit to cook the meat, but when Eamonn cast a sideways glance at her, he saw the dimple in her cheek, sending his heart to his throat. Did she not care that Dorylss might have seen them nearly kiss? Eamonn didn't care—not really. He just wished the man had better timing.

SEVEN

THE NEXT DAY WAS their last full day of travel before arriving at Avaria. Leyna, Eamonn, and Dorylss packed up camp at dawn and set off through the northern Idyrrian woodlands with few words spoken. Heavy clouds had gathered overnight and threatened snow, so Dorylss suggested they push the horses a little faster.

Leyna and Eamonn hadn't discussed what happened by the fire the night before. Dorylss never brought it up, either.

You sparked a fire in my soul that I can never quench.

She'd never imagined those words to come out of Eamonn's mouth. A chill rushed over Leyna's skin and covered her in goosebumps, her insides in a scramble like whisked eggs.

His touch spoke to his sentiments, though. The way he helped her up as she mounted the horse, the brush of his hand on hers when he took the reins, the steady comfort of his body behind her...it seemed new and exciting, laden with energy.

"There are no settlements this far north," Dorylss told them when they took a break for their midday meal. "We'll have to make do with what we have already and what we can find. I have a bad feeling the night will be harsh, what with those clouds brewing."

Leyna lifted her face upward and studied the low-hanging grey clouds through the bare, white-barked birch trees. She already didn't like them; they blocked the sun and took away its light, its warmth, and its joy. The landscape was bleak enough, turning rockier the farther they traveled. The thinning trees provided almost no cover, and the gentle slopes in the terrain would become treacherous when iced over. The last thing she wanted was a snowstorm.

"Any chance we'll make it to Avaria before tonight, then?" Eamonn asked. He took a swig of water from his canteen and offered it to Leyna. She'd finished hers that morning, but Dorylss assured them they'd arrive at another water source soon. They hadn't crossed a creek or tributary in miles. In truth, she wished they had a kettle so she could make a piping hot cup of tea. What she wouldn't give to feel the warm liquid trickle down into her stomach. Her insides curled up at the reality of drinking cold water in winter weather.

"It's unlikely." Dorylss kicked dirt over the fire before swinging his leg over Bardan's saddle. "And by unlikely, I mean, prepare yourself for a cold night."

Leyna returned Eamonn's water flask, holding his gaze a little longer than usual, and the slight grin gracing his features was enough to make her stomach flip. She couldn't help but smile in response, and Eamonn stood eagerly. His eyes flashed with something like desire, and he closed the space between them, tenderly grasping one of her hands with only his fingers.

"I meant every word." He kept his voice low enough for only Leyna to hear.

"Ready over there?" Dorylss asked as Bardan stamped in place, ready to move again.

Leyna squeezed Eamonn's hand, then she turned and hoisted herself onto the horse. Eamonn was behind her in the saddle in an instant, and as soon as he was settled, he placed a soft kiss on her shoulder.

Even through the layers of fabric that covered her, Leyna could tell it was a kiss, the purse of Eamonn's lips delicate but the pressure firm. A flutter filled her entire belly and swirled like a whirlpool, warm and fierce.

Just like that, Leyna latched on to the idea that there could really be something between them, that it could grow and flourish and become something beautiful. She hadn't allowed herself to dwell on the possibility before because she never imagined it would happen. She imagined Eamonn too scarred and emotionally unavailable after his torment at Rothgard's hand. It didn't have to define him, and he didn't seem to let it. But Leyna knew it was there, and she didn't know how long it could hide under the surface.

She'd witnessed him thrash in his sleep at Taran and Teiyn's house, presumably with nightmares he refused to acknowledge to her. She'd seen the shame in his eyes as she tended his wounds, something she now explained with his belief that she resented him for breaking under his torture and betraying her to Rothgard. And then, most recently, she hadn't missed the subtle anxiety that plagued him at unexpected times and with no discernable reason.

Leyna leaned comfortably against Eamonn in the saddle, and he responded by pressing in close to her, the reins held lazily in his hands. She wouldn't focus on the changes he'd undergone or how his trauma might show up later. Right now, Eamonn was opening up to her. He was giving her more of him than he ever had, and she closed her eyes and soaked it in.

The grey sky darkened and a biting wind picked up, whipping at their cloaks and stinging their exposed skin. The storm was imminent, and their only shelter was the bare treetops overhead. Leyna trembled as a sudden burst of cold air swirled around them and penetrated down to her bones.

"Take these," Eamonn whispered to Leyna, holding up the reins. She stuck her hands out from the cave of warmth that was her cloak, the bite of the air unforgiving, and took the reins from Eamonn. With his hands free, Eamonn wrapped his arms firmly around Leyna, holding her cloak closed against the cold and cocooning her in his body heat.

She ought to have said something. Her mind raced as she searched for words to say, for a reply she could give, but the glacial temperatures had numbed her mind and frozen her mouth.

White specks dotted Leyna's vision, and at first, she thought she hadn't had enough to eat or drink, but she soon realized the first snowflakes had begun to fall, floating harmlessly down from the sky. A layer of white steadily built as they rode, hiding the dry brown leaves that covered the ground.

"We'll have to find a place to set up camp soon," Dorylss said over his shoulder. "I don't want to get caught fighting a snowstorm."

The snowfall picked up over the next hour, piling stacks of fluffy white powder on the ground. It clung to their cloaks, their hair, and the horses' manes, and it was rapidly building.

"Over there!" Dorylss nodded toward an incline up ahead, where an overhang of rock jutted out over a clearing.

They guided their horses up the slope, careful to find their footing under the blanket of snow. The overhang was low, barely high enough for the horses to stand underneath, but it offered sufficient cover to keep them out of the snow.

Once under the broad jutting of rock, Eamonn jumped down from Rovis and helped Leyna off before hurrying back into the storm with Dorylss to gather wood for a fire. Leyna tucked herself into the deepest corner of the alcove where the wind barely reached her, keeping eyes on the two men in case they went too far and got lost in the growing wall of white. She hugged herself, the cold air reaching every inch of her body without Eamonn at her back, and she began to shiver.

Eamonn and Dorylss returned within minutes, arms full of twigs and tree limbs, and they began to build a fire near the rock wall where Leyna stood. It soon roared to life and engulfed the space with heat. Eamonn tethered the horses to a tree just beyond the overhang where they could remain under its cover, and Dorylss procured the remainder of their meal from the day before.

"Heat it up, and it'll be just as good as it was yesterday." He winked at Eamonn and Leyna as he put the meat on a spit and set it up over the fire.

Leyna retrieved the bedrolls from the horses' packs and went to work laying them out near the fire. Eamonn joined her, reaching a hand out to take one from her.

"Here, let me help."

Leyna extended one of the bedrolls to him, and he spread it out on the ground beside hers. About six inches separated them. When Eamonn left to join Dorylss at the fire, Leyna adjusted her bedroll, hoping to find a more comfortable position on the ground—three inches closer to Eamonn's.

The wind whipped and howled around them, sending a thin layer of snow inside their hovel, but the fire melted whatever came too close to them. Their bedrolls were spared the worst of it, as far under the overhang as they were. Darkness settled over the land as night arrived, giving the storm an eerie quality that sent a different kind of chill down Leyna's spine.

"You were right," Eamonn announced after swallowing his last bite of dinner. "It was just as good. I'm glad we saved some."

Leyna ate her last bite, grateful for something warm and more substantial than the hard cheese they had munched on along the way. She took a drink from her canteen, filled to the brim with water from melting snow, and rose from her place by the fire.

"I think I'm going to turn in," she said. "The day's catching up with me." Bidding goodnight to Eamonn and Dorylss, she took off her cloak and settled down onto her bedroll, her scarf and cloak serving as a makeshift pillow and blanket.

Heat from the fire filled the space under the overhang, but Leyna still shook with cold. The temperature had dropped dramatically with the storm. How could autumn be so cold? Teravale rarely felt a cold so severe, even in the dead of winter. She closed her eyes and tugged the cloak over as much of her face as she could, and she tried to let both her mind and body relax and find enough peace to fall asleep.

Minutes later, Leyna felt movement near her, and something on the ground shifted. She thought about opening her eyes but changed her mind, imagining Eamonn must have decided to get some rest as well. With any luck, just the proximity of his body might add to the heat of the fire and help warm her.

Her eyes shot open as an arm snaked its way around her waist. Eamonn had lain down beside her, yes, but closer than Leyna had expected. She had taken away three inches, and Eamonn made certain to remove the other three.

"Is this okay?"

Eamonn's breath sent a tremor through Leyna's body as he whispered in her ear. This was more than okay, but she couldn't say so. His body settling beside her had robbed Leyna of words, of breath. She slowed her pounding heart and nodded in response, her head still turned away from Eamonn on the scarf.

They had all slept close to each other the other night they had camped, making use of everyone's body heat to keep them warm throughout the crisp night. But this was different.

Dorylss must have agreed to take the first watch, but he wouldn't be far. Apparently, Eamonn had no qualms about snuggling close to Leyna with Dorylss present. Whatever this was, there was no point in hiding it from Dorylss or pretending it wasn't happening. He was as close to Eamonn as a father and to Leyna as an uncle; he would know about it, so it might as well be sooner rather than later.

Leyna no longer felt the cold, but she still shivered, her entire body aware of Eamonn curled up behind her.

"You're shaking." He tightened the arm around her waist and pressed his chest closer to her back. Leyna was grateful for the cloak that covered her and acted as the slightest barrier between her and Eamonn. Not that she wanted the separation, necessarily, but right now, while this was new and exciting, every little thing was magnified. Each touch from Eamonn sent fire through her.

She had spoken the truth when she told Eamonn and Dorylss that the day had worn her down. Between the fire and Eamonn,

Leyna was shielded enough from the cold that her mind gave in and exhaustion pulled her down into sleep.

When she awoke hours later, the storm had ceased, but the cold had returned in full force. Dorylss snored near her, and Eamonn was gone.

EIGHT

HE COULD STILL FEEL the steady rise and fall of her torso as she breathed in peaceful slumber.

He hadn't wanted to leave her, but Dorylss needed rest and Eamonn had to take over the watch. The raging winds calmed and the snowfall dwindled as he sat under the edge of the overhang, but the storm inside him still churned.

Encircling Leyna's waist with his arm and snuggling up behind her while she slept was a massive leap in their relationship.

Eamonn lowered his head and scrubbed his face in his hands, his elbows propped on his knees. He was moving entirely too fast. Just because they'd skipped the conventionalities of courtship didn't mean he got to jump to the next level. He needed to reign it in, take hold of his desires and approach them with smaller steps rather than diving in. The last thing he wanted was to overdo it and scare Leyna away before he even really had her. Her closeness had given him the most restful night of sleep since he'd fled Caen. Having her beside him had kept the nightmares at bay.

She stirred on her bedroll at the back of the overhang, and he glanced back at her. He longed to return to her, take his position beside her again, and keep the cold away. When he'd said he always wanted her near, he wasn't exaggerating. It might not always be easy, or practical, or even possible, but it was what he wanted.

The storm had thrown a heavy white blanket of snow on the ground, the powder so thick in some places that the horses stepped in past their knees. The terrain was hilly, with rockier areas that jutted out, hidden under the snow, and it slowed them down as they carefully picked out a safe path. Eamonn grew impatient. He had hoped their last leg would go much more quickly. At least the sun was out and shining again. The strong light from the cloudless day reflected off the pure white snow and made it glitter, giving the land a magical quality in its own right.

The longer they rode, the more Eamonn felt a pull from somewhere deep within him. A low throb pulsed, buried in his core, growing stronger and more defined with each step. It reminded him of the sensation he'd felt when connected to the Réalta, but magnified. He knew they were approaching the magic's source.

Dorylss slowed his horse and gestured for Eamonn and Leyna to follow suit. "It's tricky with this much snow. There's a cliff here; we don't want to get too close to the edge."

Without seeing it, or even knowing exactly where on a map they were, Eamonn could sense that they were at Avaria. The land of his mother—of her people—drew him, guiding the way from inside him.

"It's this way." Eamonn flicked the reins and took the lead, confidently directing Rovis through the snow.

"What do you mean? I thought you had never been here before," Leyna said, flashing a look at him over her shoulder.

"I haven't. It's something I can't really explain," he replied. "Somehow, I know the way to go, but only since today. It's clearer the closer we get . . . like a magnetic pull of sorts. It's as if I've made this journey thousands of times."

As the words left his mouth, the deep green of a forest canopy appeared before them. Eamonn's heart jumped, and a surge of heat passed through him. He needed to be there; he needed to go inside the forest. Every fiber of his being ached to enter the homeland of his mother. It was no longer a tug or a desire; it was a physical, mental, and emotional necessity.

Eamonn prodded Rovis with his heels, navigating the horse down the slope and to the forest's edge. Rovis stopped before the snow abruptly ended and was replaced with rich, brown earth and bright green vegetation. The horse snorted and backpedaled, trying to stay away from the trees.

"Whoa there!" Eamonn gripped the reins and kept Rovis as oriented as possible as he jigged around, head held high.

"Bring him back, lad," Dorylss called from several paces behind him. Bardan stamped even where they were, closer to the cliff face than the woods. "The forest makes them nervous."

Eamonn studied the horses, curious at their reactions. Dorylss and Leyna had told him that the magic of Avaria kept out those without magic, but to see even the horses nervous to approach amazed him. As he led Rovis to where Dorylss waited with Bardan, Eamonn remembered the uncertainty of how Leyna would feel outside Avaria without wearing the Réalta.

"What about you?" he asked, his voice a murmur only she could hear. "Does it make you nervous too?"

"No, but... it's strange," she mused. When they rejoined Dorylss, Leyna added, "I don't feel that sense of dread and foreboding that the others felt last time, but neither do I feel like it's inviting me inside again. It's just...there."

Dorylss and Eamonn shared a glance before Dorylss looked at Leyna. "So, you think you're fine to go in there?"

Leyna examined the forest ahead, as though trying to figure that out herself. "Yes, I think I am."

Eamonn lowered himself from the saddle, falling into several inches of soft snow. He reached back up and grasped Leyna's waist as she descended, and she turned to face him, his hands still holding her. Their eyes met, but neither spoke. Eamonn found himself drowning in the bright blue depths of Leyna's eyes, but it was a fate he would gladly accept.

Six heavy heartbeats passed before Leyna tore her gaze away, stepping out of Eamonn's touch and facing the forest. "Well, I guess we'd better go ahead and find out what awaits us."

"I'll hang around to make sure you make it inside all right, and then I'll be on my way to Amrieth," Dorylss said. The apples of his cheeks and his nose were pink with cold, but it only made him look endearing, like something from a children's fairy story. It struck Eamonn's memory, and he could almost recall a tale about a merry giant.

Leyna took a few steps through the snow and Eamonn started to follow her, but Rovis tugged back on the reins in Eamonn's hand. Eamonn reached up to stroke his neck, attempting to calm the horse as he stamped and resisted.

"He's too nervous to go inside. But we can't go without him; we'd never make it to Miren. And I can't leave him tethered out here."

"So what are we going to do?"

Eamonn tried to lead Rovis toward Avaria, but he snorted again and backed away. Eamonn huffed, a white cloud appearing from his mouth, and he squeezed his eyes shut. *What do I do? He has to come with us.*

Then tell him he must come.

A melodic voice filled his mind, light and airy like a song, distinctly separate from his own thoughts. Eamonn hadn't asked the question of anyone; it was more of a complaint to himself. But after the voice answered, it made him wonder.

Could I?

He waited for a reply, but the voice did not answer right away. Several moments passed, and Eamonn wondered if that was all he would hear.

Why don't you try?

Eamonn smirked, and Leyna tilted her head, eyeing him. "What?"

"It's a test. Or something. They want me to try using magic."

Leyna's brow furrowed. "What in the stars are you talking about?"

"You'll see...I hope."

Eamonn focused his attention on the horse, then delved far into himself, in the deepest recesses of his spirit. It was all he remembered from using his magic before, but it came much easier this time. Everything seemed amplified right outside of Avaria. The forest effused energy, touching Eamonn like tendrils and bringing his magic closer to the surface. The green gemstone in the center of his pendant filled with light as a new electric warmth spread throughout his body.

Come on, Rovis, you'll be all right, he commanded with his thoughts. *Let's go into the forest now.*

For a moment, Eamonn thought nothing was going to happen. The voice had never said it would work, just to try it. Maybe it was less a test of his magical ability and more a way to see how well he followed directions.

A slight pressure arose in his chest, as though his lungs ached. Right as Eamonn was about to consider what else he could try, Rovis stepped forward, calmly walking where Eamonn guided him toward the forest.

"It's your magic," Leyna whispered in awe, a small grin on her lips.

Dorylss chuckled, still attempting to calm his own nervous beast. "Well, that's one way to do it."

"Commanding him with magic didn't even cross my mind," Eamonn admitted. "A voice in my head told me to try it. I never thought about controlling the wills of animals before. It's easier than with people."

Eamonn stopped Rovis at the forest's edge and turned back to Dorylss. A hardness had settled in the lines of Dorylss's face. "Perhaps because it's not something intended to be done to people."

Unease squirmed in Eamonn's gut with Dorylss's words, but he ignored it. "Right." He wouldn't admit to Dorylss that he believed it was the best and possibly only way to ensure they stopped Rothgard—not as they were about to be separated.

Changing the subject seemed like the best thing Eamonn could do. "We'll be fine here," he said, and it was true. Ever since they'd approached, he'd been consumed with a sense that he was where he needed to be. "Take care of yourself on the way to Amrieth. It's a long way."

"Don't worry about me, lad. I'll reach a village by nightfall and have a roof over my head for the night."

Not worrying about Dorylss would be impossible for Eamonn, but he would make a good show of it and help Dorylss feel better about leaving them behind. "Well, just be watchful."

"And not overly trusting," Leyna chimed in.

Dorylss smiled at them, his mouth framed by his unruly auburn beard. "I will treat everyone I encounter as I would a stranger, even if they're someone I know. Now, be off with you! I'll expect you in the kingdom in no more than a month's time, and if I haven't heard from you by then, I'll gather a search party to come after you."

Eamonn laughed and waved at Dorylss as he directed Bardan back to the path they had taken down, silently wishing for safe and uneventful travels.

"Shall we go on then?" Leyna's soft, winsome voice turned Eamonn toward her. Even though she'd been in Avaria before, an anxious anticipation filled her features. She didn't seem to be in fear of venturing inside, and even though she'd already told Eamonn as much, he was relieved to see it reflected in her behavior.

"Let's go," he replied, leading the way toward the forest realm. To his mother's home.

NINE

FROM THE OUTSIDE, THE forest realm of Avaria appeared to be an ordinary woodland, removing the fact that the entire place was a lush green even when surrounded by snow. In a different climate, nothing about Avaria seemed unusual.

Eamonn was drawn to the forest like a moth to a flame—no, it was something greater. The pull was that of a bear's cave, a bird's nest, a cat's hovel. It was the pull of home.

They stepped from snow to soil, and once the trees encompassed them, Eamonn shed his scarf and cloak. He packed them away in his saddlebag as Leyna undid her own, the balminess of the forest covering them like a wave.

"Is it the same as you remember?" he asked, his eyes upward as they started again.

"Exactly."

"So, how far until we get to the Kaethiri?"

"I don't know. Last time, I just walked and they appeared."

Something about that filled Eamonn with an enthralling sense of mystery, and his chest rose with a deep breath.

As he stared at the treetops, he realized that the light floating down between branches and creating beams through the trees did not come from the sun beyond. This light was warmer, more like the sunlight of the late afternoon, right before dusk, and it was everywhere.

A song filled the temperate air, light and sweet like the tinkling of chimes mixed with birdsong. Glittering specks floated around them, immaterial and dazzling. Eamonn reached out to touch one, uncertain if it was a living thing or another manifestation of light. It disappeared when he closed his hand around it.

Energy thrummed in the air, in Eamonn, in everything around them. A tingling sensation filled him from his toes up to the top of his head, similar to how he felt when he used magic, but weaker, like magic waiting to be accessed. He could feel the hum of magic in everything around him. It lifted his emotions, sending an optimism flowing through him as if nothing was out of reach. Like he could be unstoppable if he tapped into it properly. The Kaethiri were an embodiment of magic, and their home was alive with it.

"Can you feel that?" Eamonn asked, still studying the forest around him. The wide-trunked trees, tall and green, grew thick together, their branches rustling against each other as the leaves swayed in a gentle breeze.

"Yes," Leyna answered, and the dappled light made her eyes shine. "It's just as it was before."

Even though she'd already been in Avaria, already felt its magic and seen its enchantments, she still beheld the realm with awe and wonder. Some things, Eamonn supposed, you didn't get used to.

He kept his eyes peeled for a figure, a shadow—anything that might be the first appearance of the Kaethiri. They kept a slow pace through the forest. There was no path to provide a clear direction, but the undergrowth was contained and intentional—almost landscaped—which allowed them to make easy work of traveling in the dense woods.

"Do you remember how long you walked before they appeared?"

"I..." Leyna pressed her lips together in a slight frown and shook her head. "To be honest, I'm not sure how much time passed. It doesn't seem to have the same meaning here."

Maybe time, or distance, or both. Eamonn looked behind them, but he only saw forest. They hadn't been traveling for more than a few minutes and should still see the snowy bank where they left Dorylss behind them, but it was as if it didn't exist.

Ever since Eamonn had commanded Rovis to go into the forest, the horse had shown no further sign of anxiety. In fact, he shook his head and nudged Eamonn when they slowed, like he knew they hadn't arrived at their destination. A subtle heat at Eamonn's breastbone drew his eyes down to see that the pendant still glowed, the brightest it had ever been.

Welcome, Son of Avaria.

Eamonn's head jerked up at the sound of the voice in his mind. He searched the forest around him, trying to find a form the voice might belong to. Still, he and Leyna seemed to be alone.

"What? Did you see something?" Leyna asked in response to his sudden movements.

Eamonn shook his head. "Heard. In my mind, again. Someone spoke to me."

We are glad to have you here. It is long overdue.

"Where are you?" Eamonn asked aloud, his eyes flitting around.

We are all around you. But if it makes things easier...

"You do bear a striking resemblance to your mother, you know."

The voice in Eamonn's mind now came from behind them, and Eamonn and Leyna whipped around, startling Rovis a little.

"It's an incredible thing, to see so much of her in you," a woman said, tall and beautiful and glowing like a moonbeam. "And not just in your features. I see her in your heart."

A wrinkle deepened between Eamonn's brows. "How can you see in my heart?"

The Kaethiri smiled at him, her eyes a striking purple. "Patience, Eamonn. You will learn."

There was a quality to her voice when heard aloud that touched at a memory, something so long ago it nearly felt like a dream. Leyna had told him all she'd learned of the Kaethiri during her time in Avaria a few weeks before, including how Eamonn had lived in Avaria with his mother's people for the first few years of his life, but he remembered nothing of it. The vague sense of familiarity that came over him now was the first indication he'd ever had of it being true.

"Welcome again, Leyna of Teravale."

"Thank you for allowing me entry," Leyna said, her gaze fixed on the Kaethiri. "I know I don't really belong here."

"You are accepted as a friend of Eamonn and a friend of the Kaethiri. You have been gifted with a portion of Avarian magic and will always have a place among us."

"I...really?" Leyna's eyebrows were drawn low over her eyes in question.

"The gift I imparted to you will never leave you. You will never be held under the control of Avarian magic, as Kaethiri cannot control our own kind."

Leyna's mouth opened with a grin. "Thank you," she said, still surprised.

"And you, Eamonn," the Kaethiri said, "I know what you seek. You seek instruction. Guidance. Belonging."

He couldn't deny it. Eamonn had said nothing to Leyna or Dorylss about his need to know more about his mother, and in turn, about himself or his longing to feel connected to some kind of family. He had a family in Dorylss, and now he might have Leyna, but there was a desire to find a link to himself he couldn't ignore.

"I am Imrilieth, Queen of the Kaethiri. Others here with us may reveal themselves at an appropriate time. As for the moment, I will see that you have food and comfortable shelter. Come with me."

The lady dipped her head in emphasis of her gentle command and began to glide through the forest on feet like wings. Eamonn and Leyna followed, the terrain easy to traverse though the woods were dense.

The Queen of the Kaethiri bore an ethereal nature, her milky skin emitting a subtle glow and her long waves of silvery-white hair adorned with strings of light-catching jewels. More of the bejeweled strands were entwined around her head like a crown. A Réalta rested against her chest, the silver swirls of the casing identical to Eamonn's, but the stone in her pendant was an opalescent white. The train of her gauzy dress trailed behind her like a moonbeam on the earth.

"We do not need settlements in the way of humans," she explained as they walked, "but you will find we have fashioned suitable accommodations for your stay."

Eamonn and Leyna shared a glance, and Eamonn found his own uncertainty echoed in Leyna's expression. What would the Kaethiri deem "suitable"?

"We refer to our dwelling place as an 'abode,' a place of concentrated magic. Avaria has always been our primary abode, but now it is the only one. When we dwelt among humans centuries ago, we had an abode in every province in Sarieth. They were not only places of residence but also of regeneration, providing us a site where we could rest. But when we withdrew magic and isolated ourselves, we closed off the others or destroyed them, hiding them within the confines of the earth, and all of us retreated to Avaria.

"The concentration of magic is what you feel in the air. It is in the very fabric of Avaria, stronger than it was now that all the Kaethiri inhabit it. That is why even you, Leyna, can sense it without a Réalta. You will not find another place like Avaria in all of Sarieth."

They continued for a while in silence, treading carefully down a slope to a crystal clear stream surrounded by moss-covered rocks. The stream flowed gently along the slope, falling over some rocks off to their right and adding the soft rush of water to the chimes singing in the air. Stepping over the stream, Imrilieth guided them to the left, where they climbed a set of natural steps blanketed with grass and dusted with leaves.

At the top of the steps, the trees opened up into a level glade occupied by four structures that resembled buildings. The circular structures, with tall, pointed roofs, seemed to be constructed out of sturdy vines that surrounded the trunks of trees.

The pale brown vines twisted together and created intricate patterns, some portions thinner than others, forming walls, doors, and windows for each structure, with various types of leaves jutting here or tucked there. Something like glass glittered in arched windows, and a heavy layer of leaves added extra covering to the roof.

"There is one for each of you, as well as a stable and a bathing house. We have directed water from the stream there to provide you a private source of fresh water. Your meals will be served out here," Imrilieth said, gesturing to a slab of white and grey stone with benches of the same material on either side. "You have nothing to worry over while you are here. You will not lack any necessities. Take rest in knowing you are safe, but know this is not merely a refuge." Imrilieth faced Eamonn, her eyes now a bright, sparkling blue. Her features were sharp and beautiful, bright and serene. "May you find comfort here as in a home."

Eamonn didn't hold back a smile as he beheld the scene before him. Leyna's plan to stay low and hide out in Avaria for a while was becoming more and more appealing. He cast a sidelong glance at her, wondering what she was thinking and if she was as content to stay there as he was. She caught his stare, smiling back at him with an exuberant glimmer in her eyes.

"The dwellings are identical and supplied with everything you need," Imrilieth added, her hands at rest in the center of her body, fingertips lightly touching each other. "You may explore the forest as much as you wish. Your horse is free to roam here. He will come to no harm within our borders, but you may stable him as you see fit.

"We may not always be discernible to your eyes, but we are always present. If there is something you require, or if you would like an audience, simply ask. Take some time to settle, and we will meet again. You will find a meal ready soon."

Imrilieth didn't move to leave, so Eamonn turned his attention back to the little huts of deftly twisted design. Leyna had already started heading toward them, and he followed after her, but when he looked over his shoulder to catch another glimpse of the Kaethiri Queen, she was gone.

He caught up to Leyna, who pulled open the door of the hut on the far left. "How do you think they did it?" she asked, like a question broken out of a train of her own thoughts.

"Did what? Make these?"

She nodded. "Of course, it had to be with magic. But do you think they just spoke them into existence, or do you think they had the vines magically weave themselves around the trees?"

Eamonn didn't have an answer for her. He stepped over the threshold after Leyna, and what awaited them inside wasn't what he'd expected to find.

He'd imagined a cot with simple bedclothes, maybe a table and chair, and a basin for washing, something similar to the village inns where he'd lodged in the past. But nothing about this hut was ordinary. A circular corridor against the tree trunk led to multiple rooms, with a rich green and gold carpet covering the wooden floor.

Leyna took a left down the hallway after she entered, coming first to a room with two plush green armchairs, a fireplace with a roaring fire, and bookcases on either side of the room filled with books. A rug in similar hues to the one in the hallway sat in the center of the room, soft like moss.

"How can there be a fire in here?" Eamonn wondered aloud, stepping across the room to the fireplace on the far wall. He held his hand out to the fireplace surround and, upon closer examination, discovered that it was stone, though it still looked like the twisted vines that made up the rest of the little house. "Are the walls over there actually vines? This is stone."

Leyna laid her hand on the wall by the bookcase where she stood. "These are vines. I suppose they wanted the same visual appearance of vines around the fireplace, but of course it couldn't be wood."

Eamonn laughed to himself, turning away from the fireplace and crossing his arms. For the Kaethiri to not reside in homes of their own, they certainly had put a lot of thought into designing the structures for their visitors.

"We don't exactly need the fire, anyway. It's warm enough to be early summer here." Leyna grinned, running her hands over the colorful spines of books. "But it gives the room a homier quality."

She went to one of the windows set into the wall beside the fireplace and leaned in close to examine it. Light from outside streamed through the etched pane, hitting the floor in a marbled pattern. Leyna tapped her fingernail on the window, and a clear, sweet tone rang out.

"I think it's crystal," she murmured with wide eyes. "This place is really unbelievable."

"It is." Eamonn returned to the doorway and jerked his head toward the hallway. "Come on, let's go check out the rest of it."

He led the way around the circle to the next room, a bedroom with more plush green and gold carpet and crystal windows. A moderately sized bed sat against one wall, covered with a comfortable-looking cream-colored duvet and topped with several pillows. A wardrobe crafted with the same twisting vines sat against the opposite wall. Eamonn opened it to find an assortment of warm-weather tunics, trousers, and dresses, along with boots, slippers, and a leather belt.

"This must be your place." Eamonn stepped back from the wardrobe and lifted his hand toward it, palm up.

Leyna joined him and tugged at the articles of clothing, pulling them out of the wardrobe just enough to get a look at them before letting them fall back into place.

"This feels like a dream," she murmured, running her fingers over the silk of one of the dresses. "How can it be real?"

"Magic," Eamonn said with a smirk, his eyes on her. She couldn't miss the intonation in his voice, the knowing way he spoke the word.

Leyna faced him, wearing a grin of her own that made her dimples show. "Says the man who never believed in it to the girl who always did."

She held his gaze, and Eamonn's cheeks burned. The seconds that passed magnified their isolation from the rest of the world, and Eamonn became acutely aware of how alone they were. Dorylss had gone on to Miren without them, and for the first time, it was truly just them. The Kaethiri were there, of course, but not physically at the moment, so they might as well have not been there at all.

"We should go see what else is here," she said, making for the hallway again. "I'm curious to see what else the Kaethiri thought we needed."

Eamonn remained like a statue in the room, rooted to the spot where Leyna had left him. He knitted his eyebrows and frowned. He'd thought they were having a moment. As intrigued as he was to see the rest of the hut, he preferred to pick up where he and Leyna had left off.

Eamonn willed his feet to move and continued around the hallway to the third and final room. It was a dining room of sorts, with shelves full of foods and utensils they might need. A small round table occupied the center of the room, and a stove sat against the wall behind it.

Leyna circled the room, barely lifting her head when Eamonn entered. "Imrilieth said our meals would be served at the table outside."

He hung back at the doorway, trying to decide whether or not she wanted him there. "This must be to make sure we have anything else we find ourselves wanting: tea, a bite here and there."

She nodded. "Makes sense."

Eamonn rocked back and forth on his heels for a minute, still unsure if he should venture inside. Leyna was investigating the items on the shelves, but something in her manner seemed off. Forced, maybe.

Then Eamonn remembered the clothes in the wardrobe. They'd determined this hut was hers. Was she waiting for him to leave but didn't know how to ask?

"I'll go on over to mine," he announced. "The queen said they were identical, so I'm sure it's not worth you seeing." He bit down on his bottom lip. *That sounded terrible*. A fleeting grimace passed over his face, and he said, "What I mean is, once you've seen this one, I assume you've seen both. I'll go freshen up at the bathing hut and see you again for the meal."

He turned on his heel and left the hut. Had he said something wrong? Was being alone with him too much for her? Or did this go back to the previous night and him curling up beside her?

Rovis grazed right outside the huts, and Eamonn changed direction when he spotted him, guiding him toward the little stable to remove his tack. He went through the motions automatically, replaying the scene with Leyna over and over in his mind. He hoped lying beside her in the snowstorm hadn't been too forward of him, but it was all he could point to. So when he saw her again, he would apologize, promise to take a step back.

Eamonn led Rovis to a bag of oats hung in the surprisingly spacious stable before he made for the bathing hut. There was no sign of Leyna. She was most likely in her hut, making herself comfortable in one of those armchairs with a book that had caught her attention. Eamonn could picture the scene: Leyna curled up in a chair, book open on her lap, but staring into the fire instead of reading.

The bathing hut had the same floor plan as the others, with a circular hallway and three rooms that came off of it. Eamonn found a supply of soaps, lotions, towels, brushes, and anything else one might need to freshen up in the first room. The back room contained an enclosed circle of frosted crystal, and as Eamonn walked around it, he found an opening on the opposite side of the room's entrance. He stepped inside the crystal encasement and water hit his head. Eamonn reversed course and jerked his head up, seeing the water come to a trickling stop from the ceiling as he left the enclosure. Once again, he found himself marveling at the Kaethiri. A rain shower from the ceiling to bathe. Ordinary things, he thought, could be magical, too.

A porcelain toilet, sink, and mirror occupied the third room. The Kaethiri had really thought of everything. They knew enough about humans to provide Eamonn and Leyna with all the necessary comforts.

As Eamonn poked his head in the door to the third room, he caught sight of himself in the mirror—the first time he had since leaving Taran and Teiyn's. Traveling had made him appear worse for the wear, to be sure, but he didn't miss the changes to his features since his time in captivity. He was still getting used to the slimmer face and sharper features, the slight hollowness around his eyes, and the tendrils of scars that crept up his neck beyond his collar. Automatically, he lifted a hand and brushed the end of a thin pink scar on his neck.

This body couldn't be his own. Clothes hung on his frame, regardless of the strength he'd gained over the past few weeks. He looked more like the boy his father had left to fend for himself than he had since he'd begun to prosper with the Thieves' Guild, but even so, that boy was different. He was happy. He was whole.

With a sudden, unexplainable urge, Eamonn tugged his shirt off and turned his back to the mirror, gazing over his shoulder at the pattern of stripes across his back. Rothgard had magically healed his wounds at the end of each whipping so he could flog Eamonn again, but every lash had left a scar.

The scars weren't limited to his back. His heart bore damage that might never go away.

Eamonn whirled away from the mirror, pulling the dirty shirt back over his head, and left the bathing hut to retrieve a clean set of clothes from his hut. He wanted to see Leyna. Her presence always chased away the memories. He resolved to go back and explain everything to her, even if he made an utter fool of himself, when he was clean and refreshed.

He'd opened the door with Leyna, but it was as though they stood on either side of the threshold. He would make his intentions clear.

And hopefully, one of them would step through the door.

TEN

EAMONN'S DARK BLOND WAVES were still damp when he came back outside. He'd hoped to find Leyna in her hut, but as soon as he stepped out of the bathing hut, he saw her sitting at the stone table just beyond the little buildings, with a variety of food spread across it.

His stomach growled at the sight. Their last hearty meal had been three days ago in a little village east of Nos Illni, where they had stopped briefly. Since then, it had been whatever game they could find, cheese, and hard bread.

When he reached the table, Eamonn saw that Leyna had already tucked in. Her eyes lifted momentarily at his arrival.

"I'm sorry I didn't wait for you." She lowered a spoon into a bowl of stew and clasped her hands together in her lap while she stared at the food.

"Don't stop," Eamonn insisted, holding out his hand as though offering her food back to her. "It's not a problem. I took a little longer cleaning up than I intended." He sat opposite her, and she picked her spoon up again, bringing a bite of stew to her lips. "You'll have to go see the bathing hut after you eat. It's fascinating. In one room, if you step in this circular area enclosed by crystal, water falls from the ceiling like a rain shower."

He was yammering, nervous to bring up what he'd been so confident about before coming out here.

"That's incredible," she mused, picking up a piece of bread and breaking off a chunk to dip into her stew. "I'm excited to see it for myself."

Eamonn fixed a plate for himself, taking helpings of roasted chicken, vegetable stew, boiled potatoes, and bread. He picked up a carafe of wine and held it out to her. "Would you like some?"

"I'm just drinking water, thank you."

Her response came so quickly that Eamonn's arm never stopped moving. He lowered the carafe almost immediately and poured some for himself instead.

She continued to eat, and Eamonn racked his brain for the right words to say. He should compliment her, but after he swallowed a bite of bread, the wrong words came to his lips. "I wonder what it's like here at night. The light doesn't seem to be from the sun, so is there even a sunset?"

Eamonn could have kicked himself. His eloquence had abandoned him.

Leyna paused and looked up, considering. "I hadn't thought of that. Hmm." She slurped another spoonful of stew. "It'll be interesting to see. If the cycle of a day is the same here as it is outside, we ought to be approaching the evening soon."

"Time here may feel as though it passes differently to you, but it is, in fact, the same."

Imrilieth's voice drew their attention to the tree line. She approached like a mist, not seeming to be quite as solid as before until she'd come much closer to them.

"And moonlight replaces the sunlight at the end of the day, but you are correct. The light here does not come from the same celestial bodies as the outside world. As you stay here, you will find that much of Avaria is not as it seems."

The Kaethiri Queen stopped a few feet from the stone table, interlacing her fingers and holding her joined hands in front of her middle. Lavender eyes watched Eamonn and Leyna as they continued their meal. Imrilieth waited in silence, the softest smile gracing her features. The sound of chimes danced through the air, and the trickling of the nearby brook murmured steadily along with it.

Eamonn felt compelled to speak and cut through the song in the background. Imrilieth had joined them for a reason. "As I'm sure you already know, I thought I might learn more about my mother while I'm here. About who I am, exactly."

"You already know yourself, Eamonn. Who you are is not something to learn. But I can tell you what you are."

He hadn't thought of it quite in that way before, but she had a point. Eamonn took another bite of his food and turned his body toward the Kaethiri—and away from Leyna—while Imrilieth remained standing beside the table.

"I assume Leyna already told you the story we shared with her about your mother," Imrilieth began. "We do not know how Laielle became entranced with your father, as Kaethiri do not, by nature, desire romantic relationships. But she created a human appearance for herself and left Avaria to be with him, and in doing so, she was exiled from our realm and stripped of her magic.

"Without her magic, Laielle was then more similar to a human than a Kaethiri, and as a human, she developed human weaknesses. Your birth was traumatic for her, and she succumbed. We had never lost one of our own before, and each of us felt as though we lost a part of ourselves.

"But we took you in and kept you here for a few years, where you would be safe. We had no way of knowing then what magical abilities you might have developed, if any, and we hoped to nurture them and bring you up in the ways of the Kaethiri if you showed signs of their manifestation. Years passed, and you showed no indication of magic, so we returned you to your father."

Leyna had told him all of that. It made him angry all over again, as it had when Leyna had related the story to him. Even though he hadn't shown signs of possessing magic as a young child, he was still half-Kaethiri. They could have kept him and raised him anyway. He might have had a happy childhood then, one where a negligent father wouldn't have forced his son to steal to fill his belly.

"Why did you?" he asked, checking the anger in his tone. What was done in the past was done. There was no use in getting worked up over it now. "Surely you could tell what kind of man my father was—*is*. Why not just keep me here?"

"With no magic, you would not have thrived here," Imrilieth answered, her eyes changing to a deep brown. "We believed your human qualities were dominant, so you needed to live a human life. Even if your magic had appeared when you were a small child, we would have returned you after you had been taught to control it and understood why not to reveal the existence of magic. With your father living, you were not ours to keep."

Eamonn released a pent-up breath through his nose. Imrilieth's answer made sense, even if he didn't like it. Something in the story stuck out to him though, hanging like a loose thread. Something he suddenly, desperately needed an answer to.

"How much does my father know about the Kaethiri? About this place?" His words tumbled over one another, racing out of his mouth before he could get his thoughts in order. "If you kept me as a child, wouldn't he know about magic?"

The brightness in Imrilieth's eyes faded and their color drained to a dull grey. She dipped her head and started walking, taking slow steps behind Leyna to the other side of the table as she spoke. "After Laielle's death, a few of us went to collect you, and your father was made entirely aware of our existence, of magic, of Laielle's true nature. He was devastated by the loss of your mother, and, needless to say, he was skeptical of our claims. We had traveled through Idyrria in the guise of humans, much as your mother had, so when we appeared at your door, he had no reason to believe what we told him.

"In the solitude of your home, however, we let the disguise fall and showed your father our typical physical form—the form you see now. We demonstrated our magic. He had no reason to disbelieve us then. Since we intended to remove the encounter from his memories, we didn't hold back in providing him evidence. He should have only forgotten the proof of magic, but..."

Imrilieth had stopped at the other end of the table, staring at her clasped hands. She had been so forthright in everything she had said to them until then that Eamonn found her hesitation odd and a little unnerving. It was as though she didn't want to give him the end of the story.

"But, what?" he asked, his heart rate ramping up as he waited and wondered.

The Queen of the Kaethiri lifted her eyes again and locked them with his as she turned her body to face him, resolved to finish her sentence. "We didn't anticipate his reaction. Things would have gone more smoothly if he hadn't resisted. If he hadn't fought to keep you."

Blood pounded in Eamonn's ears and his heart lodged in his throat. That wasn't possible. Florin? *His* father, Florin? There wasn't a bone in that man's body that would have fought to keep him. Imrilieth had to be misremembering. It was nearly twenty years ago, after all.

"The passion, the fervor with which he outright refused to let us take you, magic or no magic, got in the way." The glow that emanated from Imrilieth's skin dimmed and her hair lost its sheen. "We do not use our magic to control humans any longer, but this was one exception we had to make. His emotions were strong and at the front of his mind when we left with you and pulled the memory. We did not foresee... We did not intend for it to happen. But we held his mind so we could leave with you, and when we withdrew and took the memory of the encounter with it, so too went the memory of his love for you."

Eamonn might as well have fallen a thousand feet. All the breath left his lungs. His vision blurred as his eyes fell from Imrilieth and landed somewhere near her feet, not really looking at anything. He heard nothing but the roar of his own heartbeat and the screaming in his mind.

His love for you.

His love for you.

His love.

The emotion that gripped Eamonn was too strong, squeezing his insides until he thought they might burst. He leaped to his feet, no longer seeing Imrilieth, or Leyna, or the table covered with food. He'd lost even the remotest semblance of the appetite he'd had when he sat down. All he wanted was to get away. He couldn't listen to Imrilieth anymore, not right then.

Eamonn crossed the short distance to his hut and shut himself inside, not making it farther than the front door. He pressed his back against it, shaking in anger, and slid down as his knees buckled underneath him.

His father had loved him. Wanted him. Fought for him.

The Kaethiri had killed it all.

ELEVEN

EAMONN ALLOWED THE AMASSED tears in his eyes to roll down his cheeks. There was no one to see him cry. A part of him wanted Imrilieth to see him weep, to watch him mourn the life he might have had with his father, the life the Kaethiri had stolen.

He scrubbed his face with his hands, clearing the streams of wetness from his cheeks. What right had the Kaethiri had to take him away from his father in the first place? They may have been magic incarnate, worshipped by some as part of an ancient tradition that had lost its original meaning, but they weren't gods. Eamonn's fate should not have been up to them.

Three gentle raps sounded on the other side of the door.

"Eamonn?"

Leyna's voice came soft and low. Eamonn's eyes brimmed with fresh tears, remembering his intentions for the afternoon before Imrilieth had ruined it and weighed down his heart with a new burden.

"Would you like some company?" She paused, but he gave no response. "It's all right if you don't. Imrilieth is gone. She says you can talk more later."

Eamonn couldn't decide if he found it cowardly or noble for Imrilieth to end the conversation after upsetting him. Regardless, he would hear nothing more from her at the moment, and he was glad she had left him and Leyna alone again.

Footsteps moved away from the door and Eamonn shot to his feet, realizing he'd never given Leyna an answer. At the moment, he wanted nothing more than her company. He swung the door open, and she stopped a few paces away before swiveling back to him.

"Come in," he murmured, stepping back from the threshold to give her room.

She joined him in the hallway of his hut. He shut the door behind her, and she shifted her weight between her feet, allowing him the chance to lead. With an open palm, he gestured for her to enter the sitting room to their left. The two green chairs in the room waited for occupants, but Eamonn strode past them, going instead to the fireplace, and leaned on one arm against the stone surround. He stared into the fire, the bright orange flames licking the air and crackling with the consumption of wood.

Eamonn heard the depression of a cushion and the settling of a body into one of the chairs behind him. He kept his eyes on the fire, and Leyna said nothing. She'd offered company, and that's what she was giving. He appreciated that about her.

This would be the perfect opportunity to bring up exactly what he'd hoped to discuss with her, but his mind still spun with the revelation from Imrilieth. The Kaethiri were responsible for the life he had lived, for the loveless childhood he had endured. To know his father had loved him and that, in a different life, they might have been happy together made his stomach churn with anger, disappointment, and regret. Where might he be now? He might have gone to the College at Nos Illni, or maybe his father would have raised him to be a soldier from an early age.

A thought came cutting in, slicing through the fantasy he was creating. He knew where he wouldn't be: with Dorylss and Leyna. If his father had happily raised him, their paths would likely have never crossed. He may have purchased goods from Dorylss whenever the caravan market came to town, but that would be the extent. And Leyna. She hardly got out of Caen and never Teravale. Eamonn would not have met her. In exchange for having his father, his life would be absent of Leyna.

He turned to face Leyna, his hand still pressed to the fireplace. She looked up at him expectantly, and he studied her, from the concern in her wrinkled eyebrows, the compassion in her wide eyes, and the slight frown across her lips, to her posture in the chair. She was there fully and irrevocably for him, waiting to offer support in whatever way he needed.

"Thank you." Eamonn dropped his hand and folded his arms in front of his chest.

"For what?"

"Being here."

A closed smile replaced the concerned frown on Leyna's face. "I'm always here for you. Just like I told you that night—"

She didn't finish her thought, the words left dangling in the air like a carrot in front of a horse, enticing but just out of reach. He wanted to revisit that night under the stars with her. The firelight reflecting in her eyes brought the image of her sitting by the campfire, her cheeks pink with cold as she opened up to him.

"I will always be here for you, no matter what." Leyna seemed to adjust the ending of her sentence to stay relevant to the present alone. Whether it was for her own sake or to not detract from Eamonn's current struggles, Eamonn didn't know.

He took a seat in the chair opposite her, leaning forward and resting his elbows on his knees. "I can't even imagine a life in which my father loved me." Eamonn stared past his joined hands at the swirls of gold in the green rug. "For fourteen years—" He stopped and swallowed, emotion closing his throat. "For fourteen years, I lived with a man who didn't give a thought to my existence. Or less than that, I guess. However long I was here not included." Eamonn shook his head as he took a deep breath, the burn of tears behind his eyes again. "To know I didn't have to go through any of it... to know he loved me once..."

Eamonn choked on the words and worked the muscles in his jaw. A thought came to him, as did the image of his father's shock at seeing him in Rothgard's tower. Had a shred of his memory returned in that moment? He'd sent Hadli up after him to help him. Maybe a tiny pinprick of the love his father had once held for him was still buried deep inside. Eamonn lost sight of the rug behind the pools in his eyes, one eye clearing when a tear dropped to the floor.

It was something he'd been wrestling with ever since they'd put Nidet at their backs. Working for Rothgard seemed out of character for Florin. In all the time Eamonn had lived with his father, he'd never known the man to go above and beyond more than his required duty. Supposedly, he'd served in the War with Cardune before Eamonn was born, and though he'd remained a soldier, Florin had barely lifted a sword since.

But even more astonishing was the idea that maybe, hidden away somewhere in the recesses of Florin's heart, he'd uncovered a soft spot for Eamonn. Had the sight of his son at Roth-gard's mercy, bloodied and broken, finally touched at something long-lost in Florin?

Leyna scooted to the edge of her chair and took Eamonn's hands in her own. Her touch was tender, and Eamonn squeezed her hands back in acknowledgment of her sympathy.

"I'm so sorry," she whispered.

"You're not the one who needs to be apologizing to me."

"I know. But I hate seeing you like this. I..."

Her sentence trailed off again, but Eamonn wouldn't let their moment pass. Not again.

"Leyna." He gripped her hands again, forcing her eyes up to his. His words came out in a whisper. "Just tell me."

Leyna's throat bobbed. "It's like I said the other night by the fire. It breaks my heart to see you in pain. Physical, emotional, it doesn't matter. I want to help you however I can."

The warmth and touch of Leyna's hands in his own brought him back to the realization he'd had by the fireplace. He would go through his father's neglect all over again—he would choose to have Florin stripped of his love for his son—to have Leyna. And to have Dorylss. The Kaethiri might have been wrong in taking the infant Eamonn from his father, but the anguish of the childhood he had to endure as a result was worth it for those two people to be in his life.

"This is helping me," he said after a long pause. He ran his thumbs over the backs of her hands. "Just having you here. Knowing that it's only because of the Kaethiri's actions that you and I are both here, right now, helps."

Leyna slid off the chair and sat on her knees on the floor beside Eamonn, pulling their joined hands close to her. She looked up at him where he sat in his chair, eyes glistening.

"Then here I'll stay."

That was as good an opening as any.

He leaned closer to her, keeping their gazes locked. A fiery bolt shot through him as his heart slammed against his ribcage, and he begged his fluttering stomach to calm. The nerves he'd had before Imrilieth showed up at their meal came charging back.

"I'm sorry if the other night was too much—lying beside you in the storm. I don't want to put any pressure on you." The words were barely more than a whisper. Eamonn held her hands fast, hoping Leyna didn't notice the slight tremble reaching down to his fingers. "I'm just—" He tilted his head back and took a deep breath. If he wanted to get the words out, he couldn't look at her. "I'm afraid I'm getting ahead of myself. I want this more than anything. I want *you*. But I'm terrified of frightening you by moving too fast." Eamonn brought his head back down and found her eyes again.

Leyna's grip on his hands tightened. Time slowed and Eamonn held his breath, the only sound the occasional pop from the fireplace. Her dimples appeared as the corners of her mouth tipped up. "It's new and I'm still getting used to it. But you're not frightening me. I want you, too."

He might as well have been consumed by the fire. Every nerve, every fiber, every ounce of his being blazed as though lit with flame. His expectations had been much lower than that. He would have been satisfied knowing she wanted to take things slowly, as long as she could still be his. This sent his spirits up to the heavens. This was so much more than he had dared to hope.

"I should have said something sooner," Leyna continued, her eyes searching his. She raised a little on her knees, bringing her body even closer to Eamonn, and she lowered her voice as though she told him a secret. "You and I... well, we risked our lives for each other. That changed us."

"It did." Eamonn fell to his knees in front of Leyna without releasing her hands. "You saw a side of me that—" He stopped, remembering. He had been overcome by Rothgard, diminishing into little more than a shell of his former self. He'd all but given up, too, until he saw Rothgard shove Leyna into the tower room where he also was being held. It only took one glance at her in Rothgard's grip to instantly rediscover his purpose.

"—I never would have wanted you to see," he finished, staring down at their joined hands. "And in the weeks that followed—when you took care of me—I never would have chosen for you to see me so broken." He shook his hanging head as though ashamed.

"Your brokenness is what opened my eyes to how I feel about you." Leyna lifted a hand to his cheek, and even though her touch was gentle, Eamonn felt electricity from each fingertip, and he lifted his head. "It showed me things about myself I couldn't ignore, things I hadn't had the chance to consider properly before. I realized how much I care about you."

Bright golden sunlight streamed in through the windows on either side of the fireplace as though a sun set somewhere. It illuminated Leyna's hair, her eyes, her entire face. She looked like she came out of a dream. Her strawberry blonde curls were a shining frame around her shimmering eyes and soft smile.

Eamonn wouldn't miss another opportunity. He placed a hand along Leyna's jaw and the base of her head, and he brought his face to hers, their lips brushing together tentatively. Eamonn's pulse thundered as their breath mingled. He'd tested the waters, stepped in up to his ankles, and found it was perfect. So he dove.

Eamonn brought his free hand to the other side of Leyna's face and closed the rest of the distance between them where they kneeled on the floor, pressing his lips onto hers. She answered with an embrace and parted lips, moving her mouth in response to Eamonn's.

His heart grew wings that thrummed inside his chest, threatening to burst out and take flight. Was he even in his body anymore? This couldn't be real. Eamonn's fingers tangled in Leyna's curls and his thumbs skimmed her jawline. Her lips tasted sweet, probably from the honey butter at their meal, but he preferred thinking it was just how they tasted.

He moved one of his hands, scooping his arm around her waist and pulling her closer. This kiss was a key, unlocking something deep inside him that he had never known was there. He wanted Leyna: only her, always her. Eamonn hadn't known something this perfect and pure could exist, especially not for him. His past was messy. He wasn't proud of the person he used to be. And now...

Now he had been to hell and back and brought part of it with him. He was tainted, unworthy of any kind of favor from Leyna, let alone her affection.

Leyna shifted, moving one hand to the back of Eamonn's head. Her lips stayed locked to his, moving in a slow rhythm that Eamonn guided. He kept most of his eagerness in check, compelled to move forward in stages. This was their first kiss. There was no need to treat it like it was their last. He would rather savor it, taking in all the details so that he would never forget.

"Eamonn," Leyna murmured with her lips still touching his.

A thrill tore through Eamonn's body to hear her say his name like that. To *feel* her say his name.

"Eamonn," she said again, a little more insistently. She brought her hands around and pressed them against his chest, tenderly pushing him only a fraction away.

He pulled his mouth back but leaned his forehead to touch hers, drinking in the heat of their heavy breaths. The smell of her so close was intoxicating.

"I don't want... I know your emotions are running high right now. About what Imrilieth said. About your father."

"Leyna." Eamonn put just enough distance between them so that he could look her in the eye. "This is about you and me. That's it." He ran a thumb across her cheek. "I've wanted this for a long time, before I had any clue what the Kaethiri might say."

A corner of Leyna's mouth lifted for an instant before she dropped her hands. "I know. I would just feel better if you took the rest of the day. Separated things a little bit."

Eamonn opened his mouth to protest, but Leyna stood, and he knew the kiss was over.

"I'm not going anywhere."

She held out her hand to him, and he took it, coming to his feet as well. A grin brightened her face, a mischievous quality setting off the flutter in Eamonn's gut all over again. Her hand slipped out of his as she walked away from him, and he hung on to it by the tips of his fingers as long as he could.

"See you tomorrow, Eamonn."

Leyna left the room before he had a chance to argue, and Eamonn heard the hut's door close before he saw Leyna pass by the windows of the sitting room. She looked back over her shoulder at the windows, the grin still on her lips, and Eamonn watched her go until she disappeared inside her hut.

TWELVE

IMRILIETH APPEARED THE NEXT day as Eamonn and Leyna finished their midday meal. Eamonn glanced up at her arrival and quickly returned his gaze to the mug in front of him. He emptied it with one long swig, turning it bottom up, and sighed when he lowered it back to the table with a thud.

"I am sorry, Eamonn," Imrilieth said with no introduction and without waiting for an opening. "There is a reason we do not insert ourselves into the affairs of humans. As I said, your father was an exception. But our power is limitless. It is easy for things to get out of hand, even if our intentions are good."

Fingernails bit into Eamonn's palm from his iron grip around the mug's handle. Pain shot from his jaw to the sides of his head as he ground his teeth together, forcing back the words he so desperately wanted to say.

You had no right.

You ruined my relationship with my father.

I have no family because of you.

But he kept the thoughts to himself. For all he knew, the Kaethiri could read the words in his mind, and how he felt was no secret. Imrilieth said nothing, and Eamonn relaxed his hold on the mug. The last one wasn't entirely true, anyway. He may not have a mother or the father who begot him, but he had a family in Dorylss and Leyna.

Eamonn sighed again and let his shoulders sag. Harboring anger against Imrilieth and the other Kaethiri would do him no good or change anything they had done. But that didn't mean he had to be okay with it.

He cast a quick glance at Leyna. He'd barely been able to think of anything but her the rest of the night before, after she'd left him so abruptly. She wanted him to separate the news of his father and the emotions attached to it from their kiss, but nothing related to the revelations about his father made a reappearance in his mind. Eamonn had only thought of Leyna, replaying their kiss in his mind, remembering what it felt like to hold her in his arms.

Tearing his thoughts and eyes away from Leyna, Eamonn faced Imrilieth. "It was a lot to learn without any kind of warning, but I wouldn't have the people in my life that I do if you hadn't done it, so I'm choosing to let it go."

"An appropriate response. It is an unfortunate part of our history, but we cannot deny it. It had to be mentioned, for good or for ill. But we shouldn't dwell on it." Something like a smile formed on Imrilieth's lips, and her eyes changed from a heavy grey to a light blue. "Now, shall we try something new?"

Staring at her through narrowed eyes, Eamonn asked, "Something new like what?"

"You are here to further develop your skills with magic, are you not?"

Leyna may have suggested coming to Avaria to find safety from Rothgard, but after she had, and after Eamonn had felt the connection with the Kaethiri, he knew furthering his knowledge of magic was the best thing he could do to oppose Rothgard. He'd felt so helpless when he couldn't call his magic, unable to use the power within him to save them all in the battle on Nidet until the Kaethiri intervened on his behalf.

"Yes, I am. I want to know how to find it when I need it, how to make sure I'm doing the right things. Obviously, I thought I'd defeated Rothgard last time, but it wasn't enough."

Imrilieth nodded in acknowledgment. "Since you are half-Kaethiri, you still have a human side to contend with. Your human side is vulnerable, devoid of our magic. It's constantly at war with your Kaethiri side. We will help you learn how to silence the human side when you are in need of magic."

"We?"

"A few of the others are joining us today." Imrilieth gestured behind Eamonn and Leyna, and they turned to find three more Kaethiri who had silently appeared while they spoke.

"This is Rafella, Galicia, and Tandriel." Each Kaethiri dipped her head when introduced. "They have offered to help with various aspects of our magic."

The three new Kaethiri approached them with slow strides in unison, each possessing the same moonlit glow as Imrilieth, wearing similar pearl-colored gowns in material as delicate as foam. Their individual appearances, however, drastically differed from each other and their queen. While Tandriel had the same ivory skin as Imrilieth, hair the color of copper fell in waves down to her waist. She continued to Eamonn after the others had stopped, her bare feet poking out from the bottom of her dress as she walked.

"We are excited to have you here with us again, Eamonn," she said, a pink-lipped smile spreading across her face. "We all loved Laielle. It's wonderful to feel her presence among us once again."

"And, of course, we are happy to see you grown up." Rafella remained several paces away, though she looked no less enthused than Tandriel. "We all became quite fond of you as a small child." Her muted gown contrasted her rich, dark skin.

Galicia nodded beside Rafella. "You are just as much a part of us as Laielle was." Her lavender eyes glittered as she smiled from ear to ear. Galicia didn't seem to have the same gravity and solemnity about her as the others, especially not Imrilieth. Eamonn saw a laugh behind her eyes as she said, "I know you don't remember us, but I'm fairly certain I was your favorite."

Eamonn smiled, glancing among the three newcomers as they spoke. It was a strange feeling, to be in the presence of beings who knew him while he had no recollection of them. He studied Galicia, his supposed "favorite," looking for a hint of familiarity in her. Something about the combination of her deep brown tresses and bronze skin struck a spark of recognition, but he pushed the idea of remembering her away when he realized her features looked Idyrrian. Of course she would seem familiar, having a similar appearance to those he'd grown up around.

"We will help you learn how to find your magic and call it to you. As Imrilieth said, you may have difficulty at first since your human side is in conflict with it," Rafella said, her expression soft and kind.

"I don't really understand," Leyna interjected. She took a few steps toward Rafella, tilting her head upward to catch the eyes of the tall Kaethiri. "Humans used magic in the past. They can use magic now. We've seen it with some friends of ours. If that's the case, why would Eamonn's human side prevent him from using magic?"

"The magic humans have been granted and the magic of Avaria are different," Rafella explained. "Eamonn's human nature will always be incompatible with Avarian magic because humans are innately susceptible to our magic. No human can possess it, and all can be influenced by it."

"Rothgard's figured out how he can have Avarian magic as a human." Eamonn crossed his arms as he spat the words out. The mere thought of how Rothgard obtained Avarian magic had Eamonn's hip throbbing all over again.

"And he has performed an atrocity to obtain it." Galicia's gaze was severe as she spoke, losing all of the joy she'd previously expressed.

"We will not discuss the Evil One, not now," Imrilieth cut in. The other three Kaethiri dipped their heads in obedience. "We will help Eamonn to understand him more later, but now is not the time."

"Come, Eamonn." Tandriel led the way out of the glade with the table and huts. Eamonn fell in behind her as she struck a path through the dense woods. "Leyna, you may accompany us. You can observe, if you would like. There may even be something for you to learn."

Eamonn glanced over his shoulder to find Leyna following Galicia and Rafella, with Imrilieth bringing up the rear. Her excitement and anticipation to see more magic firsthand radiated off of her. Eamonn would be eternally grateful to her for many things, but especially for opening his eyes to the realities of magic and helping him embrace his magical heritage.

The Kaethiri were not creatures who hurried, and Tandriel kept a slow, even pace as she guided them through the forest.

They followed her down a slope into a gulley where the brook ran through, then crossed a natural bridge and continued up the other side. Treetops swayed in a warm breeze, the music of their rustling leaves wafting down to them below. Everywhere they walked, the sound of tinkling chimes played a song on the air, and the scents of earth, moss, and blooming plants filled their noses.

Up ahead, the beams of light that filtered through the leaves intensified in one collective spot. The energy in the air strengthened as they approached. The thrum of magic that filled Eamonn from the moment they had stepped foot in Avaria escalated and warmed him from the inside. He held out his hands, turning them over in front of them as a tingling sensation came over them.

"Where are we going?" he asked.

"We are going to the place of greatest magic in Avaria," Tandriel replied, briefly looking back at him. "This is the gathering place of the Kaethiri. Our magic is strongest here, so it will be the best place to access your own."

The lift in his spirits, the heightened sense of confidence he'd first felt upon entrance into Avaria, grew into something almost indescribable in this part of the forest. Nothing could hold him back. He believed in victory in every trial he faced, a victory that he would personally bring about. All the untapped potential in the magic around him gave him an exhilarating feeling of invincibility.

They broke out of a thickly treed part of the forest and stepped into a sparser one, though a heavy canopy still shielded them overhead. An open grassy area awaited them, half surrounded by a trickling stream and the other half enclosed by bushes covered with a fragrant white flower. Golden light filled the space, and the glittering specks that floated through the air twinkled like stars all around them.

Tandriel strode into the circle, and structures materialized out of thin air. Eamonn gasped, unable to withhold his surprise. Stone benches appeared, forming a circle around a small gazebo-like structure, with a slightly raised platform and three pointed arches of stone that met at the top in a peak. A brilliant array of vines and flowers covered the gazebo, and the light in the space appeared to grow brighter.

Imrilieth entered the clearing and glided to the little gazebo, situating herself inside. She gestured toward the benches for Leyna and Eamonn to take a seat. The three other Kaethiri positioned themselves around her, Tandriel in front of the gazebo and Rafella and Galicia on either side, all of them facing Eamonn.

He sat on the smooth marbled bench and rested his hands on either side of him, the stone surprisingly warm under his palms. Eamonn chuckled as his eyes ventured from the array of benches to the Kaethiri who stood before him.

"If you don't prefer your physical form, why do you need a meeting place like this? With benches for you to sit?"

A grin appeared on Imrilieth's face—the first time Eamonn had seen such an amused smile playing on her features—and she held her hands out in front of her, palms up. "We like to have the option. Even though we prefer our incorporeal form, we still choose to embody our physical forms some of the time."

"And that structure," he continued, nodding at the gazebo where Imrilieth stood. "What's its purpose?"

Imrilieth lowered her hands and her arms floated out from her sides, filling the space. "This is for the speaker or moderator. I am here now to observe and guide as necessary."

Leyna sat on the same bench as Eamonn and laid her hands in her lap, and he cast a quick sidelong glance at her. Her lifted eyes darted around the space, and her parted lips beckoned Eamonn. He threw his gaze downward. He couldn't get distracted by her now. He needed all of his focus to go to his magic.

"We shall begin." Tandriel lifted a hand. "As I said, the magic is so thick in the air here that finding it within yourself will be much easier. Know that it will not always be this way. We will change locations as you learn what it feels like to take hold of it.

"First, you must close your eyes. Concentrate on within; eliminate anything that might pose a hindrance."

Eamonn obeyed. He tried to put Leyna out of his mind, forget her presence next to him. Even among the earthy, fragrant aromas filling the clearing, he could still smell her clean, sweet scent. He pulled his mind away from it, willing himself to not think of her. That would come later.

With his mind clear, he let himself bask in the energy around him. The steady hum in the air seemed to travel through his flesh and seep into his bones. The tingle he'd felt on his skin transformed into a low vibration from within him, flowing out of him and back in like waves upon the shore.

Good. You've communed with your magic. Tandriel's voice no longer came from beyond, hitting his ears. Her words formed in his mind. *Send a breeze through the clearing. Will it with your thoughts.*

Eamonn thought of a breeze blowing past him, ruffling his hair and sending the leaves around them into song. As soon as the idea passed across his mind, the prickles of energy in the air around him unified and thrummed, then flowed into him and met his magic before exuding back out. A warm breeze rushed through the clearing as the magic and energy left his body, swirling and directionless, whipping at the edges of Eamonn's clothes.

Well done. Now, try to be more specific. Control the strength and the direction. Bring the wind exactly where you want. Set the temperature. Mold it to fit your desires.

He imagined a cool, gentle breeze this time, a soft caress over his skin, traveling from west to east. Again, just as the thought appeared, the wind came with it. This time, it came exactly as he described.

Keep your hold on it. Change it. Don't let it go simply because you have already brought it into existence. Turn it into something new.

The instructions sounded so simple when Tandriel gave them. She was right that here, in Avaria, in this spot, accessing his magic and manipulating it was as easy as breathing. In the outside world, Eamonn had fought to find his magic except for in dire circumstances when his magic appeared, unbeckoned.

He sent the wind into the trees with a force strong enough to make their top limbs sway. He made it swirl in the tree tops in a circle the size of the clearing, slowly bringing it down to their level, where it lashed at the bushes and whipped the water of the brook but didn't touch Eamonn, Leyna, or the Kaethiri.

"Very well done, Eamonn." Tandriel spoke aloud again, and Eamonn opened his eyes, releasing the wind. "We can move on."

"I have a question," Leyna announced. Her eyebrows bunched together as she looked from the Kaethiri to Eamonn. "If Eamonn was manipulating wind, wouldn't that be considered practical magic? That's something anyone could do, right?"

Tandriel smiled at Leyna's curiosity, but Imrilieth was the one to answer. "Yes, Leyna, you are correct. For humans who use magic, manipulating wind is something any could perform. But it is necessary for Eamonn to learn practical magic as well, and it is a good place to begin." She cocked her head to the side and raised her eyebrows, her lips spreading in a grin. "Would you like to try?"

Leyna's mouth fell open and her eyes widened. She stared back at the Kaethiri, unable to speak, and one side of Eamonn's mouth tipped up. Leyna had believed in magic for so long, held fast to the stories her father had told her when she was young, that even seeing magic with her own eyes had been powerful. Eamonn guessed that the idea of Leyna actually using magic was a dream she'd long since given up, wishful thinking that would never go beyond her imagination.

"Oh, no, I'm not sure I can. This is about Eamonn..."

"Give it a try," Eamonn encouraged. His voice drew her face to his, and he saw a mixture of desire and panic in her expression. "I bet you'll do better than me."

Leyna closed her mouth and swallowed, her throat bobbing dramatically. With a small nod, she faced the Kaethiri again.

"Very well. Leyna, it will be a little different for you," Tandriel said. "But we will begin the same. Close your eyes and bring your heartbeat into the rhythm of the forest."

Leyna did as instructed, and Eamonn split his attention between her and Tandriel, who stood silent and motionless. She must have been speaking in Leyna's mind, just as she had in Eamonn's. He watched Leyna as she breathed deeply and pulled her fingers into fists in her lap. Her eyes moved back and forth rapidly behind squeezed-shut lids. Eamonn was starting to wonder how difficult it must be for Leyna to tap into magic when a low rumble drew his line of sight. He watched as a small, dark grey cloud formed from nothing, and rain began to pour down in a designated spot. The cloud flashed with lightning and rumbled again, and then it was gone. Leyna opened her eyes and let out a breath as a smile lit up her face.

Eamonn gaped at Leyna with lifted eyebrows, sending lines popping out across his forehead. "That was amazing."

A pink flush crept over Leyna's cheeks as she caught Eamonn's eyes before turning back to the Kaethiri. "Did I actually do that?"

"Yes, you did." Imrilieth still grinned, and her eyes had transformed into the brightest blue. "You have an inclination for magic, Leyna. We will help you develop magic skills while you are here. You will need them against the Evil One."

The gravity of Imrilieth's words settled over Leyna, and her triumphant expression fell. "I have two friends who use magic as well," Leyna said as her eyebrows lifted, as though a sudden thought had come to her. "They held their hands up and positioned their fingers differently when they used different kinds of magic. Why did they do that?"

A memory flashed in Eamonn's mind: Rothgard holding the fingers of his outstretched hand in an odd position when he cast magic. But the Kaethiri had said nothing about it, and neither he nor Leyna had done anything like it.

"Extending a hand toward the recipient of magic can help increase the magic's focus and strength," Imrilieth explained. "Humans once taught that the position of the fingers further assisted in that increase because it may help those less inclined to magic, but it is not necessary."

Leyna dipped her head in understanding, her expression thoughtful.

"We will work on more with you in a moment, Leyna. The more you practice, the more you will build your endurance." Imrilieth looked between Eamonn and Leyna, instructing them both. "Physical endurance is critical in one's ability to hold an enchantment. As you would train for any sport or activity, so also must you train your body for the strain of using magic."

When Imrilieth had finished speaking, Galicia stepped forward and swapped places with Tandriel. Her exuberant eyes shone from behind a rim of dark lashes. "Now, Eamonn, let us try something a little different."

When she stopped speaking, her voice instantly resounded in his mind. *Now that you know what it feels like to tap into your magic, try to use it to control a creature's will. You have already done so successfully with your horse, so this should be simple.*

A squirrel scurried up the trunk of a nearby tree, and Eamonn put all of his focus on it. A slight pressure filled his chest under the glowing Réalta, much as it had when he commanded Rovis to venture into the forest. He must be connected to the squirrel's will. His senses alive with the thrill, Eamonn sent the squirrel to his nest, where he bade him collect some stored acorns and return to them. In a few moments, the squirrel appeared in the circle and presented the acorns before them.

You will develop a mastery in a short time, I believe. Galicia beamed at him as her voice entered his mind. *It will be more difficult outside of this circle, and outside of Avaria as well, but once you become familiar with what it feels like, you should be able to access your magic effortlessly.*

Here is a harder test. Rafella spoke to him now, trading places with Galicia and inclining her head toward him. *Release your hold on the animal.*

Eamonn didn't hesitate. He lost the connection with the squirrel, and the ache ceased. The squirrel scrambled, confused why its hoard of acorns lay among the grass, but in the next moment, it stilled again.

I am now connected with the squirrel. Find my connection and release it.

Eamonn blinked a few times and zeroed in on the creature. He found himself unable to reconnect, even though he had done it with ease minutes ago. He could feel a blockage of his magic, like a barrier or shield surrounding the animal's will that prevented him from reaching it. It must have been Rafella's hold. Eamonn tried to find a way around it, or a way through it, or a way to break it, but he only hit a wall.

"What am I supposed to do?" he asked aloud, frowning at Rafella. "I can feel your magic there, but I don't know how to remove it."

"It will not be easy," Imrilieth said from her place in the gazebo. "Kaethiri cannot control Kaethiri, so you cannot change Rafella's actions. You must manipulate the magic itself."

Eamonn's frown grew deeper, and he inhaled deeply and pressed his lips into a line before trying again. He closed his eyes to see if depriving one of his senses would help, and he discovered he could almost see the magic in his mind, a glow somewhere in the distance.

He tried to do what Imrilieth had said and reach out to the magic itself, rather than to the squirrel or to Rafella. A shiver passed over him as he seemed to brush it, but he couldn't grasp it. It always seemed just out of his reach.

I don't understand. He directed his thoughts to whatever Kaethiri might be listening. *How do I command the magic to do anything? It doesn't have a will.*

No, it does not. It is not alive in the sense that you are, came Imrilieth's voice, *but it is alive in the same way we are. We are magic.*

But you can't be controlled. Eamonn's frustration began to mount, but he kept his eyes closed and his internal sights didn't leave the magic's pull. *So how can the magic be controlled?*

You are disturbing the flow of magic. Do not think of it as controlling it. Rather, you are guiding it. Changing its direction.

With the new instructions, Eamonn tried again. He pushed out toward the magic, hoping to make contact, and he felt a gentle sway as the magic moved against his touch, but it didn't give way completely.

Better. Rafella's voice returned to Eamonn's mind. *Again.*

Eamonn exhaled and cleared his mind of everything but his task. He tuned out the sounds around him: the tinkling chimes, the rustling leaves, the flowing stream. He curled his hands into fists as he had seen Leyna do, straining with the effort of putting all his energy and focus into magic. Once again, he found the flow of magic and pushed against it with his mind, and this time, it wavered. Eamonn kept the same thought going, a shudder of exhilaration passing through him at sensing the magic give. It was much more tangible now, and he could feel the bond it shared with both Rafella and the squirrel. He thought distancing it from Rafella was most logical, so he pushed it in a direction away from her until the connection Rafella held on the magic broke.

A gust of wind burst from Eamonn's lungs, and he opened his eyes to find the squirrel hastily gathering the acorns and scampering away. Relief flooded him and lifted his heart, replacing his frustration with a lightness that made him almost giddy.

Imrilieth nodded, pleased. "That is not easy magic to perform for someone who is learning and half-human. It will take practice. You will want to be well-equipped to use it when the situation arises."

Power coursed through Eamonn—not the power of the forest's magic as much as the power of his triumph. The power that came with successfully using magic. He wanted more. He wanted to feel it again, the vigor of control and the thrill of success. Eamonn stood from the bench, energized and eager.

"What's next? Can we practice controlling a person's will somehow? I need to know how to do the right thing—command the right thing—whenever I can hold Rothgard's mind with my magic again."

Imrilieth's smile faded and her eyes lost their brilliance, transforming into a golden brown. "We will not train you on how to control the Evil One or anyone else. As a Kaethiri, you are not to use Avarian magic in such a fashion. It is no longer our way."

Eamonn's victorious expression fell as an incredulous breath left him. "Why not? How else am I expected to defeat him?"

"You are not." Imrilieth released her folded hands and descended the gazebo steps. Rafella moved out of the way for Imrilieth to take her place a few paces away from Eamonn.

"What?" The word flew out of him, unrestrained. He couldn't believe what he heard. "So you're fine with letting Rothgard roam free, taking over province by province until he has the whole country in his grip?"

Imrilieth tucked in her chin, eyes still boring into Eamonn. "Of course not. I said, *you* are not expected to defeat him."

Eamonn blinked and pulled his head back, his eyebrows knitted together. "What is the point of helping me learn magic if not to challenge him? Who else is going to? Who else has the ability?" He threw up a hand toward the Kaethiri. "You do, but you've already made it clear you're not going to do anything about it."

"And neither are you. At least, not in the way you are suggesting." Imrilieth's gaze turned hard. "You are one of us, Eamonn, and with that comes a certain set of principles. We do not use our magic to control humans."

"But I have, and no one stopped me. *Your voice* came to me when I was searching for my magic to do just that."

"You sought your magic, and I helped you find it. I did not know your intentions. There are other ways of using magic that do not involve controlling a person's will."

"But how else is there even a chance of defeating Rothgard?" Eamonn's anger rose, and his words strained against his throat as he tried to keep his tone in check. "He has created his own Réalta. He can control others. Any army opposing him could be his in a thought. We've seen it before."

"The Evil One has created an amulet akin to a Réalta, but it is corrupt, and his range of Avarian magic is limited. A true Réalta cannot be created, no matter the vile methods the Evil One has attempted. He possesses only a fraction of our power with the blood he stole from you, and the power he wields is incompatible with his human form. He will not have as much power as you suggest and is not as much of a threat as before."

"That's not good enough!"

Eamonn's chest heaved in the silence left by his outburst. How could the Kaethiri be so nonchalant about Rothgard? Regardless of how they perceived him, he held power he shouldn't possess. He had broken Eamonn, and though Eamonn had managed to put the pieces back together, they didn't fit in the same way they had before. Rothgard had altered Eamonn down to his very essence, forever. He deserved to lose his will to Eamonn's control. That, and more.

A shuddering breath near him caught his attention, and he swiveled his head to Leyna, where she sat on the stone bench, gutted to see her round eyes and parted lips. His loss of control had shocked her; that much was obvious. His stomach squirmed, and he dropped his head, searching the lush grass at his feet as he reined in his exasperation. "If you weren't going to help me learn how to use my magic to control him and stop him, what was your purpose?"

"You came here, Eamonn. We did not summon you. Though we anticipated your arrival after Leyna's time with us, we did not call you here. We will gladly train you in the magic that you rightly possess but not in ways we no longer use."

Eamonn met Imrilieth's gaze. The hardness had not left her features.

"You can use magic in a multitude of other ways, all of which will aid you in defeating the Evil One. We will teach you how to resist his control, since your human side is still vulnerable. You have already begun to practice removing the hold of Avarian magic on another's mind, which will be useful in freeing any under his influence." Imrilieth laced her fingers together and hung her hands in front of her, tilting her head back so that she looked down at Eamonn. "If you use our magic in the way you suggest, it can lead to the darkening of one's soul. As half human, you are susceptible to the seduction of this power and, consequently, the corruption of your being. Though you may have good intentions, you would become no better than the Evil One himself."

Imrilieth's last words made Eamonn bristle. Of course he was better than Rothgard; he would always be better than Rothgard. He was on the right side. He wanted to use Avarian magic to defeat an oppressor. Rothgard wanted power and control at the cost of innocent people's minds, of their volition. Eamonn only desired control over one person, and Rothgard was far from innocent.

He swallowed before speaking again, steadying his voice. "That *won't* happen. I am *not* like Rothgard."

"It is true that the corruption happening to the Evil One is not the same because he is not one of us, but be wary—your human side is still vulnerable. Do not be fooled into thinking you are impervious to such things because you truly are Kaethiri. You are just as truly human. Even those with the noblest intentions can be easily corrupted." Imrilieth's eyes transformed to the deepest brown and the hum of energy increased around the Kaethiri Queen. When she spoke again, her voice was heavier, and the ground seemed to tremble beneath his feet.

"The soul of the Evil One is quickly growing dark. The impure amulet he wears is accelerating its corruption. However, as I said a moment ago, he is not as powerful as you make him to be. While his new bloodstone is capable of channeling the magic within him, it has an endpoint. He does not have sufficient energy to continue to use Avarian magic without another source to revive him. The bloodstone's curse will not kill him, but it will transform him as it corrupts his soul."

Eamonn frowned, his curiosity piqued. "How do you know all this?"

"We can connect with him weakly, due to your blood. We were able to determine what he has done."

The words sent a bolt of terror through Eamonn. Could he connect to Rothgard as well? Worse—could Rothgard connect to him?

Imrilieth seemed to read Eamonn's mind. "It is nothing for you to fear. Without a renewing source of magic, he would not be able to sustain a connection." Her shoulders rose and fell in a heavy breath, and her eyes dimmed to a dark grey. "Regardless, we will step back from magic training for the time being. Take the time to consider what we have told you and examine yourself for your true motivation." Her eyes held him until Eamonn broke free and stared at the ground. When he looked up again, the Kaethiri were gone.

Lifting his face to the sky, Eamonn closed his eyes and sighed. Imrilieth didn't understand—she couldn't. It might have been the Kaethiri's choice to not use their magic to manipulate humans, but only half of Eamonn was Kaethiri. His human half couldn't reconcile with the idea. It didn't feel compelled to follow the principles set forth by the Kaethiri.

And it wasn't like he wanted to go around controlling anyone who stood in his way. He and Rothgard differed in that. Eamonn wanted to use Avarian magic to manipulate the will of Rothgard alone. As far as Eamonn was concerned, Rothgard had lost the right to keep his mind for himself.

THIRTEEN

From her seat on the bench, Leyna had watched the interaction between Eamonn and Imrilieth, keeping her mouth shut and choosing not to get involved. Maybe she would have, if she agreed with Eamonn. But as it stood, Leyna was inclined to agree with the Kaethiri.

She had never believed it was Eamonn's responsibility—or destiny, however one chose to look at it—to stand up to Rothgard.

Though she understood what drove him, his outburst in the clearing had taken her by surprise. Learning the magical skills needed to take control of Rothgard seemed less like something to help the others in their fight and more like a vendetta. From the limited details Leyna knew of Eamonn's time in captivity, it was enough to understand that much of Eamonn's motivation came from a place of revenge. Still, she had hoped he wouldn't give in to his vindictive feelings.

No matter what she believed, she wouldn't point it out to him then. He already felt a little betrayed by the Kaethiri; she wouldn't betray him too.

They had gone back to their little glade that afternoon alone, the path appearing before them as they walked. She had tried speaking to Eamonn, but the topics she chose yielded no valuable conversation. Eamonn's mind must have remained in the clearing.

He entered his hut once they had returned, and Leyna did not follow. He needed the time to process, to decompress from the argument with the Kaethiri.

Leyna, however, had no desire to coop herself up in a hut. Her body still hummed with energy. The thrill that came with using magic still hung on her skin. She strolled back through the forest the way they had come, again finding the Kaethiri's meeting place. The magic was so thick in the air there that she drank it in with every breath. Using magic for the first time seemed to have transformed something inside her. Leyna had already been able to feel the magic in Avaria; the buzz of it had always tingled her skin. Now, it coursed through her. In the meeting place especially, there was no longer a difference in how Leyna felt inside and what she sensed around her. The magic wasn't just around her; it flowed through her, filling her with an exhilaration she never knew before. It was a confident hope, a tangible optimism. Like she had nothing and no one to fear.

The Kaethiri's offer to willingly teach her magic had stunned her. Leyna still couldn't quite wrap her mind around it. She would be a magic-caster. Magic would be accessible to her, something she could use as the need arose. Imrilieth said she had an inclination for magic. A soft smile formed on her lips, and she closed her eyes as she wondered if her father might have, too. If he'd felt the pull of magic, and if that was what had kept him in search of the truth of it.

With her eyes closed, Leyna pushed away everything that struck her other senses and focused on the buzz of magic. She wanted to keep practicing. Until the Kaethiri instructed her further, she didn't know the extent of her ability, so she wanted to try something relatively simple again.

The warm beams of sunlight caressed Leyna's skin, and she reached out to them, wrapping them around her like a blanket. The heat intensified as Leyna tugged as much warmth as she could from the rays. She opened her eyes and was almost blinded, the light bare and strong and all around her. At the shock of its intensity, she dropped the magic, and the light faded back to its evening glow.

A smile broke across her face. What else could she do? She wanted to find out, but she didn't want to get in over her head without proper supervision and guidance. She considered calling back one of the Kaethiri when a voice came from behind her.

"I'm glad they're teaching you as well."

Leyna spun around at the voice, surprised that he had followed her back to the clearing. "What are you doing here?"

Eamonn shrugged. "You didn't go in with me."

Leyna's expression fell, and she shook her head quickly. "I didn't know you wanted me to. I thought you needed the time to yourself."

Eamonn crossed the circle and met Leyna where she stood, his fingers restless at his sides. He closed the space between them and took her hands, drawing her eyes to him. "I thought after last night you would know that I always want you around."

A warmth that had nothing to do with the magic blossomed inside Leyna as she held Eamonn's hands. A smile crept up her cheeks, which burned with the way Eamonn looked at her. "I'm sorry," she whispered. "You got so angry. You argued. I didn't know—"

A hardness passed over Eamonn's face and silenced her, but it was gone as quickly as it had come. His lips stretched in a small smile as he shook his head. "You don't have to apologize. And don't worry about it." Eamonn dropped one of her hands to place his fingers under her chin and lift her face up to his. "And never, *ever* feel like you shouldn't be around or that I need to be left alone. You make everything better."

The way he spoke did not reprimand her but encouraged her, and Leyna pushed aside the nagging in her mind. Sincerity filled his every word. It was all right that she hadn't joined him in his hut. She and Eamonn were still navigating what it meant for them to be together. It was new, and exciting, and everything she had ever hoped for. Leyna's heart nearly burst to feel Eamonn's calloused hands in hers as his gentle voice soothed her anxiety.

"Come on, let's go back. The evening meal will be waiting for us." Eamonn turned to leave the clearing and tugged Leyna by the hand he still held, but she released it and didn't move.

"I'm not ready to go back yet." Leyna inhaled deeply, breathing in the current of magic, and it ran all the way through her down to her fingers and toes. She couldn't deny that it was intoxicating.

Eamonn raised an eyebrow, watching her curiously. The way a corner of his mouth raised made Leyna think he knew what was going through her mind.

"I never imagined I would be able to use magic. To feel this." Leyna closed her eyes briefly and lifted her arms, palms up, from her sides. "It's like a dream. It's so hard to believe that it's real."

Eamonn's eyes glittered with mischief, and he crossed his arms. "Want to try something?"

Leyna had been ready to summon a Kaethiri to help her with magic before Eamonn had appeared, but—well, Eamonn was half-Kaethiri. And yes, he was still learning magic as well, but his magic was innate.

"You can teach me something? You're learning, too."

"I know enough."

The sunlight was fading, and Eamonn was right to go back to their glade. The food would be waiting for them on the stone table. But Leyna wanted to experience the rush of her magic again, and Eamonn was offering to help her. Her lips spread across her face, dimpling her cheeks.

"All right then. Show me."

A glimpse of triumph flashed across Eamonn's features. "First, close your eyes."

Leyna obeyed and fought to even out her grin.

"Now, take a deep breath and focus on the magic within you rather than what's around you."

Her chest rose with the breath, and her lips parted as she blew it out, bringing her attention to the hum of energy that dwelled inside her.

"Think of the brook behind you. Feel the energy in the current and pull at it. Make the water flow faster."

She imagined the gentle brook, trickling over rocks and cascading tranquilly over the short waterfall. Leyna pictured the water hurrying and touched that center of magic that warmed her core. As she reached for the energy found in the stream, she heard the growing rush of water and saw the foaming white in her mind's eye as it bubbled and crashed.

"Good." Eamonn's voice sounded like it came from far away. "Try to raise the water level."

Again, Leyna saw the brook in her mind's eye and watched it rise up the banks as she tried to alter the water's energy. She didn't feel a tug on her core this time and tried again. The water still rushed, splashing over itself as it hurried along, but even without looking at it, Leyna knew the level hadn't risen.

"Turn toward the water."

Leyna turned around to face the brook that surrounded half of the meeting space. Something shifted within her. The change in position had helped.

"Here, try this."

Hands grasped her arms from behind and lifted them both into the air, but just as they made contact with her skin, the bite of sparks pierced her flesh at each pressure point and Leyna opened her eyes. Her breathing changed from even and rhythmic to shallow and erratic, as though she'd been running and tripped a couple of times along the way. The brook instantly returned to its lazy flow. Leyna threw her head over her shoulder to see Eamonn right behind her, his arms on either side of her.

"What happened?" he asked, keeping his hands wrapped delicately around her biceps as Leyna dropped her arms.

"You." The word came out in a breath. Leyna had lost any hold she'd had on magic at the electricity of Eamonn's touch. She caught his eye from over her shoulder before casting down her gaze. He moved his face so close to hers that the air between them grew hot and thick. The hum of Eamonn's magic radiated off of him, heady and invigorating.

"I barely touched you." The wind from Eamonn's whispered words tickled Leyna's ear and sent a shiver through her.

"That was all it took."

Leyna turned to face him, bringing her eyes to his. Dusk gave way to night around them, the last golden rays of sunlight dwindling and the silver glow of moonlight replacing it. The light specks floating in the air brightened and emitted a soft luminescence that glimmered in Eamonn's eyes. Leyna couldn't tear hers away.

Eamonn dipped his head toward Leyna, and his lips met hers. The shock of his magic's sting almost made her withdraw, but it quickly eased into an energy that sucked her in and fired every nerve. It made her feel alive, and she wanted more.

Leyna tipped up her chin as she reached up to Eamonn and deepened the kiss. With her response, he moved his hands to her waist and pulled her close. Leyna twined her arms around his neck and tangled her fingers in his loose curls. Her mouth moved on Eamonn's with a fervor that surprised her, but she couldn't deny that she wanted this. His hands held her waist and his lips pressed onto hers. It was all she could do to stay on two feet.

Their lips parted in a rhythm that came as naturally as breathing. Leyna's stomach flipped when Eamonn's hands moved to her back and he stepped one leg past her, effectively removing any remaining space between their bodies. A smile pulled her mouth away from the kiss. Eamonn noticed, moving his face from hers only enough to speak.

"What is it?"

Leyna shook her head, the tips of their noses brushing. "I really am in a dream."

Eamonn grinned as a laugh escaped his lips. "Let me see if I can wake you up."

The kiss he returned with was faster, more eager—as though the time they had was limited and he was racing against it. Leyna's pulse hammered in her veins as her heart beat the same current as the brook when her magic had sent it pounding over the rocks. She answered with equal zeal, searching for something that she couldn't name and may never find. Eamonn's fingers tightened against her back and Leyna's breath hitched. The song of the chimes in the air changed, speeding up as though to match the kiss.

But the thrum of magic couldn't compare to the fire Eamonn had unleashed in her. He'd done what he set out to do: awakened her spirit.

Eamonn moved his body a step back and cupped Leyna's face as he leaned his forehead against hers. A laugh broke through his smile.

"I can't…" His breath came in deep gasps, and he took a moment to let it even before he pressed his lips to Leyna's forehead. "You're too incredible for your own good."

Leyna couldn't stop the grin that appeared on her face. "Oh, am I?"

"Well, maybe for *my* own good."

Eamonn brought his gaze to Leyna's, and the look in his eyes sent a flutter through her middle. They gleamed with a passion she hadn't seen in him before and an affection that mirrored what she held for him. He touched her jaw softly and ran his thumb over her cheek.

"You are my dawn, my midday, my dusk. You are *everything*, my love."

FOURTEEN

Eamonn didn't know which was more magical: practicing actual magic, or the time he spent with Leyna.

After their kiss in the clearing, the need to be with Leyna all the time had exponentially increased in Eamonn. They had gone their separate ways to their individual huts—at Leyna's request, and Eamonn wouldn't dare push otherwise—but he lay in his surprisingly comfortable bed awake for hours, replaying the evening in his mind until he'd exhausted himself and gave in to sleep.

My love, he'd called her. He hadn't planned to say it, but the words had formed on his lips naturally, and they felt right. He cared for her. He treasured her. *My love*.

Now, every time he saw her, he was back in the clearing, holding her, her lips pressed to his and her arms around his neck.

When the Kaethiri appeared the next day to train them both further in magic, he groaned inwardly and wished they would go away. He would rather put learning magic on hold than time with Leyna.

During the day, the Kaethiri accompanied them to the meeting place and led them both in the instruction of practical magic, but the evenings belonged to Eamonn and Leyna. Some nights they took walks through the forest or lay in the reeds by the little river, talking about their pasts and—sometimes—their future. Other nights weren't for words. They might find a hollow in a wide trunk, a thick covering of leaves, or a face of rock to have a bit of privacy and spend the evening stealing kisses in each other's embrace. Private though the forest may seem, every inch of Avaria held magic and, with it, the presence of the Kaethiri.

Leyna showed promise as she learned to use magic, proving Imrilieth right that she had an inclination toward it. She manipulated the world around them with ease, creating storms and suppressing light and levitating rocks as though she'd been doing so all her life. Practical magic came easily to Eamonn too, and the Kaethiri had them join together, directing their magic at the same things to create magnificent displays and powerful onslaughts of the elements at their disposal.

Even Avarian magic was within Eamonn's reach. He practiced using it for protection—a shield around himself and others—feeling it as a tangible thing around him that could be worked and molded into what he needed. After his success in breaking the Kaethiri's control on various creatures, they moved their training outside of the meeting place and the intense concentration of magic.

"You will find it more difficult away from the magic's center," Imrilieth told them as they settled into a new practice spot on the banks of the brook where it had flowed downstream. "Even more so outside of our borders, but we will not train you there.

In order to access magic in the world, you must come to the point where it can be summoned with the slightest thought while still in our realm."

Leyna practiced first, and Eamonn took a seat on one of the large mossy rocks by the stream. She started with her eyes open, giving her full attention to a tree in front of her. Her shoulders lifted with a deep breath, and she let it out slowly through lips pursed into a circle. Still, nothing happened.

"Raise your hand to the tree," Tandriel instructed, making a slow semicircle behind Leyna. "Remember, the extension of a hand can aid in accomplishing your goal by directing the flow of magic toward its target."

Leyna closed her eyes and lifted a hand toward the tree. Both she and Eamonn had stopped using their hands to focus magic in the clearing, but here, it seemed Leyna needed the extra funneling of magic.

The way Tandriel stopped behind Leyna and watched her made Eamonn wonder if she had switched to communicating through their minds. Leyna took another steadying breath, and any tension in her muscles relaxed. A tremor began in the tree as Leyna reached toward it, going from the base up the trunk to the thinner top limbs, making them shake and sway as if an earthquake was hitting only that tree.

With a smile, Leyna turned her hand palm up and lifted it higher, and another quake rattled up the tree. Rustling leaves and trembling limbs drowned out the soft bubbling of the brook and the ever-present tinkling song. Birds squawked and balked as they were thrown from their perches. Squirrels raced across limbs and jumped to nearby trees for safety. A gust formed from the waving branches fell upon Eamonn, Leyna, and the Kaethiri, and Eamonn's heart skidded when the groaning of wood met his ears. Instead of letting the tree crack, though, Leyna released it from her magic, and the world around them instantly stilled.

"Well done, Leyna," Imrilieth praised. "Take some time to rest, and we will try something else. Frequent rest as we practice will help to build your endurance and allow you to hold an enchantment longer." Imrilieth's eyes landed on Eamonn, their bright blue penetrating and almost severe. "We will begin with you, Eamonn, by practicing a magic block. We will focus solely on Avarian magic now that you understand the fundamentals of environmental manipulation."

Eamonn bounced his knee where he sat on the rock. Words hung on his tongue, desperate to be spoken. None of the Kaethiri had brought up his outburst from the first day, nor had they mentioned anything about the methods he wanted to use against Rothgard or the potential "corruption" they had described. But he wanted to try again. He had done what they said and examined himself for his true motivation. All Eamonn saw was a desire to rid the world of Rothgard, and using his magic to command Rothgard's will seemed to be the most obvious and effective solution, if he could learn exactly how to do so.

"Come," Galicia said with a wide smile, stepping forward. "I will try to latch on to your human side. Fully embody your Kaethiri side and protect your human half."

Eamonn stood to still the twitch in his leg, but his muscles continued to skip. He kept his mouth shut, focusing in on his core to commune with his magic and prepare for Galicia's latch. He reached for it but couldn't grasp it. Though the magic in the air still flowed through him and all around him, it seemed to slip through his fingers as he frantically clawed at it inside him. The Kaethiri were right; it was harder to use magic away from the meeting place. Eamonn hadn't expected it to be so drastic, and he reached again just as Galicia's latch found his humanness.

The Kaethiri in him dwindled, even though he fought against Galicia's hold. He tried to push it away, to resist falling under her control, but his magic dimmed like a candle in a closed jar. The attention he placed on his human side drew his focus farther away from his magic and lessened his chances of removing or even blocking Galicia's control.

Turn your mind away from your defeat. It was Imrilieth who spoke to him, not Galicia. *Put all your strength into grasping your magic. If you panic, you will surely fall.*

Eamonn tried not to panic, but he felt like the ground beneath him was opening wide and swallowing his Kaethiri side and with it, the magic that would save him. He tried to catch himself, wishing he could throw out his hands to search for any kind of purchase, but the memory of being held under Rothgard's control consumed him—an inky blackness that constricted his mind and his spirit and robbed him of his remaining strength. The thought finally snuffed out the candle, and his Kaethiri side gave way to his humanity, which fell completely under the latch of Galicia's magic.

Galicia released him the second he lost the battle, her kind eyes edged with sadness. "Do not be discouraged, Eamonn. This is challenging, and you have become used to the ease of accessing magic in our meeting place. We will try again, and now you know what to expect."

Eamonn sucked in a breath and nodded, ready to face Galicia's next attempt to latch to him. He shifted his feet on the grass, planting them solidly as if preparing for a physical attack. His hope was that the right mindset from the start would give him an advantage.

He turned all his attention inward, diving for his magic through a deep, dark pool where he couldn't see the bottom. He felt the heat, saw the distant glow, and forced himself farther, reaching until he made contact, and he held on for dear life. His pendant roared to life at his chest, shining bright green and humming with warmth, and Eamonn brought all his magic up to surround him like an invisible shield. Galicia's magic hit but did not get through.

Now hold it, she said to him. *Your enemy will not give up easily. You must be prepared to withstand.*

As he listened to her words, Eamonn's magic began to falter, so he doubled down and braced himself against the attack. Power surged through him and warmed his blood, filling him with the intoxicating sense of victory that made him never want to let the magic go. Power fueled him now as much as magic itself. He pushed back against Galicia's magic, and it broke around him like a parted sea.

Galicia smiled as she released her magic, and Eamonn felt as it passed by and disappeared. "Much better. There is so much of your mother in you."

Eamonn beamed at the comparison. He'd never felt more connected to the mother he never knew than he did during his time in Avaria practicing magic. The Kaethiri had told him more of what Laielle was like, even in her human form, and he understood why his father had always spoken of her as if she was an angel. Kind, gentle, endearing. Though the Kaethiri had exiled Laielle after she'd chosen to be with Florin, they knew she was overjoyed to be a mother. Hearing such things made Eamonn's heart swell and be filled with grief all at once, and he wished more than he ever had that she had lived. That he had known her, and she him.

Rafella took slow strides up the bank to join Galicia, while Tandriel remained closer to Leyna and Imrilieth near the tree that Leyna shook. "Yes, with you, she still lives on." A soft smile touched Rafella's lips for a moment, and then she clasped her hands together and straightened. "Let's work again on releasing someone's mind from magical control more. Your ability to commune with the magic inside you is improving, so it may come easier than you imagine."

Maybe it was the euphoria that came with the magic that pulsed through him, but Eamonn wouldn't stay silent any longer. He couldn't contain the questions that had been plaguing him since the first day learning magic, occupying his thoughts only second to Leyna.

"Can we do that later?" Eamonn asked, his heart picking up speed. "I want to learn how to place my own hold on someone." He tried to swallow but found his throat scratchy and thick. He turned his attention to Imrilieth and took two steps in her direction. "Please. I've done what you said. I took a good look at my motivations, and I think my reasons are sound. I only want to use it on one person. He has done enough to deserve it."

Imrilieth's nostrils flared as she stepped unhurriedly toward Eamonn, the jewels in her hair jingling. Her eyes turned a shocking amber. "You will not persuade us to train you in such practices. It is a violation that will lead to corruption. We have already discussed this."

"If I am as much a Kaethiri as you say I am, I have a right to know." Each word flew like a dagger from Eammon's mouth. "All of you can do it. I should at least know how to do it, too."

"None of us have human blood," Imrilieth replied, and the soft glow around her skin brightened as she spoke. "None of us carry the same temptations, the same stumbling blocks as humans. Our decision to not teach you is as much to follow our principles as it is for your protection." She shook her head in warning, eyes wide and jaw set. "Controlling a human is not something to take lightly, no matter their sins. A taste of that power can lead to an overwhelming desire for more. That is how it corrupts."

Eamonn clenched his teeth and worked the muscles in his jaw. His hands formed fists at his sides. Couldn't they see that he was their best chance against Rothgard? "Rothgard has to be stopped! There is no guarantee that any army gathered to oppose him would be enough. If you *just* teach me this magic, it can be over and done, and we all can move on!"

"Eamonn."

Leyna's voice from off to his side drew his attention. She wrung her hands, her eyes flitting from him to Imrilieth and back. "I think Imrilieth is right."

Eamonn turned to face her. "What? Why?"

She looked worried, her eyes not lingering on him for more than a few seconds, like she was afraid to say what was on her mind. When her gaze stilled on Imrilieth, Eamonn glanced back at the Kaethiri Queen over his shoulder and assumed she must be speaking in Leyna's mind.

"There's no need for secrets," he said to Imrilieth, an irritated edge to his tone. "If either of you has something to say to me, say it."

"I know you want this magic," Leyna started, her voice soft but impassioned. Eamonn whipped his head back to her as she approached him. "And we all want Rothgard to be defeated. But at the cost of your soul? Even if it's just a possibility, you would risk that?"

"Leyna, I'd be fine." He mirrored her gentleness, closing the distance between them and picking up her hands. "If that's what you're worried about, don't. Once he is gone, I wouldn't have a need to use it again."

"Are you sure?" Her brows knitted in concern as she searched his eyes. "You don't know what may happen after. You don't know who might oppose you. What would be justified? Where would the line be drawn?"

"I wouldn't—"

"I know you want revenge for what he did to you. You were beaten and abused—and it was horribly wrong—but revenge can lead people to do things they wouldn't have dreamed of." Leyna took a shuddering breath and whispered, "I don't want that to be you."

Eamonn released Leyna's hands, and they hung in the air for a moment before falling to her sides. He pressed his lips into a narrow line and swallowed, turning away from her. Staring out blankly into the forest, Eamonn rubbed a hand over his mouth and chin, his heart beating like a deep drum.

He did want revenge. Rothgard deserved nothing less than Eamonn's vengeance. But, as he had told the Kaethiri and Leyna, it would end with Rothgard.

"It wouldn't happen," he finally said as he stared off at nothing, his voice a low grumble.

Leyna moved closer to him eagerly, but he didn't turn his head. "I'm just trying to look out for you. You don't know what the future holds. All I want is for you to be safe."

"It's not your job to keep me safe!"

The minute the words had left his mouth, he wished he could take them back. They'd flown out in anger, a reaction more than a response. The injury mixed with a little fear in her round blue eyes hit Eamonn right in the heart. He squeezed his eyes shut and pressed his fingers to his forehead.

"No, Leyna. I'm sorry." The hand scrubbed down the rest of his face before he opened his eyes again. "I shouldn't have said that. I'm sorry."

Leyna closed her hanging mouth, but her expression remained as hard as iron. Eamonn took a step toward her and Leyna stepped back in sync, shaking her head. "You shouldn't have said it, but you meant it. If you're going to have people in your life, Eamonn, you have to expect them to care."

"You're right." He rushed to her, desperate, gripping her tenderly by her upper arms in the hope she wouldn't pull away. "You're right. Forgive me."

Leyna's eyes roamed all around the forest, looking anywhere except Eamonn, but she didn't fight his grasp.

"*Leyna.*"

"I forgive you," she murmured, and when she met his gaze, he found her eyes pooling with tears. "You're just so ready to throw your life—your soul—on the line for this. I'm in this with you now, too. I can't bear for you to be so reckless."

Eamonn nodded quickly and pulled her into his arms, planting a kiss on her forehead. His heart raced, but so did his mind. He didn't want to hurt Leyna; in fact, hurting her was the very last thing he ever wanted to do in life. But neither could he abandon his desire to take down Rothgard simply because she was afraid for him. Thoughts whirled through his mind, trying to form some kind of plan—a workaround that would give him both Leyna and his revenge.

One thing he knew: staying in Avaria much longer would do more harm than good.

Eamonn released Leyna with the stroke of a thumb across her cheek, and he spun to face Imrilieth again, but the Kaethiri were gone.

"You didn't have to go away!" he called, his vision wandering the space around them. "You don't have to disappear every time things get hard."

We only seek to give you the privacy you deserve.

Eamonn sighed, his shoulders falling. *That's very thoughtful, but we weren't finished.*

If you would like to continue practicing the magic we have chosen to instruct, we will return and start again.

We can finish what we were doing, but then we will prepare to leave.

Imrilieth appeared closer to Eamonn and Leyna than where she had previously stood. "You wish to leave?"

"Leave? No." Leyna frowned at Imrilieth, then turned to Eamonn. "What's going on?"

"I don't see the need to stay here anymore, not if the Kaethiri won't teach us everything." Eamonn spoke to Leyna, but his eyes didn't leave the Queen of the Kaethiri.

"We need to practice."

"We can finish our practice today. We've learned a lot, and I think we would both do well outside of Avaria."

"Eamonn." Leyna's voice was incredulous, and it forced him to look at her. "We're not ready to leave yet. There's more to learn, more to practice. Why would we go now?"

"There's not much else we can glean from the Kaethiri. Practice is practice, and we can do that anywhere. We can practice with each other. We should go on to Miren, help Dorylss and the others work on the king to form an alliance. That's the best we can do against Rothgard now."

"We'll need to join up with them eventually, but I'm sure they have that under control. Dorylss may not even be in Amrieth yet."

"At least I'll feel like I'm doing something productive. If we stay here, it's just more of the same."

"And that's a bad thing?"

Eamonn heard the intonation in her voice and knew her words had more than one meaning. She spoke of the two of them, too. Of more of the same kind of evenings they had been spending together.

"Like I said, we can still practice away from here. We'll continue what we started."

Leyna released a pent-up breath, and it seemed she understood his meaning. Their new relationship could continue—would continue—outside of Avaria. He had to admit, he would miss how Avaria made everything between them more magical.

"What if I don't want to leave?" she asked, crossing her arms. "What if I'm not ready? Why don't I get a say in whether it's time for us to go?"

"I'm sure the Kaethiri would be more than willing to let you stay, if that's what you really want. But I'm going to leave, and I'd like you to come with me."

Leyna blinked a few times, her mouth shut, like she was registering what Eamonn had said. Her throat bobbed with a hard swallow, and her nostrils flared as she inhaled sharply.

Eamonn rested gentle hands on her upper arms, stroking them with his thumbs. He hadn't meant it as a command, but it was still abrupt—even to him. He hadn't expected to want to leave today, but once he'd said it, he knew it was what he wanted. He was sick of arguing with the Kaethiri, sick of them holding a guiding hand over his life. Why would he expect anything different from the beings who had ripped him from his father as a baby?

"I *want* to go," he said more gently, stepping closer to Leyna. "I'm done living under the Kaethiri's expectations for me. If you would rather stay here, I understand, but I want you with me."

"Of course I'll go with you," she murmured, the softness in her voice a contrast to the ice in her features. "But I don't feel like you're really giving me a choice. And I don't agree with you. I don't believe we're ready to leave here."

Eamonn didn't have a response for her. What was he supposed to say? He wasn't coercing her, not really. Surely the Kaethiri would provide a way for her to travel to Amrieth safely if he left without her. Or was that, too, outside the realm of magic they were willing to perform?

"Take the rest of the day with the Kaethiri," he suggested. "We can practice magic out here and get a better feel for what it will be like after we're gone. One more night, and we'll leave at daybreak."

Leyna sighed, disappointment written all over her face. But it didn't seem to be about leaving. Something about the way she looked at Eamonn...her disappointment was directed at him.

"It's your turn," he said, hoping to break up some of the lingering tension. He gestured from Leyna to Imrilieth just as the other three Kaethiri came into view. Eamonn stepped back and returned to his seat on the boulder. Leyna moved her attention from him to the Kaethiri, and the magic training resumed.

Eamonn watched Leyna raise rocks from the ground and magically throw them into the stream one by one. His heart cracked as he recalled the hurt in her eyes after he'd snapped at her. He hadn't meant to hurt her, truly. And he didn't mean to upset her by prompting their leave from Avaria, but it had to be done. He would admit, he had pulled the rug out from under her, his decision to head to Miren's kingdom so sudden and final. Eamonn bounced his leg again as he sat on the rock with crossed arms. He would think of a way to smooth things over with Leyna. Maybe she would even come around. It had just been too abrupt, and she would understand after a while.

He needed Leyna on his side. He'd known it before: before they kissed, before they admitted their feelings to each other. But now, having her turned against him even in the slightest filled his chest with an ache different from the pang of magic. It was consuming, leaving him hollow and empty. Without Leyna, he was nothing. A shell.

He would find a way to bring her back to him.

FIFTEEN

At least Rovis seemed to be in agreement with Leyna. The horse almost snorted at Eamonn in annoyance as he saddled him and seemed to resist the tugs on his reins as Eamonn walked him away from the glade with their huts. Leyna began to wonder if Eamonn would have to use Avarian magic to command Rovis to leave the realm, just as he had to get him to enter.

Leyna didn't blame the horse. Nothing indicated that now was the right time for them to leave, except for Eamonn. She'd tried to replace any resentment building toward him with images of what awaited them in Miren. Perhaps Dorylss did need their help. If all had gone well on the road, he would be arriving in Amrieth soon. The way he, Kinrid, and Gilleth had spoken about the King of Miren didn't fill Leyna with confidence. Maybe it would take Eamonn showing the king the kind of magic Rothgard had at his disposal to persuade him to join in an alliance.

It was what she told herself to feel better about leaving, at least.

Imrilieth waited for them at the edge of the glade to guide them out of the forest. She dipped her head in greeting at Leyna and then at Eamonn, and Leyna didn't miss the flicker of grey that passed over her lavender eyes or the tightness in her expression when she looked at Eamonn. Grey, Leyna had learned, was the color that reflected a Kaethiri's sorrow. Was Imrilieth sad to see Eamonn leave? Or was she, like Leyna, unhappy about the change in his behavior that had led him to his decision?

"The way to Amrieth is long, even longer if you go off the main road to remain hidden," Imrilieth said as they walked, leading with a slow, even pace through the dense woods. "Although, if the Evil One is intent on finding you, the magic you carry with you from this realm will be easy to detect. It will dwindle over time, but not quickly enough for him to lose track of you."

Leyna furrowed her brow and looked up at the tall, radiant woman. "What do you suggest?"

"Take the main road," Imrilieth answered, much to Leyna's surprise. The Kaethiri Queen reached a hand out toward them but directed past them, and Leyna turned to find a white horse trotting in their direction. "This is Hiraeth. He is one of our own." The creature came to Imrilieth and nuzzled her outstretched hand. "He is for you, Leyna. We will cast an enchantment on the horses that will allow them to travel at maximum speed without losing endurance or requiring a pause for rest, so you will need to ride your own. We will also grant you stamina and protection from severe soreness or injury from the ride so your body can tolerate it. Take only necessary breaks, and do not linger at any inn along the road. The comfort there will provide a feeling of safety, which may prove false, so stay no longer than needed to sleep. You will arrive in the Mirish kingdom before anyone sent after you would have the chance to catch up. Eamonn, when you no longer require him, command Hiraeth to return to us. He knows the way."

Eamonn nodded in response, and at Imrilieth's gesture to the forest before them, the edge of the realm appeared, the bare rock cliff face and layer of white snow beyond.

"Thank you for your hospitality in letting us stay here and for training us in magic. I do truly appreciate all of it," Leyna said to the Kaethiri Queen. She hoped her sincerity came across. The Kaethiri did not have to allow her reentry, let alone provide protection against Avarian magic and teach her how to use practical magic. She owed them more than she could ever give.

"It was our pleasure to have you here," Imrilieth replied with a small smile. "Both of you are welcome to return. Avaria will always be a haven for you."

Leyna returned the Queen's smile, then reached for the winter clothes they had draped over Rovis.

"Thank you," Eamonn said, inclining his head. "And I'm sorry for the way I behaved. I hope I will return one day, and we can start afresh. There is still more I hope to learn about my mother."

Imrilieth nodded. "Yes, there is more to tell. Now..." The specks of light in the air concentrated and swirled around them and the horses before dispersing and once again floating aimlessly. "Your horses will be able to travel to Amrieth within three days. Follow the river down to the road and do not leave it. It runs directly to the Mirish Kingdom."

Leyna wrapped her thick scarf from Braedel around her neck and over her head, and she started to sweat under the layers she had been adding. Leaving Avaria pained her for many reasons, but one was because she had grown accustomed to the calm, temperate weather. She groaned internally as she braced for the frigid temperatures and biting wind that awaited her in far northern Idyrria.

Eamonn started to don his winter wear as well, and Leyna glanced around them, realizing Imrilieth was gone.

"Not much for goodbyes, are they?"

Eamonn looked up from the pile of clothes on the saddle, threw his head from side to side, and then huffed a laugh. "No, they are not."

As Eamonn finished with a scarf of his own and leather gloves, Leyna hoisted herself onto Hiraeth. Her stomach flipped to remember her and Eamonn together on Rovis, before they had arrived in Avaria. She hadn't been sure what they were, exactly. There had been some uncertainty, some suspense between them, never knowing what to expect from Eamonn as he sat behind her. Never knowing what to expect from herself, either.

In a few days, things between them had changed so dramatically. They had taken the next step in Avaria, and Leyna missed Eamonn's presence behind her in the saddle. She longed for the new comfort and familiarity that came with his embrace. But since the day before, there had been a different kind of tension that threatened their new and fragile status. Neither had brought up their conversation with the Kaethiri by the stream.

"They were generous to provide another horse," Leyna said when Eamonn had seated himself in Rovis's saddle. She almost wished Imrilieth hadn't offered Hiraeth. The words were on her lips, but she didn't say them aloud. If they were to ride at a gallop all the way to Amrieth, they couldn't ride together.

"They were." Eamonn rode up to Leyna and extended his hand. She gave hers in return and he brought it to his lips, placing a tender kiss on the back of her glove. A flutter awoke in her stomach. They were okay. Of course they were okay. Their feelings for each other were worth more than a disagreement about magic. "Stay close. Let me know if we need to stop for any reason."

The pair directed their horses to the border of the forest realm, and Leyna deeply inhaled the fresh earthy scents and tingle of magic one last time.

We wish you safety on your journey and success in your endeavors. Until we meet again.

Leyna's cheek tugged up one side of her mouth. "Did you hear that, too?"

"Yeah," Eamonn answered, and Leyna wondered if it was a twinge of regret that she heard in his voice. "All right. Let's go."

Hiraeth and Rovis stepped past the lush green and gold and into the stark white snow, the cold air hitting them like a wall. The hum of magic that had ebbed and flowed through Leyna immediately vanished, but the euphoria of magic remained, like a layer of sand blowing off of her as they rode.

Clouds colored the sky a milky grey and the circular haze of a sun hung to their left. The horses climbed the slope back to the top of the short cliff, and a shiver tore through Leyna. She was immediately thankful for the magical speed Imrilieth had granted them for more than just avoiding danger; their shortened travel time in the northernmost parts of Sarieth would mean less time in the cold.

Once atop the cliff, with the dense, leafy treetops of Avaria at their backs, they commanded their horses to run, and they sped away. Snow covered the ground, but not the inches of soft powder that had blanketed the earth when they had arrived. Bare brown patches spotted the open, rocky landscape, and the remaining snow did not impede the animals.

Where they left Avaria was mostly flat and dotted with trees, contrary to the hilly woods to the east where Dorylss had led them from Rifillion. It allowed the horses to pick up speed quickly and maintain it since they didn't have to navigate around trees or go up and down slopes.

The bounce of the horse jarred Leyna, and she adjusted in the saddle, taking a slight stance in the stirrups. After days of relaxing in the warm woods, the bumpy ride that sent knives of icy wind stabbing into Leyna's face was an unwelcome change. She sent another offering of thanks back to Avaria, grateful for the charm that would prevent her from becoming sore during their trip. Galloping all day wouldn't be pleasant, but at least she would be protected from pain.

Any kind of anxiety Leyna might have had about there being awkwardness between her and Eamonn as they rode flew past them at lightning speed. The horses galloped so fast that conversation was impossible. She let Hiraeth's movements flow through her body as the blistering cold enhanced by his speed sent a permanent chill down into her bones.

The Durnholm River appeared in the distance, wide and grey and powerful, funneling down into Sarieth from the Parassinian Sea in the north and providing water for their very own Lake Elaris, which separated Farneth and Teravale. Eamonn guided Rovis next to the riverbank before it sloped down into the rocky valley the water ran through. Leyna followed, keeping her horse abreast with his. That was their road.

Since Imrilieth's advice had been to only stop when necessary, they kept up their pace until the hazy sun had passed the peak of its journey. They paused to rest and eat some of the food they brought from their huts in Avaria, then set off again right away.

Night descended quickly, but the landscape around them hadn't changed much. A few bare trees punctuated the muddy rock along the bank of the river, interspersed with wilted grass under wet snow. They had come across no village or town, no sign of civilization all day, and Leyna began to wonder if they would be sleeping under the stars again. Maybe they could huddle under a clump of trees or find an outcropping of rock they could shelter behind. But Eamonn pushed on ahead, and Leyna matched his pace, trusting in his knowledge of the country to get them somewhere safe for the night.

As dusk settled over the land, the grey sky was painted in pinks and oranges where the sun managed to poke through the clouds. Mountains loomed in the distance to their left, their white-capped peaks taller than any Leyna had ever seen. Eamonn eased Rovis to a stop, pulling Leyna's attention from the mountain range. She slowed her horse and circled back around to Eamonn. Her entire body vibrated with the pounding of Hiraeth's hooves on the hard ground, even though the horse had stopped moving.

"We're almost to the fork in the river," Eamonn told her, pointing ahead toward the mountains. "There's a village right in the crook on this side of the fork. The road runs through it, connecting northern Idyrria and Miren. We'll find an inn there and cross on the ferry to Miren tomorrow." The mountain range held his gaze, and Leyna followed it to study the shadowed ridge again. "Erai is nestled just east of those mountains. My home."

Eamonn's voice betrayed a hint of nostalgia. He had told her he was from Idyrria and had mentioned Erai once or twice, but, truth be told, Leyna knew very little about the city where he grew up. To be so close to such a huge part of Eamonn's past filled her with an unusual mixture of longing and loss, as though Erai belonged as much to her as it did to him. How long had it been since he had spent time there? His and Dorylss's last caravan market had traveled through there, but that had been months ago, and the visit hadn't been pleasant. Leyna faced Eamonn and caught a glimpse of sorrow passing over his features, but he steeled his expression and turned his attention back toward the river.

"We're not far from that village, Tenier. We should be there shortly after dark." With that, he set Rovis at another gallop and Leyna joined him.

As the sun fell to their right and what little light it had cast dissolved into darkness, forms of buildings began to appear and light twinkled out at them from the dark shapes. Leyna sighed, tension releasing from her shoulders. She had trusted Eamonn when he said the village lay ahead of them, but to see it with her eyes, to know for certain that she would not be making a bed on the cold rock, sent relief rushing through her.

On the outskirts of the village, Eamonn and Leyna slowed the horses to a trot and then walked them into town past a few modest homes, with Eamonn leading the way. Leyna wondered how many times he had been to this village, especially with it so close to his home. He led them with confidence through the slushy streets, the little village growing quiet for the night as its residents returned to their homes.

They turned a corner onto a street lined with tall, flat-faced buildings, most of them with shutters drawn, and Eamonn nodded his head toward a building in front of them. A three-story structure with windows ablaze sat in the direction he had gestured, a sign painted with bright blue flowers and green vines hanging out front.

"That's where we're going. The Bluebell and Vine." A sentimental smile stretched across Eamonn's lips. "The mountains are covered in bluebells in the spring."

Leyna couldn't help but smile in return as she followed Eamonn to the inn's stable. The horses were sweaty but surprisingly energetic, like they hadn't just run more than enough miles to kill them.

Once the horses were in the care of the inn's stable hand, Eamonn and Leyna entered the front door of The Bluebell and Vine to a raucous crowd and lively music. The heat inside was stifling, with so many bodies adding to the warmth from the large hearth at one end of the room. A peal of laughter from a group at one table filled the space as the travelers stepped up to the counter to see about rooms.

A short man stood behind the counter, his belt bulging as though he had a habit of indulging in good food and—possibly—good ale as well. He beamed at Eamonn and Leyna and suddenly became taller as they approached. Leyna glanced over the counter and saw a wooden stool under the man's feet.

"Welcome, friends!" He pulled a ledger out from under the counter and slapped it down on its surface. "Glad you've chosen The Bluebell and Vine! Looking for accommodation tonight?"

"Yes, we are," Eamonn replied.

"Excellent, excellent. How long is your stay?"

"Just one night. We're passing through to Miren and plan to leave at daybreak."

"Of course. How many rooms?"

"One," Leyna answered.

At the same time, Eamonn said, "Two."

Their questioning gazes met with a magnetic pull. Leyna's furrowed brow matched Eamonn's. They weren't in Avaria anymore. One room would be safer. But Leyna wasn't sure how much money remained, so she faced the innkeeper again and changed her answer.

"Two."

"One."

Her head whipped back to Eamonn with his altered response as they again spoke in unison.

"Tell you what," the innkeeper began, his eyes flitting between the two of them under confused brows. "I'll cut you a deal. Two rooms for the price of one, with it being so late and you being out at dawn." He retrieved a quill and stooped over his ledger, muttering words under his breath that Leyna didn't miss. "Sounds like you need to talk."

He reached below the counter again and pulled out two keys, extending one each to Leyna and Eamonn. "That's two gold for the night. And I'll need names."

"I am Marielle Renville, and this is Noriden Shay."

The innkeeper copied down the names Leyna gave him and cast them another curious gaze before closing his book. Eamonn laid two gold on the counter and the innkeeper scooped them into his hand. "Well then, enjoy your stay, Marielle and Noriden. Your rooms are twelve and sixteen, on the third level. I am Babkak, if you need anything."

"Thank you, sir," Leyna said with a polite smile, and she turned to Eamonn, who gestured to the crowded dining room.

"Hungry?"

Her smile widened and her shoulders relaxed. "Starving."

Eamonn navigated through the crowd and Leyna kept close behind him, the mingled scents of roasted meat and spilled ale meeting her as she walked. Her stomach rumbled, their last meal long ago. She followed Eamonn to a small open table back in a corner away from most of the crowd, squeezing through the sweaty, ale-soaked bodies to get to it. A server approached their table and they placed an order for food and mead. Leyna grinned at Eamonn remembering that she preferred the sweet honey drink to most other ales.

"Any particular reason you used your sister's and brother's names for us?" Eamonn asked as they waited for their food.

Leyna chuckled. "Well, I didn't think it wise to give our own names."

"I agree. But why theirs?"

With a shrug, Leyna answered, "They were the first that came to mind. They're always on my mind."

Eamonn reached a hand across the table and took Leyna's. "I know," he said, squeezing her hand. "Write to them when we get to Amrieth. Hopefully by then, we'll be in a place where they can write back."

Leyna nodded, a small smile on her lips. The thought had crossed her mind to send her family a letter from The Bluebell and Vine, but like Eamonn pointed out, they couldn't write back to her there. Not to mention, she didn't want to give their location to any possible interceptors until they had secured themselves in Miren.

"So, uh..." Eamonn slid his hand out of Leyna's and interlocked his fingers, his elbows on the table. "One room?"

Leyna hugged the tankard of mead with both hands. "Half the cost."

"I just wanted you to have your own space. I didn't want to assume..." The words dangled in the air.

Leyna sighed, her lips turning slightly up at the corners at his thoughtfulness. "I appreciate that. But Eamonn, this is the real world, not"—she dropped her voice to a whisper and leaned in across the table—"Avaria. There's real danger out here, and I thought... I thought it would be safer."

Eamonn sat back a little, his eyes round and mouth open with understanding. "I'm sorry. I wasn't thinking about it that way." He shook his head.

Leyna's smile widened, conciliatory. "It's all right. Really." She loosened the grip on her mug. "Like you said, we'll be out by morning. I'm sure everything will be fine."

The server arrived with their food, and after thanking her, they fell silent. But with the heavy-laden plate of aromatic food before her, Leyna lost the desire to speak altogether.

They ate their fill of roast chicken, potatoes, and a strange purple vegetable native to Idyrria that Leyna had never seen. Eamonn told her the spices used on the food were typical for Idyrria. The savory flavors were nothing like Leyna had tasted before, and she couldn't get enough.

Some of the inn's patrons retired to their rooms or returned to their homes, but enough remained in the dining room to fill the space with noise. Thankfully, the level in between the gathering and Leyna and Eamonn's rooms helped muffle the roar. He accompanied her to her door, almost standing guard as she turned the key in the lock. She pushed the door open but didn't step inside, instead turning around to face him.

"Good night," she said softly, her eyes betraying her by falling to Eamonn's lips.

He must have noticed the glance. Eamonn leaned toward her, meeting her lips with his own and resting a hand on her waist. Leyna's stomach erupted into the flutter of a hundred wings to feel Eamonn's strong hand holding her and his delicate kiss on her mouth.

"Good night, my love."

Leyna swallowed, not certain her feet still touched the floor.

He stepped backward and left her in the hallway, unlocking the door to his room and entering before Leyna crossed the threshold into her own. She smiled, still feeling the gentle pressure of his lips against hers, and her thoughts lingered on him as she readied herself for bed.

But sleep never came. After lying in bed for what felt like hours, Leyna was certain sleep would evade her as long as she noticed every creak, every snap, every thump. The expectation of an enemy lurking just outside her door kept her mind buzzing.

There was one thing that would help, however.

Leyna slid out of bed and gathered her few belongings, as well as the blanket and pillow from the bed, wrapping the blanket around her shoulders against the cold. Hinges squealed as she eased open her door and padded down the hallway. Her quiet knock on the door to room sixteen resulted in the rustle of movement on the other side, and her heart beat a wild staccato against her ribcage. Maybe she shouldn't be outside his door in the middle of the night, but it was the only way she would get any rest.

Eamonn opened the door seconds later, his hair sticking out at odd angles and his shirt disheveled, hanging awkwardly on his shoulders as though he'd thrown it on in haste.

"What's wrong?" he asked in a near-silent breath, alarm written all over his face.

Leyna swallowed past her parched throat. "I don't want to be alone."

A small smile replaced his surprise, and he opened the door wide to allow her entry. With a soft click, the latch closed behind her. "Here, take the bed." Eamonn rushed to it and smoothed out the blankets, giving the pillow a couple of pats before gesturing toward it. "I can sleep on the floor."

"Oh no, really," Leyna protested, shaking her head. "I can. I brought bedding."

Eamonn's eyebrows raised in sincerity. "I promise, I'll be fine. Here." He took the pillow from her arms and tossed it to the floor, and she let the blanket slide from her shoulders. Eamonn settled onto the thin rug, cocooning himself in the blanket from Leyna's bed. "Go on. I'm perfectly comfortable. Trust me, I've slept on worse."

There was no point in arguing. Leyna climbed into the bed, still warm from Eamonn's body heat, and nestled into the covers. His mere presence in the room with her was already having the desired effect, and her weariness began to take her under.

In the space just before she fell asleep, where dreams and reality mix, she found enough remaining energy to utter, "Thank you."

"Anytime, love."

With a smile on her face, Leyna slipped into slumber.

SIXTEEN

IF NOT FOR THE sun that shone freely and proudly in the sky the next day, providing at least the impression of warmth, Leyna might have expected to freeze to death on their ride.

Somehow, the day was colder than the last: a dry, harsh cold that stung Leyna's bones regardless of her layers. They crossed the river into Miren and found its edges frozen. Winter would arrive soon, and Leyna didn't want to be in the wilderness or on the road any longer than necessary. Cities were always warmer than the countryside, if only for the bustle of everyday life that added heat within their borders. No doubt Amrieth would be cold, but maybe it would be a manageable cold.

At first, Miren resembled the parts of Idyrria they had just left, then transformed as they rode farther into the province. Rocky ground gave way to soft soil and groves of trees, the gentle slopes of the land reminding Leyna of parts of Teravale. But the hills were not as steep as those outside her city of Caen, and the trees stood closer together and taller, giving the impression of being more closed in than she was used to in Teravale.

Now that they were on the road, Leyna and Eamonn came across several towns and villages, as well as one of the larger Mirish cities. Leyna was tempted to stop in Nilvan and rest, but Eamonn preferred not getting comfortable in the feeling of safety that came with the city's size. They would stay in another village inn that night and leave bright and early. The horses were still going strong, just as Imrilieth had promised, so there was no reason to delay. If they limited their breaks, Leyna and Eamonn would make it to Amrieth before dark the next day. No matter how appealing another break might be, what they both truly preferred was to arrive at their destination.

The landscape wasn't the only thing that changed as they delved deeper into Miren. The architecture in the towns evolved from something purely functional to its own unique art form. Structures were crafted, not built; beautiful details in the forms of arches and columns, engravings and carvings, and even more embellished every building. Even the stables had intricate ornamentation. In Miren, the world was their canvas.

"I can't imagine what the kingdom looks like if the towns look like this," Leyna said as they dined at the inn where they would lodge for the night. Colorful paintings hung on the walls and plush, rich carpets covered the floor. Wooden trim where the wall met the ceiling had been carved with shapes of flowers and vines. Even the stair rail leading up to the rooms was shaped to look like the limb of a tree, carved to resemble bark with sprigs extending off of it.

"I've only been through Amrieth on their main road and into their largest shopping quarters, but it's pretty magnificent."

Eamonn leaned his head in closer to Leyna opposite him at the table and lowered his voice. "And the people are well aware."

Leyna copied Eamonn and dropped her volume to a murmur. "It's true what they say? That the Mirish are pretentious?"

"Pretentious, pompous, ostentatious, whatever you want to call it. In my experience..." He hesitated, flashing his eyes around them at the straight-backed people making quiet conversation. "It's true."

Leyna chuckled and glanced around at the crowd, most of them dressed in ornate clothes of expensive fabrics, their noses high in the air. Eamonn and Leyna stuck out like sore thumbs in their dirty riding clothes. "I don't think a single one of them has looked at us."

"They probably won't. We're clearly not Mirish." He dipped his head even closer to Leyna. Anyone could tell he was divulging secrets, even though no one past their table could hear him. "It's hard selling to them when we come here for the market. Unless it's an item that's uniquely from another province, they try to convince us how they do it better here."

Leyna's shoulders slumped. "Sounds like we've got our work cut out for us then. How will we get any of them to ally with Kinrid and Gilleth's army?"

The mention of the Farnish soldiers and the true nature of their mission sucked the joviality out of Eamonn's expression. "Kinrid seemed to think that we could get through to some of them. Maybe he's right. Maybe enough of them will join us even without the king."

Leyna hummed over her hot cider, gripping the warm mug tighter in her chilled hands. She surveyed the room, hoping to get an idea of whether or not there were Mirish people in the inn who weren't as conceited and snobbish as Eamonn had led her to believe. There might have been a few who looked more relaxed than others, but she had no way of truly knowing without trying to recruit them. And if the people respected their king, listened to him and followed his lead, and the king saw no need to pursue action against Rothgard, would they be able to get anyone on their side?

Taking a swig of the beverage that ran hot down her throat, Leyna sent up a wish for something that would give them an edge, enough to get the King of Miren—and the Mirish army—to join them. Their strength against Rothgard would come in numbers, and Miren's army was large and capable. Possibly their ticket to victory. Leyna doubled down and prepared for a fight against King Taularen, because whether they liked it or not, they needed him.

Rovis and Hiraeth slowed automatically as soon as the pearly white walls of the kingdom of Miren came into view. Far in the distance west of the city, hazy snow-capped peaks of tall mountains speared the sky.

Eamonn and Leyna led the horses at a trot around the lake surrounding Amrieth in a half-moon, a natural barrier for the kingdom. The city's creamy walls reflected in the rippling water, and the closer they rode, Leyna began to see details of carvings all throughout the walls.

"The kingdom's walls are a source of contention," Eamonn began, following Leyna's line of sight. "The walls are made of granite, encased by pure alabaster from the Valneria Mountains. When the Mirish excavated all the alabaster for the walls from the mountains, Wolsteadans tried to run them off, claiming they were trespassing. Miren says part of the mountains are included in their territory, but Wolstead argues that the mountains mark the border between the two provinces—on their side."

"Who's right?"

Eamonn shrugged. "I don't think anyone knows for sure. It's a struggle that has lasted since the provinces were first founded, it seems. The people of the two provinces are so opposite, they've been butting heads for as long as anyone can remember."

"Based on what you've told me, I imagine the Mirish would butt heads with just about anyone."

They branched off the roughly paved road onto one made of cobblestones that led them to the city. "You have a fair point," Eamonn said with a smirk, throwing a good-humored glance in Leyna's direction. "But it's especially bad with Wolstead. The border disputes are only part of it." Eamonn paused, the clop of the horses' hooves on the road the only sound. His voice was solemn when he spoke again.

"Wolstead is a stark contrast to Miren. It's mostly laborers, and most of the laborers are miners. The products of the mountains are their greatest export. But even then, it's a large province, and there's not always enough to go around. A lot of the profit supposedly gets funneled back into the province, for the purpose of 'improving' the infrastructure, trade—people's lives. Instead, the money ends up lining the pockets of the chancellors and friends of the king. There were even rumors the king was involved directly." Eamonn's expression hardened, the muscles in his jaw clenching. "That's what people say prompted Rothgard. They say that's why he was successful in deposing the king. The Wolsteadans were tired of their king growing rich off their struggles and turning a blind eye while they worked in terrible conditions."

Leyna's shuddered as a shiver ran through her, but it was only partly prompted by the cold. She had heard most of this before, especially the parts about Rothgard. When the King of Wolstead had fallen, news spread over the rest of the country. And when Rothgard moved on to Farneth, hoping to instill the same distrust of the monarchy and incite rebellion, the remaining provinces went on high alert. He'd been largely unsuccessful outside of Wolstead—until recently—and, as they had learned, that's why he'd sought Avarian magic so desperately. It meant the leaders of the provinces had learned not to be afraid of him.

What truly frightened Leyna, more than the knowledge that Rothgard possessed a bastardized form of Avarian magic and could insist on his dominance over the country, was that he felt justified in what he did. Rothgard believed he helped the common man, the poor, unfortunate man, by removing the current system of power.

She knew someone else who believed Avarian magic was the key to something he felt was justified.

Leyna closed her eyes and shook her head, willing the thought to leave her mind. Things had been going well with Eamonn as they had traveled; she didn't want to get into that again right then.

She broke the heavy silence that had settled over them with another topic she wondered about. "What is the carving on the city's wall?"

"It's a lot of Miren's history," Eamonn explained, his cheerfulness returning as he caught Leyna's curious eye. "Illustrative depictions of their pivotal historical moments. I think it starts with the founding of Sarieth by Amirendel and goes into the formation of Miren as the first province, then hits a lot of key parts of their history."

They were close enough to the wall that Leyna could start to make out some of the carvings, noticing the forms of people, trees, animals, and mountains, and bodies of water. The level of detail was absolutely exquisite, a work of art as well as the city's wall. Her mouth fell open as her wide eyes studied the alabaster surface.

"It's like this all the way around?"

Eamonn chuckled. "Most of the way. I think they add to it periodically." They brought their horses to a stop just outside the gate, the wrought-iron molded into swirling designs, and they waited for the guards to assess them and grant them entry. "If we have the chance, I'll take you around to look at some of it. I've only seen a small portion of it myself."

Leyna responded with a gracious smile as two guards left the gatehouse and approached them. Their gleaming gold armor was intricately engraved and polished to a shine that almost blinded her.

"Good afternoon, travelers." A guard with light blond hair flowing from under his helmet greeted them. "What is the nature of your visit to Amrieth?"

"We're here to join our friends, Dorylss Boon of Teravale, and Kinrid te Oberron and Gilleth te Inglair of Farneth," Eamonn answered, his tone confident and cordial. "Can you tell us if they have arrived?"

"Of the Farnish, I cannot say," the guard replied. "They have not passed through my gate. But Dorylss of Teravale arrived two days ago. He claimed to have business with the king."

"He does. So do we."

The guard angled his head up at Eamonn, eyes narrowed behind his helmet. "The king does not have an abundance of time to allow an audience with inconsequential travelers."

"We'll still seek one."

"Hmm." The guard strode from Rovis to Hiraeth, studying Eamonn and then Leyna. "And what is the business you wish to bring forth?"

Rovis stamped impatiently under Eamonn, as though sensing the tension. The guard's eyes lingered on Leyna, and heat crept up her neck and into her ears under his scrutinizing stare. She watched him in return, hoping she appeared more unfazed than she felt. It took Eamonn speaking again to draw the guard's gaze back to him.

"That's for the king."

The guard gave his companion a curt nod, and the other man stepped back to open the gate. "The king is a busy man and does not squander his time. Do not expect to be granted an audience." The blond guard left the road as the gate opened to allow them entry. "But please, enjoy your time in the kingdom. You may not see a sight such as this again in your lifetimes."

Eamonn dipped his head in thanks, and he and Leyna guided the horses inside the city. Leyna looked over her shoulder as the heavy gates swung closed behind them.

"I'll never see a sight like this again in my lifetime?" She raised an eyebrow and turned to Eamonn, who replied with a laugh. Afraid there was any chance the guards could still hear her, she dropped her voice to a mumble. "They sure are proud."

"And that's just the guards," Eamonn murmured back. He sat straighter on Rovis and raised his voice to a speaking volume. "Come on, I have a feeling I know where Dorylss will be staying.

There's an inn not far from the palace that he and I have visited before."

Eamonn led the way through the wide streets paved with light grey stone in an intricate pattern similar to a basketweave. Beautiful buildings lined the streets amid strips of grass, brown with winter, and earthy beds where gardens were cultivated and flowers might bloom in warmer weather, as though the Mirish sought to keep nature within the city. Entire squares of the city were devoted to treed areas where paths wound through grass and shrubbery. Bubbling fountains sprayed endless streams of water into their pools, surprisingly not frozen considering the temperature outside.

The light stone buildings were designed and carved like those in the other villages Leyna and Eamonn came across in Miren. Ornate pointed arches were featured, often enclosing sparkling glass windows, and wooden accents added warmth to the cold stone. Any open surface was carved with an image, a shape, or a scene, and tall spires prodded the sky. Grand sets of stairs led up to the heavy wooden doors of some buildings, while others were covered with arched porticos or enclosed by columned verandas.

The city rode the waves of gentle slopes, the main street curving through the city like a river. Smaller streets branched off and flowed into other areas, but Eamonn and Leyna kept to the main road that wound through the kingdom like a maze. Something prickled Leyna's senses, raising the hairs on her arms under her many layers, and she was suddenly overwhelmed with the feeling of being watched.

"Where's the palace? Do we have to go far?" Leyna asked after they had ridden in silence for several minutes.

"The palace is situated on the opposite side of the kingdom from where we entered," Eamonn answered, maneuvering Rovis through the slow-moving Mirish who glanced their way and didn't hide their scowls. "It overlooks the lake at its southernmost point. So yes, we have a long way to go."

The closer they got to the palace, the more people filled the streets around them. Leyna glanced through the people they rode among and noticed that not all of them appeared to be Mirish. Based on physical features alone, she guessed that some Farnish and Idyrrians strode through the city. Their more amiable appearances contrasted the stern Mirish and confirmed to Leyna that they were not native to the province.

Outside a stable whose wide wooden doors were set in a stone face under a broad porch, Eamonn hopped off of Rovis and walked him inside. Leyna came behind him with Hiraeth, gaping at the artistic wood and iron stall doors separated by thick columns as the horses' hooves clopped on the pavers that continued into the building. Circular chandeliers laden with candles hung above them, lighting the interior to show catwalks connecting the open walkways of a second floor. Leyna couldn't imagine the purpose of a second floor in a stable; the horses didn't go up there.

They left the horses with the stable hand, ensuring they were well taken care of, and returned to the main street. Golden light filled the city, indicating the imminent setting of the sun and the beginning of the end of another day.

"The inn isn't far from here," Eamonn said, taking Leyna's hand in his own. Her heart jumped as his fingers interlaced through hers. "We'll pass through this green space and be there in no time."

The green space in question was alive with people and activity. Lanterns hung from tree branches, and banners of bright colors painted the sky around them. People played games—proving the Mirish could indeed smile and laugh—and the song of instruments floated on the air from somewhere in the distance. Vendors under tents sold various wares, and outdoor tables surrounded the cookfires of those selling food. Wine had been passed around in abundance; very few of the jovial revelers lacked a glass in their hand, their cheeks flushed with drink.

Leyna strolled through the park hand-in-hand with Eamonn, marveling at the gaiety and lightheartedness of the Mirish. "What is this?" she asked Eamonn after taking in the scene. Then the hairs on the back of her neck stood, and she resisted the urge to look over her shoulder.

"Let's see." He stopped to think, studying the celebration. "It may be the Festival of Niira."

Leyna's eyebrows drew together as she frowned. "Niira, the Auroturan goddess of health? I didn't know anyone in Sarieth practiced any of the old Amirendelian religions."

"The old religions stuck in Miren more than anywhere else. A lot of the Mirish are Auroturans."

"A lot, but not all."

A voice from behind them sent them both spinning around, breaking the clasp of their hands. At first, no one stuck out to Leyna as the source of the voice, the people surrounding them otherwise occupied and paying them no attention.

"Some Mirish are Litrellan," the voice came again. A young woman stepped out from the crowd, a hood pulled over her eyes and a grey cloak draped around her down to her ankles. "And some aren't religious at all."

The woman stood stock still in the middle of the pathway and crossed her arms, her eyes glittering under her hood with the light from the lanterns. A half smile pulled up one cheek just as a fresh wave of goosebumps arose on Leyna's skin.

"Have you been following us?"

The woman shrugged. "Maybe. Doesn't make a difference, though, does it? I'm standing here in front of you."

Eamonn found Leyna's hand again and he tucked her in close to him. "Following us, why?"

As the woman took a couple of steps toward them, light glinted off a dagger strapped around her trousers at her thigh. Leyna squeezed Eamonn's hand, already fearing the worst. Was she one of Rothgard's?

Before she could answer, Eamonn spoke again, his voice low in the merry din of the festival. "Do all Mirish casually wear daggers so openly?"

"Only when they're a gift." The woman pulled the dagger out of its sheath and rested it in her open hands, displaying it to Leyna and Eamonn.

In the few feet of distance that separated them from the young woman, Leyna could see the engraved double-edged blade flash against an intricately designed curved handle with a white gemstone set in its pommel. Like most things of Miren, the dagger was a piece of art as much as a tool.

"My father gave it to me for my twentieth birthday," the woman said, as though she spoke to friends. "So it's still relatively new. I haven't used it for anything other than cutting cord yet."

Leyna clenched her teeth and took a sidelong glance at Eamonn. She wasn't sure she wanted to know how else the woman might hope to use the dagger.

"I don't believe you answered my first question," Eamonn said, an edge to his voice. His expression was neutral—almost pleasant—as though trying to keep a mask on for the partygoers, but Leyna noticed his eyes flitting around them, looking for accomplices and determining the threat level.

"You're interesting. I noticed you shortly after you entered the city." The woman sheathed her dagger and strode in a slow half circle around them. "You're dressed in Idyrrian garb, but you're from Teravale." She dipped her head in Leyna's direction before focusing on Eamonn. "And you could pass as Mirish, but you're not from here. You're actually Idyrrian."

Leyna blinked a few times, studying the woman as she came to a stop only feet away. "How can you tell?"

The same half-smile reappeared on the woman's face and she dropped the hood of her cloak to her shoulders. Voluminous light brown hair in tight curls framed her face, complementing her light brown skin and amber eyes. She took a couple more steps toward them, towering over Leyna and coming almost eye-to-eye with Eamonn.

"The red in your hair, for one thing," she answered, nothing unkind or impertinent in the way she spoke. She instead seemed intrigued—amused, even. Responding as though she'd studied them for her own enjoyment and took delight in her analysis. "And your lilt. And you," she continued, turning to Eamonn. "Looks alone, I would have guessed you were Mirish. But you don't carry yourself the same way, and then there's your accent. So, what? Your family moved from Miren over to Idyrria when you were young? Before you were born?"

"Something like that." Eamonn's grip on Leyna's hand didn't loosen. Of course, his family situation was nothing like that, but this strange woman didn't need to know the truth. "My mother was Mirish, but my father is Idyrrian."

A broad smile erupted on the woman's face, displaying her straight white teeth. She crossed her arms and drummed her fingers on her bicep. "We have something in common then:

coming from two different backgrounds. My father is Mirish and my mother is Farnish."

Leyna flicked her eyes from Eamonn to the woman, trying to get a read on what Eamonn was thinking. The chance that this woman was one of Rothgard's was becoming less likely. Trailing them only to reveal herself in the middle of a crowded festival wasn't the best strategy. And the way she spoke with them truly didn't seem to be hostile or false.

Movement in Leyna's hair had her flinging her head to look behind her, and her skin prickled with alarm. A tall Mirish man with golden waves of hair that hung to his shoulders had wound his fingers in the tips of her curls, half of his mouth upturned in a remorseless grin. Leyna grabbed her hair and yanked it out of the man's grasp, but he didn't seem shocked or dissuaded.

"Such a pretty thing," he said, a slight slur to his words that instantly betrayed how much he had imbibed at the festival.

"Get away from me!" Leyna exclaimed, stepping back as the man filled her space.

Eamonn whipped around to face the man and pulled Leyna from his reach. "Leave her alone."

The man might as well not have heard Eamonn. He didn't so much as glance Eamonn's way, his blue-green eyes locked on Leyna. Even though Eamonn stood between her and the man, a rising panic flooded Leyna's veins. He watched her like wolf staring at his prey.

"And where might you be from?" he continued, ignoring Eamonn. "Not from around here, that's apparent. I didn't know such beauty could exist beyond our borders."

"I said," Eamonn hissed through gritted teeth, stepping completely in front of Leyna, "leave her alone. She's spoken for."

"Like that matters." The man sneered, forced to come face to face with Eamonn. He took a shaky step toward them. "The only woman truly spoken for in Miren is the Queen, and even then—"

The mysterious woman appeared like an apparition next to Eamonn, her beautiful dagger unsheathed again and pointing at the man's belt. "If you don't want to have an unfortunate accident that ensures filth like you will never reproduce, I suggest you turn around and leave. Now." Her warning was a low hum, smooth and deadly.

The knot at the man's throat bobbed up and down as he cast his gaze to the dagger. He stumbled backward and made eye contact with the woman as he began to turn away but paused before his back faced them. Holding her stare, the man squinted at her curiously for a moment before his eyes widened, and he tripped over his feet in his haste to get away.

The woman replaced the dagger in its sheath again and gestured with an outstretched arm to a less crowded spot by a tree. Leyna didn't know what the man had seen to change his demeanor, but she wasn't exactly thinking straight. Adrenaline caught up with her and she trembled as she followed Eamonn's steps to the place the woman indicated. He must have noticed, for when they arrived under the low-hanging branches of the old tree, Eamonn squeezed her hand before releasing it and rubbing soothing circles on Leyna's back.

"Sorry about that," the woman said. She stopped close to them and crossed her arms. "The festivals usually bring out the worst in people."

"You don't need to apologize." Eamonn ran his hand over Leyna's back one last time and dropped it to take her hand again. "But thank you."

The woman dipped her head in acknowledgment as Leyna spoke, finding her voice for the first time since the Mirish man had appeared. "Why did you step in like that? Who are you?"

"The name's Ree." She extended a gloved hand toward them. Leyna stared at Ree, knitting her brows together, but Eamonn took her hand tentatively and shook it. Leyna had heard of the traditional Mirish greeting, but she'd never seen one, so it hadn't crossed her mind as to what Ree was trying to do. "And I stepped in because it was the right thing to do."

"Nice meeting you, Ree." The edge in Eamonn's voice was gone now, and Leyna wondered if Ree noticed. "I'm Noriden, and this is Marielle."

Ree laughed and shook her head. "No, you're not. You're Eamonn and Leyna, right?"

Leyna fought to give no indication of the surprise that crashed over her. She swallowed, keeping her mouth shut, not wanting to answer lest any shake of her voice betray her. Eamonn looked as though he might speak, but no sound came out.

"Relax, you don't have to hide your identity from me. Not that I know why you'd want to." She spoke in all seriousness, but her eyes sparkled with the last sentence, giving Leyna the impression that she wasn't telling them something. "You mentioned meeting up with a man named Dorylss when you came into the city. I've seen Dorylss around. The merchant with the red hair." Ree smiled again. "I've heard him speaking with some of the others with him, the Farnish soldiers. They've mentioned your names and that they're expecting you."

Eamonn dropped Leyna's hand and crossed his arms in a mirror to Ree, his brow furrowed in question. "How in the stars do you know all this?"

Ree shrugged, a coy grin spreading across her lips. "I'm incredibly observant. It's kind of my job."

"And just what *is* your job?" Leyna stretched her fingers, the cold air hitting her palm in the absence of Eamonn's hand. She curled her hands into fists and stuffed them into the folds of her cloak.

"You could say I'm Kingdom Security."

"'You could say?'" Eamonn repeated, one eyebrow raised. "You're not a guard."

Ree pulled the corners of her lips down into an expression like a thoughtful frown. "Maybe not. Doesn't mean I'm not security. Don't you feel secure after the encounter you just had?"

Eamonn shook his head with his eyes closed, as though ridding himself of any further arguments. "Fine. You are. But what made you follow us, really? Was it the mention of Dorylss back near the gate?"

"I like you, Eamonn." Ree tugged on a curl, straightening it out, and it bounced back into a perfect spiral the second she let go. "You use critical thinking. Yes, that's why I followed you."

The music stopped and applause thundered throughout the festival. Leyna had lost awareness of it, so engrossed in their interaction with Ree. The last light of the sun hung to the west, casting the green space in long shadows.

"The festival ends at sundown. Most other festivals go well into the night, but not this one." Ree chuckled to herself, raising a shoulder and then letting it fall. "Something about Niira being the goddess of health, and good sleep promotes good health." She tilted her head back toward the path. "I can accompany you to the inn, if you like. Being security, and all that. Dorylss is at Yenalt Guest House; it's not far."

Eamonn turned to Leyna in question, and she responded by raising her shoulders and pulling the right corner of her mouth into her cheek. *Might as well.*

"All right. Let's go." Eamonn's hand found Leyna's again as they continued down the path in their intended direction, walking three abreast with Ree on Eamonn's other side. "How much do you know of Dorylss's activities here?"

Ree paused for a beat, taking in a slow breath through her nose, as though considering her answer before she gave it. "I know he attempted to seek an audience with the king. His Farnish friends only arrived yesterday, actually, accompanying King Vinnerod and his grand advisor to the palace. I hear King Javorak of Teravale is expected to arrive shortly."

They broke out of the green space and left the noise behind them. Eamonn lowered his voice in the quiet street when he spoke again. "Do you know what they're doing here?"

Ree rolled her eyes up and tilted her head down, looking at Eamonn from underneath her brow. "You're fishing. Why don't you cut to the chase?"

"Do you have much to do with the palace?" Leyna asked, understanding Eamonn's hesitation but trying a different approach.

"I work closely with the palace."

"So you know they are seeking an alliance with your king against Rothgard, who has taken over rule of Idyrria."

"You may think critically, Eamonn," Ree said, grinning at Leyna, "but she gets to the point. You two make quite a pair."

Something about Ree's tone sent heat into Leyna's cheeks. It was nothing to feel embarrassed about, especially considering she and Eamonn were, in fact, a couple. But Ree seemed too in tune with both of them for knowing them less than fifteen minutes.

"What are the chances of King Taularen agreeing on an alliance?" Eamonn asked, avoiding Ree's observation entirely.

"Honestly," Ree replied with raised brows, "not good."

Eamonn ran his free hand through his hair. "Got any tips on what might win him over?"

Ree tucked in her chin, eyes still wide. "For you two? You think *you* can convince the King of Miren to use his military on something he doesn't perceive as a threat?"

The way Ree emphasized the word "you" sent Leyna's heart plummeting to her gut. It put the likelihood of getting Miren on their side in no uncertain terms, laid out in black and white. No grey. The world suddenly seemed so large, and Leyna was only a blade of grass, a drop of water. What could she do?

"Not just us. We're here to assist Dorylss and the Farnish soldiers," Eamonn retorted, his voice just as firm and unwavering as Ree's. If he felt the same as Leyna, he didn't show it. "Hopefully, with enough of us showing the king the enormity of the threat Rothgard poses, he'll come around."

"Hmm." Ree pressed her lips into a tight line. "Few in Miren take Rothgard's rule in Idyrria seriously. Most of us—the king included—believe it will fizzle out in time, and that Idyrria's army is enough to handle it." She eyed Eamonn. "But you don't."

"Not even a little bit. King Taularen needs to understand..." Eamonn shook his head and let the end of his sentence hang. They came to a stop in front of the inn, and Eamonn faced Ree outside the mahogany front door inlaid with etched glass. "I imagine we'll be seeing you around, given your apparent presence in the palace."

"And the city in general. Security is everywhere." Ree gave them another toothy grin. "Yeah, I'll be around. I'm glad I met you, Eamonn and Leyna." She pulled the hood back over her shock of curls and slipped away into the darkening streets.

Neither Leyna nor Eamonn made a move to enter the guest house, watching as Ree's shadowy shape disappeared from view. The whole interaction left Leyna with new questions she hadn't expected and less confidence than before on persuading Taularen.

"Do you think we can trust her?" she asked, looking up at Eamonn.

He met her gaze and inhaled a slow, thoughtful breath. "I think so. She may be helpful, too. Sounds like she knows a lot about what goes on in the city." Eamonn threaded an arm behind Leyna's waist, and a smile broke his clouded features. He pulled her close before guiding her to the inn's veranda. "Come on, let's find Dorylss. I'm sure he'll be happy to see us."

Leyna offered Eamonn a small smile in response and let him lead her to the front door, but not before she glanced over her shoulder one more time to see if Ree was really gone.

SEVENTEEN

THE FRONT DOOR OF the guest house opened into a vestibule with warm wooden trim and peaceful paintings of landscapes on the walls. A lantern hung from the ceiling, casting the space in a flickering light. A thick, multicolored rug spanning almost the full length of the room muffled Leyna and Eamonn's footsteps. At the opposite end of the vestibule was a mahogany desk with doorways to either side, leading to other parts of the inn, and a wide, open staircase behind it. A man with long brown hair stood at the desk, a pleasant, closed-lip smile etched on his face.

"Welcome to Yenalt Guest House," he greeted, his expression less than genuine but not rude. "How may I assist you this evening?"

"We're in need of two rooms," Eamonn requested, "and we're looking for our friend Dorylss. Is he staying here?"

"He is," the attendant answered, opening a drawer in the desk and retrieving two ornate, golden keys. "I believe he is in the dining room at the moment, to your left. May I have your names, please?"

"Eamonn and Leyna."

"Ah, yes, Dorylss is expecting you. He asked me to send you his way when you arrived." The man pushed the keys across the desk toward them. "I have two rooms near his, fourteen and fifteen. Four gold each a night. Will your stay be as long as his?"

Eamonn started to reach for the keys but stopped at the attendant's question. "Just how long is that?"

"Three weeks, or now, two and a half. That's what he paid for, at least."

"I might not have that much with me." Eamonn reached for the pouch at his belt, and Leyna could tell from the look in his eyes that his mind was whirring, trying to figure out how to cover the bill for that long. It surprised Leyna that Dorylss paid for three full weeks in advance. He expected them to be in Amrieth for longer than she had anticipated.

Of course, they could save quite a bit on lodging if she and Eamonn shared a room.

"Eamonn! Leyna! You made it!" A booming voice came from their left, and they both turned to find the behemoth of a man they loved so dearly hurrying down the hallway toward them. "Whatever their fee, Grimmel, I'll cover it. Add it to my bill."

Eamonn let the pouch fall as Dorylss wrapped him in a tight hug. "I wasn't expecting you for another two weeks, at least!" the man bellowed, beaming at them together before taking a turn to embrace Leyna. "Did everything in...the forest go well?" he questioned, dropping his voice for the second half of the sentence as he let the word "Avaria" fall from his lips.

"Let's get something to eat. We're famished." Eamonn gestured to the dining room behind Dorylss, and his eyes flicked to Grimmel at the desk before finding Leyna. He must have been hoping to take the conversation somewhere more private. Eamonn retrieved the keys from the top of the desk and handed one to Leyna. "Thank you for your assistance, Grimmel."

"Of course. Please enjoy your stay."

The three of them left the vestibule, Dorylss leading the way through the serene, half-full dining room. The cream-colored walls were surrounded by more of the wooden trim from the vestibule, and chandeliers full of candles hung overhead, their light mixing with the glow from lanterns interspersed on the walls. A quartet played in one corner of the room, filling the space with a sweet, soothing tune. Orderly tables were spaced around the room: some with two chairs, some with four.

Leyna spotted Kinrid and Gilleth sitting at a table of four chairs, and she couldn't resist the smile that naturally came to her lips. Seeing them there, with Dorylss, ready to take on the Mirish king, sent Leyna's hope soaring. They would have a good case. Surely he would listen.

Dorylss dragged a smaller table to add to the length of the table where Kinrid and Gilleth were seated, drawing stares from the Mirish throughout the room as the legs scraped along the wooden floor. Not seeming to notice, Dorylss pulled the two chairs over as well, then motioned to them.

"Sit, sit! Tell us about it! Why are you here so soon?"

Leyna and Eamonn lowered themselves into the chairs Dorylss had acquired and greeted Kinrid and Gilleth, who gave soft smiles and slow nods in return. Eamonn explained how they had left Avaria sooner than planned and how Imrilieth gifted the horses with magical speed and endurance to carry them quickly to Amrieth.

"Did you learn what you hoped to from the Kaethiri?" Dorylss asked, his eyes glittering as he spoke quietly. "Was your time in Avaria beneficial?"

Leyna turned her attention to Eamonn sitting beside Dorylss across the table, and she held his gaze until he dropped it. Eamonn was going to have to explain why they left Avaria earlier than expected and how he argued with the Kaethiri. She could tell them, of course, but it would sound accusatory. Eamonn had made his decisions; now, he had to accept Dorylss's reaction.

"It was beneficial." Instead of lifting his eyes from the smooth tabletop to his mentor, Eamonn looked at Leyna. "The Kaethiri actually instructed both of us in magic. It turns out Leyna has a predisposition for it."

A wide smile broke through Dorylss's features as he looked from Eamonn to Leyna. "You don't say! Well, that's marvelous! Were you able to learn much?"

"Yes," Leyna answered, keeping her tone neutral, "but not as much as I might have."

Dorylss knitted his eyebrows together. "Did something happen?"

Leyna didn't answer. Her eyes never left Eamonn, which drew Dorylss's attention to him as well.

"Lad?"

Eamonn sighed. "Things were going well. I was learning useful magic; Leyna was learning how to manipulate the environment. We would have stayed longer and practiced magic further with the Kaethiri, but they weren't going to teach me the magic to control Rothgard, so I suggested that we leave. They wouldn't teach me how to do it since they don't control the wills of humans anymore. So, unless I manage to figure it out myself again and use it properly, we don't have what we need to defeat Rothgard."

Dorylss frowned as he inhaled. "I imagine if they refused to teach you, there was a reason. It's crossing a line, even for someone like Rothgard. But you were able to learn other magic, yes? And Leyna, too?"

Leyna nodded as Eamonn answered for her, not hiding the frustration in his tone. "Yes, I learned a few things, but they won't be as helpful as taking over Rothgard's will would be."

"We have a good bit of magic at our disposal, Eamonn," Leyna said, trying a bit too hard to sound optimistic. "If Taran and Teiyn are able to join us, between the four of us, we'll have a lot to work with. Rothgard may have stronger magic than Taran, Teiyn, and me, but he is still just one against four."

"Maybe," Eamonn conceded, "but it all goes back to the issue of the Kaethiri not caring, not being willing to intervene. This could all be over in a blink of an eye if they got involved. *I'm* actually trying to do something about it. They shouldn't force me to ride their same moral high horse."

"Yes, but they—" Leyna pressed her lips together and sucked in a breath through her nose before continuing. She *really* didn't want this to turn into an argument, but she believed Dorylss had a right to know all sides. With a softer, more controlled voice, she said, "The Kaethiri said that Eamonn using magic to control others will tarnish his soul. It could slowly corrupt him."

Dorylss stiffened and angled his head at Eamonn. "They told you this?"

Eamonn nodded, barely making eye contact with Dorylss before dropping his gaze to the table.

"And you still think it's a good idea?"

His head still lowered, Eamonn replied, "It's a good idea because I will only need to use it one time." He slowly raised his head and met Dorylss's eyes. "It can't corrupt me that much once, and it's worth it to bring down Rothgard for good."

Leyna swallowed down her argument. There was no reason to get into it here and now. Besides, she was too tired to rehash what he had just gone through with the Kaethiri.

The wrinkles in Dorylss's forehead eased, presumably noticing the growing tension and hoping to dispel it. "Be that as it may, Leyna does have a point, lad. You may not have the need to control his will at all. You're more skilled with magic, now. Leyna has learned magic, which none of us knew was possible. Those are both great things."

At least Dorylss seemed to be on Leyna's side. Not that Leyna even wanted there to be sides, but she felt better about her stance to know Dorylss agreed with her.

Eamonn leaned back in his chair and crossed his arms. "Yes, they are. But if the Kaethiri helped me with the same kind of magic that Rothgard is *actively using*, we wouldn't even have to be here right now. We could go to Rifillion and take him down. There would be no need to try to convince the King of Miren to join in an alliance."

"Regardless, this is why we're here. It's what we planned for." Kinrid's deep voice resonated through Leyna, the strength in it enough to stop their argument. "We move forward with our original plan. King Vinnerod perceives Rothgard as a threat and came here with us to discuss an alliance. King Javorak is en route. Wolstead has had no king since Rothgard started the rebellion that led to the upheaval of the monarchy there, and several people who believe in Rothgard's cause represent the citizens.

Idyrria, of course, is under Rothgard's control, so once Javo-rak arrives, we can begin deliberations."

The mention of Teravale's king sent a spark of excitement through Leyna. She had never met the king before, though she had seen him ride through Caen once or twice when she was little. He mostly remained in Barenwitte, Teravale's kingdom, but he had always been a good, kind ruler to the people. He was getting older, preparing his eldest son to take the throne, and Leyna couldn't deny how thrilled she was to meet the king before that happened.

"Let's order some food so you two can go and rest," Gilleth suggested. "You'll need it, assuming the king grants an audi-ence with us." Her dark eyes glinted in the torchlight as she rolled them. "Prepare for battle."

"That's enough, Gilleth," Kinrid said, though he wasn't harsh. "No need to poison them against Taularen before they've even met him." Kinrid sucked in a breath and mur-mured, "He'll do that on his own."

Leyna kept mostly out of the conversation at the table as they ate their food, the exhaustion from the last few days finally catching up to her. Imrilieth's magic must have com-pletely worn off. Her back ached and her head pounded, and even though the food and drink helped, all she really wanted was to go to bed. She pushed her chair back from the table before the others had finished to excuse herself.

"I'm going on to my room," she announced, and Eamonn stood as well. "I'd like to be alone, if that's all right."

A pang of hurt washed over Eamonn's face, and Leyna averted her eyes. She didn't mean it personally—she *did* just want to be alone for the rest of the night. She was tired. So tired, she didn't even want to take the time to explain it. Eamonn would have to accept her saying goodnight a little early.

"Get some rest then." Eamonn took her hand and brought it to his lips.

In her peripheral vision, Leyna saw Dorylss's eyes widen, but she only bid Eamonn a good night before making her way to her room. She would let Eamonn be the one to fill Dorylss in about everything else that happened in Avaria.

EIGHTEEN

"Something you failed to tell me, lad?"

Eamonn stopped his glass in the air on its way down from his lips, then set it on the table with a *clink*. He held the wine in his mouth for a moment before swallowing it, and his throat bobbed dramatically.

Kinrid and Gilleth had excused themselves after further conversation, and Dorylss didn't even wait long enough for them to leave the dining room before he prodded Eamonn for information. Not that Eamonn had any issue with telling Dorylss. The man was his closest friend, essentially his father. He had planned to reveal everything about him and Leyna—well, maybe not in significant detail—but he hadn't expected Dorylss to wait only until the first possible second they were alone.

Although, Eamonn probably should have expected as much. Dorylss was mostly aware of how Eamonn felt for Leyna, and he loved Leyna dearly, as his late best friend's daughter. Without

Dorylss even saying so, Eamonn knew he liked the idea of them together.

"Turns out Leyna was only distant because she wanted to help me through everything I endured, but she was afraid bringing it up would drag me through it again. And once we got that out of the way—" Eamonn cocked his head to the side, a smile teasing on his lips. "Apparently, we've both felt the same way about each other, but she didn't know how to bring it up, and I was afraid I was coming on too strong. We're, um... we're together, now."

Dorylss's face lit up. "I'm glad to hear it. I think you two are a good match. To be perfectly honest, I imagined it would happen sooner or later, but I like that it is sooner. Although," he began, his joyful expression falling, "you two seemed a little short with each other tonight."

"We're just weary from so much travel," Eamonn said with a shrug. "Covering that much ground in three days took a lot out of us, even if the horses fared well with the enchantment. We did have a disagreement in Avaria. Leyna wasn't ready to leave."

Eamonn didn't want to get into the whole truth with Dorylss. There was no need to take time going over the specifics of how he and Leyna had argued—or how he and the Kaethiri had argued. It was better to look forward to what lay ahead instead of dwelling on the past.

"Well, I hope a few days of rest will help turn things around," Dorylss said, standing from the table. "You'll likely have some time before Javorak arrives from Teravale. I'm sure they are traveling as quickly as they are able, but it's a long way here from Barenwitte. Come." Dorylss clapped Eamonn on the shoulder and grinned at him. "Tomorrow is a new day. We have much to do, and I'm glad you're here, Eamonn."

Eamonn returned Dorylss's smile and walked with him through the dining room to the set of stairs at the back of the room. "Dorylss," Eamon said slowly as they climbed to the second floor, a new question coming to his mind. "Have you met someone named Ree? A young woman who is part of the kingdom's security?"

Dorylss furrowed his brow in thought. "Can't say that I have. Why do you ask?"

"She trailed Leyna and me from the city gates when we arrived, then spoke to us as we passed through the green where the Festival of Niira was taking place. She knew who we were because we mentioned you. Said she'd seen you around."

"Hmm." Dorylss ran a hand over his bushy beard. "What does she look like?"

"Tall, with light brown skin and hair. Curly hair."

Dorylss stopped in the middle of the second-floor hallway, two rows of doors surrounding them on either side. "And what did you say her name was?"

"Ree."

"Ree," Dorylss repeated. Something Eamonn couldn't identify passed over Dorylss's expression for only a moment, as though the name sparked some kind of recognition, but it didn't last. "I don't know anyone by that name. I'll see if Kinrid or Gilleth have had any interaction with her."

"She seems like she might be helpful," Eamonn continued, arriving outside the door to his room. "She's close with the palace and already knows what we're doing here. She might be someone good to have on our side."

"Maybe so. If you come across her again, let me know."

Eamonn nodded and turned the key in the lock. "Good night, Dorylss."

"Good night, lad. It's good to have you here, safe and sound."

Eamonn smiled again and entered his room, unlacing his boots and kicking them off as soon as he shut the door.

He had stayed at the Yenalt Guest House before, when passing through Amrieth with the caravan market. The room was not dissimilar from the one where he'd lodged in the past, and if it had been his first time in the kingdom, he might be taken by its extravagance. A thick red, cream, and gold patterned rug cushioned the polished wooden floor. Layers of thick, warm blankets covered the wide, four-poster bed topped with several squishy pillows. A comfortable-looking chair, upholstered in red velvet, sat in a corner with an ottoman in front of it, complete with an intricately crafted side table and bookcase with a small selection of texts. In one wall, a fireplace was set, already brightly burning to provide warmth for the room, and heavy red curtains bordered a window. A wardrobe with floral designs carved on the doors was present for guests to hang their clothes, and paintings of landscapes similar to the ones that greeted them in the inn's vestibule added color to the walls. The room even included its own bathing room, separate from the sleeping quarters and private for the individual.

Eamonn stripped down to his underclothes, casting his dirty garments on the chair, and slipped in between the silky bed sheets. He groaned as his back stretched, molding to the comfort of the mattress. Amrieth's lodging may be more expensive than he was used to, but it was for good reason. And worth it.

He closed his eyes and already felt sleep taking him under, but a thought stayed with him for a moment longer. Leyna's room was next to his. A single wall separated them. She was likely already asleep. Eamonn waited with half a hope for a knock on the door that would never come. Not here, in Amrieth, where they had a greater sense of protection.

So, he would soak up every moment of the time he could with her. Since they had a day or two before they met as a council, he would take Leyna around Amrieth—show her what he knew of the city and see more for himself as well. Hopefully, she would start to see past their disagreements and embrace a new kind of magic with Eamonn.

Fear.

Cold, brutal, stabbing fear.

And pain.

Relentless pain. Agony.

A whip.

A crank.

A needle.

Eamonn bolted upright, his heart ready to hammer straight through his ribcage. Sweat dripped from his hairline and the back of his neck. Cold air hit his bare chest, and he shivered. He had to get out. He had to run.

Warm embers glowed in the fireplace. A sliver of white moonlight snuck into the room past the curtains. Peaceful pictures decorated the walls.

Eamonn finally got his bearings, and the fear began to fade. He was no longer in Rothgard's clutches. His panic had come from another nightmare.

He settled back down into the soft pillows, despite the lingering anxiety, and tucked the blanket around his shaking body. It was the first nightmare he'd had in days. Not a single flash of one had bothered him during his time in Avaria, as if the forest had prohibited them. He'd thought maybe they were gone, or maybe something about Avaria had purged them from his being.

But it hadn't, and all that came to mind as he tried to relax was how badly he longed for Leyna's presence beside him.

After they took their time eating breakfast, allowing the sun to warm the city, Leyna and Eamonn set off on a stroll around Amrieth. Leyna had invited Dorylss, but he graciously declined, and Eamonn knew it was to allow him and Leyna to spend some time by themselves. He had thanked the man with his eyes from behind Leyna, where she couldn't see the unspoken words he and Dorylss shared.

The clothes they had worn in Idyrria didn't seem right for Amrieth, and they had left their magical summery clothes in Avaria, so Eamonn offered to get Leyna a few Mirish pieces. She beamed and kissed his cheek before they walked hand-in-hand to the nearest clothier.

Leyna chose two dresses, one grey and one blue, both long and full and made of a warm wool for winter, with higher necklines than the light summer dresses she'd worn in Avaria. The grey one was trimmed in cream and featured thin gold designs, and the blue dress matched her eyes, embroidered with darker flowers above the hem and dissipating as the flowers climbed the skirt.

Eamonn carried her package for her as they left the shop and headed for a café down the street for a midday meal. The road was bustling with horses and carriages and wagons, and people filled the walks on either side. The kingdoms were the busiest cities as the homes of the monarchs in each province, where the palaces were situated. Amrieth was Miren's seat of power, where rule for the entire province was centralized. Citizens of Amrieth and travelers alike—from other parts of Miren and beyond—filled the streets, on their way to do business or meet others or simply explore what the kingdom had to offer.

They made their way through throngs of people, keeping pace with the steady flow of the city. Eamonn's gaze wandered as they walked. His mind drifted to Kinrid and Gilleth's force, and he wondered how many had accompanied them to Miren when he caught sight of a familiar profile in the distance.

Eamonn blinked a few times, wondering if the blinding mid-day sun was playing tricks on his eyes. The face came better into view, and the recognition hit him like a ton of bricks. He knew that hard jawline, the tan complexion, the dark hair that fell in waves to his chin.

No.

Eamonn's stomach nearly bottomed out. His insides con-stricted into a ball that weighed heavily in his gut as white-hot knives of fear sliced into his heart. He stopped in his tracks, and Leyna jerked back with the pull from their joined hands.

"What is it?"

The stream of people parted around them, continuing on their way and paying Eamonn and Leyna no attention. Eamonn searched through the sea of heads again to find the one that had stuck out to him, but to no avail.

"Eamonn?"

Without answering Leyna, Eamonn moved again, desper-ate to spot that all-too-familiar face again and make sure he hadn't imagined it. He tugged Leyna along, diving and weaving through the crowd in the direction where he'd seen him, but he found nothing. A couple of Idyrrian men roamed the streets, but they didn't match the face Eamonn had seen. His pulse slowed, and he took a deep breath, hoping to ease the tremble that had erupted within him. Eamonn must have seen one of those men in the too-bright sun and his brain had to fill in the gaps. It was the only explanation.

Because he didn't dare believe the other.

That Hadli was in Amrieth.

"Eamonn!"

Leyna had been jogging right alongside Eamonn as he'd feverishly scurried through the crowds down the street. He stopped again and turned to her, finding her eyes wide and her cheeks flushed.

"What in the stars?"

With one more glance at the faces again, Eamonn answered, "I thought I saw Hadli." He swallowed past the rising bile in his throat. "I couldn't really tell, so I tried to catch another glimpse, but I didn't see him again. It must have been someone who bore a passing resemblance. He was far away, and I was squinting in the sun."

Leyna's chest fell as all the breath left her lungs. "Are you sure it wasn't him?"

"No," Eamonn answered honestly with a shake of his head. "Be vigilant. Hadli's good at not being seen when he doesn't want to be."

Leyna nodded, and they resumed their walk to the café, but their new unease was palpable, evident in their clammy joined hands, their quickened breaths, their flitting eyes. Eamonn might have turned back, not gone to the café, but it would prove he believed he'd seen Hadli. He wanted to keep up the assumption that they were safe in Amrieth.

Patrons of the café sat outside at small tables, basking in the sun as they ate their delicacies and watched the roamers on the street. Eamonn hastily surveyed the café's occupants inside and out, and he determined Hadli was not among them. He and Leyna ate a quick meal, taking a seat at a table under the cover of the café's porch, even though it lacked the sun's warmth and they shivered as they ate. Leyna looked suddenly haggard, as though she hadn't slept in days, and a realization hit that she was that worried over *him*.

During their stroll back to the guest house, Leyna's hand relaxed more in Eamonn's, and the tension in her shoulders decreased. With no threat materializing, they both breathed a little easier and picked up a casual conversation as they walked, admiring the city's beauty. Eamonn said something to make Leyna laugh as they rounded the last corner between them and the inn, but Leyna's laugh ended abruptly when they spotted three people approaching their destination.

Taran and Teiyn.

And Hadli.

In a flash, Eamonn spun on his heel and dipped behind the building he and Leyna had just appeared around. He pressed his back to the stacked stone wall and pulled Leyna close beside him.

"It *was* him," she whispered, fear shining in her eyes.

Eamonn's throat had gone as dry as sand, and his heart pounded in his ears. What was Hadli doing in Amrieth? Especially *with* Taran and Teiyn? Eamonn's first assumption was that Rothgard had sent Hadli after him, just as he had before.

Perhaps he had, but Taran and Teiyn had found Hadli before he got to Eamonn. They might have put him under some kind of magical control to bring him to Dorylss, Kinrid, and Gilleth. Perhaps Eamonn was safe after all.

Leyna grabbed Eamonn's hand and pulled his attention to her. "What do we do?"

"I don't know," Eamonn murmured. "The fact that he's with Taran and Teiyn doesn't make any sense. I don't imagine he'd try to capture me directly in front of them, in the middle of the city."

Leyna drew her eyebrows together. "Maybe not. Maybe he has a message from Rothgard?"

Eamonn scoffed. "Hadli's no errand boy. He wouldn't travel all the way here just to carry a message for Rothgard. They'd find a courier, or Hadli would delegate it to someone else."

"Unless he was under Rothgard's control."

Eamonn's lungs emptied. He hadn't considered that. Hadli could easily be under the command of Rothgard's magic with his new Réalta, the same one that caused a king to willingly step down from his throne. Eamonn forced a swallow down the desert that was his throat and resisted the shudder that threatened to shake his shoulders.

"I can find out," he said, looking straight ahead at nothing in particular, "but we have to get closer. If I'm close enough within Hadli's presence, I can use my own magic to determine if there is a magical hold on him. It's something they taught me in Avaria: finding the barrier of magic and removing it."

Leyna nodded eagerly, her brow still creased with worry. "Do it. I know you can. Now is the best time, with Hadli at the guest house. You have five other people there to help you if things take a turn."

Eamonn placed a quick kiss on the top of Leyna's head and wove his fingers through hers again. "Come on."

They struck a pace just below a run to cross the street and arrive at the inn. Eamonn paused for a moment at the front door, inhaled a deep breath, and pushed it open, ready for what awaited him.

But the vestibule was empty, save for Grimmel at the desk at the opposite end.

"Can I be of some assistance with something, Master Eamonn?" the man asked, watching Eamonn with a curious, if not flustered, expression. An awareness washed over Eamonn that he had flung open the door and burst into the room more aggressively than intended, his emotions running high and sending adrenaline flooding through his veins.

"Three people—Idyrrians—did they come inside a moment ago?"

"Yes, they've gone into the meeting hall and requested that Dorylss, Kinrid, and Gilleth join them," Grimmel answered with his arm outstretched to their right, indicating the direction of the hall. "I've just sent one of the house boys to retrieve them."

A knot formed in Eamonn's gut, and a lump blocked his throat as he approached the room. It was similar in size and appearance to the dining room but arranged with lounge chairs and low tables for people to meet. Eamonn scanned the upholstered chairs before spotting the Idyrrians seated by a window, silently watching passersby.

Eamonn dropped Leyna's hand and gave her the package of dresses to focus inward, shutting out the world around him to search for magic surrounding Hadli before they noticed him there. He would check Taran and Teiyn, too, for good measure, though he didn't know if their own magic would get in the way. Something he'd failed to learn in Avaria was how to detect the magic of a specific magic caster. He hadn't realized its importance while there, and a pang of regret stabbed him that he hadn't spent more time in Avaria after all.

But he pushed the thought away, reaching out for the warmth and light of his magic within him. It came to him more easily now, more naturally, and he let out a quick sigh of relief to know that he had gained at least one beneficial skill from the Kaethiri.

Magic shot through him like electricity, its heat spreading from his core and sending a tingle to his extremities. The familiar ache pressed behind his breastbone, and he knew his Réalta glowed underneath his warm layers. Eyes closed, Eamonn reached out toward Hadli, Taran, and Teiyn, and he found no wall of magic, no barrier that surrounded any of them. A heat seemed to emanate off the twins, which must have been their own magical abilities. Eamonn found nothing around any of them like Rafella's magical hold on the creatures in Avaria.

With an exhale, Eamonn released the magic and his eyes met Leyna's. "Nothing," he said, shaking his head.

The anxiety that had contorted Leyna's features vanished briefly before returning anew. "He could still be here for you," she whispered, but the entrance of Dorylss, Kinrid, and Gilleth stole away any other words she might have hoped to say. They stepped farther into the room than Eamonn and Leyna had, prompting the Idyrrians by the window to look up at them.

"Dear friends!" Teiyn beamed when she saw them, hopping up from her chair and approaching them. "We're glad to see you."

"And glad to be off the road," Taran added, standing as well. Curved lines popped out around the corners of his mouth as he grinned. His dark eyes shone, their slight upward tilt making him look perpetually mischievous: a trait he shared with his sister.

Behind them, Hadli slowly came to his feet, barely lifting his eyes from the floor. His beard had grown fuller in the weeks since Eamonn had last seen him, and it needed a trim, giving Hadli a more unkempt appearance than he'd had on Nidet. Maybe it was just the long way they had traveled, but Eamonn could discern a weariness about him. Something in his deep brown eyes gave an impression of the Hadli from before—before Nidet, before Rothgard, before Eamonn had abandoned him and the Thieves' Guild.

Eamonn wanted to join Dorylss and Leyna in greeting the twins, but his gaze wouldn't leave Hadli. With the removal of the potential threat, Eamonn's fear was replaced with a flurry of emotions that bombarded him all at once: anger for Hadli's betrayal and loyalty to Rothgard, even after reconnecting with Eamonn; bewilderment at what he was doing there, and accompanied by Taran and Teiyn, no less; and compassion, despite it all. The boy who had stolen to survive, just like Eamonn—the boy who had found Eamonn and invited him into his crew, giving him a family—that boy stood before him. A man now, but still familiar. Still his brother.

"What are you doing here?" Eamonn crossed his arms and planted his feet. Though his heart raged, Eamonn refused to display his feelings in words or actions. First and foremost, he needed answers.

With his head still slightly dipped, as though in humility, Hadli met Eamonn's gaze. The knot in Eamonn's stomach pulled tighter, twisting and tugging.

"I couldn't stay with him anymore," Hadli began. A hush had fallen over the others, and even though Hadli kept his volume low, his voice carried through the room. "After I saw what he'd done to you, how he'd treated you, and what he was becoming...

I know what I said before I left you, and I thought I meant it at the time. I wanted to believe that everything Rothgard did was right and had a purpose. But he went too far."

"You mentioned a rendezvous after the battle," Eamonn accused. He attempted to even his breathing as he shot daggers from his eyes. Hadli's final words to him still rang in his ears, crystal clear. *You underestimate Rothgard.* He'd pulled out of Eamonn's grasp, making it obvious that his loyalty lay with Rothgard, even though Hadli had helped Eamonn. Even though Eamonn had asked him to leave with them.

"That had nothing to do with Rothgard. I thought he was dead." Hadli shrugged. "That was me doing the only next thing I knew to do." He dipped his head toward Kinrid and Gilleth. "I found Rothgard at that rendezvous, alive, and I did join him again, I'll admit. I'm not proud of it. I'd lost your good opinion of me, so I didn't think I had anything more to lose. He showed me the new magic he had, the new amulet. He told me how he got it." Hadli dropped his head again and shook it. "At that point, I knew I had to get out. But then, he started telling me his new plans." Hadli's eyes found Eamonn's again, this time fiercer, as though lit with flame. "I stuck around to learn what I could, and when I felt he'd divulged everything to me, I knew I had to find you. I had to warn you."

Eamonn's heart seized. "Warn me about what?"

Hadli surveyed those around him. "We should probably sit," he said, gesturing to the chairs he and the twins had left. "It might take a little while."

Taran and Teiyn returned to Hadli, this time resting together on a settee, and Eamonn took a seat in the chair opposite Hadli. Leyna sat beside Eamonn, and Dorylss once again had no problem with dragging furniture out of its arrangement and added three more chairs to the group for Kinrid, Gilleth, and himself. No one said anything once they were all seated, waiting for Hadli to pick up where he'd left off.

"I assume you're still trying to take down Rothgard," Hadli began, leaning forward with his elbows on his knees and his hands clasped in between. He kept his voice at a murmur, and the others watched him with rapt attention. "I learned something about his plans that you need to know.

"Believe it or not, right now, he's weak. The amulet he made isn't working as well as he'd hoped. Controlling Trinfast is using most of his magical capacity, and it leaves him vulnerable. Most people don't know this. They see how he has taken over the reign of an established king and it promotes fear. A lot of his power comes from people's perception of his power.

"All that to say, he needs to refine and regenerate his new magic before he encounters resistance. He needs a way to expand his Avarian magic and ensure that he will have it when he needs it. He has an idea how to, and he's probably on his way now."

"On his way here?" Kinrid asked as he moved his hand to the hilt of his sword, apparently ready to call together his army.

"No, to Wolstead," Hadli answered, his voice a murmur. "He knows of a place...deep within Mount Iyer at the base of the Valneria mountains. He said when he was younger, Wolsteadan miners discovered what seemed to be a door in the heart of the mountain where they were mining Arithnyx, but none of them dared try to open it."

"What did you say?" Eamonn didn't mean to interrupt Hadli or blurt out his question so abruptly, but he wasn't sure if he'd heard Hadli right. Had he really said Arithnyx?

Hadli drew his eyebrows together as he watched Eamonn curiously. "The miners found a door in the mountain."

"No." Eamonn shook his head. "Did you say they were mining Arithnyx?"

"Yes."

Eamonn's heart leapt to his throat. He'd seen the name of the unfamiliar gemstone written on Rothgard's pendant sketch back in Kinrid's tent.

Hadli must have read the question in Eamonn's eyes. "It's a gem that's only found in the deepest parts of Mount Iyer. They say it hums in the rock, but once it's mined, it loses its trill."

"It channels magic."

Teiyn sat up straight on the settee, her eyes widening as her lips parted. "How do you know?"

In his peripheral vision, Eamonn saw Leyna face him, and he turned to meet her gaze.

"That's the stone in Rothgard's pendant, isn't it?" she asked.

He nodded vigorously in answer, the rhythm of his heart accelerating. "It was circled on his sketch. He must have known of it from the Wolsteadan miners, possibly for a long time. That hum," he continued, turning back to Hadli, "is the energy of magic. It must be how Rothgard knew the stone could channel magic."

"Well, he knows the place where the miners found the door is Avarian. Something about it filled them with such an overwhelming fear that they covered the door back up and moved on, never mining in the area again. Rothgard said it's the same sense of dread that keeps curious visitors out of Avaria." Hadli released the clasp of his hands to wave them in the air as though he was instructing a classroom of learners. "In his study of magic, he learned of these places called 'abodes' around Sarieth where the magical beings of Avaria used to dwell. They tried to hide their abodes—destroyed some of them—but the miners uncovered this one. The abode is full of magic. Rothgard said it's exactly what he needs to build his strength."

Eamonn turned the term over in his mind. *Abode.* Imrilieth had mentioned the abodes, but he couldn't remember any details. But even without the specifics of Imrilieth's description, he knew Hadli spoke the truth. Eamonn had heard of these dwellings from the mouth of the Kaethiri Queen herself. There was no way Hadli would know about them without having heard about them from Rothgard.

"So, Rothgard is weak until he makes it to Wolstead?" Dorylss asked as he stroked his beard.

"He's weak, and..." Hadli trailed off, bringing his hands back together and rubbing one set of knuckles. He locked eyes with Eamonn before he spoke again. "Something's happening to him. He didn't say anything about that part, but I think the amulet is causing it."

Eamonn stiffened. Imrilieth had told him the "bloodstone," as she had referred to it, was already corrupting Rothgard. "What do you mean?"

Hadli cleared his throat and shifted in his chair. He ran a hand over his jawline and licked his lips. "It's like it's draining him. Not just in strength; in appearance, too. He's done a good job hiding it from the public so far, but by the time I left him, it had gotten worse. It's almost—it's almost as if it's altering his being."

This time, the silence that covered them was heavy, as though they all wanted to speak but said nothing. Eamonn didn't know if he should celebrate or worry. Imrilieth had said the perversion of the amulet would transform Rothgard but not kill him. And even though they'd established his magic was weak, that weakness could fuel a new fury within Rothgard that may ultimately make him more dangerous.

"And you said he's on his way there now?" Gilleth asked. She gripped her baldric with both hands, the light in the room shining off her fierce eyes.

"I left Idyrria before him, but he seemed eager to go. He was gathering the followers he had in Rifillion with him, along with some of Idyrria's military from the palace to accompany him."

"So he feels like he needs protection." The words from Gilleth's mouth formed a statement rather than a question. "It will be a good time to strike, especially if we ambush him on the road. What is his route?"

Hadli sat back in the chair, bringing his forearms to rest on his thighs and loosely clasping his hands. "I imagine he'll avoid Miren. He told me the Mirish army nearly killed him on his way through the province before. So he'll probably take the lower road that crosses where the rivers feed Lake Elaris."

Kinrid turned his head to meet Gilleth's gaze. "Our best strategy is going to be an ambush at Mount Iyer. It's less than two days' ride from here, and we should have plenty of time to set up our forces there and prepare."

"Hold on." Eamonn's voice rang out. His stare was hard and zeroed in on Hadli. "Everyone just hold on. How do you know all this? About the abode, about the amulet... It sure seems like a lot of convenient information for you to happen to know to give us an advantage."

Hadli didn't miss a beat. "Rothgard trusts me. I earned that trust. I was his right hand."

Eamonn drummed his fingers on the arm of his chair. "Okay, fine. I'll give you that one. But explain this." He leaned in toward Hadli and cocked his head to the side. "How are you *here*? How did you know exactly where to find me?"

With a sigh, Hadli rested his head in his hand and rubbed his brow. "I didn't know where you might be. I didn't even know where you'd been for the last three years until Rothgard sent me to Teravale to find you. So I went back to Erai. My plan was to ask around and see if anyone had any information about you: if they'd seen you recently, if they knew where you were based now. I happened to be staying at the same inn as Taran and Teiyn on their way to join you, and I recognized them from the raid on the castle." Hadli chuckled, glancing in the twins' direction. "I think they were both ready to kill me on the spot, but I convinced them to trust me. I told them I was searching for you to warn you about all of this, and they eventually believed me and told me they were going to you. They offered for me to travel with them."

Eamonn turned to the twins, studying their expressions and sensing for any sign of magical barriers around them again. Nothing surrounded them; only the light of their own magic was present. So, they weren't being coerced into believing Hadli. That was a single good sign, at least.

"You trust him?" Eamonn asked them. He hoped they would give some insight into what convinced them to believe Hadli, when the words out of Hadli's own mouth just now had been "Rothgard's right hand."

The twins shared a look before Teiyn spoke. "He seemed desperate to warn you."

"He freely gave us all the information he just shared," Taran added

"He denounced Rothgard and cursed him for his treatment of you."

"We didn't know what to think at first, but we chose to put our faith in him."

"We have traveled across Miren with him, and he has only been helpful and true to his word."

Eamonn rested against the chair's back and crossed his arms once the twins had finished speaking. "And what's to say it's not a trap?" he continued, eyes boring into Hadli. "You would say and do all the right things to gain our trust."

Hadli shrugged again and tilted his head down to look at Eamonn from under his brow. "I guess you just have to take me at my word. Or you can ignore me, decide you don't believe me. I'm not much of a threat to you by myself."

A war waged within Eamonn. He had longed for Hadli to turn away from Rothgard, to realize the cruelty and malice in Rothgard's ways and leave him behind. Eamonn wanted nothing more than to restore his relationship with Hadli, once the closest thing he'd had to a brother.

But only a few weeks ago, he'd tried to convince Hadli to come around and had failed. Even when it seemed Hadli saw the truth in Eamonn's words, he'd still chosen to stay with Rothgard. Could he have changed that much since Eamonn saw him last and turned his back on Rothgard?

Or was Hadli just as deceitful as Rothgard now, giving Eamonn and the others a taste of what they wanted within their reach so they would fall into his trap? But what kind of trap would it be? Rothgard would have to know that a force of fighters would accompany Eamonn, and as Hadli had said, his magic was weak.

Eamonn didn't doubt the truth of Hadli's account. The Kaethiri had confirmed that Rothgard was not as powerful as before and mentioned the Avarian abodes throughout the country, as well as the curse of the stone Rothgard wore around his neck. Those were facts, and if Hadli knew them, they came straight from Rothgard.

The question that remained was whether or not Hadli was providing this information for their gain or for Rothgard's.

Eamonn stood to show his control over the situation. Hadli's fate was in his hands. "You make one move out of line, or this whole thing proves to be a trap, and you'll have our entire force turn on you. I'm not exactly happy about this, but I'll believe you...for now. Know that it can change."

Eamonn pivoted and left the circle of chairs. He needed air. He needed something to clear his head and lighten his heart. Hadli showing up to help them was on the bottom of scenarios he had expected to deal with, and it affected him more than he wanted to let on.

"Eamonn."

Hadli's voice from behind Eamonn stopped him, and he looked back over his shoulder. The emotions on Hadli's face had changed. Relief and calmness exuded from Hadli's eyes, and... was that hope?

"Thank you."

The burning pressure behind Eamonn's eyes pushed him out of the room, but not before he gave Hadli one last message.

"Prove to me you deserve it."

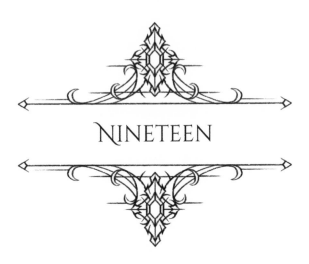

NINETEEN

KING JAVORAK ARRIVED AT the palace at sundown, which meant Dorylss, Kinrid, and Gilleth would seek their audience with the King of Miren the following morning. The kings of Teravale and Farneth had requested the presence of both Eamonn and Leyna, since they had been in the tower in Holoreath with Rothgard and saw his capabilities firsthand.

Leyna donned the blue dress Eamonn had purchased for her, weaving portions of her hair into loose braids and pinning them in place around her head. She had bathed and put on a light floral perfume provided for her in the bathing room, and she even added color to her lips and cheeks in preparation for the council.

The Mirish loved beauty, so Leyna used it as a tool, a weapon in her arsenal. King Taularen would never take them seriously if they came to him at less than their best. She viewed it as a tactic, a strategy, and if Eamonn happened to notice, too, then so be it.

Leyna opened the door to her room to find Eamonn waiting just outside, leaning against the wall between their doors. He pushed himself off the wall as soon as she'd stepped out, dropping his crossed arms and taking in her appearance. Leyna's ears burned under Eamonn's gaze, but not in a bad way.

He cocked his head and a half-smile tugged at his mouth. "Miren suits you," he said, reaching out to take her hand. "You look lovely."

"Thank you," Leyna replied as he pulled her close and stole a kiss. "It suits you, too."

Eamonn had dressed in a clean white shirt and brown trousers, with a structured green jacket trimmed in gold that made his mossy eyes stand out. "Well, I had to put my best foot forward. The king wouldn't take us seriously if we didn't look like we belonged here."

A grin erupted on Leyna's face, but she pressed her lips together to suppress some of her enthusiasm that she and Eamonn shared the same idea. "That's exactly what I was thinking."

Eamonn took her hand, his eyes glittering. "Let's just hope it works."

They met Dorylss, Kinrid, and Gilleth in the vestibule of the guest house, ready to depart. Taran, Teiyn, and Hadli would not be attending the meeting. Hadli had no business there, and while Taran and Teiyn might be included later, they didn't want to make the king feel like they were ganging up on him right at the start.

"We have a carriage waiting out front," Dorylss said as Leyna and Eamonn entered. "It's not far, and we could walk, but it shows more class to arrive in a carriage. King Taularen will notice."

Sounds like I had the right idea. Leyna ran a hand over her waist to smooth her bodice, hoping to keep everything about her appearance pristine.

The only person who didn't seem extraordinarily put-together was Gilleth. She still wore leather armor over her usual shirt and trousers, her black hair twisted into thick braids that she had piled expertly on her head. She was notably missing her weapons—a usual staple to her attire. Another difference, Leyna noted, was bright golden lines around her eyes, luminescent against her dark skin. Leyna was curious about their significance, as she'd never seen Gilleth draw the lines around her eyes before, but she decided then was not the best time to ask.

The blustery winds when they stepped outside made Leyna grateful for the carriage, even to carry them such a short distance. Thin clouds glided across the sky in the cold breezes, and Leyna gripped her cloak and embraced herself in its warmth.

Though not impressively ornate, the carriage was large, and the group was able to fit comfortably inside. Dorylss and Kinrid shared a seat opposite Leyna, Eamonn, and Gilleth, and Dorylss spent the short ride briefing them on what to expect and how to behave.

Leyna barely paid attention. She watched the city go by from the window beside her. She was in awe of the artistry of the city and the way nature had been woven throughout. The whole kingdom felt like a massive garden, the roads its winding paths and the buildings its monuments and benches.

A glint of sunlight up ahead caught Leyna's eye, and she peered through the trees, buildings, crowds to discover it came from sunlight bouncing off water. In glimpses as they rode along, Leyna saw rippling waves that glittered in the light—the lake that surrounded the entire kingdom. They must be close to the palace; Eamonn had said it was situated at the southernmost point, overlooking the lake.

The carriage crested a hill, and the palace came suddenly into view, shining like a beacon against the choppy waters. Built much in the style of the other structures in the kingdom, the palace was truly a sight to behold. The cream-colored stone of the walls was full of elaborately detailed carvings, making the palace look more like a massive sculpture than a building. Artisans' tools had touched every fragment of stone. Balustrades, columned porches, and curving staircases had been designed across the palace's facade with overwhelming ornamentation. Arched windows lined three levels, their panes shimmering with the reflection of the morning sun. The roof was higher in some places than others and came to multiple points, with spires that stabbed the sky. Two spires on either end of the long roof bore the flag of Miren, green with the provincial emblem in white—a great tree full of thick branches and adorned with leaves, contained within a circle—and the royal family crest flew on a flag from a spire in the middle.

They passed through golden gates onto a long, curving drive that ran right up to the palace's massive front steps. Surrounding the palace were exquisite gardens, blooming with winter flowers in purple, white, red, and pink, and filled with dark green shrubs and leafless trees. Beyond the garden, the lake hemmed the grounds in on all sides, vast and deep blue. Leyna understood now how foolish it would be for anyone other than the Mirish to cross the lake. They would be seen coming for miles and stopped before coming close to the kingdom.

The carriage came to a stop at the huge, curved steps, where footmen opened the doors and assisted Leyna in her exit. She tried to keep her eyes straight ahead as much as possible, hoping to not gawk at the palace in front of anyone who mattered, but the exquisite beauty of the palace continued to pull her gaze.

She was beginning to believe the guard who had allowed her and Eamonn entry into Amrieth; she might never see a sight like this again.

"Right this way, if you please." A Mirish man with long, straight brown hair guided them into the palace and down a long corridor to a room on the ground floor. Soft piano music drifted through the air from somewhere behind them, a light, merry tune that made Leyna's heart swell. An unexpected confidence rose within her, as though the song imbued her with a new hope. They could do this.

The man paused outside the door, turning to face the group. "The kings of Farneth and Teravale and their advisors are present with King Taularen now. He has agreed to meet with you per their request. When you have been dismissed, someone will come to retrieve you and escort you back to your carriage."

At least King Taularen had granted their audience. Leyna was grateful the kings of the other two provinces had made the journey to meet with Taularen. Dorylss had sought an audience on King Javorak's behalf and was denied. It took the physical presence of the other kings to sway Miren's sovereign.

The Mirish man opened the door and stepped just inside, announcing to the room beyond, "The rest of the party, Your Majesty." He introduced them all by name as they entered at his instruction, and as Leyna passed the man, she glanced at him with a knitted brow, curious how he knew her name.

The question vanished from Leyna's mind as the room captured her attention. Her eyes were drawn upward to the ornate ceiling that rose two stories, painted with scenes that must have come either from Mirish history or legend. Intricate carvings and gilded details surrounded the painted ceiling. Leyna's gaze lowered to a row of arched windows made of stained glass, and below was another row of arches enclosing small sculptures. At the ground level, windows of clear glass lined one wall and paintings in gold frames large enough for Leyna to walk into hung opposite. A chandelier, heavy with candles and dripping in crystals, hung from the center of the ceiling, providing additional light for the room.

Seating for at least a dozen people was tastefully arranged in the room around low tables, grouped near a fireplace blazing with life. A rug with swirls of red, cream, blue, and gold covered almost the length of the room's polished wooden floor.

"Join us," a man standing by the fireplace said, clothed in deep purples and blues trimmed in gold, a crown of gold inlaid with white jewels resting on his head. Another man, burlier than the king with hooded eyes and dark brown hair, stood at attention nearby, staring mercilessly at the visitors.

Leyna nearly tiptoed to the seating area, careful not to damage or dirty anything she came across. She recalled her visit to the palace in Rifillion with Dorylss on their way to rescue Eamonn, and she almost laughed at how she'd thought it grand. By all regards, it *had* been grand in comparison to what she knew. But this…this palace left her breathless.

Four other men had taken positions near the man who spoke, two Teravalen and two Farnish: the kings and their advisors. The two provinces' kings were so opposite in every way it was almost comical. One man had grey hair down to his shoulders and wrinkles folded throughout his fair skin, and shorter than Eamonn. The other was less than ten years older than Leyna and Eamonn, his dark head bald and encircled with a simpler gold crown, the tallest in the room beside Kinrid and Dorylss. Leyna recognized

King Javorak from seeing him in her childhood, even though he had aged, so she assumed the other to be King Vinnerod, who had taken over the throne of Farneth after his father's sudden and mysterious death.

Dorylss and Kinrid gave respectful bows to the three men, and Gilleth stiffly lowered her head. Leyna glanced to Eamonn, who caught her gaze and spoke through his eyes in that moment.

Bow.

Leyna dipped into a curtsy, keeping a watch on Eamonn out of the corner of her eye as to how low to go and for how long to stay down. She should have listened closer to Dorylss in the carriage on their ride over.

"Be seated, please," said the man who Leyna assumed to be King Taularen. His light brown hair was cropped short and his beard neatly trimmed. He was arguably an attractive man, about the same age as Dorylss, though Taularen seemed much more devoted to his appearance.

"So," Taularen continued after everyone—including the two other kings—had taken a seat, "let's cut to the chase here. Hyfell tells me that you and your little band seek the aid of the Mirish military because you are afraid of what's happening in Idyrria." It wasn't a question, and he continued without giving anyone else a chance to speak after a quick gesture to the man beside him, who must have been Hyfell. "Well, I am sorry that your provinces aren't as stable or strong as Miren to withstand any potential front from this Wolsteadan, Rothgard, but I don't see how this is my problem."

Leyna's lips parted as a silent breath escaped them. Right out of the gate, King Taularen was dismissing their request. He might actually be worse than Kinrid and Gilleth had made him out to be.

"Your Majesty," Kinrid began, his tone even and respectful, "we are afraid you don't understand the true gravity of the situation. There is a greater depth than is apparent on the surface."

King Taularen narrowed his eyes. "You seek to insult me with your first breaths, Kinrid te Oberron? You think me too dense to understand what is happening at my doorstep?"

"Of course not, Your Majesty. But some of the things happening are known by very few. We are here to share the information and urge you to ally with the provinces free from Rothgard's control."

Taularen took a seat in a high-backed gold chair with green velvet cushions near the fire. He tilted his chin up and brought his fingertips together in front of his chest. "Tell me, then. What do I not know that will change how I view this matter?"

Kinrid glanced at King Vinnerod and his advisor before speaking as though to specifically remind them of what he was about to tell Taularen. "Rothgard has sought magic from the beginning. He requires magic to accomplish his goals. Not only did he obtain ancient texts that he used to teach himself magic that once existed centuries ago, but he has done something abhorrent and perverse to possess the magic of Avaria as well."

Leyna expected Taularen to laugh, or scoff, or give some indication that he didn't even believe in magic, much less that Rothgard had acquired magical abilities. He leaned back and whispered to the tall man behind him, then looked down his nose at Kinrid and tapped his index fingers together.

Kinrid gestured to Eamonn, who faced the king and dipped his head once again.

"Eamonn is the son of a Kaethiri, one of the magical beings who inhabit the realm of Avaria. The magic of Avaria flows within him. Rothgard discovered this and took Eamonn captive to withdraw his marrow and inoculate himself in order to possess the same magical abilities."

Taularen's eyes widened, but beyond that, he offered no evidence that the information surprised him. Few people in the entire country seriously believed in the previous existence of magic—though Mirish made up a large portion of that number, the belief of magic entwined with some of their religion—and even fewer thought magic was present and accessible in their world.

"Rothgard is using that magic to control the will of anyone he wishes," Kinrid continued. "That is how he was able to take over Idyrria's throne. He forced King Trinfast to abdicate, making him believe it was his idea. He went into the minds of our entire army all at once to turn them to his side. With this magic, Rothgard can be truly unstoppable. He can change the very will of anyone who gets in his way."

King Taularen brought a finger to his lips, laden with a large silver ring with a natural-looking milky white stone, and he tapped it against them. The hint of a smirk played on his mouth. "You, Eamonn. You are Kaethiri?"

"Half, Your Majesty."

The King of Miren relaxed back into his chair, stretching his arms along the armrests and gripping the ends in his hands. "Show me this magic. Prove your claim."

"Your Majesty?" A crease formed between Eamonn's eyebrows with the command.

The smirk on Taularen's face fell, but the cunning in his eyes remained. "Do what your companion attests. Take over my mind. Make me do something against my will."

Leyna's gaze swung to Eamonn. His jaw fell as he stared incredulously at Taularen, giving a small shake of his head. "It's not something to be taken lightly."

"I'm aware. Which is why I want to see exactly what Rothgard can do."

Leyna wrung her hands in her lap, sweat forming along her brow. Since the Kaethiri would not teach him such magic, there was no guarantee Eamonn would be able to summon and demonstrate it for Taularen. Nevertheless, he rose and closed his eyes, inhaling deeply through his nose as he sought his magic.

Leyna's pulse throbbed in her neck as she watched in anticipation, her eyes flitting back and forth between Eamonn and Taularen. Eamonn's eyelids were squeezed shut, and his chest rose and fell with heavy breaths. The King's sly smile returned, and Leyna's heart dropped to see Eamonn failing.

Taularen clicked his tongue three times. "What a shame. And I *so* wanted to believe you."

Eamonn opened his eyes, his jaw clenched and redness rising to his cheeks. Leyna swallowed past the lump of empathy in her throat. Taularen had humiliated Eamonn, but he didn't understand the deeper meaning of Eamonn's defeat. If the Kaethiri had taught him, he would have taken the king's mind and shown him the truth of the threat.

Eamonn's chest still heaved, and a low hum of energy flew through the air past Leyna like a gust of wind. Her chest tightened. Eamonn was still going, and Leyna feared what he might do in his embarrassment.

He curled his fingers into fists, and a shockwave burst from him, jolting everyone in the room and shaking furniture, loosing smaller objects and toppling an empty chair. The fire in the hearth whooshed and dust filled the air, pushed from everything it had settled on.

Taularen cocked his head and his eyes hardened, the grin present but fading. "While it's quite something to witness magic in use, that's not what I asked for. It's not accompanied by the same level of threat."

"With the proper training, I would be able to take control of your will. I've done it before," Eamonn said through gritted teeth, clearly fighting to keep his composure. "Rothgard is actively doing so to the King of Idyrria. It would be wise to heed our warning."

Leyna's eyes darted around the room. No one moved to defend Eamonn. Her heart raced with anticipation as she tried to get up the nerve to stand, to say something, to support Eamonn. But her body was like a sack of rocks in her seat, too heavy to lift, and words never made it to her tongue.

The king studied Eamonn for a lengthy moment before addressing the kings on either side of him. "Javorak, Vinnerod...what do you make of these claims?"

The men glanced at each other, as though waiting for the other to speak first, and then at their advisors. Javorak cleared his throat and took the lead.

"Just because the boy cannot does not mean Rothgard cannot. It does seem hard to believe, but I cannot imagine Trinfast giving away his throne without influence."

"Blackmail is influence, Javorak," Taularen hissed. "The threat of attack is influence."

"We don't know that Rothgard used either of those," Vinnerod spoke up, something in the deep cadence of his voice honest and reassuring. "I believe the words of Kinrid. He was a loyal soldier to my father and has proven himself to me. It would seem Rothgard is using magic, but to what extent is yet to be determined."

"It's not something you'll want to wait around to find out," Eamonn interjected. His eyes flashed hot over the kings. "If you do, you're just giving Rothgard time to invade each of your provinces and do to you exactly what he did to King Trinfast."

Vinnerod and Javorak watched Eamonn with interest, but Taularen glared at him. "Miren is not Idyrria. Our military outmatches that of any other province. We prevented Rothgard from taking root here once already. I have no doubt we will do so again, if necessary."

"Rothgard didn't have the magic then he has now." Anger laced Eamonn's voice. "It's unlikely he would have been able to take Idyrria without it. You're just as vulnerable."

"You may take a seat, Eamonn." Taularen spoke calmly, but the spite was still evident in his words.

Eamonn fell into his chair, seething, and crossed his arms as his leg bounced. Leyna longed to reach out to Eamonn beside her and comfort him somehow, provide him reassurance. Again, her body was paralyzed with the intimidation of the Mirish King and the tension thick in the room, and she remained still.

"And what do you say, Dorylss?" Javorak asked, shifting the focus of the discussion. "I am curious to know your perspective. You are close to the situation, and you bear a wisdom that has proven true and helpful to me in the past."

"Your Majesty," Dorylss said with a dip of his head in King Javorak's direction, "I too have seen Rothgard's capabilities. With the magic he has at his disposal now, he would be able to take every kingdom and set himself as ruler of them all under his own banner, which is what he intends to do." He glanced at his company and shifted in his seat. "We have it on good authority that Rothgard is weak at the moment but seeks a way to enhance his power. If we step in now and ally together against him, he can be stopped before he gets to that point."

Leyna's eyes shot to Eamonn, gauging his reaction to Dorylss's pronouncement that Hadli's assertion was their "good authority." He continued to bounce his leg, still fuming from the interaction with Taularen and apparently oblivious to what Dorylss had said.

"Come now, Taularen." Javorak turned back to the King of Miren with a hand held out in Dorylss's direction. "If Rothgard is weak as they say, what harm can come from allying with us and sending troops against him? We could be done with this once and for all."

Taularen scoffed, sitting straighter in his seat and gripping the arms of his chair until his knuckles turned white. "The *harm*, Javorak, is coming off as weak to every person in Miren, as well as all the other provinces. To ally together means that I believe there is a threat we cannot overcome in our own strength. But that is not so. The Mirish military is stronger than both of yours combined, and I will not have rumors floating around of anything else."

"Then be the savior," Eamonn interrupted, speaking when he hadn't been addressed. Taularen scowled, but Eamonn didn't stop. Leyna pressed her lips together, as if doing so could close Eamonn's mouth and prevent him from speaking. "Step in and help Teravale and Farneth in their time of need. Come to their rescue. I'm sure their kings are less concerned than you about appearances and would rather have Rothgard defeated, regardless of how it makes them look."

A vein bulged in Taularen's forehead as his face deepened to a red hue. "You mock me. I will *not* be mocked, especially by some boy who claims the magic of Avaria yet cannot perform a simple act." The king picked up a small hammer near him and struck a chime that let out a clear, low hum. "This council is adjourned. Miren will come to no one's aid."

The door to the room opened and the Mirish man who had announced their arrival stepped into the room, waiting. Eamonn stood and marched out the door first, not hiding an ounce of his anger, disappointment, and humiliation. Dorylss and Leyna followed after him, but Leyna stopped when King Taularen addressed Gilleth.

"And Gilleth, before you go," he began, and Leyna spun around to see a wicked grin pull at his lips, "Milena sends her regards. I had hoped she might be present for the council, but she was otherwise occupied."

Gilleth said nothing as she turned away from Taularen and almost stomped to the door. Leyna watched them both, hoping she could put the pieces of their interaction together into something that made sense, but to no avail. The casual nature with which Taularen spoke her name pointed to a familiarity, but the spite in his smile and Gilleth's refusal to respond indicated some bad blood. Curiosity prodded Leyna, but she at least had the good sense to know it wasn't the right time to ask.

She glanced one last time over her shoulder as Gilleth and Kinrid passed her. Taularen was dismissing the other kings as well. He leaned back in his gilded chair, stretching out his fingers before wrapping them one by one around the chair's arms, his nose in the air and a look of contented arrogance on his face. Taularen probably believed he'd rid himself of them and the subject of Rothgard forever. He would soon find they weren't that easily thwarted.

Leyna was the last to return to the corridor, where the piano music carrying on the air had transformed into a slow ballad, heavy with sorrow and loss.

TWENTY

"Eamonn!"

He strode right past the carriage, hugging himself against the cold as he exited the palace grounds on foot. He was tempted to turn back and look to the source of the voice that so sweetly spoke his name. She didn't have to follow him; he wished she would ride in the carriage, but not because he didn't want her company. He didn't like for her to walk in the cold and wind because of him.

Leyna's footfalls came quick and heavy from behind him. Eamonn glanced at her and sighed, but he didn't say anything. Once he'd made it past the gates, he would talk to her. He had to at least feel like he'd put the palace behind him.

Leyna respected his silence as she walked with him, keeping his pace down the stone drive and out the massive gates.

The carriage rumbled past them and Eamonn caught Dorylss's eyes, riddled with concern. His mentor was letting him walk, giving him the time to let his emotions cool off, but he knew Dorylss would address it later. Eamonn sucked in a breath through his nose, as though the air beyond the boundaries of the palace grounds was fresher. It was laced with subtle florals, smoke from wood fires throughout the area, and the clean crispness of cold. He breathed it in, purging himself of the foulness left behind by King Taularen.

Eamonn's failure to prove his magic to Taularen was bad enough, but the strange unease had unexpectedly returned just as Eamonn began to search for the king's consciousness. It filled his mind with a fear that occupied his thoughts and distracted him from what he was trying to do.

"I sincerely hope the Kaethiri didn't just ruin our chances of getting Miren to help us," Eamonn said after a while, his voice no more than a murmur amidst the noise of life in the street. He didn't want to worry Leyna with the unexplained foreign feeling that spiked his anxiety, so he blamed his difficulty solely on the Kaethiri's refusal to train him.

His sudden words pulled Leyna's gaze toward him, and she frowned. "I have a feeling King Taularen was just looking for an excuse to dismiss us. He probably believed that would be the easiest way." She rested a hand on Eamonn's bicep, squeezing it gently. "You have to remember, even among those who believe in magic, Avarian magic is known to be inaccessible. Taularen might not even believe that you're half-Kaethiri."

Eamonn worked the muscles in his jaw as he looked away from Leyna. "I know. But I could have proved it to him. I *am* Kaethiri, and I could have shown him. He wouldn't have had a choice but to believe me."

"But then he would have found something else. Eamonn." Leyna tugged him to a stop and turned him to face her. "This isn't your fault."

He would give Leyna that. It wasn't his fault.

It was the Kaethiri's fault.

He inhaled deeply again and closed his eyes, taking Leyna's hand and continuing their way to the inn. "Let's try practicing some with Taran and Teiyn. I think it will be good to feel magic in the world." He didn't say it, but he hoped any kind of magic practice outside of Avaria could help him better grasp magic that would allow him to control wills. He *had* done it before. True, he didn't know how, but he'd done it. Twice. He could do it again, without the help of the Kaethiri.

"Magic, you say?"

Eamonn and Leyna broke their handhold and whirled around in the direction of the voice. Ree leaned on her right side against the column of a building, her arms folded and her right ankle crossed in front of her supporting leg. Underneath her hood, her face bore a crooked grin that struck a nerve in Eamonn. It sent a fire of embarrassment through him, but he didn't know why. Ree's smile was mischievous and intrigued, not cruel and condescending like the look Taularen had given him.

"How long have you been following us?" Eamonn asked, more curious than angry.

Ree pushed herself off the column, giving a shrug as her only answer.

"Since the palace?"

Ree's grin widened as she closed the short distance between herself and Leyna and Eamonn. "I told you I'd be around."

"I didn't know that meant in hiding."

"I wouldn't call it 'hiding.' I'm just particular about who sees me and when." Her hood fell to her shoulders as she tugged it, revealing her curly mane. "An especially helpful skill as a member of Kingdom Security."

"You know, the guard typically uses their presence to deter criminal activity," Leyna said, her voice a knife's edge, and she narrowed her eyes. "It's hard to do that when you don't have a presence."

"Ah, but I'm not the guard." Half of Ree's mouth curled into a smile and her eyes glittered. "But if you would like, I'll accompany you to the guest house and perhaps my 'presence' will help keep you safe."

Leyna huffed and rolled her eyes at Ree's usage of her words, but she didn't refuse. Eamonn extended a hand to invite Ree to join them, and they turned back in the direction of the inn.

"So, how much of our conversation did you hear?" Eamonn wondered, casting a sidelong glance at Ree. "Were you in the council chambers with us?"

Ree chuckled. "No, I wasn't in the room with you, but I have been following you since the palace." She tilted her head and eyed Eamonn. "What's this about you being half-Kaethiri? I thought you said your mother was Mirish."

Eamonn's eyes flew wildly around them, searching for listening ears. "It's not exactly common knowledge," he murmured. He hoped she picked up on the sternness in his tone and understood to keep it to herself. "I wouldn't have said anything if I'd thought someone was listening."

"That's why I didn't want you to know I was listening," Ree replied with a quick raise of her eyebrows. "I've never met anyone who can use magic, much less a Kaethiri. It's not a surprise the King didn't believe you." She sent her gaze straight ahead. "He doesn't put much credit into those kinds of things."

Eamonn puffed out a breath, still frustrated with Taularen, but he couldn't deny the relief that passed through him as well. Leyna might have been right about the King of Miren; even if Eamonn could have followed through with his command, Taularen might not have bought into it anyway.

But if he'd been able to follow through with the command, Eamonn could have *made* Taularen buy into it.

"Who are Taran and Teiyn?" Ree asked.

"Uh..." Eamonn blinked and spluttered, unprepared for the question. Ree had heard everything, apparently. "Friends of ours. Idyrrians."

"Magic users?" Ree watched Eamonn, waiting for confirmation. "You said you would practice with them."

"Yes," Eamonn whispered. Leyna grabbed his hand and squeezed, and when he turned to her, he found her eyes wide with alarm. "She already heard us," he said, his forehead creased. "Besides, I believe we can trust her. And if she spends a lot of time in the palace, she might find out eventually. I don't see the point in denying it."

Leyna looked past Eamonn to Ree. "They're outcasts where they're from because they use magic. I don't want them to get into any trouble here where they have a chance to start fresh."

"Don't worry, I'm not going to tell anyone anything I've learned," Ree said with a sincere warmth in her eyes. "I'm not in the habit of spilling secrets or ruining people's lives. But I do think they'd have a better reception here than in Idyrria. There are a lot of people here in Miren who believe magic does still exist in the world, but they don't know how to access it."

Leyna sighed and nodded, seeming a little more at ease with Ree's new knowledge.

"So, you need to practice magic with them. Why? Because of Rothgard?"

Eamonn felt Leyna tense beside him, and he studied Ree with a furrowed brow.

"Oh, come on, it's not that hard," Ree continued, a playful smile lighting her face. "I already knew your crew was here to persuade King Taularen into an alliance against Rothgard. Then you said you were trying to convince the king you're Kaethiri, and when we met before, you said Rothgard was a greater threat than people realize." She shrugged, amused. "I can put the pieces together. Rothgard has magic. Powerful magic."

Eamonn stopped at a corner, the guest house just across the street. Leyna and Ree followed his lead and faced him, and Eamonn turned his attention to Ree. "You seem familiar with who the Kaethiri are."

She nodded in response. "I grew up Litrellan. A lot of the religion is drawn from the belief in magic. The Kaethiri are Light Bringers."

"Okay, so if you know of the Kaethiri, you know what they can do. The type of magic they have is different from what humans can use."

"Well, they *are* magic. They can manipulate magic itself, which no one else can do," Ree replied. Her expression lost any remaining merriment. "But I know they can bend the wills of humans. It's magic they never gave to humans because it could be so easily misused."

Eamonn locked eyes with Ree, the gravity of the situation settling over them like nightfall: dark and unavoidable. "Rothgard has obtained Avarian magic. Using me. And it's how he took Idyrria's throne." He took a step closer to Ree, lowering his voice further. Leyna held his hand with both of hers, her grasp tight. "He's coming for the other provinces. We need an alliance with Miren to stop him before it gets that far."

"Hmm," Ree mused, her narrowed eyes staring out at something distant, a thoughtful expression on her face. Eamonn waited as she said nothing for several seconds, apparently turning something over in her mind. Finally, she returned from her reverie and nodded her head in the direction of the guest house.

"Those Idyrrian friends of yours staying with you?"

"Yes," Eamonn answered.

"You'll need a place to practice magic, I assume. I imagine you won't want to openly use magic in the guest house or outside in one of the gardens."

"No, we can't," Leyna said, stepping closer and tightening their small circle. "We don't want to draw attention. Even here in Miren, I doubt people would expect to see actual magic performed."

With a slow nod, Ree said, "That's what I thought." She flung her hood over her curls and stepped away from them. "Come back to the palace tomorrow, midmorning. But not the main gate—follow the wall around the grounds to the lake on the eastern side. I'll be there waiting."

Eamonn drew his eyebrows together. He hadn't yet fully decided if Ree could be trusted, but something about her made it seem like she was truly on their side. Agreeing to her suggestion would be taking the plunge and choosing to put faith in her.

Before he or Leyna had the chance to say anything in response, Ree turned on her heel and disappeared into the crowd.

TWENTY-ONE

THE NEXT MORNING WAS cold, wet, and dreary. A rainstorm
had rolled in overnight, leaving a hazy mist and a dense fog
over the city. Eamonn and Leyna strode through the streets
side by side on their way to the palace, and though Eamonn
longed to feel the warmth of her palm against his own, they
both had to use their hands to clutch their cloaks against the
cold.

Taran and Teiyn followed closely behind them, wearing heavy
wool shirts over their clothes in the typical Idyrrian style, with
thick scarves wrapped around their necks and heads. Sand-
wiched in the middle of the two pairs was Hadli, whom Eamonn
had argued against bringing. If Hadli was lying—if he was still
loyal to Rothgard—Eamonn didn't like the idea of showing him
exactly what kind of magic he was capable of. But Hadli had been
under the close eye of the twins; and with Dorylss, Kinrid, and
Gilleth meeting again with the kings of Teravale and Farneth to
discuss their next moves after Taularen's rejection, Hadli would

be left to his own devices. Eamonn liked that idea even less, so Hadli was joining them for their magic practice.

With Eamonn's lead, the group bypassed the gates to the palace and followed along its eastern wall. They couldn't see the vast lake through the dense fog, but Eamonn knew they were going the right way. The crowds were sparser there, with only the ports and a nautical shop or two in that direction. It meant less curious glances at their odd assortment of people but a greater opportunity for them to stick out.

Eamonn stole a glance at Leyna as they meandered casually down the street. She caught his movement and looked at him, giving him a small smile of reassurance. She had been wanting to practice magic again since leaving Avaria. Even though she had difficulty trusting Ree, she jumped at the opportunity to use magic outside Avaria, as Eamonn had promised when they left.

"You're early," said a voice to their right. Eamonn came to a halt, stopping the group, and he peered through the grey fog in search of Ree. He knew her voice well enough by then to know it was she who spoke.

She stepped into view, the grey of her cloak a camouflage in the mist. Her bright eyes gleamed from under her hood and locked with Eamonn's.

"I find it noble to be early," he said, almost a challenge. "You're early, too."

A grin pulled at one side of Ree's mouth. "Follow me."

She spun and strode away from them, heading for the wall. Eamonn wrinkled his brow in confusion, and Ree seemed to pick up on his hesitation without even turning around.

"Keep up," she said. "You won't want to get lost."

Eamonn obeyed and discovered a small door hidden behind shrubbery, the same color and material as the wall. Ree passed through the doorway and the others stuck to her heels, entering the palace grounds through the low hole in the wall. More shrubbery covered the wall on the other side, as though it was supposed to be hidden on the interior as well. Ree led them down a path through the tall shrubs until they finally emerged into a garden with neatly manicured hedges, bountiful trees thoughtfully arranged, and winter flowers that painted the garden with color. The hedges grew tall in many parts of the garden, at least two heads taller than Eamonn. Ree seemed to know exactly where she was going, with no hesitation to her steps, but to Eamonn, the garden was turning into a maze.

As they followed Ree through the winding garden paths, Eamonn wondered why someone would bother to hide the little door on the inside wall. It made sense to conceal it from the outside, so curious passersby wouldn't try to force their way into the palace grounds, but concealing it on the inside must have meant that not everyone in the palace knew it existed. Perhaps it was special access for "Kingdom Security".

And then there was this maze. Ree seemed to know every twist and turn, every choice to make following the hedges, and Eamonn was certain he wouldn't be able to find his way out on his own. Though after a while, yellow and white tinged leaves started sticking out to him, appearing every so often in the maze. He made a mental note of them but didn't say anything.

"Where exactly are we going?" Leyna asked behind him. Eamonn looked back at her to catch her glimpse past the hedge maze where the palace walls stood tall off to their right. "This can't be the way to the palace."

"It's not," Ree replied without turning her head. "I know somewhere much more secluded."

After a few more paces, the maze widened and they stepped into a grassy area surrounded by hedges and shaded with trees, though the brown leaves were strewn on the ground around them. A structure stood in the center of the space built in the elaborate Mirish style. It wasn't quite a building, having a shingled roof and stone walls but open entryways and windows.

"Well," Ree said, turning around to face the group with her arms spread wide, "here we are."

"Which is where, exactly?" Hadli asked as he took in their surroundings.

Ree crossed her arms and cocked her head to the side. "A place very few people know about. You can practice safely here without fear of onlookers."

"And how do we know we can trust you?"

Eamonn scoffed and glanced at Hadli. "Look at you, talking about trust."

"Excuse me for looking out for your best interests."

"You're only here because you have to be. You can just fade into the background, all right?"

Eamonn stormed away from the group up the pavilion's few steps, crossing the structure's wide veranda and stepping over the threshold inside. Ree jogged after him, catching Eamonn before he got too far.

"I was expecting four of you." An intrigued grin played on her lips, and she flashed her eyes back at Hadli, still outside. "Who's your friend?"

"Someone you need to stay far away from," Eamonn replied, his gaze hardening as he pulled his eyebrows low over his eyes.

"Oh, come on, it's just a question. I'm not about to throw myself at him just because he's attractive." Ree glanced outside one more time before meeting Eamonn's gaze again, and her expression sobered. "I do need to know who he is, though. You haven't told me about him. Does he know magic too?"

Eamonn shook his head and scrubbed a hand over his face. "No, he doesn't use magic. He works for Rothgard." The almost imperceptible widening of Ree's eyes didn't slip past Eamonn's notice. "Well, he claims not to anymore. Says he left. He's given us some inside information, supposedly. We're still deciding if he's good for it."

"And how does he know you?"

A sigh left Eamonn's lips before he hardened them into a line. Hadli and the others were about to enter the pavilion, so he didn't have time for a full explanation. Not that he wanted to give one, anyway.

"We were friends growing up. Close friends. But he turned his back on me when he joined Rothgard."

The intensity of Ree's expression softened as a sadness welled in her eyes, and she laid a gentle hand on Eamonn's forearm.

Leyna was the first to come into the pavilion, and she stopped just inside the entryway when her gaze landed on Ree's hand touching Eamonn's arm. Her eyes flitted between the two of them.

"Let's keep it moving," Hadli said from behind her. Leyna threw her gaze to the floor and continued inside. Taran and Teiyn brought up the rear, and all eyes turned to Eamonn.

"What shall we do first?" Teiyn asked.

Eamonn studied the space, a large room with a tall ceiling in the center of the pavilion. Walls in the space designated two other "rooms" on either side, though none of them had doors. The purpose or function of the structure was unclear, having no light, furnishings, cook stove, or ritual objects. The architecture and layout first made him think it might be a temple, but the interior was plain. The only feature was a round pit in the center of the room for a fire surrounded by four stone benches. It clearly wasn't a guest house, and it didn't appear to be a gardener's shed. It was an open space, a blank canvas, the beauty of which was that they could use magic without feeling like they might mess up some part of their practice room.

Across from him, Leyna shivered, and Eamonn resisted the urge to cross to her and wrap her in his embrace. "Let's get a fire going and we'll begin."

Taran and Teiyn set to work on the fire, using wood from a pile Ree showed them out back to start a flame. Once Taran lit the spark, Teiyn curled her fingers into her palm and the fire burst to life. Leyna knelt beside Teiyn, watching her closely.

"You'll have to show me how to do that," Leyna murmured, her forehead wrinkling with awe. "I never worked with fire in Avaria."

Teiyn smiled brightly back at her. "That sounds like a good place to begin."

"It's always helpful to know how to manipulate fire," Taran confirmed, turning his palm upward as the flames grew higher, showing his control over them.

Leyna's blue eyes sparkled from the light of Taran's flames, and she looked up at him and his sister eagerly. "How do I start?"

Eamonn should have gone over to her and listened to the twins' instruction. He had never controlled fire with magic either, and it would be a useful skill to have. Instead, he kept to himself on one side of the room and closed his eyes, searching for his magic. Away from the continual fountain of magic that was Avaria, Eamonn had a much harder time finding and drawing on his own. But, since practicing so much in Avaria, he knew what he was looking for and how to get there—the point the Kaethiri had been making during their training.

Eamonn soon touched the low thrum of energy nestled within him: quiet, waiting, ready. As he pulled the magic out of the recesses of his being and into his chest, the familiar ache arose behind his pendant again. He sent the wind outside to rustle the leaves scattered over the ground with his eyes still closed, basking in the warmth of magic spreading down his extremities.

Now one with his magic, Eamonn could feel the blatant pulse of magic in the air coming from Leyna, Taran, and Teiyn. It was easier to discern this time as they used magic themselves. He knew exactly where they were: how far away from him, their positioning with each other, everything. Each person's magic gave off a light and a heat that he could see without his eyes and feel from inside his body.

He opened his eyes and watched as a tongue of flame flicked up from the rest and sparked, following the direction of Leyna's finger. She cheered and beamed at the twins before looking for Eamonn. When she found his gaze, she closed her smile and lifted her hand in the air, drawing the flame upward, and he grinned back. Leyna turned to Teiyn to ask what to do next, and Eamonn scanned the room. Ree's figure filled the back entryway, where she watched the magic users with a fascinated expression. Hadli sat on one of the stone benches and added another small log to the fire, seemingly uninterested in what the others were doing.

Eamonn longed to read his mind and find out if Hadli was trustworthy. Was that even possible? Was that something he could do if he knew how? The Kaethiri had never mentioned it. Controlling minds meant injecting their own thoughts and commands into a person's subconscious, not learning what they thought.

He would try, at least. If he failed, it made no difference; but if he succeeded and was able to learn Hadli's thoughts, he would know how honest his former friend had been with them.

Eamonn stoked the magic in his being like Hadli stoked the fire, and the magic consumed him with a heated buzz. He rested his eyes on Hadli before closing them, focusing all his energy on him. Eamonn pushed his mind and magic out to Hadli, searching, looking for some way to get into his head. Nothing changed, and Eamonn worked harder to shut out the world around him. How was Rothgard able to use Avarian magic so easily when he wasn't even a true Kaethiri?

Eamonn stifled his questions as he continued to reach out with his magic. Getting into Hadli's head would be the only foolproof way of learning his motivations. It was the only way they would know if what he'd told them was true. They needed that information almost as much as they needed to defeat Rothgard.

The buzzing within Eamonn grew louder as the vibration of magic nearly emanated from his fingertips, consuming him more than he'd ever felt in Avaria. In fact, he'd felt it that strongly only a couple of times before. An intense pressure filled his chest, becoming almost uncomfortable until it vanished in an instant.

And without warning, Eamonn found himself in Hadli's mind.

As he suspected, he couldn't read Hadli's thoughts, but the connection between them was like a rope, with Eamonn at one end and Hadli at the other. Or perhaps it was more like reins in Eamonn's hands leading to a bit in Hadli's mouth. The magic flowed off him like an extension of himself, easy and natural once he'd tapped into it.

Eamonn's mouth twitched with the slightest smirk and his eyes flew open. Hadli sat just as he had before, but Eamonn picked up on the vacancy in his eyes. His heart raced and pushed adrenaline through his veins, warming him even more, and he forced himself to deepen his shallow breaths. He'd actually done it: on his own, outside of Avaria, no thanks to the Kaethiri.

Eamonn needed to test this out, see what he was capable of, but he would start small. No need to rush things.

Hold your hands out to the fire.

Hadli raised his hands, palms forward.

The thrill of success shot through Eamonn like a lightning bolt.

Stand up and walk to the front entryway.

Eamonn hadn't finished his thought before Hadli stood and began to walk.

Now come closer to me.

Hadli left the entry and came to a stop a few steps away from Eamonn. The other heads in the pavilion followed Hadli.

Tell me what you're doing here.

"I had to tell you about what Rothgard plans to do," Hadli said, his tone even and his glazed-over eyes locked onto Eamonn. "I had to tell you about the abode in Wolstead. Rothgard said—"

"*Eamonn.*"

The severity of Leyna's voice captured Eamonn's attention, and he lost connection with Hadli's mind. Hadli blinked a few times and his eyes darted around as he likely put the pieces together of what just happened.

"What are you doing?"

Leyna had rushed over to him and stood just behind Hadli, her face drained of color and her brows knitted together in alarm. Her chest heaved as though she had been running, and she leaned slightly toward Eamonn, not releasing his gaze as she waited for his answer.

Eamonn knew Leyna agreed with the Kaethiri that he shouldn't use magic to control a person's will. It wasn't new information to him. What surprised him was the intensity sharpening her voice and bathing her features.

"You did the thing, didn't you?" Hadli asked as he furrowed his brow and folded his arms. "You were controlling me."

As his eyes flitted back and forth between Leyna and Hadli, Eamonn breathed out an incredulous laugh and dropped his shoulders, turning his palms up in innocence. "It was an accident. I was just practicing magic. I didn't mean to end up in your mind."

Taran and Teiyn joined them, and even Ree angled her head in their direction, watching them closely while she leaned against the wall with her ankles crossed.

"I've never been able to figure it out, really," he continued, Leyna and Hadli especially staring him down. "The few times I've done it, it just kind of happened."

"It may have just 'happened,' but you didn't let me go when you realized it." Hadli's expression changed from shocked to severe as he drew his eyebrows farther down. "You took advantage of it. You started controlling me."

Leyna's lips became a straight line and her nostrils flared. She didn't bother trying to hide her displeasure. The anger in her eyes sent heat to Eamonn's face, and he looked away from her, finding Ree at her post.

Ree had witnessed him control Hadli and heard it verified from Hadli's own mouth. She was close with those in the palace. She might have some sway with the King. Perhaps Taularen would listen to her. Believe her.

The warmth in Eamonn's cheeks continued up to the tips of his ears as he realized he was more concerned with Ree getting this information to King Taularen than he was at how upset his actions had made Leyna. A new wave of shame overcame him, and he dropped his head.

"I did. I'm sorry," Eamonn said, pinching the bridge of his nose with his face to the floor. "I thought I could use it to find out whether or not you were telling us the truth."

A long breath left Leyna's nose, and she seemed to relax a little, straightening and hugging herself against a cool wind that blew through the pavilion.

"I know it's hard for you to trust me. I wouldn't trust me either." Hadli's glare only deepened as he spoke. "But you either have to choose to trust me or send me packing. Getting in my head makes you no better than Rothgard."

Has he been talking to Leyna? Eamonn doubted Hadli and Leyna had shared many words at all, let alone discussed Leyna's issues with Eamonn using Avarian magic. Maybe they were on to something.

"I'm sorry. It seemed like the right thing to do in the moment." Eamonn had been looking at Hadli, but his eyes were drawn to Leyna as her deep frown returned. With an exhale, she turned on her heel and strode through the pavilion and out the front, her clipped steps echoing off the high ceiling.

"Leyna, wait!" Eamonn called after her, following close behind. She had descended the steps leading to the front entry when Eamonn reached her. He took her hand and swirled her around to face him. "I was trying to help. I thought that if I—"

"It should *never* seem like the right thing to do, Eamonn." Leyna's chin quivered, and she worked the muscles in her jaw. Her eyes moved back and forth as she bored into Eamonn's. Loose curls framed her face and blew in the breeze, but Leyna didn't move to tuck them away. "Taking over a person's mind is *never* the right thing to do, regardless of the information you could learn. The Kaethiri gave it up for a reason. I didn't understand at first, but I do now. It crosses a line."

"I know, it was wrong. I said I was sorry," Eamonn said, his raised brows wrinkling his forehead. "I got caught up in it once I realized I'd gotten into Hadli's mind, but it really was an accident." He didn't have to include that he'd been trying to see if he could read Hadli's thoughts before he found himself in control of Hadli's will. Leyna clearly wouldn't understand.

Leyna didn't say anything in response. She crossed her arms and turned her head, looking off into the garden as the wind continued to blow strands of blonde hair across her face.

"Leyna."

The single word pulled her gaze back to Eamonn, and her throat bobbed as she swallowed. Eamonn saw her mind whirring behind her eyes, putting together sentences that may never find her lips.

"I really am sorry."

Leyna sighed and closed her eyes as she dipped her head briefly. "I'm not convinced you understand why it bothers me."

"We went through this in Avaria." Eamonn's voice came out as a murmur, keeping the words in the space between him and Leyna. "Hadli just said it, too. It makes me no better than Rothgard."

"I agree. So do the Kaethiri. And you know it's true, too. The thing is, Eamonn..." Leyna's piercing stare found him again. "You think you have a right to it where Rothgard doesn't. You think you have a valid reason where Rothgard doesn't. What you're missing is that no matter what, it's wrong."

Eamonn inhaled through his nose and bit back his next words. He didn't want to argue with Leyna, but she didn't understand. He did have a right to the magic, and he did have a valid reason to use it. He shouldn't have used it on Hadli—that was never his intention or his goal—but if he could access Kaethiri magic when he and Rothgard met again, he wouldn't hesitate to use it.

"See?" Leyna said, throwing her hands into the air. "You won't say anything because don't think it's wrong!"

"Only when it comes to Rothgard." Eamonn tempered the passion of the words that begged to be spoken. A biting, unfamiliar fury threatened to rise up within him, but Eamonn stopped it. He wasn't angry at Leyna, so where was this coming from? "I swear to you, I didn't mean to take control of Hadli. It was wrong of me to keep control once I had it. But Leyna," he said, lowering his head closer to hers so that their white puffs of breath mingled in the air between them, "it's the best way to make sure Rothgard is stopped for good."

Leyna stepped back, her chest rising with an incensed breath.

Before she could say anything in response, Eamonn continued, letting fervor ripen his tone. "Rothgard is weak, but if he gets to the abode, he won't stay that way. If I can do this, I can end it. No army. No bloodshed. Just me and him."

"But—"

"Just *listen* to me, Leyna. Please." He gripped both of her hands and stared her down. "If we plan this well, we don't have to get Kinrid and Gilleth's army involved. No one else has to become a victim of Rothgard. I can use the magic I was born with to bring an end to this."

Leyna said nothing, but her nostrils flared again, and dense puffs of white appeared in front of her nose as she pulled her eyes from Eamonn.

"What about his amulet?"

Eamonn spun to see Hadli behind him, stopped halfway down the steps of the pavilion where he watched them, his hands on his hips.

"What?"

"Rothgard's amulet. The one he made. Or *had* made, rather." Hadli came down the rest of the steps and strode closer to Eamonn. Taran and Teiyn appeared in the entryway, with Ree in the shadows behind. "Would that prevent him from being controlled?"

Eamonn didn't have a quick response. The thought hadn't before occurred to him. Rothgard had some of Eamonn's own blood. Would it be enough to protect him from another Kaethiri's control?

"So there's not even a guarantee it would work," Leyna said, and Eamonn glanced back at her before finding Hadli again.

"I don't think it would be a problem," Eamonn said after a moment. "The Réalta doesn't contain Avarian magic. It channels it, amplifies it. Amulet or not, he has some of my blood. I already held his mind twice, and he was able to control me; well, the human side of me. I had to learn how to resist that control on my human side, and it's not easy. I doubt that's something Rothgard has taken the time to consider."

"You doubt?" Leyna's voice was as sharp as a hawk's talons and cut just as deep. "You're willing to face him alone based on what you *think* Rothgard has or hasn't taken into consideration?"

This time, Eamonn only looked back at Leyna through the corners of his eyes with his head half turned to her. His jaw worked as he bit back an argument. He tasted the irritation on his tongue, and he knew whatever he said to her would be in anger.

"If it helps," Hadli said slowly, pulling Eamonn's attention again, "I don't think Rothgard has thought of it, either. He was so consumed with having the new amulet and the fact that it worked that I don't think anything like that crossed his mind. He's aware it doesn't work as well as yours, but I think he sees that as his only problem."

Eamonn's eyes narrowed as he studied Hadli, his head slightly tilted. That was convenient, especially considering Hadli brought up the problem only to provide a solution. He had put some trust in Hadli—enough to bring him here and have conversations like this with him—but was it enough to believe every word that came out of his mouth?

If he was going to believe anything Hadli said, Eamonn realized he would have to believe all of it. He couldn't pick and choose what he assumed might be the truth. He might be entirely led astray about some things and miss the truth in others. No, if he was going to put his faith in Hadli, it had to be all his faith. And if Hadli was lying about any of it, Eamonn would have to deal with the consequences later.

"Let's say I believe you," Eamonn said, crossing his arms tightly over his chest. "If that's the case, I could still command Rothgard. He's mostly human. And if he's not prepared to defend himself from Avarian magic coming after his human side, I'll be able to get him under my control."

A sigh from behind turned Eamonn around again. Leyna's face and shoulders had fallen. Any distress or vexation had evaporated from her features. Her gaze was hard but had transformed from blistering to icy, as cold as the wind that gusted around them.

"So that's it? You're listening to *him*," she said with a pointed glare at Hadli, "and you're still planning on doing this." Her eyes softened as she said, more tenderly, "Don't you remember what Imrilieth said? Using magic in that way corrupts your human side. It damages your soul."

Eamonn touched Leyna gently on her shoulder before taking both of her hands in his. "I promise it won't," he murmured. "It's just for Rothgard, and never again."

Leyna's face of stone returned, and she stepped back from Eamonn, her hands slipping out of his grasp. Her eyes shone as she pulled her cloak against the wind. "You think you're incorruptible, Eamonn. You're not."

She passed Eamonn and Hadli on her way back to the pavilion, speaking quietly to Taran and Teiyn as she ascended the steps. The twins turned and entered with Leyna, but Ree remained just inside the entryway, still watching Eamonn and Hadli. A rush of embarrassment tore through Eamonn's body as the realization sank in. They'd had an audience for their debacle, and he probably said more in front of Ree than he should have.

Her narrowed eyes were fixed on Eamonn, watching him with her head tilted slightly back. What was running through her mind? What did she think of Eamonn now, of who he was and what he believed?

And, more importantly, what would she pass on to her king?

TWENTY-TWO

King Taularen sat in his green velvet chair, lounging to the side with his weight resting on one of the chair's arms. He looked truly bored, as if wondering why Eamonn and his group were there, yet it was the King himself who had invited them back.

After Dorylss, Kinrid, and Gilleth had pleaded with the kings of their respective provinces to seek another audience with Taularen, trying new arguments to better appeal to his ego, they had received word from the palace that Taularen would see them again. They were a little surprised, given the finality of his refusal at their previous council, but thankful.

Eamonn had a sneaking suspicion that it wasn't his friends or even the other provinces' kings that had convinced Taularen to grant them another audience. Though Ree never defined her official role at the palace, Eamonn had begun to gather that she was more important than she let on.

A robust allegro on a faraway grand piano had met them when they'd stepped foot in the grand entrance hall, accompanying them through the corridor and into the king's council chambers, but was promptly cut off as the door to the room closed behind them.

"We sincerely appreciate the opportunity to return, Your Majesty," Kinrid began as everyone took a seat.

"Silence," Taularen said, his boredom replaced with irritation. "I only care to see Eamonn's magic."

Eamonn's throat bobbed. *Definitely Ree.*

Kinrid did not object or attempt to speak again. Eamonn met Taularen's scrutinizing gaze and took a deep breath. Once again, their meeting hinged on him. It could easily end in further embarrassment for him and a quick dismissal of their group.

"I can't imagine you would intentionally withhold your magic from me last time, Eamonn, so I am giving you another opportunity to prove it to me."

All eyes turned to Eamonn, and as he scanned them, he paused momentarily on Leyna. She, like the others, watched eagerly to see what he might do, but a distinct sadness lingered behind her eyes.

They'd barely spoken in the day since he had accidentally used magic on Hadli. She always found reasons to excuse herself from his presence or engage someone else in conversation.

Eamonn had hurt her—hurt them. This was something on which they might never see eye-to-eye. Having her so distant from him again, after finally learning what it was like to have her as his own, nearly ripped Eamonn's heart in two. He was counting on the hope that it would only take a little time for her to come around. She would see. She would learn that Eamonn was right, and he was just doing what was necessary. His soul would remain fully intact.

But he couldn't dwell on thoughts of her. He had to show King Taularen his magic this time. It was their last chance, and they all knew it.

Eamonn slowly stood from his chair and stared at the King of Miren. Hyfell stood to the king's right, his interlaced hands hanging in front of him. Something in the advisor's manner rubbed Eamonn the wrong way, but not in the same manner as Taularen. Hyfell seemed out of place in court. His large frame and scarred skin seemed more befitting for a battlefield than a king's council.

No distractions. Eamonn shut out his thoughts of Hyfell, of Taularen, of Leyna. They would only get in the way. All that mattered now was finding his magic again.

Eamonn quietened his mind and focused his spirit. The hum of magic built in his body like the approaching hooves of a hundred horses. It filled him to his fingertips, and he felt the energy around him as though it were a tangible thing, but it ended there. He could whirl the wind, fan the fire, even put space between his feet and the ground, but Eamonn couldn't find Taularen's will. He struggled, searching through the air between them behind closed eyes, but the more he fought to put himself in Taularen's mind, the further from it he became.

Not again.

Panic closed Eamonn's throat, and he tensed all the muscles in his neck and jaw, but as he'd learned in Avaria, panicking made things worse. He tried to steady his breathing and ease his anxiety. Why wasn't it working? He'd managed it effortlessly the day before, hoping to learn if Hadli was being truthful with them.

But wait—that was it.

He was trying too hard.

In every instance of Eamonn's use of Avarian magic, it had happened as an extension of himself without even really trying. It hadn't been something he had to figure out how to do.

The trouble was, the pressure on him to succeed this time made him want to do nothing *but* try as hard as he could. He had to do this. He had to show Taularen what kinds of things Rothgard was capable of. Every fiber of his being *tried*.

So he changed his perspective. He let go of his expectations, decreased the thought he put into the magic. Instead, he immersed himself in his magic and dwelled there. Eamonn felt the energy reaching every ounce of his being, and he soaked his consciousness in it.

Magic wasn't simply within him.

He *was* magic.

Energy from all parts of the room centralized on Eamonn, filling him to capacity, and he found himself in Taularen's consciousness.

He opened his eyes as a smirk pulled at his cheek. The euphoria he'd felt in Avaria crashed over him like a wave. He was unstoppable. The magic coursed through his blood like a drug.

Now, Eamonn had to show everyone else in the room. He wouldn't do anything too drastic, respecting King Taularen as Miren's sovereign, but he wanted to do something out of character so that no one in the room would question who was in control.

"Fantastic, Eamonn!" Taularen cheered, beaming, as he stood and clapped in awe. "I have to concede; Rothgard must be as formidable an adversary as you say. I will admit, I was wrong." The king then spun in a circle with his arms spread wide, laughing. "I never thought I could be so wrong."

The other kings and their advisors gawked at Taularen before turning their attention to Eamonn. Kinrid's jaw rippled, Dorylss straightened and rested his hands on his thighs, and Gilleth openly snickered with her hand covering her mouth.

Then Eamonn found Leyna, her eyes fixed on her hands folded in her lap. Her shoulders rose and fell with deep breaths, but she didn't look at Eamonn. All the power and overwhelming feeling of success vanished. Everything within him wilted, and he cut the connection.

King Taularen came back to himself, inhaling sharply and blinking before his eyes locked on Eamonn, cutting him like razors. He pressed his lips together and the tendons in his neck stood out as though he suppressed anger. Whether it was anger at Eamonn for how he showcased his magic or more general displeasure at having less of an argument against them, Eamonn wasn't sure.

"How dare you humiliate me in such a way," Taularen said through clenched teeth. "You could prove your power without the theatrics."

"I needed the others to see it, too," Eamonn said with a shrug.

Taularen fell into his seat, fuming, and pushed himself forward with a white-knuckled grip on the arms of the chair. "I said before," he muttered, his voice guttural and deadly, "I am *not* mocked."

"You can't deny our plight now, Taularen," King Vinnerod spoke up. "You have seen for yourself the magic that Rothgard possesses. He could do that to you, and worse."

Taularen continued to glare at Eamonn, not acknowledging the Farnish King. Hyfell dipped his head down to Taularen's ear and whispered something. As the advisor spoke, Taularen's glower slowly eased and was replaced with his usual haughty defiance.

"You are mistaken, Vinnerod," he said, his voice as slippery as ice under a spring sun. "I have seen no evidence of this magic within Rothgard. I have merely heard claims of his possession of it." A sneer spread wide across King Taularen's face. "Even if this boy is half-Kaethiri, as he claims, there is no reason to believe Rothgard shares his blood."

King Vinnerod tried to interrupt. "But—"

"Besides," Taularen added with a dismissive wave of his hand, "as I said before, Miren's army is more than enough to not only withstand Rothgard but to vanquish him. Should he, in fact, possess such magic, and he conquers you and your provinces before coming to Miren, our army will put a stop to him and release you of his control." His sneer turned wicked as he looked again at Eamonn. "After all, I believe Eamonn himself suggested Miren play savior to you lot."

"With all due respect, Your Majesty, that's not what I meant."

"*Respect*," Taularen snarled. "Clearly, you don't understand the meaning of the word. This is *my* kingdom. You are my guests."

King Javorak cleared his throat. "Taularen, if I may—"

"You may *not*." Taularen shot a look at Javorak before glaring at the rest of the room's occupants in turn. "I have made my position abundantly clear, and no magic tricks or ancient sorcery will convince me otherwise." His gaze landed on Kinrid and Gilleth and his voice lowered to a growl. "If Farneth and Teravale fall and Rothgard comes here to make his claim on the country complete, I will send our army to fight. Until that time, Miren will not get involved."

A silence as heavy as lead settled over the room, magnifying the crackle of the fire. Eamonn sank back into his seat, his knees giving way to the decisiveness in Taularen's words. Their last hope, gone. He dropped his eyes to the luxurious rug at his feet and balled his hands into fists. The anger that welled within his heart felt sharper, more intense than before, as though it fed off the remnants of magic left behind from holding Taularen's mind.

Now, Leyna and the others would have to understand that Eamonn was their only choice. In Eamonn's mind, this had always been his battle. Maybe it was better this way. Lives might be saved if he was able to face Rothgard alone.

Gilleth sprang to her feet, her hand fisted on her hip where her sword might otherwise be. All the attention of the room fell on her.

"You're a coward, Taularen," she said through gritted teeth. "Despite your claims of might, you're a coward hiding behind the strength and numbers of your army."

"Gilleth," Kinrid warned in a low voice beside her.

"Your inane arrogance blinds you to the threat before your eyes. You care more for your reputation and your appearance than you do for anyone else, even the people of your own province. Even your family."

"Gilleth, that's enough."

Taularen slowly rose and lightly interlaced his fingers in front of him, watching Gilleth like a hawk does its prey. "You would be wise to listen to your companion, Gilleth te Inglair. You cannot protect yourself with the shield of your sister. I will grant you no clemency for her sake."

Gilleth closed her mouth and spoke no more, but her eyes eviscerated King Taularen from behind their gold-lined lids.

"I don't want to see any of you in my council chambers again concerning this matter. The door is closed and locked. I have given my final terms, and I will not change them."

King Taularen struck the chime and the door to the chamber opened, the footman waiting just inside for their exit. Eamonn stayed in his seat, trying to control his deep, shuddering breaths. Leyna had been right. Even with the demonstration of Eamonn's magic, Taularen still did not see the threat. Or he saw but refused to believe it.

Some of the guilt fell from Eamonn's shoulders, knowing that Taularen would have denied them regardless of whether or not Eamonn could prove his magic, but a new burden settled upon him in its place. He was their best chance against Rothgard. Kinrid and Gilleth's army could be his backup if anything went badly. Eamonn wouldn't send them into an avoidable battle and risk lives when he could attempt to take hold of Rothgard's mind and rid the world of his presence.

Dorylss and Leyna rose to leave, and Kinrid took Gilleth by the elbow to guide her out of the room. She still fumed, her stare shooting daggers at Taularen, but she went with Kinrid. It had been obvious since before they ever came to Miren that Gilleth had some kind of issue with the king, and now they knew Taularen had a connection to her sister. Eamonn followed Kinrid and Gilleth, wondering if Taularen's link to Gilleth's sister might be prompting some of his resistance to them.

In the hallway, Eamonn was met with silence. The music—a constant every other time they had walked through the palace—had ended.

The party had taken a carriage to the palace again, and this time, Eamonn had no desire to walk back. One foot was inside the carriage, Eamonn the last one in, when a soft hand grazed his arm and he stopped in his tracks.

"There's something you need to know." The shadowy, hooded figure of Ree had appeared out of thin air behind Eamonn. Sunlight barely reached her eyes in the darkness her cloak created, her face almost entirely hidden. "Come back after dark, same place as before."

Eamonn stepped down from the carriage and faced Ree. "What is it?"

She was already backing away from Eamonn. "I can't linger. Come back tonight."

"Just me? Or everyone?"

Already clinging to the shadows of the palace gardens, Ree replied, "The same ones who came before, but be discreet."

Ree hung right past a tree and slipped into the beginnings of the hedge maze, gone as quickly as she had appeared, more like a mist than a human.

Eamonn blinked, not quite sure if he'd imagined her, then he turned to enter the carriage, sliding onto the bench beside Leyna as the coachman closed the door behind him. She was looking at him for the first time that day, something foreign in her expression. It wasn't curiosity—Eamonn could see in her eyes that she knew who the hooded figure was. Her throat bobbed and she turned her gaze away from him. Was she still distrusting of Ree? Eamonn was under the impression Leyna didn't like her very much.

"Who was that, lad?" Dorylss asked quietly after the carriage had pulled away.

"Remember the girl I told you about?"

In his peripheral vision, Eamonn noticed Leyna look at him out of the corner of her eye.

"Ree?"

Eamonn nodded. "She said there's something we need to know, and she wants me to come back tonight."

"Just you?"

Leyna had turned her head to look at Eamonn with a deep crease between her eyebrows, the terse astonishment in her question unmistakable.

Eamonn locked eyes with her, something in his stomach flipping unexpectedly at the fierce hold of her stare. "No," he replied, keeping his voice soft and matter-of-fact. For some reason, he felt the need to defend himself, but not so much that Leyna might wonder why. "She said those of us who were in the garden yesterday."

"Who is Ree?" Kinrid asked, and Eamonn gave what little backstory he had of her. "We're certain she can be trusted?"

"I believe so, yes," Eamonn answered. The carriage pulled up in front of the guest house, so he had to wrap up his explanation. "She does some kind of work for the palace. I think she was the one who got us the audience with Taularen today. She saw me use magic, and she seems to understand the threat Rothgard poses."

Dorylss nodded. "Go tonight, then. See what she has to say."

Eamonn left the carriage first and extended his hand behind him to help Leyna out. Her eyes remained on his outstretched hand for a moment, as though contemplating, and then she placed her hand in his own. Eamonn's heart soared to feel the warmth of her palm against his. A sudden, overwhelming desire to be alone with her rushed through him. He wanted to explain himself, show her all the good of his intentions, and repair whatever little crack had fractured them the day before. And then, he wanted to hold her, breathe in the scent of her hair, find his lips on hers. Know everything was okay. It had been too long since they'd had a private moment, constantly in the presence of one or more of their other companions, and he needed to slip away with her somewhere.

Leyna didn't release their grasp as they entered the guest house, and Eamonn ran his thumb over the back of her hand. Maybe they would find some time.

TWENTY-THREE

THE GARDEN WOULD BE too dark to navigate if not for the pale light from the waning crescent moon. Not that it was easy to navigate in the daytime. They still fully relied on Ree to guide them through the tall hedges to the pavilion where they had practiced magic. Without light in these parts of the garden, they were almost entirely concealed, but they also had a hard time finding their way.

Leyna stuck close to Eamonn, her hand firmly in his as he walked in front of her. She'd hoped they would have a chance to find some time to themselves after leaving their council meeting at the palace, but the opportunity never arose.

Now that Eamonn had been able to control not only Hadli's will, but also Taularen's as well—and intentionally, at that—a growing fear rose within Leyna that Eamonn would insist upon attempting his magic against Rothgard. He probably believed he even had a stronger argument now, too, with King Taularen refusing to ally with them under no uncertain terms. She was both afraid for him and furious at him, wishing he wouldn't endanger himself under a high and mighty notion of being the "only one" who could defeat Rothgard, and still upset that he didn't see the inherent wrongness of what he wanted to do. Maybe Rothgard deserved it, but that wasn't up for debate. Eamonn wouldn't give up his claim to Avarian magic, even though he understood the risk to his soul. Even the slightest corruption that might stem from the times he'd already used Avarian magic terrified Leyna.

If only she could make him understand just what he was risking. She hated how their disagreement had pushed them apart, especially when Ree was continually making her presence known.

"Take a seat," Ree said once they had entered the pavilion. A fire blazed in the firepit in the center of the floor, and six thick logs had been arranged in a circle around it.

"You're sure no one will find us here? Not even with the fire going?" Hadli asked, the last besides Ree to sit down. He narrowed his dark eyes at her, the dance of the flames sending mysterious shadows across his face.

"Only two other people even know this place exists, and they don't come here anymore," Ree answered, the slightest edge of sadness in her voice. "So no, no one will find us out here. We can speak freely." She lowered to a log, returning Hadli's questioning gaze. "Or I suppose, I can speak freely to everyone who isn't you, considering your allegiances."

"*Past* allegiances." Hadli sat up straighter and crossed his arms. "Eamonn has decided to trust me. Doesn't that mean you should, too?"

"I have my own mind. I get to make it up how I choose. And if you must know, I haven't decided how I feel about you yet. Why exactly are you here?"

Hadli shrugged. "Because I was here last time."

"Because," Eamonn cut in, his gaze zeroed in on Hadli, "I've decided that if I'm going to trust you, I have to trust you fully."

Ree mirrored Hadli and crossed her arms, drumming her fingers on her upper arm. "Then I'll choose to put my faith in Eamonn's faith in you, for now. But just know"—she leaned forward, peering with skeptical eyes at Hadli across the fire—"I'm watching you."

Hadli smirked and seemed to relax some, bringing his elbows to his knees. "Be my guest."

"The *reason* we're here," Eamonn interjected, shifting his glare at Hadli to a questioning look to Ree. "What is it that we need to know?"

Ree released a heavy sigh, and her fingers mindlessly beat a rhythm on the hilt of her dagger. "I was in the palace before your meeting with the king. I overheard a conversation between him and his new advisor. They were discussing a plan. It sounded like they've been working on it for a while, possibly since Hyfell joined the court.

"King Taularen has no intention of allying Miren with your forces. He never had. When I overheard them, Hyfell was questioning Taularen's decision to bring you back to the council chambers today, but the king said it was only to—" Ree shook her head, her curls bouncing, as if she changed her mind about the end of her sentence. "He said it was only to see if you were telling the truth about your magic. But the point is, his decision was already made before you stepped foot into the palace again."

"We didn't know that for certain, but I'd thought that might be the case," Leyna said with a quick glance at Eamonn. She'd told him as much after their first council with King Taularen.

"Well, that's not the important part," Ree continued, and she leaned toward the fire, resting her forearms on her thighs. "Hyfell was questioning the king's decision because they had already made another plan." Ree waited a beat and took a breath. "King Taularen *wants* Teravale and Farneth to fall. Hyfell says he knows Rothgard's plan, which is to take Farneth next and Teravale shortly after. Taularen is just biding his time."

An unyielding vice clutched Leyna's heart. In her mind, of course, she already knew Rothgard wanted control of every province in Sarieth. But to hear it said out loud that he planned to force himself upon the people of Teravale as their new ruler... the thought made her sick.

"I swear, I didn't mean what I said the first time about him playing savior," Eamonn interrupted, panic flooding his features. "I was just trying to stroke his ego and see if that got him to at least halfway offer to help."

Ree scoffed. "Don't worry. I don't think he got the idea from you. I'm under the impression Hyfell fed it to him before you ever arrived. He and the king have formulated a plan that will have Taularen defeat Rothgard and step in as an alternative to him. He seeks to bring all the provinces under his own rule."

Around the fire, faces gaped back at Ree. An incredulous breath left Leyna's lungs, and she faced Eamonn to find him looking at her as well. So Taularen wanted Rothgard's power. He was likely jealous of him. Leyna couldn't understand why he'd agreed to meet with them at all if this had always been his plan.

Ree allowed a moment for her words to sink in before she spoke again. "His argument—if Rothgard conquers Teravale and Farneth—will be that clearly, the other provinces in Sarieth are too weak to be ruled on their own; that Rothgard was flawed in his methods and motivations, but his idea of uniting the country under one banner isn't a bad one. King Taularen wants to fulfill that goal: the first King of Sarieth." She spoke the last words with mock regality that dripped with contempt.

"Surely people won't go along with that," Teiyn said, furrowing her brow. "Rothgard is getting away with it because he has magic. King Taularen does not."

Taran turned to his sister, frowning. "No, but if all the provinces fall to Rothgard and King Taularen brings Mirish forces to eliminate him, the provinces will owe him a debt."

"Recognizing Taularen as king over all Sarieth is too high a price for such a debt." Teiyn didn't hide the worry etched in her features.

"Maybe not," Taran replied with a shrug. "It's possible that many *will* see him as a savior. They won't know this was his plan from the start. People might be happy to have him as an alternative to Rothgard rather than restore the monarchies."

Teiyn's eyes searched the fire and she swallowed hard. A pang of worry stabbed at Leyna's heart to see Teiyn so crestfallen. Bubbly, optimistic Teiyn, disheartened. Leyna didn't know it was possible. Apparently, the prospect of having their entire world turned upside down—whether with Rothgard as a ruler or the King of Miren—was what would finally quell her spirit.

New questions emerged in Leyna's mind, and she brought the conversation back to Ree. "How were you in a position to overhear all of this? I understand you work with the palace, but the King and his advisor wouldn't be careless with their words, would they?"

Ree chewed on her lip as she stared into the fire. Seconds passed and she didn't answer Leyna's question. There was something she wasn't telling them, something she didn't want them to know.

Eamonn sat up straight and whipped his head to face Ree. "You aren't just 'Kingdom Security.' To be that close to the king... You're in the king's personal guard, aren't you?"

Ree lifted her eyes to Eamonn but said nothing. Leyna assumed she couldn't admit it, which was probably why she had given them the vague occupation of "Kingdom Security" when they first met.

"Well," Leyna said, lifting her eyebrows, "that really gives new weight to what you've said."

With a sigh, Ree sat back and propped her foot against the side of her log. "Trust me, since Hyfell put the idea in his head, it's all the king can see. He won't let anything get in his way, but he's letting Rothgard do the dirty work."

Eamonn dipped his head a fraction closer to Ree. "And you disagree with what he's doing." It was a statement, not a question, as though Eamonn had already concluded it himself.

Ree nodded, her lips pressed into a thin line. "But I can't openly oppose him. Not until it's dire."

The pops of wood in the fire echoed off the pavilion's high ceiling. Leyna didn't know what to say, and it seemed neither did anyone else. Her blood started to boil as she thought of Taularen, not just unwilling to come to their aid but awaiting their defeat.

Hadli's voice rose in the quiet, and Leyna found him staring intensely at Ree. "But wouldn't it be better to have Taularen over Rothgard?"

A fierceness overcame Ree as she leveled her gaze with Hadli. "Taularen might be better than Rothgard in many ways, but believe me, you still would not want him to be the leader of this entire country." Hadli backed down from her challenge, and Ree scanned the circle. "You all have already seen how Taularen only wants to be viewed as great: to be respected, feared, no matter what he has to do to achieve it. Most Mirish are too blind to see it. They want the same greatness for Miren: 'Miren above all.' They give little thought to anyone else." She snapped her attention back to Hadli. "Is that the kind of ruler you want? Do you want a king who only cares about proclaiming his might and the might of his people? He would strip the other provinces of their best resources and let whatever remained fall to ruin."

A painful silence settled over them. Hadli slightly bowed his head as though put in his place by Ree's speech, but his eyes flicked up from under his brows to watch her again. He didn't seem upset or even in disagreement, but something in his stare caught Leyna's attention. Hadli seemed to hang on Ree's every word. She wanted to point it out to Eamonn, but she couldn't, not right there.

Eamonn's voice brought Leyna back to the present. "Those are strong words for a Mir. Especially strong for the king's own guard."

Ree slightly lifted her chin but dropped her eyes, and her throat bobbed. "I'm not disloyal," she said, her voice soft but strong, "but I'm not blind either. Being close to the palace gives more insight than many other Mirs are granted. But he's still my king." She pulled the dagger from the sheath at her thigh and turned it over in her hand, examining it in the orange light of the flames. "Miren is corrupt, but by appearances, you'd never know it. But that's kind of the point. As long as things look grand and extravagant and wonderful, and the people are well off, no one cares if the king is less than honest in his dealings."

Firelight glinted off the blade in shards across Ree's face as she studied it. Her expression was downcast, and Leyna believed every word she had spoken. She may have had an issue trusting Ree at first, but she heard the conflict riddled in Ree's words and saw it written on her face. Ree's disdain for the king's intentions was as palpable as her loyalty to her province. Maybe King Taularen hadn't always been so power-hungry. Maybe he would have been happy to remain—in his mind, at least—as the ruler of the most stable and prosperous province in Sarieth, had it not been for his new advisor.

His *new* advisor.

"Ree," Leyna began slowly, the questions forming in her mind as she spoke, "how long has Hyfell been the king's advisor?"

The blade stilled in Ree's hands as she met Leyna's eyes. "A few weeks."

"And how did he come to be in the palace?"

"The king's previous advisor died. He was old; he'd been an advisor to Taularen's father as well."

Eamonn jumped in, possibly following Leyna's hunch. "Where did Hyfell come from?"

"He was a lower member in the king's council, but Taularen chose him because he liked his ambition and loyalty. He'd only been in the king's service about a month or two, but he'd made enough of an impression on Taularen to be chosen as the replacement when the old advisor died."

"Huh." Leyna shared a look with Eamonn, glad she wasn't the only one suspicious of Hyfell.

"If he's the one putting these ideas in Taularen's head, I bet he has an agenda of his own," Eamonn said, and Leyna nodded vigorously.

"The question is," she continued, "what does Hyfell have to gain from it?"

"Nothing." The single word from Ree deflated Leyna. "At least, nothing more than the king does. The Mirish want to see Miren prosper. You could take a poll on the street and find out that the majority of people—if not all—would be elated to have their king as King of Sarieth."

Leyna tapped the toe of her shoe against the cold, hard stone of the pavilion's floor. Ree had a point. Maybe she and Eamonn were following a hunch that led nowhere. She looked at him again, and he shrugged.

"So, where does that leave us?" Teiyn asked, despondent. Taran reached out to her and rested a reassuring hand atop her shoulder. "Where do we go from here?"

Eamonn straightened, opening his mouth and taking a breath to speak. Leyna closed her eyes. She already knew what he was about to say, and she didn't want to hear it.

But it was Ree's voice that followed, not Eamonn's. "I have some ideas about that."

Leyna's eyelids flew open. She stared at Ree expectantly, but not before her eyes slid over Eamonn. He frowned at Ree, his mouth still open, but he didn't retort.

"There's one more thing that goes along with all this, and it might be your ticket to allying with Miren, whether Taularen likes it or not. Hyfell is writing missives to send to our military's generals detailing their plan and the king's intent to let Teravale and Farneth fall to Rothgard. They want the generals preparing their battalions for war with Rothgard after that happens. The king is supposed to sign them and seal them with his ring tomorrow evening, and they will be distributed the following day."

"So, what exactly are you suggesting?" Hadli asked. His stare never left Ree, though it had transformed from curious to concerned.

Ree met Hadli's eyes. "Those missives are proof of King Taularen's plan to seize control of the country for himself, which is the same thing Rothgard is attempting. The kings of Teravale and Farneth would view it as an act of war. If we can get our hands on the missives, we might be able to blackmail Taularen into joining the alliance. Since he's refusing to join of his own accord, we'll have to force him."

"And how are we obtaining these missives?" The suspicion in Eamonn's voice was unmistakable. He must have guessed Ree had something specific in mind.

"You're going to need to get in the palace and steal them," Ree replied, so evenly and matter-of-factly that she might have been detailing what she'd eaten for dinner. "After the king has signed and sealed them, of course."

"Why don't you just take them?" Leyna furrowed her brow and angled her head. "You're already in the palace."

Ree's confidence shattered and she dropped her eyes, wringing her hands in her lap. "I can't be more implicated than I already am. I may not agree with what the king is doing, but the most I can do is help you here, now."

Eamonn rubbed his chin. "Wouldn't it be easier to get the missives after they leave the palace? We could catch the courier on his route or wait at the military headquarters to intercept."

Ree shook her head, her free curls bouncing with the movement. "No, that won't work. The courier will have the letters on his person and hand deliver each one to the generals. Unless you're planning on taking out the courier." She crossed her arms again and raised her eyebrows as a small smile played across her lips. "But I imagine you're not exactly the killing type. And if you're not, then you have a loose end who may get back to the king before you do."

Eamonn's knee bounced as he studied the orange flames dwindling in the firepit. He looked thoughtful, like he was considering their options, but what other choice did they have? This was their best course of action. They had no more cards to play against Taularen. As it stood, all they could do would be to move against Rothgard themselves and do their best, which no doubt included Eamonn again arguing to control Rothgard's will.

"What are you worried about?" Hadli asked, and Leyna found that his gaze had finally moved from Ree to Eamonn. "We've pulled off harder stuff together."

Eamonn's mouth fell open as his eyebrows lifted, and he sat ramrod straight. "Oh, no," he said with a shake of his head. "No, no, no, no. You are *not* getting involved in this."

"Why not?" Hadli asked, and he seemed genuinely offended. "I'm the only other person in this group who was actually a thief, and a good one at that."

Leyna's breath caught in her throat. She watched Eamonn gawk at Hadli. He was still ashamed of his previous life as a thief, and here came his old partner in crime making it seem like an accomplishment.

Ree's lashes lowered over her eyes as another smirk curled her lips. "I'm not sure that's something you want to brag about."

"It's out of the question." Eamonn shot to his feet and stared Hadli down, his hands balled fists at his sides.

Hadli stood in response to Eamonn, slower and with purpose. He folded his arms against his chest. "I thought you said you trusted me."

"I did. I *do*." Eamonn squeezed his eyes shut and pinched the bridge of his nose before rubbing fingers across his forehead and down the side of his face. "But this is *big*. And it could go really, really wrong."

"Which is exactly why you need me." Hadli didn't back down. He shifted on his feet and tipped his chin up. "Come on, it'll be like old times."

Leyna saw the muscles in Eamonn's jaw work as he briefly closed his eyes and murmured, "That's what I'm afraid of."

"You *did* say you had decided to trust him. Fully." Ree shrugged. "I don't know your history, but accomplished thieves are exactly what's needed for the job. Better chance of you getting in and out with the letters without being seen."

The way Ree said "accomplished thieves" made Leyna's stomach flip as she worried about how it affected Eamonn. He'd been desperate to put that part of his life behind him, and he'd succeeded, so Leyna hated seeing him faced with it again. And she wasn't particularly thrilled to be reminded of it herself, either.

A grimace flashed across Eamonn's face before he raised his hands, palms turned out in defeat. "Fine. But we'll need a good plan. We have to be in sync every step of the way."

A wide smile spread across Hadli's face, and he sat back down. "Like I said, it'll be just like old times."

Eamonn rolled his eyes before taking his seat again.

"Don't worry. We'll come up with a plan and make sure we're all on the same page," Ree said, leaning to her left toward Eamonn.

"We?" Leyna asked. She certainly didn't have the skill set to attempt thievery. "It's just Eamonn and Hadli doing this, right?"

"Well, we can make the plan together, just so we all know what's going on. But I do have an idea how you, Taran, and Teiyn can play a role."

Leyna's heart leapt to her throat. She didn't want to be anywhere close to this. She would only get in the way. Nothing about her was sneaky or sly. Her going along would give them a greater chance of being caught and be an unnecessary distraction for Eamonn, who would no doubt feel obligated to keep her safe. No, she was happy to let Ree, Eamonn, and Hadli handle it.

"What would you have us do?" Taran asked, sitting up. At least someone was eager to help.

"I don't think we would make very good thieves," Teiyn chimed in. She'd regained some of her typical enthusiasm, her eyes brightening as she spoke.

"And too many people sneaking around the palace have a greater chance of being noticed."

Taran had a point. In something like this, having fewer people go after the missives would be smarter.

"You won't be doing the sneaking," Ree answered. The low flames caught the twinkle in her eye as she added, "Well, not the same sneaking."

Leyna's stomach squirmed again, the thought of whatever it was Ree had in mind for her already making her nervous.

"Let's meet again tomorrow." Ree stood and doused the fire. "I'll bring diagrams of the palace's layout, and we'll go from there. We'll wait for nightfall to go in; the cover of darkness and fewer people around the palace will work to our advantage."

The cold struck Leyna with a new sharpness, and she shivered under her heavy cloak. The thought of going to Eamonn and linking arms with him crossed her mind, but before she could even talk herself out of it, Eamonn had stepped away from her and closer to Ree.

"Why are you helping us?" he asked. His voice was quiet but not so low that the others didn't hear.

Ree rolled her shoulders back as she kicked the ashes around the fire pit. "Because, despite what the king believes, you've convinced me that Rothgard has to be stopped. I have it in my power to do something about it, so I am."

She raised her shoulders in a slight shrug and led the way out of the maze again. Eamonn walked beside her, whispering with her about something. Leyna kept close behind them but couldn't figure out what he said. Maybe he wanted to understand Ree's motives better. Maybe it was misgivings about Hadli he hadn't made known to the group. He might want Hadli to believe he trusted him even if he didn't. Or maybe it was about his past as a thief.

Whatever it was, it had pulled Eamonn to Ree's side, with Leyna following them in the brisk moonlit night. An emotion she couldn't quite name seized her heart with an iron grip. Was it jealousy? Leyna shook her head. She had nothing to be jealous about. It was silly, especially given everything else they faced.

"I wouldn't worry about that if I were you."

Hadli's whispered voice came closer to Leyna's ear than she'd expected, and she jumped. She whipped her head over her shoulder to find him right behind her, and she took a few steps to add a little distance between them. One side of Hadli's mouth lifted, amused.

"What are you talking about?"

"Oh, don't give me that," he said good-naturedly. He nodded toward Eamonn and Ree. "Them. It's not a thing, don't worry."

Leyna blew out a breath. Hadli was the last person she wanted to talk to, especially about this. "Why do you say that?"

The grin pulled Hadli's mouth even more, and his eyes glinted in the silver light of the moon. "Because," he whispered, coming close to Leyna again, "she likes me."

The laugh escaped Leyna in a burst before she could think to stop it, and Eamonn and Ree turned around.

"What's funny?" Eamonn asked, and Leyna watched his eyes travel from her to the man at her shoulder.

Leyna cleared her throat and shook her head, dropping her eyes to her feet to regain her composure. "Nothing at all," she said, allowing herself to meet Eamonn's gaze.

Eamonn arched an eyebrow, but he only said, "We need to be quiet. We can't be noticed." He fell behind Ree as they continued through the hedges.

Leyna hoped Eamonn wouldn't bring it up later. She didn't have a good alternative to the truth, which she wasn't interested in sharing. But after they had slipped through the low door in the palace wall and returned to the street, the same low voice floated to Leyna's ear again.

"It wasn't *that* funny."

Leyna fought a smile and didn't look back at Hadli.

TWENTY-FOUR

"Okay, so here's the layout of the parts of the palace that you need to know."

Ree pulled a piece of paper from her trouser pocket and unfolded it several times until it covered a good chunk of the pavilion floor in front of them, and she laid stones on the corners to hold it down. She sat by the map on folded knees. "Here is the Strategy Room, which is where the missives should be." She pointed to a square in the hand-drawn depiction of the palace's ground floor. "Hyfell will have written them in here and left them for the king to seal, but I can't tell you exactly where in the room they'll be."

The fire roared in the middle of the space, giving the group light and heat to work by as a black night overtook the fading grey of dusk. Eamonn had taken a seat on the pavilion floor by Ree, and Hadli leaned over their heads behind them. Taran and Teiyn stood on the other side of the diagram close to Leyna, who hugged herself and ran her hands up and down her arms to warm them.

"This corridor that leads to the Strategy Room runs the length of various official rooms, and it meets up with this corridor here," Ree said as she traced her finger along the map, "which connects to an entrance on the side of the palace near the gardens. That's where you'll go in. You'll be hidden if you take the path through the hedge maze to the palace."

"How will we find the way?" Eamonn asked. He kept his head hunched over the map but flicked his eyes up to Ree. "If you're not going to be involved in this, we need to know the path through the hedges to this door."

Ree nodded as if she expected the question. "Look for the leaves edged in white. There will be one in the hedge beside the correct path at each intersection. But make sure it's white, and not yellow."

"Where does yellow lead?" Leyna wondered, crouching down beside them. She hadn't noticed any such leaves on their way through the maze when she'd traveled through it, so she couldn't begin to wonder how Eamonn or Hadli would spot them, especially in the dark.

"Here," Eamonn replied automatically. Leyna drew her brows together and met his gaze. So he'd already noticed them. "I'd been wondering where the white ones led."

Leyna's lips pulled in a grin, but then she made a connection in her mind and her smile faltered. *It's a skill from him being a thief.* She wouldn't deny that Eamonn's previous, dishonest life was coming in handy for them now, but it still managed to unsettle her that he was, in a way, reverting to his old ways.

"Okay, so, for a little more detail," Ree continued, shifting on her legs to point to the other side of the paper, "you follow the white path of the hedge maze, and you'll come to a service door. I'll unlock it for you. It's primarily for gardener access, but they aren't the only ones who use it, so you'll want to be cautious." The corner of her mouth tilted, and she huffed out a laugh. "Of course, that goes without saying. But you two are well-acquainted with the necessities of a good heist, yes?"

Eamonn drew his brows together and nodded, but Hadli cracked a grin. "You don't even know the half of it." He clapped a hand on Eamonn's shoulder from behind, and Eamonn winced. "We got away with some of the most astounding thefts Erai has ever known—and not known. I'm still not sure old Jarrus knows what happened to that family dagger of his."

"And *I* still don't understand why you held on to it," Eamonn retorted as he rolled his eyes. "There was almost no point in stealing it if you weren't going to try to get what it was worth."

"The dagger was too high profile to get back into someone's hands in the city, even if it was through the black market." Hadli cocked his head as he explained with his palms turned up. "I trusted our buyers, but not who they sold to. It would be too easy to get back to us."

"So, again, why steal it in the first place?" Eamonn stood and turned to face Hadli's crooked grin.

Leyna heard the ire growing in Eamonn's voice and stepped forward before Eamonn could, holding up her hands to both men. "Can we focus, please? That's not important right now."

"I agree. You two are a team right now, and you have to behave as such." Ree swiveled on her heels toward them but didn't stand, prompting Eamonn and Hadli to return their attention to the diagram. She resumed dragging her finger in a path on the sketched map. "So, once you're in the palace, you follow this corridor until it ends, then turn here, and then you follow this one to the second door on your left. They should be empty; none of these rooms should be in use till morning."

"What if King Taularen and Hyfell are meeting about the missives in the Strategy Room?" Leyna gripped her arms again to control the trembling in her core. "They might be up late discussing their plans."

"I'll expect our thieves to make that call in the moment," Ree said with a gesture toward Eamonn and Hadli. "It's a possibility, but not a likely one. Unless something has changed, their plans are made. Once Taularen signs the missives, all he has to do is sit back and wait."

"What are we to do?" Teiyn grasped the top of the bag slung across her body, as though ready to open it and prepare a tonic of some kind from her assortment of ingredients. Teiyn had made healing elixirs for both Eamonn and Leyna before, using both knowledge and magic to add a special potency, and Leyna wondered if she could mix something to increase stealth or add protection or provide another benefit to their heist.

"You three I want waiting in the king's study, here, on the second level." Ree pointed to a square far from the Strategy Room. "There is a hidden door that connects to his library, which is where he should be that time of night."

Leyna's stomach twisted into unpleasant knots. What could Ree possibly have in mind that would put her so close to the king?

"There is a secret staircase that leads from the first level to the king's study. There is a long painting here"—she rested a finger on a nondescript part of her map—"that hides a door to that stairway. Eamonn and Hadli, once you have the missives, meet the others in the study. Distribute the letters among you.

That way, if Taularen manages to take the one you show in your possession as blackmail, you still have backups."

"Wait—we're confronting him with it tonight?" Leyna had assumed they would steal the missives to blackmail Taularen later, preferably with people like Dorylss and Kinrid and Gilleth there to do the actual blackmailing.

"You won't have another opportunity. He won't meet with you again. Ree sat back on her rear, propping an elbow on one knee and sliding her other foot under her bent leg. "Besides, you'll already be in the palace. I'll make sure the guards posted outside his chambers are otherwise occupied. Taularen will be taken by surprise with no one to come to his aid. It will be on your terms, not his, and that in itself will throw him off balance."

Leyna looked at Eamonn, wanting a different opinion, but he shrugged. "What other choice do we have? With any luck, we could have Miren joining the alliance by morning."

Or, the five of us could suddenly go "missing" for getting in Taularen's way. But she said nothing, regardless of her misgivings, since she seemed to be the only one opposed.

"So, what does that mean for us?" Taran asked. He absently waved his hand over the flames and made them dance in captivating movements.

"You, Teiyn, and Leyna are there for support of the magical variety." Ree nodded her head toward Taran's manipulation of the flames. "One against five, four of whom have magic, isn't good odds for the king."

"I can barely use magic," Leyna blurted, her confidence in Ree's plan crumbling more and more with every word. "Taran and Teiyn can, sure, but I haven't practiced nearly as much as I would like."

"But the king doesn't know that. A small display of magic might be all it takes to keep him in his place and prevent any attempt he might make to call the guards."

Teiyn nodded as her cheeks lifted slightly and orange light flickered wildly in her eyes. "And Taran and I can draw his attention to us."

"Don't worry about being convincing or intimidating. Just do what you are capable of so the king knows you can use magic, and then leave the rest up to us," Taran said.

Ree continued giving instructions, but Leyna's mind whirred so fast that she had difficulty keeping up. She didn't like Ree's plan at all. They all seemed to give Leyna much more credit than she deserved in regard to her magical abilities.

But, if this was the best they could come up with, Leyna would do as instructed. There was more on the line than successfully blackmailing Taularen into joining their alliance. Their lives could be at stake. Leyna didn't know the laws of Miren or what would happen to people snooping around the palace with the intent to blackmail the king, but she imagined it wouldn't be anything good.

"You have to make sure two things happen." Ree paused, locking eyes with each of them in turn. It brought Leyna back to the moment and she listened more closely. "Aside from getting in and out without being seen by anyone but the king, of course. One"—she held up a finger—"you take as many missives as you see to have plenty of backups. Two, you get the king to agree to join the alliance *in writing*. Do not expect to take him at his word. You need something that he signs and seals with his ring. Otherwise, the next time you confront him, he'll deny it."

Hadli nodded and crossed his arms. "We can do that."

"Good."

A low breeze blew through the pavilion, pushing loose leaves across the ground outside, and Leyna jumped. She closed her eyes and sighed. It was too early to be nervous.

"What do we do now?" she asked. The sooner they got this over with, the better.

"We get ready," Ree said with a nod. "We need the moon to rise and the palace to go to sleep before we go in, so we have a little time. I'll go on and lay the groundwork, and the rest of you should go back and change into something... more appropriate for sneaking. Meet back at the wall in an hour."

Ree spoke a few quiet words to Eamonn and Hadli while Leyna melted to the floor and scooted close to the fire, letting its heat bake her face until it was almost uncomfortable. She wrapped her arms around bent knees to keep her body heat from escaping. Taran and Teiyn sat near her, diving into conversation about their part of the plan. Leyna probably should have joined them, but she couldn't move. She'd frozen to the pavilion floor.

A hand reached out from Leyna's right and lightly touched her elbow. She turned to find Eamonn by her side, a soft, reassuring smile on his lips. He must have sensed her anxiety. Leyna took a deep breath as he moved his hand from her elbow to her fingers resting there and squeezed them.

"We've got this. Hadli and I know what we're doing, and you only have to do a little bit of magic."

The bite of tears stung Leyna's eyes, but she refused to let them build. They would give Eamonn the wrong impression, making her look more afraid than she felt. She was nervous about the heist and confrontation, but not to the point of tears. No, the tears came with the emotion that welled unwillingly inside her with Eamonn's touch.

A divide had wedged its way between them, and Leyna hated it, but neither could she accept Eamonn's approach to defeating Rothgard. She hadn't missed the increasing ire in him, noticing him so close to letting his anger get the best of him lately. He'd used Avarian magic to control others three times now—twice lately—and it wasn't a stretch to believe his change of temperament was the beginning of the corruption the Kaethiri had mentioned. Eamonn was changing, whether or not he saw it or would admit it.

But Leyna let him hold her hand, taking a moment to find comfort in his presence and forget how he wasn't quite the same. She tightened her fingers around his and wondered what they would look like going forward, if all went well and they could put this part of their lives in the past.

Eamonn took the pressure of her grip as an opening and sat closer to her, twining an arm around Leyna's back at her waist. To hell with their disagreement. Leyna rested her head on Eamonn's shoulder and felt—for the first time in days—that nothing had changed between them.

She pressed her eyelids closed and scrunched her eyebrows, praying it would last.

"I hope it works," Leyna finally whispered in response to Eamonn.

Eamonn leaned his head on top of Leyna's. "I think it will. I have faith. As much as I hate to say it, we *are* good at things like this, Hadli and me. We can do it."

"That's not the part I'm worried about."

Eamonn inhaled deeply through his nose. "He won't have a choice," Eamonn murmured as he let out a breath. "He'll have to set aside his ego this time."

He moved to kiss the top of Leyna's head, and it sent her heart racing. Maybe Hadli was right after all, and Eamonn had no interest in Ree.

But she couldn't dwell on it. They had work to do.

"We're going to blackmail the King of Miren," she said, lifting her head and looking at Eamonn, his face illuminated orange. "Are we insane?"

That got a smile out of him, and he dipped his head down. "Yeah, maybe. But I would expect sane people to give up."

Leyna chuckled and stood, wiping loose dirt from the seat of her dress, and Eamonn rose with her. "At least we've got that going for us." She gave him a smile—a true, genuine one that she didn't have the heart for even five minutes before—and joined Taran and Teiyn to review their part of the plan.

What they were doing was risky, possibly foolhardy, and not guaranteed to work, but they could all say they didn't give up. Whether that would land them in an alliance with Miren or in a Mirish prison remained to be seen.

TWENTY-FIVE

EAMONN HAD TRULY DRESSED for the occasion tonight: a tight dark shirt and matching trousers, a black hood to cover his sandy hair, and soft-soled shoes he'd purchased earlier that day to keep his footfalls silent.

It frightened him just how easily he could fall back into thieving, even after years away from it. Aside from the recent incident in Caen when he stole the medicine Leyna's mother needed, Eamonn hadn't stolen anything since his time with the Thieves' Guild over three years before. It didn't matter, though. His muscle memory came back as though it had never gone, and his body recalled how to quieten nerves before the theft.

He and Hadli fell into a familiar rhythm, picking up on each other's silent cues and body language without skipping a beat. They traveled through the maze from the pavilion to the palace, following the trail of white-edged leaves until they arrived at the service door. Hadli entered first and checked for late-night stragglers before waving Eamonn inside. Hadli had offered to take the lead, which he said had nothing to do with being the former head of their Guild and everything to do with the fact that he hadn't been seen at the palace before. He claimed if he ran into someone, he could better convince them he belonged there. He'd even shaved his beard to give him a more groomed, Mirish-adjacent appearance.

Eamonn kept several paces behind Hadli, following his signals through the quiet palace corridors. Deep red carpets covered white marble floors and further muffled their footsteps. Scents of jasmine and lavender perfumed the air, and the faint ticking of a large clock floated to their ears even though no clock was in sight. They came across no one in the dimly lit hallways, and Eamonn was thankful.

Hadli paused outside a set of white doors, identical to the other doors they had passed, and he raised his hand. Eamonn flattened his body against the darkest part of the wall as Hadli leaned against the door and listened. He nodded once, and Eamonn joined him.

With the slightest pressure, Hadli pushed down on the door handle to find it locked. Eamonn pulled a set of makeshift picks that Ree had procured out of the pouch at his waist and he went to work, his fingers remembering the lock-picking dance without trying. In seconds, the latch clicked, and they were inside.

The room was dark, so Eamonn located a lamp on a table inside before they shut the door soundlessly behind them. He struck a match and lit the lamp's oil, giving them just enough light to work by.

Alone in the room, they were willing to risk quiet speech. "I'll start at the desk, you look at the shelves," Hadli instructed in a low murmur, and Eamonn set the lamp on the desk to illuminate it and the shelves behind it.

The books and documents Eamonn searched through on the shelves offered proof that they had found the Strategy Room. Volumes on various histories, battles, and tactics filled the bookcases lining the walls of the room. Most of the books were relatively worn, and the shelves on which they sat were free of dust. Either the maids came through regularly and did an immaculate job, or the books were often pulled from their spots. Eamonn looked closer and found thin lines of dust on the empty part of the shelf between volumes, confirming the latter theory.

Why was Taularen perusing books on war and strategy so frequently? Was he preparing for a confrontation with Rothgard? Or with the other provinces, if they didn't readily accept his rule? Maybe his regular study was why the Mirish military was regarded as the strongest in the country.

"Here," Hadli whispered behind him, and Eamonn spun to face the desk. Hadli had lifted a false bottom in a desk drawer to locate several letters, along with a small leatherbound book, a coin, a heavy ring, and a piece of paper that appeared to be some sort of official document.

Hadli took a sealed letter off the top, opened it, and began to read, while Eamonn fingered the ring. It was masterfully crafted silver, the band formed to resemble the tree so commonly found in Mirish design. Where the branches converged was inlaid a large, round, milky white gemstone, translucent enough for light to shine through but not enough to see through. Eamonn slipped it on a finger and the heavy stone pulled the too-large ring upside down. He recalled seeing the ring on the king's finger in their meetings. It might be a king's ring, passed down through the generations of Miren's sovereigns.

Eamonn replaced the ring in the drawer and glanced at the other items. He could make out Taularen's name on the document ornately bordered with gold foil, as well as the name "Milena te Inglair." Eamonn's breath caught, recognizing Gilleth's surname.

Her sister.

The memory of their last time in Taularen's council chambers came back to him. *I will grant you no clemency for her sake.* Eamonn pushed the other items in the drawer aside and pulled the lamp over to better read the document at the bottom. At the top of the document, in flowy gold script, was written "Certificate of Marriage."

Eamonn's eyes widened and his stomach dropped. The King of Miren was married to Gilleth's sister.

"Look," Eamonn whispered, nudging Hadli to take his attention away from the missives. He pointed at the certificate in the drawer, and Hadli furrowed his brow.

"So?"

"Gilleth's sister," Eamonn explained. He realized Hadli barely knew either Gilleth or Kinrid and probably didn't know their family names. "The Queen of Miren."

Hadli's confusion instantly transformed into shock, and he met Eamonn's eyes. "How did we not know this?"

"I'm starting to think Gilleth isn't happy about it, so she doesn't talk about it," Eamonn replied. "There must be something deeper there. It would explain the issues she has with Taularen."

Hadli nodded, his mouth hanging open. "Yeah, it would."

Eamonn pointed to the letters in Hadli's hand. "That's them?"

Nodding again, Hadli handed one of the letters to Eamonn. "Six of them. I assume that's how many generals he has."

Eamonn tugged the wax of the seal off the letter and unfolded it, scanning his eyes over the contents. Just as Ree had said, Taularen and Hyfell's plan was laid out there. It was the perfect evidence, incriminating the King of Miren in a plot to allow the other provinces to fall at Rothgard's hand, only for him to step in after the fact and battle Rothgard, then declare himself Sarieth's king after Rothgard's defeat.

"All right," Eamonn whispered, tucking the missive into his pocket before holding his hand out for more. "Let's get to the king's study. The others should be waiting there now."

Hadli split the letters with Eamonn, and Eamonn blew out the lamp and returned it to its previous spot as Hadli listened at the door.

"Sounds quiet," he murmured when Eamonn rejoined him. "Let's go."

Hadli pulled the door open a fraction to listen more clearly for a second, then he swung it wide enough for Eamonn and himself to slip out. Eamonn swiftly set the lock back into place with his picks, and they crept down the hall in the direction of the hidden staircase to the king's quarters.

A sudden tightness gripped Eamonn's chest as he thought about Leyna waiting in the king's study, presuming she and the twins had made it inside all right. Fear for her safety rose within him like water filling a basin, but he stopped it before it could take over his senses. He needed to stay focused. Leyna had Taran and Teiyn and the bit of instruction Eamonn had imparted to her earlier. While they had waited in the pavilion for night to deepen, he had given her a few pointers about how to remain unseen and what to do if they came across someone. He hoped they'd had no trouble and hid in the shadows of the king's study even now.

Eamonn's thoughts came crashing to a halt as the soft thump of footsteps on carpet met his ears. Hadli must have heard them as well, freezing where he stood just ahead of a corner. Eamonn ducked behind a wide marble pillar that held a tall vase with a bountiful floral arrangement. It wasn't much cover, but it was something.

Hadli stuck a foot behind himself as though about to retreat to safety, but a deep voice carried through the quiet corridors and stopped Hadli before he had a chance to hide.

"Who's there?"

Eamonn watched from his cover as Hadli stiffened, then took a neutral stance where he stood.

Hyfell rounded the corner and came into Eamonn's line of sight. Eamonn pressed himself against the pillar and peeked through the gaps in the arrangement to see what was happening.

"What are you doing in here?" Hyfell questioned, no less intimidating than he'd been in the council chambers.

Some of Hadli's tension appeared to ease as he lifted his arms before gesturing down the corridor. Eamonn heard the low rumble of their voices but couldn't make out words. Since Hyfell hadn't immediately called the guard or captured Hadli on the spot, Eamonn assumed that their plan for being caught was working. Hadli was supposed to act as if he'd recently been taken on as a gardener and lost his way in the palace while tending to the numerous arrangements. Although, Eamonn had to stifle a laugh as he considered how Hadli had lost his touch. None in the Thieves' Guild had ever been caught in their years of thievery, and one mission back after so long away landed Hadli in the lap of people they were trying to evade.

The conversation continued longer than Eamonn would have expected, and he frowned. What kind of lies was Hadli having to spin to get away from Hyfell? Was Hyfell not buying it? Eamonn's heart fluttered with nerves, and the warmth of adrenaline started to pour through his veins.

Hadli's back was to Eamonn, so Eamonn couldn't read his expression. Hyfell drew his eyebrows together and crossed his arms as Hadli spoke. Hadli leaned in closer to the king's advisor and lowered his voice, and an alarm went off in Eamonn's head. Something had gone wrong. There was no way Hadli was still working the "lost gardener" ruse. Eamonn's heart thumped against his ribcage and a thin line of sweat formed along his brow.

Hyfell relaxed his expression and looked Hadli up and down before uncrossing his arms and waving one down the corridor where Hadli had gestured. He was letting him go.

Eamonn held his breath as Hyfell continued on his way, passing right by him, and Hadli disappeared around the corner after a brief glance behind him. Eamonn glided along the smooth surface of the pillar, his body practically molded into it, keeping opposite Hyfell as he walked by. He didn't dare move a toe until he no longer heard Hyfell's footsteps, and then he bolted in Hadli's direction.

Hadli hadn't gone far, waiting in a dark corner for Eamonn to catch up. He nodded once, wordlessly asking if Eamonn was all right, and Eamonn reflected the nod. Eamonn willed his heart to slow down as he and Hadli resumed sneaking.

Navigating the rest of the way to the secret stairs where Ree had directed them was less eventful. They located the painting she had described, which opened to reveal a narrow, circular shaft and a tight, spiral staircase. Eamonn breathed a little easier once they had closed themselves in the passage, embracing the concealment of the space. Ree certainly did have a thorough knowledge of the palace layout, but then, she would have to as part of the king's personal guard. She probably knew the entire city just as well, or close to it.

"What happened back there?" Eamonn asked in the quiet confines of the hidden staircase. "What did you say?"

"Oh, uh..." Hadli coughed. "He bought the 'new gardener' thing. Just told me I'd better not be wandering so late at night in the future."

Something in Eamonn's gut twisted, but he wasn't entirely sure why.

The circle of the ascent left Eamonn a little dizzy at the top, where a simple door awaited them, but he steadied himself and nodded to Hadli to open it.

They stepped into a room full of furniture, books, shelves, and paintings, and as Eamonn pushed the door closed behind them, he discovered that the other side was not a door but a shelf. Moonlight streamed through the tall windows that lined the wall beside the door, their long curtains having been pushed aside. Ree had instructed Leyna, Taran, and Teiyn to push back the curtains in the study for two reasons: to have a little visibility without lighting a lamp, and so Ree would know from the outside that they had made it there safely.

Eamonn released a deep sigh of relief at the sight of the open windows and started surveying the room, searching for its hidden inhabitants.

"Did you find them?" asked a soft voice to his right, and Eamonn looked in the direction of the sound. Teiyn.

"We have them," Hadli announced quietly, raising his three in the air. Taran and Teiyn approached him, the moonlight illuminating the white teeth of their victorious smiles, and Hadli handed them each a letter.

Eamonn's eyes had adjusted to the minimal light in the room in no time, but as he peered through the darkness, he couldn't spot Leyna. His heart stopped for a fleeting second, his mind wildly painting a picture of her being caught and captured, but he realized just as quickly that if Taran and Teiyn were there and smiling, nothing had happened to Leyna.

"Are there any more?"

Her voice came from directly behind him and he spun on his heel, a strange crash of surprise and relief flooding him all at once.

"I didn't see you there," he whispered, lifting a hand to rest on her jawline. With a grin, he added, "You might make a pretty good thief yourself."

Leyna's expression remained impassive, and Eamonn's smile fell.

"Yes, there are three more. Here." He handed her one of the missives, ignoring his attempt at humor that she clearly didn't appreciate.

"Were you able to figure out if Taularen is in his library next door?" Hadli asked the twins.

Taran lifted his overshirt, then tucked the letter Hadli had given him between his shirt and his belt. "We've heard movement in the room, but we weren't able to determine if it was, in fact, the king."

"It has to be him," Teiyn insisted, more to her brother than to Hadli. "Who else would be in *the king's private library* at this time of night?"

"Any number of people." Taran held up fingers as he rattled off options. "His wife. His daughter. An advisor."

Hadli held up a hand to stop Taran. "Well, we're about to find out, one way or another. We didn't make it this far to sit in his study in the dark."

Eamonn took two deep breaths to steady his racing heart. Nerves hadn't affected him before now, but this wasn't something in which he was well-versed. The goal of a good theft was to remain hidden, to get in and out with your prize and leave no one the wiser. This was different. He had obtained his quarry, and instead of sneaking back out, he was about to flash it in the face of the person from whom he'd stolen it.

Hadli stood at the hidden door to the library, a piece of wall hung with a painting and half obscured by a small table. A sconce, identical to others in the room, would release the latch to open the door. The only clear indication the wall was false was the thin rim of light that came from the room beyond, outlining it.

Hadli glanced at their crew over his shoulder. "One."

They fell into line.

"Two."

Hadli gripped the camouflaged handle.

"Three."

He swung open the door and made straight for his target—the door leading out to the main corridor—blocking the king's escape before the man could think twice. King Taularen sat in an armchair near the fireplace in a navy blue dressing robe, and his head shot up from the book he'd been reading at the sudden entrance of the intruders. The twins and Leyna took their posts at other possible exits and raised their hands. Taran lowered the fire, Teiyn sent a blast of icy air through the room, and Leyna pulled the book from the king's hands and caught it in her own.

As Eamonn entered, he noticed the triumphant smile that momentarily pulled at Leyna's lips, and he almost smiled himself.

But his eyes fell on King Taularen, and any pleasantness Eamonn possessed evaporated. Taularen had straightened in his chair, sitting stock still and watching the others carefully, especially the magic-casters. He hadn't noticed Eamonn yet; the embers Taran had left in the fireplace did not provide enough light to expose him. Every vertebra in Eamonn's back stiffened, and he tilted up his chin, the mere sight of Taularen sending a surge of contempt through him.

We have him.

Finally, the King of Miren would not be the one who had the upper hand.

"What is the meaning of this? Who are you?" Taularen demanded. "What do you want?"

The strength of the shock and outrage in his voice didn't fool Eamonn. Taularen had been taken fully by surprise, and he was nervous. He was a mouse caught in a trap, and Eamonn had the power to set him free or snap his neck.

Once Eamonn had taken several steps into the room, Taran brought the fire back and light fell on Eamonn, scattering the shadows cast by his hood. The king's gaze had been flitting back and forth over the intruders, not recognizing any of them—even Leyna, who had sat twice in his council chambers—but deep-seated anger settled over his features when his eyes landed on Eamonn.

"And to *what* do I owe this pleasure?" he snarled, tendrils of flame reflecting in his fierce eyes.

"We're here to make sure you join our alliance," Eamonn said simply, stopping a few feet from Taularen.

The king sneered and laughed once bitterly. "What do you think you're doing? You think a little magic from your friends is going to intimidate me?" He stood from his chair, and both Taran and Teiyn took a half step forward. The flames grew hotter at the same time ice crystals formed in the air. A warning.

"No, I don't," Eamonn replied, holding his ground. "You've already shown us that you aren't intimidated by magic. They're just here to make sure you don't go anywhere or try anything while I present you with our offer."

Taularen curled his lip in mocking curiosity. "Your offer?"

"I'm giving you the choice. You can join the alliance and help us fight against Rothgard before his influence spreads, *or*"—Eamonn pulled the missive from his pocket and held it out to Taularen, letting it fall open so that his signature and Hyfell's words were visible—"we show this to the kings of Farneth and Teravale."

Taularen clenched his teeth and narrowed his eyes at Eamonn, but he said nothing.

"I don't think Kings Vinnerod and Javorak will be very pleased to know what you're planning. You're not just against joining our alliance; you want to take over rule of Sarieth for yourself. You want what Rothgard wants. It's an act of war against the other provinces."

The tendons in Taularen's neck stood out and a vein bulged in the middle of his forehead. Redness crept into his face as he scowled at Eamonn. "You're blackmailing me? The King of Miren?"

Eamonn tipped his head to the side slightly without breaking eye contact. "That's exactly what we're doing."

Taularen inhaled sharply through his nose and opened his mouth to speak again, but he stopped before the words formed.

His expression transformed as though a new thought overcame him, and his eyes widened for a moment. A cruel sneer slowly spread across his face, his fury melting away. Taularen regained his composure, gently touching his fingertips together in front of him as his typical cool superiority returned.

"I applaud your attempt," he said, his words drawn out and dripping with scorn, "but I'm afraid you should have considered all implications of your plan more thoroughly before going to all this trouble."

Eamonn's gut twisted at Taularen's self-assurance, and his mind raced to pinpoint what the king was saying they had missed. He hoped his face didn't give away his second-guessing; he didn't want to lose any of their advantage. But Taularen remained silent, clearly waiting for Eamonn to speak first. Eamonn conceded.

"And why is that?"

Even in his nightclothes, King Taularen's sudden confidence endowed him with authority. Eamonn felt the shift in control in the room, and he didn't like it.

"If you had given more thought to this idea of blackmail, you might have considered the war you're already facing. The kings of Teravale and Farneth have already approached me for help because they know they will lose if they face Rothgard alone." Firelight shrouded Taularen in a sinister mixture of orange and shadow. He meandered across the open floor to Eamonn, an aura of triumph radiating off of him. The mouse had escaped the trap and had managed to turn it toward his captors. "They do not have the resources to spare to turn against me, nor do they have the time. Especially without Miren in their alliance, they must devote all their attention to the more imminent threat of Rothgard. Your blackmail is worthless. Even if you show the kings my plan, even if they learn what I intend to do after their inevitable defeat, they're powerless to stop it."

Eamonn could have crumpled to the floor. Taularen was right. He couldn't attempt to deny it or work around it. How had none of them seen the flaw in their plan? Of course, Javorak and Vinnerod would be appalled and want to stop Taularen, but with the threat they already faced, there was nothing they could do. If, against all odds, they managed to emerge victorious from the confrontation with Rothgard, they might then move the remainder of their forces against Miren. Even then, there was no guarantee of victory, and their blackmail would be useless. King Taularen was in the perfect position, no matter the outcome.

Eamonn had failed, again.

There was, however, an obvious alternative.

Rage seized Eamonn and he rushed toward Taularen, all the energy in the room connecting to him in streams. Taularen crashed against the wall behind him with a surge of energy that Eamonn sent his way, and Eamonn was upon him in seconds, his palm facing Taularen as he pinned the king against the wall with magic.

"*Or*," Eamonn snarled through clenched teeth, "we can do this *my* way."

He heard his name called out by someone behind him, but he didn't acknowledge them. He was tired of being put down by Taularen. He wasn't going to let him win again.

Taularen's throat worked as he swallowed, his eyes wide with fear. He struggled to move against the force of the magic pressing him into the wall.

"I can take control of you and have you join our alliance." Eamonn's top lip curled up in disgust as he spoke. Each word spewed from his mouth was laced with revulsion, and he meant every one. "I can have you command your generals to follow the orders of the other kings. You won't have a choice but to agree with us."

"And then what?" Taularen spat with choked breaths. "You won't hold on to my mind forever. You can't." He managed to tip his chin up and glare at Eamonn down his nose. "And once I'm free of you, I'll have every Mirish soldier turn on the other provinces. I'll tell all of Miren the lengths you would go to for the sake of your alliance and have every citizen poisoned against you. Who would be the aggressor then? There would truly be war, and it would be because of *you*."

Eamonn's throat went dry. He was out of options. There would be no victory against King Taularen.

"He's right," a rough voice murmured in the background, and Eamonn realized it came from Hadli. "You don't need to do it, Eamonn. It won't end well."

Eamonn ground his teeth, holding back renewed rage, and he scowled at the king a moment longer before he released his magic and stepped back.

Taularen rolled his neck, cracking a couple of joints and rubbing the back of it. "As it stands," he said, looking at every person in the room in turn, "you're trespassing in the king's private quarters. I can call my guards and they would be here in seconds to arrest all of you."

If Ree had done her job, the guards wouldn't be there. But King Taularen, of course, didn't know that.

"And how skilled are your guards against magic?" Eamonn asked, waving his fingers in front of him in a showy display. "Because we're ready to defend ourselves."

Taularen's eyes narrowed again as he surveyed the three other magic casters, and he pursed his lips. He shot an icy glare at Eamonn.

"If I ever see you on my palace grounds again, I will not hesitate to use force. This is your final warning."

Eamonn swept his eyes over the rest of his crew and jerked his head toward the door. He would be the last to leave, ensuring a safe exit for each of the others. Magic still hummed throughout his body. He kept it close in case Taularen had deceived them or changed his mind. But the king remained still, and once the others had slipped back into the study, Eamonn moved to the door.

"I eagerly await the day reign in Miren passes to your successor," Eamonn said in all seriousness. He didn't know the king's heir, but he believed anyone had to be better than him. "Maybe Rothgard will decide to come for Miren first after all, and that day will come sooner than we think."

Eamonn expected another glare or an angry retort, but a snide grin played across Taularen's face, and for the first time in their interaction, he seemed to completely relax.

"Oh, I can guarantee he won't."

The blood drained from Eamonn's face and he froze where he stood. The satisfaction in Taularen's expression sent Eamonn's heart hammering in his chest. *What is that supposed to mean?*

He wanted to question Taularen, but his friends waited for him in the next room, holding their escape until he joined them. It wasn't as though the king would answer him anyway. He probably took a sick pleasure in saying something like that and then letting Eamonn wonder. So, he turned his back on Taularen and regrouped with the others.

Eamonn had just shut the door and was about to give instructions for their escape when a voice belonging to none of them cut through the darkness of the study.

"What happened in there?"

It only took seconds for him to recognize Ree's voice, but in that time, he nearly jumped out of his skin.

"What in the stars are *you* doing in here?" Hadli asked in a sharp whisper.

Eamonn took a deep breath to try to slow his jumping heart. "I thought you couldn't be involved in this."

"I'm not."

"You're pretty damn close," Hadli replied, his voice tight with irritation and colored with distrust.

"I thought you'd be happy to see me."

"I can't be anything until I figure out why you're here when you said you *wouldn't be involved*."

Now that his eyes had adjusted to the dark, Eamonn could easily see Ree's furrowed brow and her mouth hanging agape. She huffed, appearing genuinely offended. "You still don't trust me?"

"I don't know *what* to think about you, to be perfectly honest." Hadli ran a hand through his hair and rested it on the back of his head.

It caught Ree's attention, and she tilted her head, moonlight glinting off the whites of her eyes and giving her a mischievous look. "You shaved."

Hadli shrugged, his brows furrowed in question. "Yeah."

Ree crossed her arms. "I liked the beard."

A reluctant half-smirk tugged at Hadli's open mouth, but Eamonn didn't allow him the chance to respond. "We can all talk about Hadli's facial hair once we're out of here. Just because the king let us leave doesn't mean we're in the clear."

"Let you leave?" Ree asked, abruptly losing the lightness of her voice. "The blackmail didn't work?"

"Again, we can talk about it somewhere other than here." Eamonn motioned for the group to move to the bookcase that hid the stairs. "Hadli will lead. You three stay close and let Hadli stay a little ahead of you, just in case. I'll bring up the rear."

"I'll meet you in the pavilion," Ree murmured before turning and disappearing into the shadows of the room.

Hadli opened the door but stopped short, casting his eyes back to Eamonn.

"You so sure we can trust her?"

I hope so, he wanted to say, but he couldn't convey any misgivings in the moment. There was too much happening, too much he needed to figure out, and he didn't want to add to the confusion by giving the others any hint of doubt in Ree after such a spectacular defeat. So, Eamonn simply nodded in answer, thankful for the darkness that shrouded his expression.

Hadli shook his head. "I hope you're right." He led the way down the spiral stairs, and while Eamonn gave Hadli a head start, he looked over his shoulder in the dark where Ree had vanished. How long had she been in there? She must not have heard much if she didn't know the blackmail hadn't worked. Eamonn had assumed she would be posted outside the king's suite, ready to act if Taularen had called for the guards. But now that he thought about it, Ree had never said where she would be for the mission or what she would be doing.

He'd lingered too long in the room alone. Eamonn brought his mind back to the present and skulked out of the palace the way they'd come.

TWENTY-SIX

As if it wasn't bad enough that their blackmail hadn't worked, a crushing weight now sat on Leyna's heart, finding a permanent home in her chest. Eamonn had lost all sense of control and threatened the King of Miren with Avarian magic. Something he swore was reserved only for Rothgard. Something Leyna was terrified he would begin to lean into more and more. Her fears for the corruption of Eamonn's soul were playing out before her eyes.

While they waited for Ree, and Eamonn started to discuss with the others what their next move might be, Leyna sat staring into the fire and remained silent. The shock of Eamonn's actions in King Taularen's library had settled and left her feeling hollow.

The tears that had pricked her eyes in the palace never fell, and holding on to them left Leyna pressurized, her emotion restrained but just under the surface. She hadn't said anything to Eamonn to know if he would try to defend himself. He could claim that it was just a threat, and he didn't intend to take control of Taularen, but that would be a lie. Leyna had heard in his voice how ready Eamonn was to make the king join their alliance with his magic. Taularen had belittled him one too many times.

But what broke her heart the most was why Eamonn jumped so effortlessly to retaliation. He might not see it, but it had been unmistakable to Leyna: the change in him after his torture at Rothgard's hand. Eamonn had left Rothgard's captivity tormented, bitter, and vengeful.

Hadli and Eamonn turned their heads toward the back of the pavilion as if in response to a sound, and moments later, Ree appeared.

"Okay, so what happened? Did you get the missives?"

"We got them," Eamonn replied. He pulled one out of a pocket and handed it to Ree. "They just ended up not being good blackmail."

Leyna pressed a hand against her trouser pocket, and paper crinkled under the fabric. They had left with all the missives. Maybe they'd bought themselves a little time before Taularen informed his generals of his plan.

Ree took the letter from Eamonn and scanned it. "It says just what we expected it to. So why didn't it work?"

"*Your king* made an excellent point," Hadli said. "It may be enough to start a war between Miren and the other provinces, but none of them can afford a war with Miren right now. All their attention is already on Rothgard."

Ree jerked back like she'd been punched in the gut. She dropped her eyes to the ground, searching for answers. "How could I have missed that?"

"We all missed it," Eamonn said with a shake of his head, but Hadli crossed his arms and pointed his gaze at Ree.

"Did we?"

Ree's head shot back up. "What's that supposed to mean?"

"You were conveniently not around." Hadli leaned toward Ree. "You sent us in there with a plan that could have ended with all of us thrown into a Mirish prison."

"You think I did this on purpose?" Her whisper sliced through the night, sharp as a knife. "What would I have to gain?"

Hadli shrugged off her piercing reply. "You could have made us think you were against the king when you're still loyal to him. What was it you said? 'Miren above all?' You got close to us to find out what we were willing to do for the alliance and then set us up to have us arrested. You were hiding in the study when we left, probably waiting to help walk us to the prison yourself."

Ree lunged at Hadli, her face contorted in rage, but Eamonn stepped in and grabbed her shoulders to stop her. Leyna jumped to her feet, all her despair vanishing with the glint of fire reflected in Ree's eyes. Even after Hadli's suspicions in the study, she hadn't questioned Ree's motives, and now, she was sure there was no need. The indignation pouring from her expression at Hadli's accusation seemed completely authentic.

"I would *never*," Ree hissed as Eamonn held her back. Her fingers danced over the hilt of her sheathed dagger, the firelight flickering over its intricate details and filling the white stone in its pommel with a subtle orange glow. "I'm trying to help you, *and* your alliance. I, unlike the king, understand that Rothgard has to be stopped." Ree shook Eamonn off, taking a couple of steps back. "So, what happened, then? How did you get away without using blackmail?"

Eamonn inhaled and Ree turned her attention to him, waiting for a response. Leyna held her breath as her pulse started to pound. What would he say? Would he defend his actions?

Hadli cut a glance at Eamonn. "That's where it gets a little dicey," he said, apparently unaffected by the girl in his face a moment before. "Eamonn *might* have threatened to use his magic against the king to force him into joining the alliance."

Ree's eyes became circles as she slowly angled her head at Eamonn beside her. "You did *what*?"

Leyna pulled her arms tightly against her middle. Eamonn had nowhere to hide. He had to own up to what he did.

"I was angry," he admitted with his eyes on the fire. "I didn't want Taularen to win again. I wanted it to be done."

"And that didn't work either?"

Eamonn explained the interaction between himself and the king, and Leyna's heart painfully hammered without apology against the inside of her chest. Hearing how nonchalantly he recounted his threats to the king brought back her anger and disappointment in him. He didn't have to outright say he believed his actions were justified—his tone and body language displayed as much. Her eyes burned again, and her throat swelled, but she shoved her emotion down.

"So, he just let you walk out of there?" Ree asked, her fingertips dancing on the hilt of her sheathed blade.

"He would have called the guard, but I think he was too unsure of our magic to risk it. At least that part of our plan worked." He rubbed his fingers across his forehead. "He said he would use force against us if he caught us on the palace grounds again."

Ree nodded several times. "He will." She cracked her knuckles and blew out a breath. "That was our last chance, then."

The sound of wood popping in the fire filled the quiet that followed. Taran and Teiyn shared a glance, communicating with only their eyes. Hadli grabbed a stick and tossed it into the fire before resting his hands on his hips and turning to pace around the pavilion.

"I could try getting the soldiers themselves," Eamonn murmured, his brow furrowed as he studied the fire. "I can't guarantee it will work; I've never tried it on more than one person before. But if the king won't—"

"Are you *serious*?" There was venom in the bite of Leyna's whisper. She dropped her arms and balled her hands so tightly her nails cut into her palms. "You would take over the wills of Mirish soldiers now? What happened to 'It would only be Rothgard?' You were prepared to control the will of Miren's king, and now its soldiers?" Leyna released an incredulous breath and barely shook her head. "What's happening to you?"

Eamonn's nostrils flared, and his chest heaved with a deep breath. He stepped past Ree to come closer to Leyna, and Leyna tried to swallow despite her tight throat. "I'm just doing what has to be done. If we need the Mirish army to defeat Rothgard, then we have to get them somehow."

"Even if the cost is your soul? Your goodness? You say when Rothgard does it, it's wicked and evil and wrong, but if you need to take over the minds of innocent people, it's necessary? It's 'what has to be done?'"

The muscles in Eamonn's jaw tightened and he momentarily closed his eyes. "It's unfortunate, but this is what we've come to. Rothgard takes over people's wills for his own personal gain. This is to stop him; it's for the safety of the whole country."

"Do you hear yourself?" Leyna's words came out in a breath. "You're still trying to justify it, even now. You'll never understand, will you? This is something that doesn't have a justification."

She couldn't hold the tears back any longer. Leyna spun on her heel, anxious to get away, to leave Eamonn's presence, to go anywhere but there. He grabbed her hand and whirled her around to face him, and the tears streamed freely down her cheeks.

"Leyna." Her name was a plea.

She pressed her lips together, her chin quivering, and she pulled her hand out of his grasp. "Let me go."

Her vision blurred as she left the pavilion, stumbling down the steps into the cover of the garden maze. She'd come this way enough now to think she knew the way out, but the heat of her emotions made her head swim. It would be easy to get lost in the darkness.

Footsteps pounded behind her, and her heart rose again to her throat. She couldn't speak to Eamonn right now. She didn't want to be near him.

But it was two sets of footsteps, even in rhythm and pace. Leyna glanced over her shoulder to spot the forms of Taran and Teiyn approaching her, and she released a sigh of relief.

"We're coming with you." Teiyn reached Leyna and picked up her hand, giving it a squeeze before releasing it.

Taran came alongside his sister. "We're not in the business of taking sides, but we think you're right, for what it's worth."

Teiyn nodded to show her agreement. "Eamonn is letting his magic get the best of him."

"We might be able to show him that our magic can still be powerful against Rothgard if we plan ahead and use it together," Taran explained, guiding them through the maze.

"But now isn't the time," Teiyn said softly. "Eamonn needs a chance to see his actions from the outside, somehow."

Taran offered Leyna an attempt at an encouraging smile over his shoulder. "We can try to find some way to make him see what we see."

More tears fell and Leyna sniffed. She was thankful for the twins and how they tried to offer solutions, but Leyna knew they wouldn't find something that worked. If Eamonn couldn't see what Leyna saw—and would let her walk away because of it—only something truly drastic might be able to bring him to his senses.

TWENTY-SEVEN

EAMONN BARELY SLEPT. IN the remaining hours before sunrise, he tossed and turned, unable to get the image of Leyna's tear-streaked face out of his mind. She'd been the angriest he'd ever seen her. He would admit, his suggestion to take over the minds of the soldiers was too far. They were bystanders and didn't deserve to lose control of their wills because Eamonn had tried other methods and failed.

But Taularen had deserved every ounce of threat that Eamonn had made. He would gladly take hold of the king's mind and order all Mirish forces to join the alliance, if it didn't mean there would be retaliation when Eamonn inevitably let the control go. Eamonn had no doubt Taularen would follow through with his warning, so Eamonn would only trade running from one enemy for another.

He must have fallen asleep, because the sky outside his window changed from a pale grey to a light blue in the blink of an eye. Eamonn didn't feel refreshed, but he was invigorated with the desire to do something—anything—that might make him feel like less of a failure.

Eamonn threw on a clean shirt, tugged on his boots, and slung his jacket over his shoulders. Some of the others should be up and about by now, especially those who weren't involved in the midnight escapade.

He flew down the stairs and entered the dining room, and the smells of fried bacon, smoked sausage, and freshly baked muffins greeted him. His stomach rumbled at the aromas, but food would come later. He had to see about some business first.

It must have still been fairly early in the morning; only four of the tables in the dining room were occupied. Around one of them, with cups of tea and plates of steaming breakfast, sat Dorylss, Kinrid, and Gilleth, just the people Eamonn wanted to see.

"Morning, lad!" Dorylss called cheerily when he caught sight of Eamonn. "Have a seat. We'll order you some breakfast."

"In a minute," Eamonn said as he sat beside Gilleth. He lowered his voice, though he spoke with urgency. "We need to move on Rothgard. There's no point staying here any longer. We'll just waste our time."

Kinrid frowned, drawing his eyebrows close together. "What's changed? What did you learn from this Ree?"

Eamonn brought the others up to date in a flash, summarizing what they'd learned from Ree to the attempt at blackmail. Their curiosity changed to surprise when Eamonn told them what Taularen planned to do behind their backs, and in Gilleth's case, surprise changed to barely-contained fury.

"It's exactly the kind of thing that blackguard would do," she muttered. She clenched her hands into tight fists on the table, a passionate spark dancing in her eyes.

Gilleth's ferocity reminded Eamonn of the other surprising information he had learned the night before: that Taularen was married to her sister. An entirely new vault of questions had been unlocked with the revelation, and Eamonn wanted answers. He didn't know the best way to go about it; there probably wasn't a good way, so he forwent propriety and asked.

"Your sister is the queen, isn't she?"

The muscles in Gilleth's neck tensed for a split second as she sat up straighter. Something in her air became regal, and Eamonn remembered the gold that had lined her eyes whenever she was in Taularen's presence.

"Are you Farnish royalty?"

Gilleth picked up her cup of tea and took a long swig. Dorylss and Kinrid eyed her carefully, as though waiting to see how she would answer Eamonn.

They already know.

It wasn't a surprise that Kinrid knew—he and Gilleth had known each other for years. But Dorylss? How long had he known and kept it a secret?

Gilleth swirled the tea in the cup before setting it down and staring at the table. She cut her eyes to Kinrid, and in his peripheral vision, Eamonn saw Kinrid dip his head a fraction. The porcelain cup clinked against the smooth wood as it met the tabletop.

"We're distant cousins of the Farnish king," she finally answered, so quiet Eamonn almost couldn't hear her. "It makes us part of the royal family, but I wouldn't call us 'Farnish royalty.'"

Eamonn waited for more, but Gilleth said nothing else. So Eamonn prodded. "And your sister?"

A scowl passed over Gilleth's features. "King Taularen chose my sister to be his wife twenty-one years ago. At the time, my family was thrilled. It was thought to improve relations between the two provinces and give Farneth more legitimacy in dealings with Miren, which has always been strained due to Miren's own sense of superiority. Every province needs some kind of 'in' with Miren... this was ours. But Taularen wanted her more for show than anything." She stabbed a piece of sausage on her plate with such force that she must be imagining it was the Mirish king. "To gain favor with Farneth and to look almost like a martyr for his people. He could have had any number of Mirish women, but he chose Milena as though he was making a sacrifice by marrying a Farnethan to improve diplomacy. Marrying my sister, a *sacrifice.*"

That perfectly fit Taularen's character—choosing a wife based on diplomatic reasons, and then making a show of it to his entire province to gain their sympathy, simply because the Mirish viewed their people as the greatest. Eamonn shook his head. Who else but the King of Miren would seek sympathy for the circumstances of his marriage—circumstances he chose himself?

"Why doesn't Milena leave?" Eamonn couldn't help himself. He was in this rabbit hole now; he might as well ask the hard questions.

"She could." The fury in Gilleth's features faded to a familiar sadness. "But they would remain married. Miren's marriage laws are strict. But despite all of Taularen's vileness of character, he treats her well, so she doesn't have a valid reason to seek dissolution of the marriage. And then there's the princess, of course. My sister would never leave Karina behind, and I'm not sure she would go with her mother."

Every glare Gilleth had given Taularen, every ounce of disgust in her voice when she'd spoken his name... all of it made complete sense. Eamonn didn't blame her for any of it, now that he'd become better acquainted with the King of Miren. He would be furious to have a sister essentially finagled into marrying a man like him. Knowing Taularen, the resentment between himself and his wife's family might have been enough to keep him from joining an alliance with Farneth, regardless of anything else.

He slouched against an arm propped up on the tabletop. "King Taularen was never going to join our alliance, was he?"

Gilleth sawed her sausage in two, only opening her mouth to take a bite, so Kinrid answered Eamonn's question.

"We hoped the larger threat of Rothgard would be enough for him to set aside his personal grievances with Gilleth and fight with us, even if it only lasted until Rothgard's defeat. I'm not entirely surprised he didn't agree to join us, but I never would have guessed what you learned." Kinrid leaned back in his chair and crossed one arm against his abdomen, resting the elbow of the other on his forearm and stroking his chin with his raised hand. "It's a bold move to make, even for him. He would have to be certain Rothgard would seek to conquer the other provinces before attempting to overthrow Miren."

The last sentence struck another memory from the night before, as well as a passing remark Ree had made. Hyfell had been the one to give King Taularen that exact information. Eamonn jerked back from his supporting arm to sit straight as a board. "He is." Eamonn's breathing sped up and his wide eyes flashed to each of his companions. "It was the last thing he said to me. I told him that maybe Rothgard would come to Miren first after all. Then he said he could guarantee he wouldn't."

Beside Eamonn, Gilleth sucked in a breath. Kinrid and Dorylss shared a concerned look.

"He said that to you?" Dorylss pressed.

Eamonn nodded emphatically. "That exactly. Ree said his advisor, Hyfell, told him so."

Kinrid's throat bobbed and the muscles in his jaw tightened. His deep voice was troubled when he spoke again. "If King Taularen has made some kind of deal with Rothgard, he's fooling himself. He's in Rothgard's hand."

The unmistakable alarm around the table opened the floodgates of adrenaline in Eamonn, and he itched with the desire to act. "If Rothgard is truly weak, we need to leave here and confront him while we still have the chance. We have to stop him, *now*."

"We can't," Dorylss said with a sharp shake of his head. "Not yet."

A crease formed between Eamonn's brows. "Why not?"

"Our army is in Farneth," Kinrid answered. "The Teravalen forces King Javorak was sending to aid us should be with them in Swyncrest by now, but we still have to contact them to set out for Miren."

"They don't need to come here. They can meet us in Wolstead where Hadli said Rothgard was headed, at Mount Iyer."

"Even then," Gilleth said, restraining the anger in her voice even though it was clearly filled with renewed indignation, "they won't arrive before we do if we leave now. The order would take time to arrive, and they have farther to travel than we do. Their numbers mean they would move slower, too."

"We don't have that much time!" Eamonn shot up from his seat, nearly toppling the chair backward onto the floor. A few more patrons had filtered into the dining room during their conversation, and all eyes turned to Eamonn. "We don't need the army. I'll go. No one else has to get involved."

"What do you mean?" Dorylss asked, his tone as urgent as Eamonn's. "You can't go alone, of course."

"That's exactly what I mean." Eamonn gripped the back of his chair till his knuckles turned white. Going alone was the best solution. He could find Rothgard, sneak up on him, and gain control of his mind to send away any soldiers that were with him. Then he would make sure to end Rothgard's life. He would watch him die. Eamonn would keep a firm grasp on Rothgard's will until he watched the light fade from his eyes. He wouldn't mess up like last time.

Then, with Rothgard taken care of, Eamonn's life could finally go back to normal. He would no longer need to use Avarian magic, and he would show that to Leyna. Perhaps, in time, Leyna's anger would dissipate. Eamonn would hold true to his word and not use it again, and Leyna would forgive him for what he had done. She would come back to him.

Another vision of her from the night before, angry and hurt, reappeared in Eamonn's mind. It had been the final straw, and Eamonn knew it. *Let me go*, she'd said. He hoped she only meant to release her hand in that moment. If she'd meant more than that...

Eamonn's stomach tied itself in knots at the memory and heat rose to his face. After he did this—after he took care of Rothgard once and for all—he would get another chance at her love.

Love he probably didn't deserve in the first place.

His eyes burned, and he pushed off the back of the chair. The others protested as Eamonn sped out of the dining room with no regard to them. He took the stairs two at a time back up to his room, and he started throwing his belongings into his bag. Yes, this was their best choice all the way around. He would clean up the mess he'd left, and no one else had to be put in danger. Eamonn knew the way to Mount Iyer from his travels as a merchant, but he didn't know where to access the mine that led to the abode, or where Rothgard might even be. He—

Movement from the room beside his stopped Eamonn's flurry of packing and he paused to listen. Soft footsteps padded across the floor. Leyna must be about. She would likely be down for breakfast soon. He wanted to be well on his way by then. He couldn't bear to see her after last night, to see the pained disappointment in her eyes and know she wouldn't speak to him unless necessary.

A hand closed around his heart, and he stuffed the rest of his things in his bag. He would give her a reason to forgive him.

Eamonn had barely slung his bag over his shoulder when someone pounded on his door. His mind immediately went to Leyna, picturing her waiting for him on the other side, but he realized just as quickly that it couldn't be her; she would never knock so loudly, and he still heard faint movements in the next room. Eamonn gripped the door handle and swung the door open, expecting to see Dorylss, but he stopped short at the sight of Hadli.

"What are you doing?" Hadli blocked the doorway with crossed arms.

Eamonn adjusted his bag. "I'm going to Mount Iyer. I don't need armies to stop Rothgard. If I can get to him, I can do it alone. I'm ending this."

Hadli nodded a few times, chewing his lip. "Want some company?"

Eamonn was prepared to object to whatever Hadli might say and shoulder his way past him, but his unexpected response got his attention. He snapped his mouth shut and gave Hadli a sideways glance. "Why?"

"If this is how you think it needs to be done, I stand by you. I know you can do it."

A warning rose in Eamonn's heart, but he pushed it back down. Old habits. He'd decided to trust Hadli, and he'd only been helpful to him. Maybe they were reconciling. Hadli might want the chance to prove himself to Eamonn.

"How quickly can you get a horse ready?"

A confident grin so familiar to Eamonn spread across Hadli's face. "In no time."

One of Eamonn's cheeks lifted, and he gave Hadli a nod. "Let's go, then."

Hadli backed out of the doorway and let Eamonn exit the room. "I'll grab my things and some food for us first and meet you in the stables." He jogged over to the room he shared with Taran as Eamonn hurried to the stairs.

The latch of a door behind him pricked his ears, and he turned his head to look back down the hallway. Leyna appeared from her room. She took one step out and stopped. Their eyes met, and an invisible force tethered them.

Fear filled Leyna's red-rimmed eyes and her mouth hung slightly agape. She must have overheard him speaking with Hadli. So, she knew what he planned to do, then. Eamonn inhaled a slow, deep breath, never breaking her gaze. She pressed her lips together and swallowed, but she didn't move, didn't speak, didn't try to stop him. Not that he would change his mind, anyway. Eamonn was resolved to see this through.

Eamonn pulled his eyes from hers and rushed down the stairs without so much as a word of goodbye.

Dorylss, Kinrid, and Gilleth waited for Eamonn at the bottom of the stairs. He saw them from the second-floor landing and groaned as he descended the staircase into the vestibule.

"There's no need to run off by yourself, lad," Dorylss said before Eamonn had even reached them. "We only need a few days to get a letter to Swyncrest and give the army a head start."

"And what are we supposed to do in those few days? Allow Rothgard the chance to make it to the abode and increase his power? We are very quickly running out of time." Eamonn paused in front of them, but he saw the slight turn of Grimmel's head from behind and continued on through the vestibule. This wasn't for Grimmel's ears.

"It's reckless, Eamonn. You don't know what you'd be facing." The gravity of Kinrid's voice gripped Eamonn, but he shook it off and pushed open the front door of the guest house. He strode outside into the bright morning light, the other three close on his heels.

"You expect to take on Rothgard and all those who accompany him?" Dorylss asked, keeping pace as Eamonn made for the stables.

"If I defeat Rothgard, I don't have to worry about the rest," Eamonn said. Even he had a hard time believing his own overconfidence, but he was determined. Surely, if he brought about Rothgard's end, any remaining force he'd traveled with would be nothing more than a body without its head.

"You're so sure?" Gilleth asked. "There will be more than those coerced into protecting him. Plenty are loyal to him. They might not take kindly to the loss of their leader."

Eamonn stopped in the middle of the path and turned on them. "All I care about is taking down Rothgard. With him gone, everything will work itself out. And I won't be alone... Hadli is coming with me."

"Hadli?" Dorylss clamped a hand on Eamonn's shoulder and leveled his eyes with him. "I'm not sure that's such a good idea."

Eamonn huffed and placed his hands on his hips. "I made a decision to trust Hadli. All of you seemed to think we could trust him. Did you really think we shouldn't but not say so?"

Dorylss squared his shoulders. "I think his information was trustworthy. I don't know how I feel about you running off to face Rothgard with only him."

Shifting the strap of his bag, Eamonn pulled out of Dorylss's grasp. "It's all or nothing to me. He's either earned our trust, or he hasn't."

The stables weren't far now, and once Eamonn saddled up his horse, there was nothing the others could do to stop him. They continued to protest as he strode down the path that ran from the inn to the stables. A heavy, rhythmic pounding sounded behind them on the main street, growing louder as seconds passed, and Eamonn whirled around. Before he even saw anything, his heart constricted. It was unmistakably the thunderous march of soldiers.

Eamonn left the others behind, rushing back the way he'd come. The path spilled out into the street, and Eamonn froze at the scene before him. Enough soldiers to make up a company had filled the street just beyond the inn. They wore the shiny gold armor of Miren's palace guards, their breastplates engraved with the province's official seal. Had Taularen sent them to arrest Eamonn and his friends after all? Fear lodged in his heart and sent it racing. He thought about reaching for his magic, prepared to defend himself, when he spotted the leader at the front of the troops.

Ree.

"What are you doing?" she asked him, continuing toward Eamonn after the soldiers had stopped.

Sunlight glinted off the soldiers' reflective armor, and Eamonn shielded his eyes. They stood obediently in formation as though awaiting Ree's orders.

"I might ask you the same question."

Ree came to a halt only a couple of feet from Eamonn, and with the sun out of his eyes, he noticed that she wore armor, too, though not quite the same as the soldiers. Hers was lighter in weight than theirs and somewhere in between gold and a silvery-white, the great tree of Miren crafted in artistic patterns across her breastplate. Ree's usual grey cloak was replaced with a white cape that attached to the armor's shoulder pieces, and her light brown curls, backlit by the sun, framed her face like a halo.

People in the street parted around the soldiers, catching quick glances and then dipping their heads to whisper to a companion. For someone who had always been hidden in the shadows, preferring to see rather than be seen, Ree had certainly pulled out the theatrics.

"I asked first." She propped her right hand on something at her hip, and peering closer, Eamonn noticed her sheathed dagger was now strapped to a belt at her waist rather than her thigh.

Eamonn closed the remaining distance between them so he could lower his voice. "Hadli and I are going to Mount Iyer," he replied, scanning the pedestrians that passed by.

Ree arched an eyebrow. "Just the two of you?"

"I don't want to wait around and waste time." He proved it in the urgency of his voice. "If it's just us, we won't endanger anyone else. But what about you? What are you doing with all these soldiers? And what are you wearing?"

"If King Taularen won't help you, I will. You don't have to do this alone. These soldiers have chosen to side with me instead of the king. To side with us."

"Ree, you *can't* do this. It's treason. He'll have you arrested." Eamonn couldn't let Ree risk her position in the king's guard—and more importantly, her life—to provide a company of Mirish soldiers behind the king's back. "He could have you *killed.*"

To Eamonn's surprise, Ree laughed. "I don't have to worry about that, trust me. Having me killed is one of the last things the king would ever do."

Eamonn knitted his brows and studied Ree's amused expression. He didn't understand. Ree had made off with what looked like most of the king's palace guard, blatantly against his wishes to not join the alliance. She knew King Taularen better than he did, it was true, but he didn't imagine being in the king's personal guard—or even the head of that guard—would save her from such treason.

"Uh..." Hadli's voice came from near the inn, and all heads turned to him. He carried two wrapped bundles beside his own bag. "What is happening?" He spotted Ree, his eyes traveling down her form and then back up as he came to Eamonn's side. "Someone explain."

A sparkle at Ree's waist caught Eamonn's eye, and he spotted the dagger as it moved in her grasp, the white stone glimmering in the sun.

He'd seen that same white stone recently.

The night before.

In King Taularen's ring.

My father gave me this dagger.

Eamonn's jaw dropped, and his gaze shot back up to meet Ree's. Her lips twitched with a smile and a mischievous twinkle played in her amber eyes.

"You're Karina," Eamonn said in a breath. He took in the rest of her new attire again with the revelation, and it all made sense. "You're the Princess of Miren."

Hadli nearly dropped the packages as his mouth fell open. "You're the—Wait, what?" Bewilderment flooded his dark features as he attempted—and failed—to regain his composure. "The *princess*?"

Ree rolled her eyes and groaned. "'*Princess*.' I hate that word. There's such an ostentatious expectation behind it. It sounds like all I do is embroider and play the piano and wear gaudy dresses and swoon over eligible men."

A smirk tugged at Hadli's open mouth. "Do you not?"

"No, I do," she confirmed with raised eyebrows and a quick nod. "It's just not all I do." She dipped her head, her eyes focused past Eamonn and Hadli. "I'm surprised my Aunt Gilleth didn't tell you about me."

Eamonn turned his head and saw Gilleth, Kinrid, and Dorylss approaching them. He laughed and ran his hand over his mouth before facing Ree again. "You were mentioned, but only briefly. I didn't even know Gilleth's sister was married to the king until last night." *The king*. Eamonn's eyes widened. Obviously, if Ree was Princess Karina, then King Taularen was her father. But putting it together now... trying to recall everything Ree had ever said about the king... Eamonn needed it to make sense.

"You asked us to blackmail your father." It wasn't a question but a revelation in Eamonn's mind as he traveled along his memory. "You're even bolder than I thought."

Ree raised one shoulder and angled her head toward it. "It's a lot easier to blackmail someone when you don't have to fear repercussions. I can't get everything I ask for, but"—she brought up her other shoulder to join the right one—"I'm the princess, his only child. His only successor. He won't harm a single hair on my head."

He remembered the second audience with the king that had confused him. Eamonn had already guessed Ree was the reason why it took place, but he'd assumed it was because she'd seen his magic in person and informed the king. After they met with Taularen again, it was clear he had planned to refuse them before he ever invited them back. He must have done it solely as a favor to his daughter.

"I'm sorry... and why did you never tell us this?" Hadli's shock had begun to fade, and his eyes were narrowed in fascinated scrutiny.

"Please." Ree nearly laughed out the word. "Like you would have taken me seriously—let alone trusted me—if I told you Taularen is my father."

Hadli nodded, conceding. "Fair point."

The two Farnish soldiers and Dorylss had joined them, and Gilleth reached out to grip Ree just before her elbow with a smile: an actual, full smile. Eamonn hadn't seen such joy in Gilleth's face before. Ree returned the gesture, clasping her aunt's arm in the traditional Farnish greeting.

Eamonn nearly laughed, remembering his first encounter with Ree. She'd mentioned a commonality she and Eamonn shared: parents from two different backgrounds. The signs had been there all along.

"I never considered that the Ree you met might be Princess Karina," Kinrid said to Eamonn, almost smiling himself. "I would have known her at once, if I'd seen her."

"How you've grown," Gilleth murmured before pulling Ree into a momentary embrace. "Ready to take the throne, I presume."

Ree's admonishing glare at Gilleth was negated by the hint of a smile on her lips. "Now, Aunt Gilleth, you shouldn't say such things. Especially not in the kingdom."

Gilleth suppressed a grin and stepped back from her niece. "Of course, of course. How foolish of me." A spark shone in her eyes. "Though I'm ready for that day."

"So, you're... coming with us? With all of them?" Hadli dipped his head toward the soldiers at attention behind her.

"That's the plan. Go, ready your horses," Ree commanded, and the new superiority in her voice was distinctly that of someone used to having a natural authority.

Hadli headed toward the stables, but Eamonn remained and shook his head; not in refusal of her request, but in disbelief as he still wrapped his mind around Ree's identity. "How are you getting away with this?"

Ree crossed her arms. "I'll explain on the way. I thought you were anxious to leave?"

He was. Eamonn turned away from Ree, ready to run after Hadli, but he pivoted back around when a new question came to him.

"If you don't like the word 'princess,' what do you prefer?"

"Heir," Ree answered without hesitation, tilting her chin up. "It's much more dignified."

TWENTY-EIGHT

Ree had brought just under a hundred soldiers, and though they traveled slower than Eamonn and Hadli would have alone, Eamonn was grateful for them. He'd been prepared to go on to Mount Iyer by himself, and then with only Hadli, but his brain knew it wasn't smart. Impatience had gotten in the way and silenced logic. With Ree and her soldiers now, Eamonn truly believed they could win.

Dorylss, Kinrid, and Gilleth insisted on coming as well but would be a few hours behind, having to finish some business and tie up loose ends in Amrieth before they could depart. They promised to bring Taran, Teiyn, and Leyna with them. Eamonn almost wished they would leave Leyna at the guest house, perhaps with Dorylss so she wouldn't get lonely and Eamonn could be certain she would stay safe. It wasn't just because Eamonn couldn't focus, couldn't think, couldn't breathe when she was near. She had no business trekking across Miren to a mountain in Wolstead where Rothgard and other unknown dangers might lay ahead.

Though she'd done exactly that through Idyrria to rescue him from Rothgard mere weeks before.

Eamonn shook his head to clear the thoughts of Leyna and turned his attention to Ree riding alongside him.

"Your father's going to notice half his palace guard is missing pretty quickly," he said, his voice edged with concern. "What will he do?"

Ree brought her brows low over her eyes. "Oh, he'll be angry. He probably already knows what happened, to be honest. One of the other guards could have ratted me out, or he might have figured it out himself once he realized I was gone."

Eamonn's pulse quickened and a thin layer of sweat formed on the back of his neck despite the cool afternoon. "So, he'll know where we're going? Will he send more soldiers after us?"

Her curls bounced as she shrugged. "He might. He's used to these kinds of things from me. He's always allowed me my freedoms, but this might be pushing it. I imagine he'll send a small force after us, but to do what? Take me prisoner? He wants his line—our line—to rule Miren, and I'm all he's got. Just consider anyone he sends after us backup." A sly smile curled at the corners of her lips. "I've never been the most well-behaved princess, but he always encouraged my spirit and creativity. That's how I got the playhouse in the hedge maze."

"Playhouse?" Eamonn repeated. Ree's assurances washed away his anxiety, and curiosity took its place. He hadn't been able to figure out the function of the pavilion in the garden. "That's what that was supposed to be?"

A wide, toothy grin spread across Ree's face. "When I was a child, I wanted a place outside of the palace to play that could be my own. I wanted to be queen of my own domain, so my father built the hedge maze and the playhouse. I know it doesn't look like much now, but back then, it was filled with furniture and toys and all sorts of homey things. My parents would come out there sometimes to play with me." Ree's eyes carried a wistful, faraway look. "Some of the best memories of my childhood were out there. But they haven't gone in years, so I knew it would be safe for us to meet there."

Hadli's horse came trotting up behind them, and he fell in step on Ree's other side. "I've been talking with one of the captains," he said, a little breathless. "How did you get so many of your father's soldiers loyal to you, Princess?"

Ree shot a good-natured glare at Hadli. "You can drop the 'Princess.' And I didn't have to 'get' any of them. I'm the heir to the throne. Loyalty is automatic."

"Okay, yes, but you're not currently the reigning sovereign. These soldiers have actually turned their back on the king in power to support you."

Ree squinted in the bright sunlight, her gaze straight ahead. "You've met him. He's not exactly agreeable, or the most reasonable. Some of the soldiers have been around since my grandfather's reign, and they serve my father out of a sense of duty, biding their time for me to take the throne."

Eamonn smirked, chuckling to himself to know that not all the Mirish loved and admired their king. "And the guards who are loyal to you... they don't mind you running around the kingdom in disguise?"

"Who do you think helped me do it in the first place?"

Hadli scoffed and made a show of rolling his eyes. "So, the guards who had sworn to protect you and are anxiously awaiting the day you become queen were helping you traipse around the kingdom where you could easily get yourself in trouble?"

Ree angled her head toward Hadli, giving him a look that shut him right up. "The guards are all over the kingdom—more than just these," she said with a jerk of her head to the company behind them. "They knew I needed the freedom to be more than the Princess of Miren. And no matter how much I 'traipsed' around the kingdom, someone always had an eye on me. None of them would let me get in over my head."

"But your father never knew?" Eamonn asked.

"Oh, he knew." Ree tipped up her chin. "He also knew he couldn't stop me."

Maybe it was the Farnethan in her, but Eamonn had never expected a Mir to be like Ree, especially not the heir to the throne. He still saw a bit of the Mirish pompousness in her, but it came across more as overconfidence and idealism than egotistical arrogance.

"I think I'll actually like Miren whenever you come to rule."

"There's plenty to like now," she said sternly, but her eyes twinkled with good humor.

"Name three things," Hadli challenged, grinning. "I dare you."

Ree didn't hesitate. "My mother, the queen; our extensive gardens; the determined practice we put behind everything we do. Artists and craftsmen aren't just born, you know." She watched him for a while before a slow grin spread across her lips. "You're growing your beard back."

Hadli scratched his hand across the stubble shadowing his jawline. "I'm used to having one."

Eamonn didn't miss the flash of a smile on Hadli's face before he smoothly covered it with the stroke of his hand. He'd cautioned Ree against Hadli, but he was starting to wonder if she'd listened, or if there was even anything to warn her about. Hadli was defying all his expectations, but Eamonn couldn't decide if he was glad for it or if it was too good to be true.

The closer to Wolstead they rode, the more the land lost its lushness. Soft soil was replaced with hard clay, groves of trees grew increasingly sparse, and grass—already brown from winter—covered the ground in brittle patches.

Eamonn understood why there were few villages out there. The land was unforgiving, much like the rest of Wolstead, and they relied on resources from Amrieth. It would make sense for the border of Miren to fall just west of the lake surrounding Amrieth, but then the Mirish wouldn't have access to the mountains and the mines that lay within.

The company rode into the night, hoping to cover as much ground as possible. As it stood, they wouldn't arrive at Mount Iyer until the day after next, so they chose to travel late and start early. They kept to the road, though in this no-man's-land where the borders of Miren and Wolstead were disputed, they came across no other travelers. The transport of goods from the mines to the rest of Miren came out of Sirvan, their mining city nestled in the mountains far to the north. Eamonn had only been through the mountain pass from Wolstead to Miren on his caravan journeys, so this part of the country was entirely foreign to him.

Ree stopped them long after nightfall at the edge of a thin copse of trees. Mountains loomed ahead of them, their white-capped peaks acting as beacons in the night sky. They were a constant in the changing landscape. At a glance, the size of the Valneria Mountains suggested they were close, but Eamonn had ridden in the shadow of those mountains before. They were some of the largest in the country, second only to the colossal Dragonback Mountains in the south. The mountains outside Erai, where Eamonn had lived in a cave with the Thieves' Guild for two years, were little more than foothills compared to them.

Lightweight canvas tents punctuated the drab earth, surrounding small fires in a few groups. Eamonn and Hadli had no tents, but they'd been prepared to spend their nights under the stars anyway. They laid their bedrolls close to a fire, the encircling tents providing a sense of security.

Eamonn sat on the bedroll as the soldiers taking the second watch settled down to sleep, propping his arms on his knees. Hadli appeared from somewhere within the camp and lowered himself to the hard ground. He threw his head back with a swig from a leather flask and held it out to Eamonn.

"What is it?" Eamonn asked, noticing the way Hadli squeezed his eyes shut as he swallowed and then let out a tight breath.

"A Mirish special," he answered with a gleam in his eyes. "Nicked it from the inn before we left."

Eamonn had started to tip the open end of the flask to his lips, but he yanked it down when Hadli spoke and gave him an icy glare. "You what?"

Hadli chuckled, and he nudged Eamonn with his shoulder. "I'm kidding. I bribed it off a soldier with some of the food I *bought* before we left. Turns out their travel rations are pretty meager."

The flask hovered above Eamonn's mouth as he considered Hadli with a sideways glance, then he brought it to his lips and took a drink. The liquid burned his throat, leaving a tingling trail down to his stomach. He winced and involuntarily closed his eyes.

"Ahh," he groaned, and he studied the flask before passing it back to Hadli. "The Mirish like it strong."

Hadli accepted it and took another gulp, sucking air through his teeth after he swallowed. "Yeah, I think it was well worth the apple cinnamon pastry." In the silence that followed, the air around them grew heavier. Hadli sniffed loudly, then angled his head toward Eamonn. "Have you got a plan? Or was your plan to figure it out as you go?"

"I have a plan," Eamonn replied, and it was mostly true. He knew what he wanted to happen, but the specifics might not be figured out until the time came. "If I can find Rothgard, I'll take over his will and have him hand over his amulet. Then, I'll have him disband any forces he came with, and then..."

He trailed off, because he wasn't sure if he could say the words out loud, the words rattling in his head since the moment he came out from under Rothgard's grasp. Eamonn wanted one thing more than anything else, and until then, the desire had unsettled him, but now... now, with the possibility of achieving it so close, it both frightened and emboldened him. It was the only way to ensure Rothgard would no longer be a threat, the only way to give Eamonn the satisfaction of his own revenge.

"I'm going to kill him."

Hadli looked from Eamonn to the fire, nodding, but he didn't speak. Silence stretched between them until it became an almost tangible thing, building like a wall. Eamonn wanted to tear it down, but he didn't know how. He couldn't find what he wanted to say to Hadli—what he *really* wanted to say.

But he didn't have to. Hadli stepped in and tore down the wall.

"I know what he did to you." His voice was rough and quiet, and something about it gripped Eamonn's heart. Hadli grasped the flask with both hands and ran his thumbs along the smooth leather, watching their movement. "I understand why you want that. And I don't think it's unreasonable, or too much." He lifted his eyes to Eamonn, and the look in them was like a punch to the gut, forcing all the air out of Eamonn's lungs. He so resembled the Hadli from their past, the one Eamonn had looked up to and been close to so long ago. They could easily be sitting around the fire in the secret hideaway of the Thieves' Guild instead of the wilds of Miren.

"If I confront him, I can't let him walk away."

Hadli nodded once. "I know." His throat worked as he swallowed, and he tipped his head down closer to Eamonn. "I'm so sorry. For all he did to you, for everything I said." He shook his head and turned back to the fire. "There's things I wish I could do differently...things I wish I could take back..."

Words seemed to linger on his tongue, but a slender form lowered to sit on the other side of Eamonn, and Hadli glanced over and shut his mouth. His face transformed, wiping away the vulnerable Hadli that Eamonn once knew to instead become the self-assured Hadli from a few moments before. Half his mouth tipped up at Ree's arrival.

"Taking the first watch as well, then?" he asked, angling his head around Eamonn.

Ree responded with a smug smile. "It's actually one of the privileges of being royal; I don't have to take either watch."

Hadli scoffed but reached across Eamonn to hand Ree the flask nonetheless. "Well, aren't you special?"

She took the flask and sniffed. "Theralas? Really?" Ree held the leather skin out to Hadli. "That's a quick way to get in trouble."

"What? You don't think I can handle it, Princess?"

Ree tucked in her chin and looked knowingly at Hadli from under her brows. "I don't think now is the time to find out."

Hadli retrieved the flask, but he didn't take another sip. Instead, he pushed the cork back into the flask's mouth and set it on the ground beside him. He and Ree engaged in casual conversation while Eamonn became lost in his own thoughts.

When he'd first spotted Hadli in Miren, he'd felt sure he was done for, that Rothgard had sent Hadli to find him and capture him again. But nothing about Hadli's actions or character resembled the man Eamonn had encountered only a few weeks before. A sliver of hope had planted itself in Eamonn's heart, without him even wanting it: hope that Hadli may yet be his friend—his brother—once again.

At first light, the company rode away from the grove where they'd made camp. Ree situated herself in the front, her natural leadership ability on full display now that she'd exposed her true identity. Eamonn had been a little skeptical of the soldiers at first and doubted their unyielding loyalty to Ree over King Taularen, but as he watched them interact, he began to realize how much these men and women respected her. Not all Mirish must be as high and mighty as he'd always presumed if this many of the palace guard were willing to betray their king to follow the princess.

Clouds rolled in on the second day of travel, hiding the sun and amplifying the cold. Worse, there was nothing in that part of the land to offer protection from the wind that rippled across the desolate plains. Eamonn shivered under his thick wool over-shirt and scarf from Idyrria, the warmest items of clothing he'd brought.

The low-hanging clouds settled in the mountains before them, hiding their snowy peaks from view. They threatened snow, according to murmurings through the company. Eamonn groaned when the speculation made its way to his ears. One of the very last things they needed was snow.

Eamonn did his best to stay alert as the weather deteriorated, keeping his nose under his scarf and cutting off any potential conversation. The wind pricked at his cheeks and made his eyes water.

Two of Ree's soldiers graciously offered to share their small tents with Eamonn and Hadli so they wouldn't be so exposed overnight, and Eamonn was grateful. Gusts beat the thin canvas and made it flap sharply throughout the night, but every time it woke Eamonn, he reminded himself it was better than sleeping on the open ground outside. Not to mention, the close proxim-ity of the solider sharing the tent provided a warmth he would otherwise be lacking.

The man's body heat brought memories to the forefront of Eamonn's mind—memories of sleeping close to Leyna on their way to Avaria, of her leaning against him as they rode on Rovis together, of sharing his room with her in the inns as they traveled to Amrieth.

The warm embrace of the memories didn't last as the vision of Leyna's face on their last night in Amrieth swam in his mind's eye yet again. Eamonn squeezed his eyes shut, wanting nothing more than to rid his thoughts of that night. The distress in Leyna's expression. The disappointment glistening in her eyes. The finality overwhelming her voice.

Let me go.

Her voice sounded so close, it could have been whispered in his ear. He tried telling himself that all she'd meant was to let her go away from the pavilion. But he knew—in the deepest part of his heart, he knew—she meant to let *her* go. The idea of them together. The relationship they had begun to build. If he continued in his chosen path, if he followed his darkest desires, there would be no reconciliation. He would lose her.

And yet, they were traveling to the same destination. She would bear witness to his darkness, watch him exact his revenge with her own eyes. For no good reason at all, she would join him at the mountain to see him hammer the final nail in the coffin that had been their love.

Love.

Was it love?

Eamonn had never been in love before, but he didn't know what else to call it. He would offer up every fiber of his being to keep her safe, to ensure she had anything she lacked, to keep her close to him. Even with his plans to defeat Rothgard in the way she despised, that was still true. It would always be true.

The wind whistled and the tent shook, and Eamonn curled up tighter under his thin blanket, willing the thoughts from his mind. He needed sleep. They would arrive at the mountain the next day, and he would require a clear mind and refreshed spirit if he was to locate the mine that led to the abode and bring an end to Rothgard. He couldn't do anything about Leyna until then, anyway.

This was the best way—the only way. He was potentially saving lives to confront Rothgard alone. He would meet him with the magic Rothgard had stolen from him and use it to vanquish him.

Eamonn gritted his teeth, tucked his chin into his chest, and listened to the howling wind until sleep finally overtook him.

TWENTY-NINE

MOUNT IYER COULD EASILY be identified in two ways.

Firstly, it was the mountain at the southernmost tip of the range, and secondly, it was far and away the largest of the Valneria Mountains.

The clouds still clung to the peaks and a fog hung on the air, hiding most of the mountain from view, but anyone near it could grasp the enormity of the mountain and how it dwarfed those to its north.

No snow had fallen from the heavy grey clouds above, but an icy mist showered them. It sent a chill to Eamonn's bones through his layers. Even as he shook with the cold, he thought of how much worse snow would make the conditions, and he tried to appreciate the flecks of ice that adhered to the fibers of his clothes.

Eamonn, Hadli, Ree, and the Mirish soldiers had only to travel a short remaining distance from their last camp to their destination, reaching the northern side of Mount Iyer by mid-morning. Ree directed her company to halt at its northeastern face, nestling into the space between Mount Iyer and its neighbor to the north. Her intention, she told Eamonn and Hadli, was to remain hidden there in the shadow of the mountain. The fog provided additional cover none of them had expected, as though it had been granted in their favor.

Scree from the mountainside crunched under the horses' hooves as Eamonn and Hadli approached Ree. She'd positioned her force in a pocket of rock, the rough mountain faces with their sparse, winter-bare trees acting as walls around them. Some of the soldiers guarded a pass between Mount Iyer and the rest of the range in case anyone came through from the Wolstead side, and another trio of soldiers had been left in sight of their route to keep watch for the others who should arrive shortly.

"We can count on there being an entrance to the mines on the Wolsteadan side of the mountain," Ree said as soon as Hadli and Eamonn were within earshot of her lowered voice. Ice crystals glittered in her hair. "The city of Devrenden is on the opposite side of the mountain, and most of the people there are miners. They'll likely be in the mines at work, so you'll have to take care to avoid them. If they catch wind of our soldiers, they'll retaliate. The last thing we need is renewed hostility between Miren and Wolstead."

Eamonn and Hadli nodded in understanding. Hadli's eyes traveled upward along the sheer rock face before them, and he shielded them from the sleet. "So, what's our best course of action? Exploring the perimeter until we find a way in seems impractical. It would take at least another whole day."

"It would—even longer since you'll have to go on foot." Ree led her dappled grey horse away from the soldiers and into the protection of the mountains. "Through the mountain pass is probably the place to begin. With all the mining along this range, it's not outlandish to think the Wolsteadans would have a series of tunnels connecting the mountains, which might be found in the pass."

"But what if they go under the mountains?" Hadli asked, squinting at Ree.

"We'll figure out pretty quickly if there's no exterior openings anywhere between the mountains. It's the best place to start, at least. Less ground to cover."

Eamonn swallowed past the lump forming in his throat. He was beginning to see the cracks in his plan, the flaws he didn't allow himself to notice before storming away from Amrieth. Eamonn and Ree had pieced together a slipshod plan on their journey, and now it was glaringly obvious how little he'd thought it through. Ree commanded the soldiers, but she had followed Eamonn's lead when it came to what needed to happen at the mountain.

"We don't even know if Rothgard is here," he admitted, his voice breaking. "Looking for a way inside the mountain might just waste time and get us lost."

Ree watched him earnestly, no judgment in her gaze. "What do you suggest?"

Eamonn whirled Rovis around to face the wider opening that led east away from the mountains. "If Rothgard and whoever accompanies him aren't here yet, they'll come from the south, right?" He looked at Hadli as he asked the question.

"Yes, they'd travel through Farneth and approach the mountain from the south."

"So, we need soldiers posted somewhere they can watch the southeastern plains. At least that way, if they haven't arrived, we'll have some warning when they do."

Ree nodded once. "I can station some soldiers to keep watch."

"But"—Hadli's voice was hesitant—"what if he's already here, and we don't know it?"

Eamonn wished he had a good answer. Part of the reason why he'd bolted out of Amrieth in such haste was because he wanted to avoid arriving second. It already gave the advantage to Rothgard.

"Well," he said after a while, his eyes roaming the land around them as though it might give him the answer, "if we send watchmen to the south, they might spot them. But if he's under the mountain already..."

Eamonn chewed on his lower lip. There was no way they could scour the entire network of mines in the mountain. They could lose their way, walk into a trap, or wander for hours and find nothing. He ran a hand along his face, wishing he could tap into Rothgard's mind without seeing him, without knowing where he was, just to pinpoint his location.

Wait.

Eamonn sat straight in the saddle, and Rovis seemed to notice the change in posture, prancing around underneath him. Was he really that brainless? How had he not thought of it before?

Magic leaves traces.

He couldn't access Rothgard's will without laying eyes on him, but that didn't mean he couldn't use other magic. Eamonn could track Rothgard the same way Rothgard had found him in Caen. He had to find the trail of magic.

He flashed his gaze to Hadli and then to Ree, who watched Eamonn with raised brows and questions in their eyes.

"If he's here, I should be able to tell," he said in a rush. "I can track him by his magic."

One side of Hadli's mouth curled, but Ree frowned. "How?" she asked.

"I..."

How? Truth be told, he didn't know. It was another magical skill he hadn't waited around to learn in Avaria.

But then, he had felt the magic coming off of Taran and Teiyn when they'd first arrived in Idyrria. Maybe he knew more than he thought.

Eamonn directed Rovis closer to the mountain and faced it before closing his eyes and calling his magic. It welled within him like water bubbling up from a spring. He allowed the magic to course through his veins for a moment, filling every inch of his body before he tried searching for the magic of another.

Something like a twinkling star floated somewhere ahead of him, bobbing in and out of his knowledge. Weak, but it was there. Eamonn could find no trail leading to it, nothing other than the pinprick itself. It was magic, and it was deep within the mountain, but he didn't know where it was exactly or how to find it.

A faint warmth prodded the back of his mind, and for an instant, his heart dropped. It was another magical aura somewhere behind Eamonn, and he got the sense that it was approaching. He was about to whirl into action, expecting Rothgard to sneak up on them, but the single aura split into three distinctly separate ones. And they were familiar.

He opened his eyes and turned the horse back around to face the northeast. He could see nothing from their hiding spot beside the mountain, but he still detected their magic.

"The rest of our people are close," Eamonn murmured. His stomach flipped at the comfort of Leyna's aura and the thought that she had almost arrived. He wasn't ready to see her. "They'll be here shortly."

"And Rothgard?" Ree asked behind him.

Eamonn sighed and dropped his head, shaking it slightly. "I don't know. There's something in the mountain, but it could be the abode itself. I... I didn't learn how to trace magic."

Hadli rode up beside Eamonn and earnestly met his eyes. "It's a start. You think you can get us to whatever magic you feel inside?"

In truth, Eamonn had no idea. Assuming they even found a passage inside the mountain, he didn't know if he would be able to guide them through a potential labyrinth of mines and find the source of the magic he had detected. But he faced Hadli, hoping he didn't display his uncertainty. "I can try."

Hadli gave a curt nod and tugged at his horse's reins. "All right," he said, turning the animal's head toward the mountain pass. "Let's give it a shot."

Hadli rode around the troops to the place between mountains, with Eamonn and Ree close behind. He hopped down and handed over the reins to a soldier nearby, and Eamonn did the same. Eamonn thought about taking his pack off the saddle, but he didn't know what to expect in the mines. As much as he wanted to prepare for anything, he also didn't want to lose everything he'd brought with him somewhere in the mountain.

"How long should we give you before we send someone in?" Ree asked the question so placidly, but when Eamonn met her eyes, he saw the concern there. If she didn't like their plan, she didn't say anything.

Eamonn looked at Hadli, who shrugged before turning back to Ree. "Two hours. That gives us some time to travel back as well, in case we don't find anything."

"And what if *we* don't find *you*?"

Eamonn picked up on the implication in her words, asking more than what to do if they got lost in the mines. What if something happened to them, either at Rothgard's hand or the hands of Wolsteadan miners?

After a heavy breath, Eamonn said, "If we can't be found after another two hours—or we're found, and we're not walking back out—then seek counsel from Kinrid and Gilleth. They might advise you to wait for their army, or possibly go back to Miren to give the army more time."

Ree dipped her head in understanding, and Eamonn was about to set off before her voice grabbed his attention. This time, he heard weight in it.

"Eamonn. Hadli."

Her mare fidgeted impatiently, but Ree steadied her as she held their gazes in turn.

"Good luck."

She didn't linger after her farewell, and Eamonn wondered if it was so she could prepare for the arrival of their friends or because she didn't want to watch them disappear between the mountains.

The suddenness of Ree's departure sent Eamonn's heart into a wild thrum. There was nothing else left for them now but to go searching for this abode in the mountain. For Rothgard.

As much as Eamonn had wanted to be at this point—in a position where he could take Rothgard's will captive and make him pay for all he'd done to Eamonn—he was afraid. What lay before them was a mystery, and their plans were shaky, at best. For the first time, Eamonn found himself regretting not waiting for the army of Farnish and Teravalen soldiers that had allied together for this exact purpose. Eamonn rubbed his fingers along his brow and studied the passage ahead. He could be walking into a death trap.

The rising unease within him transformed into a fear he didn't understand, something of himself and yet not. He hadn't felt it in a few days. His stomach clenched with nausea and his hands began to tremble. Eamonn tried to control the dread, tried to push it out of his innermost being, but it remained, as though it didn't respond to his commands.

When he finally forced his feet to move over the slick scree from the mountainside despite the overwhelming fear, Eamonn caught Hadli's eyes on him. He watched Eamonn with a cool scrutiny, but his expression wasn't hostile. He looked like he had seen Eamonn's anxiety written all over his face and now expected him to turn back.

"You all right?"

Eamonn nodded, probably too quickly to be reassuring. "I'm fine."

Rocks crunched under their boots as they traveled down the narrow, winding passage, barely wide enough for the two of them to walk side by side. A moment of silence passed between them before Hadli spoke again.

"We could go back, you know." His voice was low and sincere, and it brought Eamonn to a halt. "We can keep watch for Rothgard and his army while we wait for the forces in Farneth to arrive."

Eamonn tried to swallow, but his throat had gone dry. Part of him wanted to latch on to that idea, to take a step back and reevaluate what they were doing. But he didn't want to look like a coward.

He started walking again, brushing off Hadli's words with a shrug that he hoped looked more carefree than he felt. "If

Rothgard isn't here and we can find the abode, we'll have an advantage. There's no point in sitting around to wait."

Hadli didn't give a reply, and they continued down the mountain path, softening their footfalls until the wind above them covered any sound they made. They dissolved into no more than ghosts, silent surveyors of the rocky crag.

The fog around them shrouded the sky, so Eamonn couldn't keep track of how long they traveled. He and Hadli melted into the misty shadows, and he was grateful for the cover, but it made spotting any kind of opening in the mountain face more difficult. He still felt the hint of magic in the mountain like an ember, pulsing with a low heat, but he had no way of knowing how to find it.

Time stretched and lost much of its meaning. Nothing about the mountainside changed as they crept along, and Eamonn started to feel stuck, like they were traveling in circles. The only blessed benefit was that his unexplained fear had finally gone.

Eamonn nearly jumped out of his skin when Hadli's sudden whisper seemed to shout through the silence.

"Look, there." He pointed to a shadow in the distance, a possible opening in the rock. "That might be our way in."

Hadli took the lead, creeping forward cautiously, and Eamonn followed close behind him. He peered ahead to the apparent crevice, watching for any flutter of movement. Nothing. They were alone.

As they approached, Eamonn realized the opening was much more than a crevice; it was a squared-off entrance, deliberately cut out of the rock. The hard-packed dirt path leading inside told of frequent use. Hadli must have noticed as well, because he stopped and turned to look at Eamonn.

"I think it's clear, for now."

For now was the operative phrase. "We have to stay sharp."

Hadli gave a nod of agreement, and they slipped through the entrance into the mountain.

Just inside, a series of torches hung in rows on either side of the tunnel. Hadli took one out of its sconce and paused for a moment. The deep, consuming darkness of the mine yawned before them, their only light the flickering flame in Hadli's grasp. Eamonn's heart skittered, and a thin film of sweat formed on his palms as fear unexpectedly gripped his heart. Eamonn wiped his hands on his trousers, hoping Hadli didn't notice. Hadli, however, seemed entirely at ease. A grin split his face and he met Eamonn's eyes.

"This is just like old times, too, huh?"

It wasn't quite the same, of course, because the opening to the cave was broad and manmade instead of a thin, hidden split in the rock. But, with Hadli by his side, the dark, dank mine did remind him of the cave in Erai where the Thieves' Guild had been based.

"Let's just hope there's no one other than us in here, either."

Hadli nudged Eamonn with his elbow, exuding confidence. "Come on. Let's go find out."

For a while, their journey was easy and unhindered. A wide path led down into the cold heart of the mountain, and, to Eamonn's surprise, occasional torches on the cave walls lit the way, making the iron and other metals in the rock sparkle. Ruts had been ground into the dirt by the wheels of carts. Tunnels diverted off the main path every so often, but Eamonn didn't feel magic drawing him down any of them. No, he felt the pull to go farther, deeper.

The main path began to narrow and slope upward, with fewer small tunnels branching off. Soon, the walls lacked torches and came closer in to them on all sides, forcing them to walk in single file. This time, Eamonn led the way. Though it didn't give a clear direction, the heat and thrum of magic steadily grew as they traveled down the path. They came across no one, heard no sound other than the quiet thud of their own boots. It couldn't be right; it seemed too easy. Unless magic had been drawing Eamonn the entire time.

Hadli and Eamonn had kept conversation to a minimum, fearing their voices would carry through the tunnels of stone. It gave Eamonn too much time with his thoughts, and somehow, even with the unknown ever looming ahead of him, they always went back to Leyna. It didn't matter that they were trekking through a mountain with no clear direction and possible enemies awaiting them. Eamonn continually had Leyna on his mind. She would be with Ree and her soldiers by now. Eamonn's stomach growled, and he hoped Leyna wasn't hungry. He shivered, and he hoped she was warm enough.

Something in the atmosphere of the mine changed. Magic was close.

Eamonn came to an abrupt stop, and Hadli almost ran into him.

"What is it?" Hadli's voice was barely a whisper.

Eamonn didn't answer but turned around and reached his hand out to Hadli's torch. Hadli relinquished the torch, and Eamonn fanned it out slowly in front of him. The tunnel they followed continued up, but another tight path descended off to their right, the unmistakable hum of magic emanating from within. Eamonn lowered the torch toward the descending tunnel, barely large enough for one man to walk upright, and a faint red glow shone back at him.

"I think that's Arithnyx," Eamonn murmured as his wide eyes took in the glittering red specks in the tunnel. "This has to be the way."

A racing heart and trembling limbs replaced the calmness that had settled within him after their uneventful travel in the mines. Eamonn shook, but he didn't think the cave's cold dampness was the cause.

He dipped his head and extended his arm with the torch in front of him, and he took careful steps down the slope of the tunnel. The rock walls enclosing them sparkled deep red in the light. Much as it had in Avaria, magic was no longer only a hum Eamonn felt within himself; the vibration of magical energy came from their surroundings as well.

"Do you feel that?" he asked Hadli over his shoulder.

"Yeah." Hadli's reply came out in a breath. "Is that magic?"

"It is," Eamonn answered. The ember of magic that had been tugging him the whole time had burst into a flame. It was magnetic, inviting, forcing his feet forward. He had no doubts now that the tunnel would bring them to the door the Wolsteadan miners had discovered and then abandoned: the door that led into the Kaethiri abode.

In the snap of a finger, the energy of the magic shifted. The enchanting, optimistic lure of the magic around them darkened as though polluted by something else. Something evil. Something... cursed.

The blood drained out of Eamonn's face, and his stomach dropped. He stopped short again. Behind him, Hadli tripped but quickly regained his balance.

"Now what?"

Eamonn couldn't swallow past the lump in his throat. "He's here."

THIRTY

Relief twisted with anxiety in Leyna when two Mirish soldiers met them outside the mountain to lead them to the rest of their force. The past two days had been nothing but hard travel and little sleep, and she was grateful to have arrived at their destination, but her heart constricted to know she was that close to seeing Eamonn again. To witnessing what he had come to do.

Dorylss had requested that she stay behind, saying there was no point for her to needlessly endanger herself. He suggested she could stay in the palace as a guest of King Javorak and, therefore, under his protection. As an ambassador—even though he didn't always embrace the title—he could arrange it. But Leyna had outright refused. It didn't matter how much she and Eamonn disagreed. She wouldn't be left in Amrieth to worry and wonder and imagine all the horrible things that could be happening. Eamonn didn't have a plan. He had anger, impatience, and an intense longing to bring Rothgard to an end, but that wasn't enough. He didn't seem to see it—or if he did, he didn't care—but Leyna did. So, she would not sit in the Mirish palace, waiting anxiously for news while Eamonn risked his life and his soul.

When they reached the company of Mirish soldiers, Leyna's heart soared to see fires built in the camp, their smoke obscured by fog and clouds. She restrained herself from leaping off her horse and running across the hard-packed dirt to warm herself by one. The biting cold had chilled her down to her bones, made only worse by the frost covering their camp in the morning and the ice that rained down on them for the last leg of travel. If she'd stayed in Miren, she could have been sitting in front of a roaring fire in one of the massive fireplaces, comfortably reading a book while lounging on a plush chaise. Leyna shook her head. No. This was where she wanted to be. Where she *needed* to be.

Ree rode up to greet them, her shining royal armor a stark contrast to the muted neutrals she typically wore. Dorylss, Gilleth, and Kinrid had filled Leyna in on the discovery of Ree's true identity, and she realized at that moment that she hadn't fully believed them until she saw Ree in an outfit more suited to the heir to the Mirish throne. The shock washed over Leyna again as Ree approached them, sending her mind into a flurry of recalling their interactions and piecing together the signs.

"Welcome," Ree said, a white smile brightening the gloom. "How did you fare?"

"Well," Gilleth answered, returning her niece's smile. She rode her horse alongside Ree's and grasped her arm near the elbow, and Ree did the same.

Where's Eamonn? Leyna wanted to say, to scream, but she kept her mouth shut. Her eyes flitted over the crowd before them, looking for anyone not dressed like the Mirish soldiers. Too many horses stood in the way, and the people stretched far back to the face of the mountain. If Eamonn was around, she couldn't spot him.

"I'm glad you made it here safely. Come over to a fire and warm up. Siluria and Tevner can take your horses and tie them off." Ree motioned toward the two soldiers who had ridden up to meet them.

Leyna and her group dismounted, and though she, Taran, and Teiyn left their horses in the care of the Mirish soldiers, Dorylss, Kinrid, and Gilleth walked their mounts to a tie-off point with Ree, presumably to get an update from her. Taran and Teiyn headed straight for the closest fire, but Leyna was tempted to turn on her heel and follow after the others to find out the latest news. Where was Eamonn? She hadn't spotted Hadli either. Did that mean they went somewhere together?

Lagging behind because of her indecision, Leyna jogged a few paces to catch up to the twins, and the small crowd of soldiers shuffled around the fire to make room for them.

"Here," one to Leyna's right said as she dug through her pack. "We don't have much, but we have tea." The soldier found a cup, spooned some leaves into it, and poured hot water from a small, travel-beaten kettle over the leaves. "It'll help warm you."

She held out the cup and Leyna took it with an appreciative smile. "Thank you," she said before blowing over the steaming liquid. *Bless them*. Eamonn had given her the impression that all Mirs were haughty and entitled, but not this woman. With a glance around the fire, she didn't believe any of the soldiers fit the stereotypical Mirish profile. Perhaps that's what set these soldiers apart—why they had turned on their king and followed Ree in the first place.

Leyna sipped her tea, and even though it burned her tongue a little, she was grateful for the heat filling her insides. She examined the area where they had set up camp, mostly enclosed by the imposing mountains, and a shudder ran down her spine. It might be a good place to lay low—or a good place to get trapped.

She puffed a white breath over her drink again and took another sip. The cold air around them quickly brought the tea to a more drinkable temperature, and Leyna drained the cup. She returned it to the soldier with more thanks, then surveyed the crowd again. No Eamonn or Hadli, but she spotted the rest of her companions with Ree at another fire.

"I'll be right back," she said to Taran and Teiyn, but she didn't wait for a response before leaving the circle and striding over to where Ree spoke to the others.

"...so he thinks he can find it. He couldn't tell if Rothgard was—" Ree caught sight of Leyna approaching and cut herself off.

"If Rothgard was what?" Leyna repeated as a question. Dorylss shifted at the fire to make room for her. She locked her eyes on Ree.

A flicker of hesitation passed over Ree's face as she pressed her lips into a line and studied Leyna, and Leyna's insides burned. Did Ree want to keep things from her? Leyna had been involved in everything leading up to that point, and Ree had never seemed to distrust her before. But the look on Ree's face didn't betray a lack of trust as much as it did something else, something that took Leyna a moment to place.

Pity.

"Where's Eamonn?" she demanded, the heat in her middle rushing to her face.

"Inside the mountain with Hadli," Ree replied without pause. "He felt magic deep in the mountain, and he thinks it might be the abode Rothgard is looking for, but he couldn't determine whether or not Rothgard was already there."

All the warmth she'd acquired from the tea and her own embarrassment drained out of Leyna's body, and she clutched her arms to suppress a shiver. "They don't know if he's there? And just the two of them went?" Her eyes shot from Ree to Dorylss to anyone else, unsure where to land. Her voice was ripe with panic. "It could be a trap. Or even if it's not, it's too easy for them to get lost, or if Rothgard arrives before they make it out, he could pin them in, or—"

"They've been in the mountain just under an hour." Ree interrupted Leyna, but not unkindly. The look of pity had returned. Or was it more like compassion? "If they don't make it back before two, I'll send people in."

Leyna rolled her lips together and nodded quickly, not sure what else to say. Eamonn had chosen to do this. He probably didn't understand all the implications surrounding what he was doing, but he never truly had. He wasn't one for thinking things through before taking action; at least, not lately. Leyna feared he might face the consequences of not taking the time to construct a thorough plan. They all might.

Gilleth peppered Ree with more questions, but Leyna couldn't stay focused on the conversation. She sat on the cold dirt by the fire and curled around herself. In the time it took them to travel from Amrieth to Mount Iyer, Leyna had hoped Eamonn would consider what he was doing. She thought that after the intensity of his emotions after the failed attempt at blackmail died down, he might think more clearly. Apparently, he was determined to follow through, foolish as it was. He had no idea where Rothgard was or if he had even reached the mountain. They had no real army and no clue what size force Rothgard might bring with him.

There was a chance they could get lucky. Eamonn could find the abode first, and their army from Farneth might join them before Rothgard arrived—even shortly after would be helpful. But those scenarios seemed like far-off possibilities, and the thought of the alternatives made Leyna's stomach churn with unease.

Leyna rested her chin on her knee and tugged her cloak around her like a blanket. At this point, there was really, truly nothing she could do but wait.

She sighed. Wait for what? For Rothgard to arrive? For Eamonn to get in trouble? Running off to Wolstead had left them so vulnerable. Ree and Eamonn seemed to be heading up this expedition, and neither of them had any real military or strategy experience. Their "plan," if they dared to call it that, was like trying to catch the wind. Even with Gilleth, Kinrid, and Dorylss there, they hadn't come up with anything better than to let Eamonn see what he could find in the mountain and go from there.

But that might get them all killed.

Leyna stood so abruptly that she drew the attention of everyone at their fire and nearly toppled over as the blood rushed from her head. She briefly closed her eyes, steadied herself, and faced Ree.

"We can't stay here."

Ree knitted her brows low over her eyes. "What?"

"I know you said you'd give Eamonn and Hadli another hour, but you need to send people in to find them now. Bring them back out." Her heart sped up, galloping in her chest as she found her mettle. Words that had lived in her mind finally reached her mouth. "We don't have any way to know when Rothgard might show up, or what kind of force he has with him. We don't *really* know what he's capable of right now. And this"—Leyna lifted her hands, gesturing to the mountain faces half-surrounding them—"is a trap waiting to happen. We need to leave, go to the nearest city or village with the capacity to house everyone, and strategize there."

Dorylss and Gilleth watched Leyna with wide eyes. Kinrid, impassive as ever, regarded her coolly. Ree's frown deepened for a moment, and she crossed her arms, but her face began to relax before being flooded with concern.

"I saw the mountains as protection, not as a prison, but you're right. We've boxed ourselves in. We could make for the Wolsteadan city of Devrenden on the other side of the mountain," she said, her voice low and even. "A contingent of Mirish soldiers won't go unnoticed; we will probably have targets on our backs from the minute we make it to the city." Her eyes flashed to Gilleth. "Dunhurst is to the south: their kingdom. But that's one of the last places in all of Sarieth we need to be."

Gilleth nodded her agreement. "Dunhurst is publicly loyal to Rothgard. Their leaders are sympathizers and only have power because Rothgard helped to remove their king."

Leyna waited for a moment, expecting someone to offer up an alternative. "Is there nowhere else? Nothing along this side of the mountain range?"

Ree looked to Gilleth again, as if seeking answers or advice from her aunt. She was a couple of years older than Leyna, but the uncertainty in her eyes betrayed her youth and inexperience. "Sirvan is a Mirish mining city, but it's far to the north. We might as well go back to Amrieth if we go there." She swallowed and found Leyna again. "There are a few mining communities here and there along the range, but they're not big and do most of their business in Sirvan. They don't have the infrastructure to support our numbers."

"There are small towns and villages near the western borders of Farneth, but they aren't far from the road that we presume Rothgard is taking," Gilleth added, and she shook her head. "We might walk right into him on the way."

Leyna curled her fingers into fists to stop her hands from shaking, her nails biting into her palms. A tight knot of fear rose in her chest. Her only comfort was seeing her own desperation mirrored in Ree's expression and to know that she now seemed to understand how dire their circumstances could easily become.

"Send the soldiers into the mountain," Leyna said over Ree and Gilleth's continued discussion. Both women swiveled their heads to Leyna. "We need to get Eamonn and Hadli out first. We can deliberate while we're waiting."

"I'll go," Dorylss said, squaring his shoulders. "I'll find them."

"Take a couple of my people with you," Ree insisted as Dorylss took a step to go. "I don't want anyone going in there alone."

Dorylss gave a quick nod and strode swiftly away, recruiting soldiers to accompany him as he went.

"We could try going through the mountain pass," Ree suggested, following Dorylss's path with her eyes. "It would be slow going with the horses, but we might not be detected that way."

Kinrid rubbed a hand over his chin. "What would we do then? Make for Devrenden?"

Ree chewed her lip. "Possibly. I don't like it, though. The Wolsteadans are going to see us as intruders, whether we oppose Rothgard or not. Being Mirish soldiers is enough to cause trouble."

"Perhaps one of the smaller mining towns on the Wolstead side of the mountains would be more hospitable." Even as Kinrid said it, doubt consumed his features.

"We might have to—"

Ree's words were lost in a growing thunder, the roar of horses' hooves against the hard ground. Leyna's head shot to the opening between the mountains, and in the fog, she saw nothing. But she didn't have to. An army was upon them.

"Get to the horses!" Ree yelled, and soldiers scrambled to untie the leads. The chaos spooked many of the beasts and they whinnied and struggled against their bridles. Through the mass of moving bodies, Leyna searched for Dorylss. She couldn't spot him in the bedlam, so she hoped that meant he'd made it to the mountain pass. When she turned back to locate Ree, Gilleth, and Kinrid, she only found Ree atop her dappled mare, kicking the horse into a canter and riding around the perimeter of her forces, shouting orders.

Leyna didn't know where Hiraeth had been tied off, and she would never find him through the soldiers mounting their own horses and the dust they kicked up. She glanced again to the wide opening between the mountains as the rumble of hooves grew to be deafening. Kinrid and Gilleth rode in the direction of the invasion, leading the few soldiers who had managed to get atop their horses.

A long, dark shadow appeared in the fog seconds before dozens of riders on horseback, dressed in uncoordinated blacks, greys, and browns, burst through the cloud, stretching the length of the opening. Their ranks extended into the mist behind them; how far, Leyna couldn't tell.

The Mirish soldiers rushed to mount horses and ride to defend, but Leyna knew it was already too late.

The invading force stopped, creating a wall between the mountains to prevent their escape, and Kinrid, Gilleth, and Ree did not lead the soldiers into an attack. Even without seeing how far the opposing force extended, it was clear they were vastly outnumbered.

Enemy horses pressed in, pushing the Mirish back. Leyna scanned the crowd of Mirish soldiers for Taran and Teiyn, who should stand out among the soldiers, but she didn't spot them. She flung her gaze toward the mountain pass, praying it could still serve as an escape. Her eyes landed on Dorylss with his hands raised at the tip of a sword; he must have been pushed out of the pass by more of the dark-clad riders who now filled the space.

Leyna's breath left her lungs in a gust, and worry closed around her middle, making her stomach squirm. Their backup plan was not an option.

They were trapped.

Ree directed her horse back and forth in front of the enemy riders, who jeered and threatened but didn't strike. Kinrid and Gilleth weren't far behind her, their heads tilted low toward each other as their horses jigged. Maybe they were coming up with a plan. Maybe they had some ideas. Maybe—

A hand grasped Leyna's forearm and she whirled to see who had taken hold of her, but as she whipped her head, the world spun entirely too much and turned black. When the vertigo stopped and she looked behind her, she realized she was no longer outside at all. Dark rock walls that glittered red surrounded her on all sides. What little warmth there had been in the air had evaporated and was replaced with a chilly dankness.

The hair on the back of Leyna's neck stood on end and her skin broke out in goosebumps as her eyes adjusted in the dim torchlight.

She was inside the mountain.

And the hand that held her belonged to Rothgard.

THIRTY-ONE

EAMONN TRIED TO CONTROL the heavy pounding of his heart as it threatened to beat right through his chest, creeping through the sparkling red tunnel with Hadli right behind. He didn't have to see Rothgard to know he was there. The darkness he felt in the magic told Eamonn everything. What he didn't understand was how it appeared so suddenly. Had Rothgard teleported inside moments ago? He must have already been somewhere around the mountain, his eyes on the Mirish force from the moment they arrived. Eamonn's stomach knotted. All that hope of them having the upper hand, and it was just a lie he told himself to feel like they had a chance. Now, nothing else stood in the way of him facing Rothgard again.

He slowed to a stop before the tunnel opened into another passage, and Hadli came close and whispered in his ear.

"You're really going to do this?"

Eamonn swallowed, searching for the resolve that had helped form his grand plans and sent him running off to Mount Iyer in the first place. "Yeah," he replied in a low murmur, and he sucked a breath through his nose.

A sharp female gasp followed by a harsh, "Let go of me!" sounded from the passage before them. Eamonn's blood ran cold.

Leyna.

A new panic overtook his heart, and he burst through the end of the tunnel. He didn't have to search for his resolve anymore; any apprehension he'd felt to face off with Rothgard disappeared at the sound of Leyna's voice.

The next passage was both wider and taller, still full of the sparkling Arithnyx, and the moment Eamonn's feet landed outside the tunnel, he had his magic at the ready. His Réalta glowed bright green in the red cavern, cutting through the dimness like a beacon.

Rothgard clutched Leyna's arm a few feet away, the colored lights shining off his glossy black hair and casting competing shadows on his pale skin and dark clothes. Eamonn stormed toward them. It was easy for Eamonn to feel Rothgard's magic with his own—it was overwhelming. The wickedness of Rothgard's cursed magic pulsed around his aura like a black flame, its unseen tendrils long and whip-like. Eamonn reached past it with his own magic, easily pushing it out of his way, but when he got to Rothgard's mind, his magic stopped.

He didn't want to close his eyes for fear of what Rothgard might do while he wasn't looking, but he concentrated better that way. For a brief moment, Eamonn's eyelids flickered shut, and he reached for control of Rothgard's mind again. And again, the magic was blocked.

"It won't work," came Rothgard's silky smooth voice, and Eamonn opened his eyes. "Have you forgotten I have your very own blood? Kaethiri cannot control Kaethiri, and I've discovered how to use my magic to protect me where I am vulnerable."

In the plane where their magic was tangible, the tendrils of Rothgard's magic rushed toward Eamonn, and he set up his own defense. His breath came in tight gasps as the magic parted around him, and he wordlessly thanked the Kaethiri for teaching him that skill, at least.

A snarl curled Rothgard's lips. "I see you have learned the same."

Eamonn tensed his neck as he tried to control the wrath overtaking him. Through gritted teeth, he growled, "You are *not* Kaethiri."

"Oh, I am as much Kaethiri as you, Eamonn."

The muscles of Eamonn's jaw rippled as he ground his teeth and held his tongue. It wasn't true. Rothgard was baiting him, trying to provoke a reaction or a response. Or... did he actually believe that?

Regardless, Eamonn's plan—his hope of defeating Rothgard—was gone like a vapor. What could he do if he couldn't take over Rothgard's will? He'd had no doubts it would work. He'd been counting on it. He'd envisioned this moment for so long, yearning for the time he would see Rothgard again and seek revenge on everything he'd done to him. But Eamonn's strategy was going up in smoke. He'd come to the end of a rope where he hung over a void, unable to climb back up, and Leyna had been set on the rope with him.

Now, he faced Rothgard with ineffective magic and no support but Hadli. No other magic caster, no army, nothing.

Eamonn studied Rothgard, desperate to find susceptibilities, but what he did notice about Rothgard distracted him—details that had been difficult to spot in the weak light of the mine.

Rothgard's skin was tinted grey and striped with black veins going up his neck, just grazing his jaw, and extending down into his hands. The sunken hollows of his cheeks pulled skin tight over his bones, making him look withered, as though the life had been sucked out of him. His once icy blue eyes had transformed to a sharp gold color, cutting through Eamonn like a sword.

A bright red gem blazed at his chest, pointed at both ends and the same color as the stones in the cavern. A rough casing of unpolished gold enclosed the large gemstone. Images flew to Eamonn's mind of the sketch Kinrid and Gilleth had found. The metal casing was nearly identical to the sketch they believed Rothgard had made. Seeing the product from that sketch right in front of him made Eamonn's head swim.

The thrum of the Arithnyx surrounding them had intensified with Eamonn's and Rothgard's use of magic, flowing through Eamonn similar to the way magic had in Avaria. He longed to draw deep into his well of magic and pull out something catastrophic, but he couldn't do anything that might also harm Leyna. Rothgard held her left wrist in a vice grip, and Leyna didn't struggle. He must have threatened her somehow before Eamonn appeared because Eamonn had heard her resist, but now, she stood there complicitly, her chin tipped up in defiance but her body still.

Rothgard's eyes moved from Eamonn over his shoulder to Hadli a few paces behind him. His snarl transformed into a wicked smile, and he looked down his nose at Hadli through narrowed eyes.

"Well done, Hadli."

Eamonn's heart stopped with those three words. Willing it to beat again, he spun on his heel to meet Hadli's gaze. Hadli's jaw tightened, and he didn't look at Eamonn, instead dropping his eyes to the ground.

Eamonn searched for words, but he couldn't find anything to appropriately convey how the razor-sharp knife of betrayal had stabbed his heart. He could only release a pained breath and murmur, "Hadli."

Hadli didn't reply and stepped past Eamonn, his attention ahead on Rothgard. Before reaching him, Hadli paused, turning his head toward his shoulder and casting a quick glance back at Eamonn. Something hovered in his eyes: an emotion Eamonn couldn't place. If there was something Hadli wanted to say, he didn't say it. The moment was over in a flash, and Hadli continued on to stand behind Rothgard.

"If you wish to save your friend," Rothgard announced, yanking Leyna's wrist into the air for effect, "you will open the door to the abode."

Eamonn had been so consumed with trying to control Rothgard and failing that he'd entirely failed to notice the peculiarities of the cave wall where Rothgard stood. Flickering firelight from a torch on the opposite wall softly illuminated the passage and drew Eamonn's gaze. The walls of the passage had been excavated by miners seeking Arithnyx, coming to an end at a slab of rock devoid of gems but detailed with intricate carvings. A design of loops, lines, and swirls on the smooth stone highlighted it against the rough rock of the mine. The distinct straight sides and arched top of the design gave it the indisputable appearance of a door, though it had no handle or hinges or any visible separation from the stone of the mountain.

"I don't know how to open it," Eamonn spat, and it was true. The pulse of Avarian magic wafted through the air from the area around the carved stone, so it had to be the door to the abode

Rothgard sought, but Eamonn didn't have the first inclination of how to open it. He assumed Rothgard must know but lacked the power. *He's weak*, Hadli had said. Eamonn's insides burned with indignation at Hadli's duplicity. He still believed that what Hadli had told them was true—or, at least, most of it. He'd told them the abode was exactly what Rothgard needed to build his strength. Rothgard must have been too weak to open the door, and he needed Eamonn—the only other being with Kaethiri blood who didn't dwell in Avaria—to open it for him.

So he'd used Hadli to lure him to the mountain on the pretense of having an advantage.

Rage seeped from Eamonn's heart and flooded his soul. If Leyna wasn't there, he would pull this mountain down on them and end them all. But Rothgard had thought ahead there, too. He needed to ensure Eamonn wouldn't try anything.

"You do," Rothgard countered, not an ounce of hostility in his voice. He could have been chatting with a friend. "You may not realize it, but you can open that door almost without even trying."

Eamonn's chest heaved as he sucked in the damp mine air through his nose. He had to come up with a plan, and fast. He stood completely alone against Rothgard, now that Hadli had betrayed him yet again.

"If she's not enough incentive to open the door, then you should know my people have your entire little band outside the mountain surrounded." Rothgard laughed once humorlessly, and the blacks of his eyes seemed to push out some of the gold. "I'm actually insulted you truly believed a force that small would be enough to protect you—enough to stop me."

Eamonn's face and neck were on fire, no doubt the same color as the gems glittering all around them. By the stars, he should have waited for the army Kinrid and Gilleth had been building for this exact purpose. If he wasn't careful, Eamonn would get them and Dorylss killed, too. And Taran and Teiyn. And Ree.

"I can tell you exactly what you need to know to open that door. And if you don't," Rothgard threatened, giving Leyna's arm another jerk, "she goes first."

"You can't do it, Eamonn." Leyna shook her head wildly. "You can't let him in. Ree's soldiers will fight. His magic is too weak—"

"It is *so* disappointing that I can't take over your mind," Rothgard said with exaggerated annoyance. He rolled his eyes before boring them into Leyna. "But since I cannot, I will have to resort to other methods to shut you up, so I *suggest* you be quiet."

Leyna sealed her mouth shut and pulled her eyes from Rothgard's glare to find Eamonn. Her eyebrows were scrunched together, pleading. She didn't want Eamonn to open the abode's door, even with her own life at risk. Did she have a plan? Even if she did, there was no way for her to let Eamonn know.

"To open the door—"

"I won't do it." Eamonn's quick response took Rothgard by surprise, his eyes widening. Eamonn stood his ground, squaring his shoulders and tilting back his head. Rothgard recovered quickly, a mocking smile tugging at his lips, but Hadli's gaze flicked between Eamonn and Rothgard as his mouth fell slightly agape.

"So noble," Rothgard said, derision dripping from the words. "But it's wasted, I'm afraid. Let me be plain." Blackness consumed Rothgard's eyes and his smooth voice lowered to a guttural snarl. "I will stop at nothing to get through this door. You can do as I say and open it now, or you will have to forever live with the consequences of finding out firsthand that I follow through with my threats."

A cascade of ice sent a shiver down Eamonn's spine, and he looked again at Leyna. Her boldness had waned, indecision and fear creeping into her face.

"Now, are you going to open the door, or not?"

Eamonn swallowed hard and he began to speak, the words rising unbidden to his tongue. "The Kaethiri told me that amulet with my blood is cursing you." His chest rose and fell with quick breaths. "They told me your power has a limit, and that's why you need to get into the abode. I'm not sure your threats have as much weight as you're leading me to believe."

Eamonn assumed Rothgard would fly into an outburst, start shooting some kind of magic around in a chaotic response to Eamonn's prodding with a show of power, and in his focus on attacking Eamonn, he would release Leyna. Then, Eamonn and Leyna could come back with their own magic. Leyna was inexperienced, but it might be enough combined with Eamonn's to help them escape.

Anger flared in Rothgard's features for a heartbeat, but then he collected himself and smiled.

"The Kaethiri." He drew out the word. "That's what they told you, eh? And you trust the Kaethiri?"

It felt like a trap, but Eamonn nodded nonetheless.

"And what did the Kaethiri tell you about your mother?"

Eamonn's mouth went dry. Not much, yet, but he wouldn't admit that to Rothgard. "That she was good, and kind, and that her only crime was falling in love with a human." Emotion threatened to close Eamonn's throat and his eyes burned, but he pushed down the rising sob.

"They didn't tell you *how* a Kaethiri could fall in love in the first place?"

"They don't know." The words left his lips automatically. It was true, but Eamonn felt like he'd been put on the defensive.

"'They don't know,'" Rothgard mimicked, scowling. "Have they pulled the wool completely over your eyes, boy? Did they tell you of your father?"

Eamonn didn't know why he felt the compulsion to answer Rothgard. Maybe it was seeing his father in Rothgard's service in the tower at Holoreath. "They told me they took my father's memory of his love for me." It stung his heart to hear himself say it, even though he'd processed it back in Avaria.

"Ah, yes, they'd given up the practice of manipulating wills but were willing to make exceptions when necessary. You think the same thing, do you not? Certain situations call for an exception to their prohibition of tethering to a consciousness."

How would Rothgard know he believed that? He had blocked Eamonn's attempt to gain control over his mind the moment they'd met in the passage, so he knew Eamonn was willing. Was that, along with his own knowledge of the Kaethiri, enough to put the pieces together?

"You put your faith in the Kaethiri, but there is much they've kept from you, and not just in the use of magic. They may be powerful, but they are not great. If you believe them faultless, they have deceived you." The way Rothgard spoke was filled with genuine contempt rather than taunting jeers designed to topple Eamonn's high regard for the magical beings. "I'm certain they failed to tell you they *allowed* your mother to die. It was within their power to save her, but they did not."

Eamonn's fingernails cut into his palms. Rothgard was just trying to get to him; there was no truth in his accusations. There couldn't be.

"The Kaethiri are not to be trusted," Rothgard continued, the fervor in his speech causing him to jostle Leyna where he still clutched her arm. "I know you feel it deep inside. They were too resistant to training you in all the ways of Avarian magic. They are choosing to keep things from you under the guise of protection. They don't want you to learn the truth."

A storm raged within Eamonn, everything he thought he believed warring with his mistrust of the Kaethiri and Rothgard's claims. The Kaethiri had given Eamonn plenty of reason to turn against them, though they had appeared good and just on the surface. Somehow, what Rothgard was saying made sense, and it struck a chord within Eamonn. He still hated Rothgard and believed he needed to be stopped, but why did that mean the Kaethiri automatically deserved his trust? What if they didn't want him to open the abode? What might *he* gain from the dwelling's magic?

Eamonn found Leyna's eyes and saw a new worry flash over her face. She could see right through him; she'd come to know him too well. Her chest heaved with a deep breath, and he noticed a slight shake of her head.

She also ought to know he would *never* sacrifice her, even if it meant stopping Rothgard.

"Do you want to find out what lies at the end of this passage, Eamonn?" Rothgard's tone had shifted again, now cool and slick and enticing. "The magic of the mountain is meant for you as much as it is for me."

It wasn't meant for Rothgard at all, but Eamonn wouldn't say so. If anything, the abode would supercharge Eamonn's magic,

as Avaria had, and it should fill him much more quickly than
Rothgard, given Rothgard's current state. It wasn't just the
only way out of this mess... it might actually give Eamonn the
upper hand.

"To open it—"

Eamonn cut Rothgard off. He would take as much control
of the situation as he possibly could. "If you say I can open
the door without trying, then let me." Eamonn held back
most of his disdain. He needed Rothgard to think he'd won
him over enough to open the abode. Rothgard had piqued
his curiosity, it was true, and had given him new misgivings
about the Kaethiri, but he wanted Rothgard to believe that
was all there was—not that he planned to use the magic of
the abode himself.

Rothgard didn't release Leyna as Eamonn passed, making
for the end of the passage. Hadli stepped aside, and Eamonn
didn't so much as grace him with a glance. He'd crossed Eamonn for the last time. Eamonn wouldn't make the mistake
of trusting him again.

Magic hummed so strongly the closer he came to the door
that it made every inch of Eamonn's skin buzz, as though a
constant current of electricity ran over him. The door drew
him like a magnet, and his hands lifted involuntarily. Eamonn
pressed his palms into the cool, smooth stone, and he followed
the trail of one of the carved designs with a finger. He closed
his eyes and summoned his magic again to the surface, bringing his heartbeat to the rhythm of the magic around him.

The power on the other side of the door was so intense, it was
staggering. The magic of the abode couldn't be stronger than
the magic in Avaria. The Kaethiri had said as much, but now,
Eamonn wasn't sure what to believe. Maybe being hidden away

for so long had concentrated the magic. Maybe, without anyone to channel it, the magic had accumulated.

But something about it felt different.

The door, however, acted as a shield that prevented him from accessing it. He would have to get inside for any of it to flow within him. With his eyes still closed, Eamonn inhaled slowly and deeply, his palms flat on the rock. He concentrated all the magic inside him on the door, willing it to suffuse through the shield. Heat rose at his breastbone where his pendant lay, and the stone began to warm under his hands. He felt a release of magic, as though a dam had been broken, and Eamonn opened his eyes to find glowing white light spreading through all the carvings and illuminating the door. The stone dissipated and vanished, leaving only the swirls and lines of white light between him and a dark opening. The abode awaited them.

THIRTY-TWO

THE PASSAGE THAT LAY before Eamonn was pitch black past the swirls of light. It didn't look like he had opened into anything more than a dead end, but his heart and the heavy concentration of magic that lay before him convinced him otherwise.

Eamonn glanced over his shoulder at the group behind him. He half-expected Rothgard to come surging past him, desperate to get to the magic. Instead, he remained where he was, motionless, not yielding his grip on Leyna's arm.

Rothgard nodded his head in the direction of the opening. "Go on."

Eamonn fought the urge to scoff. Did he think it was rigged with something, ready to unleash some attack on the first unsuspecting person to breach its border? Whether that was the reason or not, Eamonn had nothing to fear entering this place that called him inside. The irresistible pull that tugged at his heart was the same as that of Avaria, making him eager to venture through the door of lights. If Rothgard had Eamonn's blood, shouldn't that give him the same feeling? Eamonn wondered, too, if Leyna felt as she had the last time she was outside Avaria: neither drawn nor deterred.

"I'll stay out here," Hadli murmured to Rothgard. A shard of anger shot through Eamonn, but he didn't turn around, letting the feeling pass just as quickly and allowing himself to be lost in the overwhelming exuberance coming from the abode.

He stepped through the light that wavered around his form, and he was lost in total blackness. He saw nothing, heard nothing, and he extended his hands to feel his way through the dark. The rock walls of the cave surrounded him almost too tightly for comfort. Eamonn took slow, careful steps forward, checking the ground for dips or other hazards. A new thought crossed his mind, and bile rose to his throat. What if he went to take a step and there was nothing there? He stuck his hands farther along the cave walls in front of him in anticipation of the tunnel's end.

As though he thought it into existence, Eamonn's fingertips curled around the end of the tunnel. His heart slammed like a chunk of lead inside his chest, and beads of sweat formed along his hairline. Still, he saw nothing. Only formless black awaited him.

Eamonn stretched out a foot, scraping his toe along the solid ground in front of him. Even past the edge of the tunnel, there was still something beneath his feet. It gave him enough hope to take another step forward, and soon, his hands found only open space around him. The hum of magic was consuming, vibrating in waves all around him, making his skin prickle. And while it was almost exactly same as the magic in Avaria, an unmistakable contrast tinged the edges of it. The energy was the only thing that gave him a feeling of existence in this vast nothingness.

He *was* inside a mountain, he reminded himself. Without an external light source, none of them would be able to see their surroundings. He recalled the torch outside the door and was about to turn back to retrieve it when he heard measured footsteps coming up behind him.

"A light," he said, turning his head to cast his voice to whomever approached. But when he faced forward again, Eamonn remembered the pendant at his chest. Its glow had vanished once he'd opened the door and stepped in the tunnel. He summoned his magic, the ripple of energy around him focusing in on him like a moth to a flame, and it rushed through him, freeing him, uplifting him, and strengthening him.

The green stone of his Réalta brightened and cast an eerie light in the space, revealing a massive open cavern with high ceilings. Except calling it a cavern wasn't quite right. It had been built into a room, with smooth walls and a level floor. A giant set of stone steps sat opposite them, delving further into the mountain's depths. Enormous pillars had been carved from top to bottom of the cavern, surrounding a space in the center of the room where a dais was encircled by stone benches, with a small gazebo-like structure in the center, almost exactly like the gathering space where they had practiced in Avaria. That was all Eamonn needed to know without a doubt that this place was of the Kaethiri.

Rothgard must have been the one who followed Eamonn because he entered the abode with a torch in one hand while maintaining his grip on Leyna's arm in the other. He raised it high, taking in the wonder of their surroundings, before tipping the torch to a dark inset line that seemed to run the entire perimeter. Fire jumped to the deep indention in the rock and traveled all the way around the room, giving much needed light to the entire space. The walls glittered red in the firelight, abundant with Arithnyx.

Rothgard set the torch in a sconce before he closed his eyes and inhaled a long, deep breath through his nose. The bloodstone at his chest eased into a steady glow. The black veins on his neck and hands drew back to his core, and the greyness of his skin began to brighten to his natural pale tone.

Alarm spiked in Eamonn's heart. He wouldn't have long before Rothgard's power had returned enough to pose a real threat.

Eamonn locked eyes with Leyna. She was still in Rothgard's grasp, but his fingers didn't seem to grip as tightly as before. Rothgard's attention must have been on the concentration of magic flooding his body. It was the perfect time—the only time—to strike.

Eamonn nodded once at Leyna, praying she understood that this was their chance. She nodded back, and Eamonn's pulse surged, sending magic rushing through his veins.

If he couldn't take control of Rothgard's mind, he would have to do the best he could with practical magic—what Leyna had suggested all along.

Opening his palms to the ground, Eamonn communed with the powerful magic of the abode and sent energy rippling through the cave floor. The ground shook violently beneath their feet, sending rocks tumbling from the ceiling and shrouding the room in dust.

Leyna slipped from Rothgard's hold as his eyes snapped open. She stumbled to the ground with the force of the quake, but as Rothgard reached for her, Eamonn used magic to pull the fire from the crevice along the wall and shoot it at him. Rothgard's clothes caught for a moment, but just as quickly, he magically snuffed out the flames.

Leyna scrambled across the few remaining feet of distance to Eamonn, meeting his eyes for only a moment before they both readied a new onslaught of magic. She gathered loose rocks that had littered the ground in the quake and shot them toward Rothgard like arrows, but he stopped them with an open palm and flung them back, forcing them to drop to the ground.

Eamonn wore a dagger on his belt, but against Rothgard, it wouldn't do much good. As he tried to think of another magical attack, Leyna threw a hand out from her prone position on the stone floor and magically pushed Rothgard back, slamming him into the abode wall. She jumped to her feet and extended her hands again, and Rothgard's arms and legs pressed into the rock as though bound to it.

The Kaethiri weren't wrong to say she had an inclination toward magic. It helped that the abode was heavy with concentrated magic like when they practiced in Avaria, where Leyna had excelled, but even Eamonn—actually half-Kaethiri—hadn't been as quick on his feet.

Rothgard struggled against Leyna's magical bonds, the glow of his red stone undulating as he pulled on the abode's magic. They might only have a few seconds before Rothgard was strong enough to counter. Eamonn attempted to control Rothgard's will again, hoping his defenses were down as he fought Leyna's attack. But Eamonn only met a wall as hard and unyielding as the mountain around them.

Leyna couldn't hold Rothgard there forever, so Eamonn needed something efficient—something quick and effective—to bring an end to Rothgard. Every passing moment grew his strength and made his defeat less likely. Eamonn directed his energy to holding Rothgard in place while ideas ran through his mind.

He could crack the side of the abode and bring down a slab from the mountain on top of Rothgard, but he would have time to see that coming and cast an enchantment to shield himself. If he doused the light of the fire to hide in a shroud of darkness, Eamonn could slip close to Rothgard and drive the dagger through his heart. And, with Rothgard disoriented, he might not know which direction to cast an enchantment. But no, their competing amulets would illuminate the area around them, regardless of the lack of light from the fire. He could always enchant the dagger and magically propel it across the distance to pierce Rothgard, but the last thing Eamonn wanted was Rothgard deflecting it and turning it on them.

Their combined efforts kept Rothgard from drawing on magic himself, but as soon as Eamonn let go to attack, Rothgard would likely be able to form an assault of his own. What they really needed was someone to sneak up on Rothgard from behind, someone who Rothgard wouldn't notice, being absorbed in his battle with Eamonn and Leyna. If only Taran and Teiyn had come with him. Or even Ree, or—

Hadli.

Eamonn couldn't access Rothgard's mind, but he could access Hadli's. And Hadli was waiting outside the abode—behind Rothgard. His fear of the magic kept him beyond its borders, so Rothgard wouldn't expect him to enter.

Rothgard pulled a hand free and extended it toward Eamonn and Leyna as if readying an attack. Eamonn return his focus to Rothgard and poured all his magical energy onto the bonds. Taking control of Hadli would pull some magic away from Rothgard again, so he would have to be fast.

The ground rumbled again, threatening to grow into a quake. Rothgard's renewing energy was starting to surpass their own. Eamonn shot a worried glance to Leyna, and he found her brow creased and lips pulled back with effort as she strained to hold the magic. She was running out of steam; he was running out of time.

"Hold it," Eamonn encouraged, needing a little extra boost from her as he split his magic in two places, but it came out more like a command.

"What do you think I'm doing?" Leyna shot back through clenched teeth. Sweat trailed down her temple. "We've got to try something else."

"I'm about to." He concentrated his efforts as much as he could on restraining Rothgard so that the dip in power hopefully would be less noticeable when he shifted to Hadli.

Then he reached out for Hadli's consciousness. Eamonn found it where he expected, just beyond the door to the abode. His lesson learned from his control of King Taularen, Eamonn didn't try hard to access Hadli's mind. He let the magic of the abode ripple through him and carried it to Hadli, wrapping around his being.

Eamonn felt Hadli's consciousness tied to his own and knew it had worked.

Draw your dagger.

He could almost feel the cold steel in his own palm.

Go into the abode and wait in the tunnel.

Eamonn kept his eyes on the entryway, and in seconds, Hadli's shadowed form appeared.

They would have to release Rothgard from the bonds that held him to the wall for Hadli to come up behind him. Eamonn faced Leyna, about to tell her to let go of the magic, but she gritted her teeth in one final grimace before she dropped her arms and stumbled back, the strain of holding the magic finally too much—like a heavy weight she wasn't trained to carry. Eamonn barely held the bonds himself—his focus turned to Hadli—and Rothgard stepped away from the rock wall, ripping himself away from the last of the magic as though it were paper.

Leyna straightened and inhaled as if to prepare another enchantment, but could she manage it? The magic of the abode was like a waterfall, a constant rush of energy around them that wouldn't deplete, but Leyna's own physical endurance might not be enough to cast another attack.

The quake roared, becoming violent now that Rothgard was free. Eamonn barely held his footing as the shaking and cracking of the ground threatened to topple them and Rothgard approached. This was his only shot. He returned his attention to Hadli.

Use your dagger to stab Rothgard in the heart.

It wasn't the ending Rothgard deserved. Eamonn wanted Rothgard's tormented death to be at his own hands, but given the circumstances, this was the best he could do.

Hadli burst from the shadowy tunnel opposite Eamonn at the command and rushed toward Rothgard from behind. Eamonn's breath caught in his throat to see his plan working, finally about to see the life drain from Rothgard's eyes, but Hadli didn't stay behind Rothgard. He came around in front of him, dagger raised, and Eamonn's heart constricted.

What was he doing? Making himself seen ruined everything. Rothgard spotted Hadli steps away and threw out an arm to magically fling him aside. Hadli hit the ground hard and rolled, the dagger clattering on the rock and sliding away from him.

Eamonn ran the phrase he'd given Hadli back through his mind, searching for what went wrong. His gut twisted as he realized he hadn't been specific about how to approach Rothgard, just as he hadn't been clear enough with Rothgard during their battle on Nidet.

How could he have been stupid enough to miss that?

Rothgard stopped moving and lowered his hands. A wicked smile twisted the corners of his lips. Eamonn froze, startled by Rothgard's change in demeanor. He kept his magic at the ready but couldn't seem to form an attack, curiosity getting the better of him.

"Why, Eamonn," he began, his voice like silk, "you surprise me. I knew you were willing to invade my mind, but this—" He gestured to Hadli's motionless body. "This was unexpected. Although he deserved it, didn't he, for betraying you?"

Eamonn couldn't tear his eyes from Rothgard, only partially because he was afraid of what he might do in the seconds his gaze left his form. Aside from that, he couldn't handle the full view of what he saw from his peripheral vision. Leyna gaped at him as her chest fell with a heavy exhale. Even from the corner of his eye, he didn't miss the shock and disappointment written all over her face.

Rothgard's voice pulled Eamonn's focus forward, the wry, calculating smile still on his mouth. "Yes, you will be quite useful."

Rothgard lifted his hands, and the air around them seemed to vibrate as chunks of rock came plummeting down from somewhere high above. Eamonn jumped and ducked, pushing Leyna out of the way of a falling boulder. He landed half on top of her, protecting her from the assault, and finally met her eyes. Even in the midst of the danger and Eamonn using his own body to shield her, Leyna looked at him with a hardness that cut him to the bone. The obvious disapproval, the surprise, the heartbreak—it was worse than Rothgard having the magic of the abode.

Eamonn lost himself so deeply in Leyna's expression that he didn't realize rocks no longer dropped from above. The grating of stone on stone sliced through the air, and he found Rothgard turned half away from them stacking the rocks in the abode entrance.

He was trying to trap them inside.

Eamonn jumped to his feet and pulled all the energy from the space around him to blast a stream of magic at the rocks, crumbling them to pebbles that battered Rothgard. With Rothgard momentarily occupied, Eamonn yanked Leyna to her feet and shoved her toward the tunnel.

"Go!" he shouted over the dying thunder of pebbles crashing to the ground. Without questioning him, Leyna ran to the exit as Eamonn pulled the fire away from the inset in the wall, adding it to a whirlwind that circled Rothgard while Leyna dashed past him.

The magic controlling the fire was pulled from Eamonn's grasp and the fire flared, sending Leyna crashing to the ground again to take cover. Heat consumed the space and the light of the flare was momentarily blinding. Eamonn blinked to bring his eyes back into focus, only to see Rothgard making long strides toward Leyna. Eamonn readied a blast of wind—hopefully enough to push Rothgard away and not injure Leyna—but Rothgard took Leyna's arm again and vanished with her just as the gust flew by.

Three heartbeats passed before the shock caught up with Eamonn. They were gone. In an instant, both of them had disappeared.

Eamonn's heart dropped to the very bottom of his gut, the weight of it settling there and making him nauseous. His hands trembled where he still held them out before him. What could he do? Surely there was something. He was in the presence of Avarian magic at its strongest. He could do almost anything.

What would bring her back?

Eamonn's eyes flashed around the room, searching for an answer. The room was as unadorned as the gathering place in Avaria, a deception to its magical potency. It gave him nothing.

Hadli stirred but didn't stand. So he was alive. He may not have been able to use magic, but he could still pose a threat. Eamonn watched him for a moment, waiting to see if he would move again.

Dark magic oppressed Eamonn as Rothgard's form reappeared before him. An all-consuming rage mingled with the abode's magic in Eamonn, and a shockwave burst from his feet, scattering the pebbles.

Rothgard stumbled but didn't fall. The black veins had started to snake past the lines of his clothes again, and the gold of his irises only bordered his dark pupils. His chest rose with a breath, and he raised his palms from where his arms hung at his sides.

"You bastard!" Eamonn yelled, his fury causing him to shake. "What did you do to her?"

Another shockwave shot from where Eamonn stood, sending loose rocks flying and causing the fire to whoosh, but Rothgard remained unaffected. The blast, rocks, and flames met an invisible force surrounding him.

Rothgard raised a hand and waved his fingers into a fist. Eamonn felt the air around him constrict, as though all the oxygen had been sucked out of his lungs. He gasped for a breath, but he only strained, tendons popping out in his neck.

"I took her away from here." Though Rothgard's voice still possessed his usual smoothness, a new malevolence dripped from his words. "You won't be able to get her back."

Fear and fury crashed over Eamonn, but he had to push it aside for the time being. He still couldn't draw a breath, and he wouldn't be able to if he didn't focus and do something about it. He shoved away his thoughts and concentrated. Magic smothered him like a blanket, like a fire consuming all the air near him. Eamonn used his own magic to strike at it, and it shattered. He gasped, long and deep, drinking in the air.

"You should thank me, really. Things here were getting too heated. She could have been hurt."

All of Eamonn's wrath and worry fueled the magic within him, and he reached out again for control of Rothgard's mind, a desperate attempt to have Rothgard lead him to Leyna.

Under his magic, Eamonn felt Rothgard's mind give for the briefest of moments, but he was soon pushed out, left scraping at the barricade Rothgard had formed around his being.

The shock showed for a split second in Rothgard's face, his eyes widening and his lips parting, but it was instantly replaced with malice. So, it was possible for Eamonn to take control of Rothgard's will, and Rothgard believed it wasn't. It struck a match in Eamonn and fanned the flame of hope he'd all but lost.

"If you want her back, you will surrender. Become my prisoner, and she will go free."

Eamonn spat. "I'm not about to put my trust in anything you say. I did that once before; it didn't end well."

Rothgard angled his head to one side, quickly cracking his neck. "Always choosing to do things the hard way."

The mountain shook again, and this time, the rock of the mountain wall moved, slowly stretching and expanding across the tunnel opening. Teleportation, and now this? How was Rothgard's magic strengthening so quickly? Yes, he was more practiced as a magic user than Eamonn, but considering the state he was in before they entered the abode, Rothgard was regaining power at a staggering rate.

Eamonn had to act fast. He readied an attack at Rothgard, but a tug at his arm sent him stumbling to the side and he lost his momentum.

Hadli gripped Eamonn's arm, his face wild with fear. A single line of blood trickled from his hairline. He was back to himself but clearly overwhelmed with the dread that came with the magic of the abode.

Eamonn began to send one of the rocks Rothgard had loosed into Hadli's chest, but a strong quake knocked him off his feet, and Hadli fell into him.

"We have to get out of here!" Hadli shouted, taking Eamonn by the arm again.

"I'm not going *anywhere* with you!" Eamonn spat. He tried to shake Hadli off of him, but his grip held firm.

"He's closing the abode!" Hadli jerked Eamonn's arm, and Eamonn looked past Rothgard to see their exit narrowing. "He's trying to trap you!"

Eamonn couldn't trust Hadli—he wouldn't trust Hadli—but he also couldn't ignore fact. He was a dead man if Rothgard shut him inside the abode. A dead man, or a tool—a pawn to be used by Rothgard as long as he decided to keep him alive. With Leyna somewhere inaccessible to Eamonn, she made the perfect bargaining chip. Rothgard would have Eamonn do whatever he wanted.

Eamonn could try to blast the rock out of the way and open the tunnel back up, but Rothgard's power was growing too fast. Eamonn wouldn't be able to last like this forever, one-on-one against Rothgard. He needed backup. That was why his plan had always been to manipulate Rothgard's will instead of engaging in a magic battle with him. He was too well-studied, too knowledgeable in the practice of magic. Even being a true Kaethiri, Eamonn couldn't match him.

"We have to go now!"

Eamonn grunted through his teeth. Hadli was right, as much as Eamonn didn't want him to be. If he wanted to save Leyna, Eamonn had to get out of there. Reconvene with the Kaethiri. Plead with them to step in and finally do something.

The entrance to the tunnel had seconds before it was closed off entirely. Eamonn hauled as much magic toward him as he could muster and knocked Rothgard to his back, sending him skidding across the rough ground. As Hadli sprinted to the tunnel, Eamonn formed a fireball from a mass of fire from the wall and shot it at Rothgard to gain a few extra seconds.

Hadli dove through the space in the rock before him. Eamonn followed hot on his heels, climbing over the bottom. Hadli reached a hand back and tugged Eamonn through before the rock came together with an ear-piercing crunch.

In the tunnel, Eamonn moved as quickly as he could in the dim green light his pendant cast as it faded with his magic. The white light of the door still glowed, at least, so he had a point he was traveling toward. The remaining torch in the sconce on the wall illuminated the part of the passage where Eamonn had first confronted Rothgard, providing light there as well.

They passed through the door, and Eamonn turned to face it, sending magic surging back through. Stone reformed in the midst of the light. When the entire space was solid rock again, just as it was before, the white designs faded, and the door blocked the entrance.

"We have to keep moving. He might still come after you."

Eamonn whirled at Hadli's voice behind him. It still shook, but whether it came from panic or their escape or something else, Eamonn couldn't determine.

"What's your game?" he snapped, closing the distance between them until he was almost touching noses with Hadli. "You're working for Rothgard after all, but you help me get out of there? What are you playing at?"

"What am *I* playing at? You were using me to kill Rothgard!" Hadli's chest heaved and his eyes blazed, matching Eamonn's fury.

"I didn't have a choice! *You* did!"

"You know nothing about my choices, Eamonn! You wouldn't believe—"

Hadli stepped back from Eamonn and inhaled, briefly closing his eyes. He jerked his head in the direction of the passage. "I will help you make it out of the mountain and find Leyna, but you have to trust me."

"Oh, I do? That worked out really well for me before."

"Eamonn—"

"You can't talk your way out of this one." It took all of Eamonn's willpower to keep from slugging Hadli right then and there. "I was stupid to trust you in the first place."

"No, you weren't." Hadli shut his eyes and dropped his head, shaking it and running the fingers of his left hand across his eyebrow. "If you'll let me explain—"

"I won't." Eamonn shoved past Hadli and strode to the tunnel of Arithnyx that led to the main passage.

"You can't go that way."

Eamonn cringed at Hadli's voice as his footsteps caught up to him. "Why not?"

"Rothgard's army has your people surrounded. They'll take you as soon as you step foot in the mountain pass."

"So? I can use magic," Eamonn countered, his voice thick and full of disdain. He might not be a match for Rothgard, but he could take out his magic-less soldiers. He turned from Hadli and stepped inside the sparkling red tunnel.

"Not against the whole army." Hadli grabbed Eamonn's wrist to pull him back. Eamonn yanked his hand from Hadli's grasp, but Hadli didn't stop. "You'll make it through the first few, but you can't take them all down. Rothgard's numbers are greater than you think. And stronger. They may not have magic, but they're still deadly."

Eamonn didn't want to put any faith in Hadli's words. This could be as much a deception as anything else. But, again, he was no good to Leyna if he found himself again in Rothgard's captivity. Even if he thought he could make it through more than the "first few," he wouldn't risk it for her.

He swallowed hard and left the tunnel. "So, where do we go, then?"

Hadli dipped his head in the direction of the passage opposite the door. "These tunnels will lead into the Wolsteadan mines eventually. It's not good, but at least it's a way out."

Eamonn huffed and ran a hand over his face. How had everything gone so horribly wrong?

He raised a hand toward the end of the passage. "Lead the way, then. But as soon as we make it to Wolstead, we go our separate ways."

Hadli opened his mouth as if to protest, but he closed it and nodded. With the torch extended in front of him, he lit the way through the dim cave passages down a path they only guessed was right. They scurried through the damp mines, ghosts in the dark, choosing their way based on what seemed the most traversed.

Eamonn was thankful Hadli took the lead because his mind wouldn't engage with the present. It was with Dorylss and the others outside the mountain, surrounded by Rothgard's soldiers. It was with Leyna, wherever she had been taken. It was with Rothgard, who, as they traveled, soaked up the magic of the abode. Magic he had no claim to. Magic that only flowed through him because of Eamonn's blood.

One day, Eamonn would see him burn.

EPILOGUE

Power.

He finally had access to the power he needed, the power he had dreamed of.

Losing the boy was a momentary setback. He had the girl, and that would be enough to get him back.

He needed the boy still. He had served his purpose in opening the door to the abode, but he was the only one of his kind, and that made him valuable. Only he possessed the pure magic of the Kaethiri outside the confines of Avaria.

He'd grown stronger, no doubt from his time with the others of his race. But it was obvious he still had more to learn, both from them and about them. He didn't know the whole truth.

Rothgard sat on a chair of stone at the top of the wide steps in the abode under the mountain. The magic of the abode coursed through him like fire sparking in his veins. The Kaethiri had said a fabricated Réalta would never be able to channel magic, yet there he sat with the glowing red gem at his chest.

It was time to bring the girl back. Rothgard had waited, and the boy hadn't returned, but he could still trace his pulse of the boy's magic within the mountain. He had either been captured or was trying to find a way to her. He wasn't dead. Rothgard would know the second his life ended, and it hadn't yet.

Rothgard stood and lost himself to magic, allowing it to consume him and meld into his essence, carrying him in the blink of an eye to the place he'd hidden the girl. With his sudden appearance, the pitch-black space was illuminated with the red glow of his amulet. The girl did not shrink or cower. Instead, she rose to her feet and faced him, determination etched in her face.

"So," Rothgard said, closing the distance between them, "you can use magic now." A smirk curled his lips. "This will be interesting."

Note to the Reader

Dear reader, I have to share my sincere thanks and appreciation for you. The mere fact that you picked up the second book in my trilogy means you wanted to come back for more, and that is truly humbling.

A simple review and star rating from you goes a long way. Reviews connect me to the right readers, so if you enjoyed *The Bloodstone's Curse*, one of the most helpful things you can do is to write a review. The QR codes below will take you to pages where you can copy and paste the same review.

The story will continue with one final installment, where lingering questions will be answered and secrets you never even suspected will be revealed.

Until then,

-Angela

Review on Amazon

Review on Goodreads

Acknowledgments

I wasn't sure this book would be written. To be perfectly honest, for a long time after the release of *The Thief's Relic*, I was fine to let it dangle as the first book in a "trilogy" that may never see another installment. The fact that you are holding it in your hands is only thanks to a number of people who either renewed my passion for writing, helped to encourage me along the way, or refused to let me give up.

First, I want to give all glory to God for this book. I can tell you with absolute confidence that this is not a product of my strength or ability, but that of Christ through me. I would have been (and was) a crumpled heap of a person trying to make this book come into being on my own. I never would have made it this far without the Lord. "But he said to me, 'My grace is sufficient for you, for my power is made perfect in weakness.' Therefore I will boast all the more gladly of my weaknesses, so that the power of Christ may rest upon me." 2 Corinthians 12:9

There is a multitude of people to thank for helping me or encouraging me at some point in this process, and if I leave someone out, please know it was unintentional. My brain has been mush lately.

To the original Discord group, Julia, Marae, Teresa, Ashley, Tessa, I never would have found that spark again or decided to write this book without you. It is truly because of that Discord and the community I found within that I continued this trilogy at all. Thank you for helping me rediscover my love of writing and see the need for me to write this story.

To my sprinting friends, Emerie, Abbi, Isabel, Georgia, you were the cheerleaders I never knew I needed. I wouldn't have written this book without the countless late nights for four months straight as we sprinted into the wee hours of the morning (for me at least). You are the reason this story idea turned into words on a page.

To Amanda and Kayla, how can my thanks to you ever be put into words? What started as a support group turned into the most incredible friendships, and I cannot thank you adequately. You aren't just author friends. The Lord intentionally placed the two of you in my life for similar but uniquely appointed reasons, and at this point I don't know what I would do without you.

To my editor, Caitlin, thank you for polishing a very rough manuscript and being so flexible with me. One of my favorite things you did in your edits was point out Scripture truth that I didn't even intend to write, showing me how the Lord can be evident in my writing without even being explicitly stated. I am so thankful that I found you.

To the creatives who brought the visuals to this book, Aamna (and team), Andres Aguirre, Laura, Adelyn, and Teresa, thank you for your incredible artistic contributions to this book. Each of you have helped bring what I could only imagine into reality. Thank you for your hard work on all my requests and being so incredible to work with. I will recommend you forever.

To my readers, you seriously bring me so much joy. Having people read words I wrote about characters and worlds that once only existed in my head is the definition of a dream come true. For years, I believed it was impossible. Now, here I am, handing you a book I wrote for the second time. It's still hard wrapping my mind around. From the bottom of my heart, thank you.

To my family, my parents, my brother, and my in-laws, thank you for always being excited for me and encouraging me to pursue this dream that I always consider one of the less-important things in my life. Thank you for believing in me.

To my husband, my wellspring of inspiration, the shovel to dig me out of plot holes, the creator of half of this book. You may not have sat at the computer and typed out words, but so much of the time, you put them in my head. I don't know how I would have ever come up with some of the events of this book without your help. You are a constant source of encouragement when I'm ready to throw in the towel, and you support me even when I'm afraid writing is taking up too much of my life. Even though I was insane and decided to start writing every single night with a one and a half month old, you stepped in to make sure I got my writing time. Thank you is not enough. You are why I continue to write. I love you.

KICKSTARTER
ACKNOWLEDGMENTS

This book has come into being in part due to pledges made by backers of my Kickstarter campaign. Thank you all for your incredible generosity and support!

Abby McGinn
Adelle Williams
Ben Nichols
Billye Herndon
Brendan Papz
Brianna Welch-Martin
Cheryl Williamson
Chuck Cofty
Courtney Yarbrough
Debi Batchelor
Ellen Pilcher
Ethan Greer
Gerald P. McDaniel
Hannah Riechers
Ian Locklar
Isabel K.
Jen Woodrum
Joe Hwang

Kandle Y.
Kasey Sargent
Kayla Ann
Kosuda-kun
Laura Edwards
Leslie Twitchell
Liz DuRoss
Marybeth Martin
Melissa Giddens
Natasha Rueschhoff
Nijeara "Ny" Buie
Patrick M
Sarah Grace
Shanon M. Brown
Solyana Marusda
Teresa LaFrance
Toby Otto
Valerie Galderisi

Angela Knotts Morse is the author of *The Thief's Relic* and *The Bloodstone's Curse*, the first two books in the *Son of Avaria* trilogy. Her love of fantasy began with *The Lord of the Rings*, and fantasy continues to be her favorite genre to both read and write.

When not writing, you can find Angela reading, snacking, binge watching a TV show, or (most likely) wrangling her two small children. She has a special place in her heart for musical theatre, performing in and attending shows when she can. *The Phantom of the Opera* is her favorite.

Angela currently resides in Birmingham, Alabama with her husband, daughter, son, and cat.

You can keep up with Angela on social media and through her newsletter at www.angelamorse.com

Instagram: @angelakmorseauthor • Facebook: Angela Knotts Morse - Author • Twitter: @angelakmorse • Goodreads: Angela Knotts Morse

Milton Keynes UK
Ingram Content Group UK Ltd.
UKHW012155091123
432302UK00016B/168/J